Dead Men

STEPHEN LEATHER

Dead Men

HODDER &
STOUGHTON

First published in Great Britain in 2008 by Hodder & Stoughton
An Hachette Livre UK company

5

Copyright © Stephen Leather 2008

A CIP catalogue record for this title
is available from the British Library

Hardback ISBN 978 0 340 92170 8
Trade Paperback ISBN 978 0 340 92171 5

Typeset in Plantin Light by Palimpsest Book Production Limited,
Grangemouth, Stirlingshire

Printed and bound by
Mackays of Chatham plc, Chatham, Kent

Hodder & Stoughton policy is to use papers that are natural, renewable
and recyclable products and made from wood grown in sustainable forests.
The logging and manufacturing processes are expected to conform to the
environmental regulations of the country of origin.

Hodder & Stoughton Ltd
338 Euston Road
London NW1 3BH

www.hodder.co.uk

For Bridie

ACKNOWLEDGEMENTS

I am indebted to Mark McKay for briefing me on the work of the Police Service of Northern Ireland, and to Alistair and Rosemary for their advice on police and SOCA matters. Sam Davies was generous with his knowledge of handguns. Any errors of fact are mine and not theirs.

Denis O'Donoghue, Barbara Schmeling, Andrew Yates, Alex Bonham and Hazel Orme helped turn my story into a novel, and Carolyn Mays made me realise yet again how lucky I am to have one of the best editors in the business at my side.

Irish Republican Army Ceasefire Statement
31 August 1994

Recognising the potential of the current situation and in order to enhance the democratic process and underlying our definitive commitment to its success, the leadership of the IRA have decided that as of midnight, 31 August, there will be a complete cessation of military operations. All our units have been instructed accordingly.

At this crossroads the leadership of the IRA salutes and commends our volunteers, other activists, our supporters and the political prisoners who have sustained the struggle against all odds for the past 25 years. Your courage, determination and sacrifice have demonstrated that the freedom and the desire for peace based on a just and lasting settlement cannot be crushed. We remember all those who have died for Irish freedom and we reiterate our commitment to our republican objectives. Our struggle has seen many gains and advances made by nationalists and for the democratic position.

We believe that an opportunity to secure a just and lasting settlement has been created. We are therefore entering into a new situation in a spirit of determination and confidence, determined that the injustices which created this conflict will be removed and confident in the strength and justice of our struggle to achieve this.

Two years later.
28 August 1996

There were five in the car, and between them they had killed more than a dozen men. The man in the front passenger seat was Joe McFee, the oldest of the group and the most experienced. He had killed two British soldiers, three policemen and a drug-dealer, and had slept like a baby after each murder. He had a kindly face and ruddy cheeks, like a beardless Father Christmas, and the only sign of his tension was a tendency to crack his knuckles.

The clouds had been threatening rain as the men had driven across East Belfast, and now the first flecks hit the windscreen. Willie McEvoy flipped the wipers on and they swished back and forth, leaving greasy streaks on the glass. The digital clock set into the dashboard told him it was just before eight and there were few other cars on the street. They had chosen the time carefully. Late enough to miss the rush-hour, early enough that five men driving around wouldn't attract the wrong sort of attention. 'Great weather for ducks,' he mumbled.

Gerry Lynn checked the action of his semi-automatic. It was his operation. He'd researched the target and planned the hit, and he'd gone to the Army Council for permission. It had been readily granted. The target had long been a thorn in the side of the IRA and they would be happy to see the back of him. Lynn was sitting behind McFee. As leader of the group, his rightful place was in the front, but he'd wanted to show respect to McFee, who had been his mentor for more than a decade. McFee had seen him throwing rocks and petrol bombs at British Army Land Rovers, taken him to one side and told him that there were more fruitful ways of striking at the occupying power. He had taught Lynn to kill, and Lynn had been a willing pupil.

Sitting directly behind McFee was Adrian Dunne. He was in his early thirties, and all muscle. During the day he worked as a drayman, delivering beer barrels around the city, while most evenings he was in the gym, lifting weights. Dunne had been Lynn's first choice for the operation. They had worked together several times and there had never been any problems. Dunne slid his gun out from its holster under his left armpit, ejected the magazine, then slotted it back into place.

'Nearly there, boys,' said McEvoy. The rain was falling faster now and he upped the pace of the windscreen wipers. It was a good sign, thought Lynn. It would cut down visibility and keep people off the streets. He took a black woollen ski mask from his pocket and pulled it over his face. Dunne did the same.

Sitting between Lynn and Dunne was Noel Kinsella, the youngest of the group, barely out of his teens. He had the looks of a young Pierce Brosnan, with jet black hair and a strong jaw. He was breathing heavily, his eyes flicking between McFee and Lynn. 'Are you all right there, Noel?' asked Lynn.

'I'm grand,' said Kinsella.

'It's the boy's blooding,' said McFee. 'He'll make his dad proud.' Kinsella's father was in the Maze prison, serving life for the murder of two Ulster Defence Force activists.

'Put your mask on, lad,' said Lynn, 'and check your weapon.'

Kinsella did as he was told. McEvoy brought the Saab to a gentle halt at the roadside. They were in Casaeldona Park, a suburb with well-tended gardens and mid-range saloon cars parked in the driveways. Lynn had spent weeks watching the semi-detached house and knew that once the man who lived there arrived home he was usually in for the night. The target was careful. He always parked his car in the garage and used the internal door to enter the house. The sitting room was at the front, as was the first-floor bedroom where he and his wife slept. Their young son was at the back of the house in a room overlooking a large garden. An old couple lived in the house to the left. The husband was almost deaf and the wife was in a wheelchair. At the house on the right, the middle-aged owners had just left for a two-week holiday in Spain. No one would interfere with the men and what they had planned.

Lynn took a deep breath. His heart was pounding – with anticipation, not fear or anxiety. McFee put on his ski mask, then massaged his gloved hands. He looked at Lynn expectantly. 'Let's do it,' said Lynn. 'And remember, Carter's a hard bastard. Don't give him any room to manoeuvre.'

McFee got out and walked to the rear of the car. McEvoy pressed the button to unlock the boot and gunned the engine. 'Easy, Willie,' said Lynn. 'This isn't Formula One.' McFee reached into the boot and took out a sledgehammer.

'In we go then,' said Lynn. 'Let's go get the bastard.' He opened the passenger door and climbed out of the Saab. Kinsella followed and stood with his gun held close to his leg. Dunne got out at the other side as McFee walked down the path, cradling the sledgehammer. Lynn and Kinsella hurried after him.

Lynn looked over his shoulder and saw Dunne heading for the front door. There was a narrow strip of grass between the garage and the fence and McFee squeezed through. Lynn motioned for Kinsella to follow McFee. Kinsella's eyes were wide and he was panting. Lynn squeezed his shoulder. 'You're doing fine,' he said. Kinsella rushed after McFee. Lynn followed.

At the back of the garage a small paved yard was overlooked by a large kitchen window but the lights were off inside. A motion-sensitive security light was fixed high on the wall but McFee stopped before he stepped into its range. Kinsella and Lynn joined him. They crouched in silence. Lynn looked at his watch and counted off the seconds. On the other side of the city, a man should have been making a call from a phone box. They waited.

They stiffened as they heard the phone ring inside the house, then someone answer it. Dunne pressed the doorbell.

It buzzed. He pressed it again. They heard Carter shout, 'Get the door, will you, love?' and Lynn pointed at McFee. He walked quickly across the yard to the kitchen door. The halogen light clicked on.

They heard Carter on the phone, asking who was calling.

McFee raised the sledgehammer and swung it. The wood round the lock splintered. He stepped aside and Lynn kicked the kitchen door wide, then rushed in, his gun arm outstretched. As he reached the door that led to the hallway he saw Carter standing with the phone to his ear, a surprised look on his face. He pointed the gun at Carter's chest. 'Put down the phone and put your hands behind your head.'

Carter replaced the receiver.

His wife was standing by the front door. She was a good five years younger than her husband, with long red hair framing a freckled face. She was wearing a pale green silk dressing-gown with a dragon on the back. 'Open the door, now!' Lynn barked at her.

She reached slowly for the lock, her hand trembling.

'Do it!' said Lynn, gesturing with his gun.

The woman fumbled and the door crashed open. Dunne pushed her back into the hallway, kicked the door shut behind him and pushed the muzzle of his gun under her chin. 'Don't move,' he warned.

Kinsella joined Lynn and aimed his gun at Carter's face. 'Hands behind your head, now!' yelled Kinsella.

Carter did as he was told.

A small boy wearing pyjamas came out of the sitting room holding a teddy bear by one leg. 'Mummy?' he said. His mouth fell open when he saw the men in masks. 'Mummy!' he cried.

The woman moved towards him but Dunne grabbed her hair. 'Stay where you are,' he said.

'Let her get the boy,' said Lynn. 'Carter, in the kitchen.'

Dunne released the woman's hair and she scurried over to her son, picked him up and hugged him. 'It's okay, Timmy,' she said. 'It's okay.'

'Don't worry, Timmy,' said Carter.

'Kitchen – now,' said Lynn, brandishing his gun.

Carter backed into the kitchen and McFree closed the door. He stood in front of it, still holding the sledgehammer.

'Get out, you bastards!' screeched Carter's wife. 'Get the fuck out of my house!'

The child began to cry.

'You're upsetting the boy,' said Dunne, pushing her against the wall.

'Don't you touch me!' she said.

'Keep your mouth shut or I'll shut it for you,' said Dunne, raising his gun.

'Elaine, leave it be,' said Carter. 'Don't antagonise them.'

'Do as your man says.' Lynn kept his gun aimed at Carter's chest. Carter had his hands up but his eyes were darting from side to side, looking for something, anything, to use as a weapon. 'Don't even think about it,' said Lynn. 'Start anything and your wife and the boy will get hurt.'

'You scum,' said Carter.

'Pot calling the kettle black, is it?' said Lynn.

'Robbie, tell them to go, please,' said Elaine.

'I warned you,' said Dunne. He raised his hand to slap her and she flinched. 'One more word.'

'Turn around, Carter,' said Lynn, gesturing with his gun. 'And lie down on the floor.'

'Not in front of my wife and child, lads,' said Carter. 'For God's sake, have a heart.'

'Turn around,' Lynn repeated. Carter did as he was told. Lynn pointed his gun at the back of Carter's left leg and pulled the trigger. Carter's kneecap shattered and blood splattered across the kitchen floor.

'No!' yelled Carter's wife. She buried the child's face in her neck before he could scream. 'You bastards!' she shrieked. The teddy bear fell out of the child's grasp to the floor.

Carter's left leg collapsed and he grabbed at the back of a chair in an attempt to keep his balance.

'I told yez, down on the floor,' said Lynn. 'Now do as yer feckin' well told.'

Elaine glared at Lynn, her upper lip curled in a snarl. 'Four of you against one man,' she said. 'That's the way you fight, is it? You cowards.'

The gun barked again and Carter's right knee buckled as blood soaked through his trouser leg. He pitched forward, face down, and slammed into the tiled floor.

His wife screamed again, an animal howl from deep within her. Lynn pointed his gun at her face. 'Shut the hell up or I'll do you too, you bitch,' he said.

'Elaine, no!' said Carter. He tried to push himself up as blood ran down his legs.

'Robbie!' she gasped.

'It's okay,' said Carter. 'Just leave them be.' He fell forward and lay face down, panting. 'Leave her be, lads. This is between you and me.'

Dunne stepped forward and pushed his pistol against the back of Carter's head. 'Shut the fuck up,' he yelled.

'Leave him alone!' said his wife. 'He hasn't done anything.'

'Elaine, please, don't talk to them,' said Carter. 'Don't give them the satisfaction.' Blood was pooling round his shattered knees.

Dunne stood up and looked at Lynn. Lynn patted Kinsella on the shoulder. 'Okay, lad,' he said.

Kinsella was trembling. He aimed his gun at the back of Carter's head. His breathing was coming in short, sharp gasps. The gun wavered and he used his left hand to steady it.

'Get a feckin' move on,' said Dunne.

'I can't,' said Kinsella.

'You have to,' whispered Lynn.

'Jesus wept,' said Dunne. 'Get on with it.'

'Okay, okay,' said Kinsella, his voice shaking. His finger tightened on the trigger.

'Take a deep breath,' said Lynn.

Kinsella inhaled. His legs were quivering, and Lynn could

hear his metal watchstrap rattling on his wrist. 'Now do it,' ordered Lynn.

Kinsella pulled the trigger. The gun jerked in his hand and the bullet thwacked into the floor by Carter's shoulder, then ricocheted into the cabinet under the sink. Carter's wife screamed.

'Again. Fire again,' said Lynn. 'Come on, just pull the bloody trigger.'

Kinsella took aim at Carter's head but then his chest heaved and vomit sprayed across the tiles. He staggered against the fridge and threw up again. He fell to his knees as vomit trickled down the front of his jacket.

'Jesus wept,' said Dunne. He stepped towards Carter and fired. The back of Carter's head exploded.

Lynn grabbed Kinsella's collar and yanked him to his feet.

Dunne pointed his gun at Carter's wife. She was sobbing into her son's neck. 'Say anything to anyone and we'll be back to do you and the kid.'

McFee headed for the front door, still holding the sledge-hammer. Lynn pushed Kinsella after him. 'Come on,' he said to Dunne, who was staring down at Carter's body.

'Let's shoot the bitch as well,' said Dunne. He took aim at her face but she didn't flinch.

'We've done what we came to do,' said Lynn.

'She called us cowards,' said Dunne. 'I'm no feckin' coward.'

'Sticks and stones,' said Lynn. 'You've killed her man. You've done enough.'

Dunne's lips tightened, but he followed McFee and Kinsella down the hallway. The little boy was crying and the woman rubbed the back of his head and nuzzled his ear.

Lynn slid his gun back into its holster. A thick, treacly halo of blood had formed round Carter's head. He felt no sympathy for the dead man, and no remorse for what he'd done. He was at war, and Carter had been the enemy.

'I swear before God Almighty, I will find you,' said the woman, through clenched teeth. 'I will find you and I will kill you.'

Lynn turned to her. She was glaring at him with a fierce intensity, still clutching the child to her neck. Tears were running down her face and he could see a vein pulsing in her temple. Lynn opened his mouth to speak, then hurried out of the room.

They left through the front door and got back into the car. 'How did it go?' asked McEvoy, putting the car into gear and pulling away from the kerb.

'How it always goes,' said Lynn. 'Bang, bang, he's dead. Now get us the hell out of here.'

McEvoy stamped on the accelerator and the Saab leapt forward.

Lynn took off his ski mask as McEvoy drove down the hill to the dual carriageway that led to the safety of the Republican Falls Road area of West Belfast. 'Well done, boys,' he said. 'You done me proud.'

Kinsella had his head down and was wiping his mouth with the back of his hand. 'I'm sorry,' he muttered.

'It's okay, Noel. The first time is always hard, no matter what anyone says.'

'I fucked up, I'm sorry.'

'You pulled the trigger, lad, and there's a lot can't even do that.'

Kinsella was trembling and put his head into his hands. McFee opened the glove compartment and handed a bottle of Bushmills whiskey to Dunne. 'Give the boy a wee dram,' he said.

Dunne unscrewed the top and tapped it against Kinsella's shoulder. 'Here, lad, this'll help.'

'I'm sorry, Adrian. I let you down.'

Dunne put an arm round his shoulders. 'Like Gerry says, the first time's the worst. You've been blooded now, that's all that matters. The next time will be easier, trust me.'

Kinsella nodded gratefully and took the bottle of whiskey. He drank deeply, then coughed as the alcohol burnt into his stomach. 'I'll do better next time, lads, I promise,' he said.

'That's for sure.' Lynn laughed.

Present day

The barmaid put a pint of John Smith's and a vodka and tonic in front of the two men and smiled professionally. 'Can I get you anything else, gents?' she asked. She was Australian, in her mid-twenties, with a sprinkle of freckles across her upturned nose, and breasts that rippled under her black T-shirt.

The younger of the two men raised his beer and winked. 'Your phone number?'

The barmaid's eyes hardened, but the smile stayed in place. 'My boyfriend doesn't let me give it out,' she said.

The older man laughed and slapped the other on the back. 'She's got you there, Vince.'

Vince Clarke took a long pull on his pint and scowled at his drinking companion as the barmaid walked away. 'Probably a lesbian,' he said. Clarke's head was shaved and a pair of Ray-Bans was pushed high on his skull. He was wearing a long black leather coat over a black suit and a thick gold chain hung round his bull neck.

'Yeah, the boyfriend was the clue.' Dave Hickey sipped his vodka and tonic and chuckled. 'You never stop trying, do you?' His hair was close-cropped and, like his companion, he had a pair of expensive sunglasses perched on his head. He wore a sovereign ring on his left hand and a bulky signet ring on the right.

'It's playing the odds,' said Clarke. 'If you ask often enough, you'll get lucky.'

'Yeah? How often do you get lucky?'

'One in five,' said Clarke. He wiped his mouth on his sleeve.

'Seriously?'

'Thereabouts. What about you? You're not married, are you?'

'Who'd have me?'

'Girlfriend?'

'No one special.' He looked at his watch, a gold Breitling with several dials. 'Where is he, then?'

'He'll be here when he's here,' said Clarke.

'How long have you worked with him?'

'Long enough to know that he'll be here when he's here,' said Clarke. He drained his glass and waved at the barmaid to refill it. 'You're a slow drinker, aren't you, Dave?'

'I'm on spirits,' said Hickey. 'If I kept up with you I'd be flat on my back and no use to anyone.'

'All right, lads,' said a voice from behind them. The two men twisted on their bar stools to face a broad-shouldered man in his mid-thirties. He had a long face with a hooked nose and hair that was receding at the front but grown long at the back and pulled into a ponytail. Peter Paxton was wearing a grey leather jacket over a black polo-neck and blue jeans. 'You ready for the off?'

'Where are we heading, boss?' asked Hickey.

'Need to know, Dave,' said Paxton. He gestured at the door. 'Come on, the engine's running.'

'What about this?' said the barmaid, holding up Clarke's pint.

'Put it back in the pump, love,' said Paxton.

Hickey and Clarke slid off their stools and followed Paxton out of the pub. Clarke tossed the barmaid a twenty-pound note and winked at her. 'Catch you later, baby,' he said.

A Jaguar was waiting at the kerb. Paxton climbed into the front seat while Hickey and Clarke got into the back. Paxton nodded at the driver, a big man with a boxer's nose. 'Nice and steady, Eddie,' he said.

Eddie Jarvis grunted and eased the Jaguar forward. Paxton said, 'Nice and steady, Eddie' to him at least a dozen times a day and had done every day for the two years or so that Jarvis had worked for him. He seemed to find it as funny now as he had the first time he'd said it.

'What's the story, boss?' asked Hickey.

Paxton turned in his seat. 'You writing a book, Dave?'

'I don't like riding into the dark, that's all.'

'We're going to check that an investment of mine is paying off. Why? You're not late for an appointment, are you?'

'No rush here,' said Hickey, settling back in the leather seat.

'Glad to hear it,' said Paxton.

They drove across the city, and after half an hour Hickey saw a sign for Stratford, the site of the 2012 Olympics. There were cranes everywhere, and trucks full of building materials packed the roads. Billions of pounds were being poured into the area in anticipation of the sporting event – new buildings were going up, existing houses were being gentrified and restaurants were opening.

'You should all buy places here,' said Paxton. 'Prices are going through the roof. I bought six flats as soon as they announced the Olympics were coming here.'

'Where am I going to get that sort of money?' said Clarke.

'Stop playing the horses for a start,' said Paxton. 'Gambling's a mug's game.'

'I win more than I lose,' said Clarke.

'That's what every punter says. The only people who make money out of gambling are the bookies. Put your money in property instead.' Paxton pointed at a set of traffic-lights ahead. 'Hang a left, Eddie. Then pull in, yeah?' Eddie made the turn, parked the Jaguar at the side of the road and switched off the engine. 'Right, lads, pin back your ears,' said Paxton. 'The guys we're paying a call on are Algerians, two brothers, Ben and Ali. They're the key to getting heroin right into London. Problem is, the delivery they were supposed to make didn't happen and I want to know why.'

'What are they, boss? Algerian Mafia?' asked Clarke.

'They work at the Eurostar depot at Temple Mills on the edge of the Olympic Park.'

'They're bringing heroin in on the Eurostar?' asked Hickey.

'They're cleaners,' said Paxton, 'and part of their job is emptying the toilet holding tanks. They've got family at the French end where security's lax. Their relatives put the gear in the tanks in France and Ben and Ali are supposed to get it out at Temple Mills. Except so far they haven't done what they're supposed to do.'

'You want us to get heavy with them?' asked Hickey.

'You've got it in one, Einstein,' said Paxton. 'I had the North Pole sewn up for years, so I want to make sure no one gets the jump on me at Temple Mills.'

'I thought Santa Claus had the North Pole sewn up,' said Hickey.

Paxton glared at him. 'The North Pole is the old Eurostar depot near Paddington. We were bringing in dozens of kilos a month and then they decided to move to Stratford. My guys at the North Pole weren't moved to the new depot but they introduced me to Ben and Ali. What we've got here are just teething problems, and we're the dentists.'

Paxton climbed out of the Jaguar and went to the boot. Eddie popped it open. Paxton moved aside a tatty sheepskin jacket to reveal a nylon holdall. He unzipped it, then glanced over his shoulder to make sure no one was watching and pulled out a sawn-off shotgun. He passed it to Clarke, who hid it under his coat.

'Shooters?' asked Hickey.

'You are on the ball tonight, aren't you?' said Paxton. He took a revolver from the bag and gave it to Hickey. 'Not a problem, is it?'

Hickey looked down the barrel of the gun, checked the sights, then flipped out the cylinder. It was fully loaded. 'No problem here, boss. It's just that I'm more comfortable with automatics.'

'Automatics jam and they spew cartridges all over the

place,' said Paxton, dismissively. He zipped the bag and closed the boot.

Hickey slid the gun into the pocket of his jacket. 'You're not carrying, boss?'

'There's no point in having a couple of dogs and barking myself, is there?' said Paxton. 'Right, stick with me. I'll do the talking, you look mean, and only pull the shooters out if I say so.' He walked down the pavement. Hickey and Clarke hurried after him.

The Algerians were living in a row of terraced houses, several of which had for-sale signs by the front doors. It was early evening and the street-lamps came on as they headed along the pavement. Three Asian boys with gelled hair and earrings walked towards them, stepping into the road to get past. 'Bloody suicide-bombers,' Paxton muttered. 'Should ship 'em all back to Paki Land.'

'They were probably born here, boss,' said Clarke.

'Yeah, well, just because a dog's born in a stable it doesn't make it a horse,' said Paxton. He jerked his head at the door they were approaching. The black paint was peeling and the wood was rotting at the bottom. The window frames were also in a bad state, and one of the panes on the upper floor had been broken and patched with a sheet of hardboard. 'This is it,' he said. He jabbed at the doorbell, then kept his gloved finger on it until the door opened. They caught a glimpse of a man in his early twenties with a goatee, then the door started to close. Paxton forced it open and the man inside swore. 'Slam the door on me, would you, you bastard?' yelled Paxton. He used both hands to push it wide, then Clarke and Hickey followed him into the hallway. The Algerian scrambled for the kitchen but Paxton grabbed him by the scruff of the neck. 'Where the fuck do you think you're going, Ben?' He slammed the man against the wall.

Hickey closed the door and stood with his back to it. 'Where's my fucking drugs, Ben?' said Paxton. He put his hand round the man's throat.

'Leave him alone!' shouted a voice from upstairs.

A second Algerian was at the top of the stairs, a big man with forearms that bulged in his sweatshirt. He wore a thick gold chain round his neck and a bulky watch.

Paxton kept his fingers tight round Ben's throat. 'Get the hell down here, Ali, and fetch me my drugs or I'll snap this little shit's neck.'

'We haven't got your drugs,' said Ali. 'They didn't arrive.'

'Yeah, well, I heard different,' said Paxton. He pulled Ben away from the wall, then shoved him backwards down the hallway towards the kitchen. 'So come down here and we can get things straightened out.' Ben's feet scrabbled along the threadbare carpet as Paxton kept him off balance. He tried to speak but, with Paxton's grip on his neck, could only grunt. Paxton forced him into the kitchen. 'Check the rest of the house, lads. Make sure there's no surprises.'

'Will do, boss,' said Clarke. He kept the sawn-off shotgun pressed to his side as he opened the door to the living room.

Hickey looked up the stairs at Ali. 'You'd better do as he says and get down here,' he said. Ali glared at him. 'Don't make me come up there and get you,' warned Hickey.

As Clarke stepped into the living room, a third Algerian appeared from behind the door and stabbed at him with a flick-knife. Clarke yelped and staggered back into the hallway, clutching his left arm. The shotgun clattered to the floor. 'He stabbed me,' said Clarke, in disbelief. 'The bastard stabbed me.'

Hickey ran down the hallway. The Algerian with the flick-knife bent down, reaching for the shotgun with his free hand. Hickey kicked out, his foot catching the man in the chest. The Algerian roared as he fell backwards, arms flailing.

Clarke slid down the wall, his face ashen. 'He stabbed me,' he whispered, his hand pressed to the injury. 'I can feel the blood,' he whined. 'I can feel it running down my arm.'

The Algerian in the sitting room got to his feet and went into a crouch, the knife darting back and forth. Hickey heard Ali rush down the stairs behind him.

'What the hell's happening?' shouted Paxton.

The Algerian with the knife lunged at Hickey, who stepped back, hands up. Ali reached the bottom of the stairs and charged down the hallway. Hickey fumbled for his revolver but couldn't get it out of his pocket before Ali slammed into him, shoulder first. Hickey stumbled over Clarke's legs and staggered against the wall, trying to regain his balance.

Ali picked up the shotgun. Hickey threw himself towards the man and clamped his right hand over the weapon's hammer. Ali tried to force his index finger into the trigger guard but Hickey twisted the gun down.

Again the Algerian with the knife slashed at Hickey, who twisted the shotgun so that Ali was between him and the knife-man. Ali tried to pull the gun away from him, but Hickey tightened his grip round the hammer. So long as he kept his hand on it, the weapon couldn't be fired.

Paxton let go of Ben and rushed to the kitchen door. 'What the hell's going on?' he roared.

Hickey pushed Ali towards the Algerian with the knife, then twisted the shotgun free.

A scraping sound made Paxton turn – in time to see Ben snatching a breadknife from a wooden block. Before he could react Ben thrust it to his neck. Paxton stood still, the serrated blade against his flesh. 'Don't do anything stupid, Ben,' he said.

In the hallway, Hickey levelled the shotgun at Ali's stomach. 'Stay where you are or I'll blow a hole in your gut,' he said.

Ali sneered at him. 'You don't scare me,' he said.

'Then you're as stupid as you look,' said Hickey. 'Put your hands on your head.'

'I'm bleeding to death here,' whimpered Clarke, on the floor.

'You're fine,' said Hickey, his eyes locked on Ali's. 'If he'd hit an artery you'd be dead already. Just keep pressure on the wound and you'll be okay.'

'Easy for you to say,' said Clarke. 'You're not the one who's been stabbed.'

'Hands on your head, Ali,' said Hickey, slowly. His finger tightened on the trigger. Ali started to lift his hands but as they got to shoulder height, the Algerian behind him shoved him in the small of the back and Ali staggered forward.

Ali's eyes widened in horror as Hickey raised the shotgun. He opened his mouth but before he could say anything Hickey took a step back, reversed the shotgun, and slapped the butt against the side of his head. Ali slumped to the ground. Hickey reversed the shotgun again and levelled the shortened barrel at the Algerian's groin. 'Drop the knife or I'll blow your balls off.' The knife clattered on the floor and the Algerian raised his hands. 'Turn around slowly,' said Hickey. The Algerian did as he was told. As he turned, Hickey hit him on the back of the head with the shotgun and the Algerian fell without a sound.

'I need an ambulance,' said Clarke.

'If you don't stop whining, I'll shoot you myself,' said Hickey, striding towards the kitchen door.

Ben had dragged Paxton to the sink, the breadknife pressed to his neck.

'Shoot the prick, why don't you?' said Paxton.

'Well, first of all, if I pull the trigger on this, the neighbours are all going to start dialling three nines and there'll be an armed-response vehicle outside before you can say, "life sentence". And, second of all, the shot from this will rip you both apart.' Hickey put the shotgun on top of the fridge and took the revolver out of his pocket.

'Just get this prick off me!' said Paxton.

'That's the plan,' said Hickey. He weighed the gun in his hand as he stared at Ben. The Algerian's face was bathed in sweat and a pulse was throbbing in his forehead.

'I'll kill him,' said Ben, but his voice was trembling.

'The thing is, Peter, if I shoot him and he doesn't die right away, he can still slit your throat.' Hickey pointed the gun at Ben. 'Drop the knife,' he said.

'You shoot me and I can still cut him,' said the Algerian. 'I'll slit his throat.'

'Which affects me how exactly?' said Hickey.

'What?'

'Listen to yourself,' said Hickey. 'I shoot you and you stab him. Where does that leave me?'

Ben frowned.

'I'll tell you where it leaves me,' said Hickey. 'Standing here with a shit-eating grin on my face while you bleed to death on the floor. So stop being an arsehole and drop the knife.'

'I'll cut him,' said the Algerian again, but with less conviction now.

'That's no skin off my nose, is it?'

'He's your boss.'

'I'll get another,' said Hickey. 'Bosses are easy to find.'

'Hickey, you are starting to piss me off in a big way,' said Paxton. 'Shoot him in the leg.'

'Peter, best thing you can do right now is to keep quiet. If I shoot him in the leg he'll cut you. If I shoot, I'll have to shoot to kill, which means blowing his brains out.'

The Algerian pressed the knife harder against Paxton's neck. 'He's going to cut me,' said Paxton.

'No, he's not,' said Hickey. 'He's stupid, but he's not that stupid.' Hickey walked slowly across the kitchen, his eyes locked on Ben's.

Ben had backed up against the sink so there was nowhere he could go. 'Stay away!' he shouted.

'Stay calm, Ben,' said Hickey. 'I just want to talk.'

'Stop moving!'

Hickey raised the gun and pointed the barrel at the man's face. 'I'm just talking, Ben. Just chewing the fat.'

'If you're going to shoot him, just shoot him,' said Paxton.

Hickey ignored him. He continued to hold Ben's eyes as he moved slowly across the kitchen floor. 'Listen to me, Ben. Listen to me carefully. We can still stop this without anyone getting really hurt. Vince there will need a couple of stitches but he'll be okay. Your two friends will wake up with sore heads but they'll be fine. But if you cut my boss there, everything changes.'

'I want you out of the house, now.'

'That's fine,' said Hickey. 'That's what I want.' He took two steps towards Ben and placed the barrel of the gun against the man's forehead. Ben tried to move his head away but Hickey kept the gun pressed to it. 'Stay calm, Ben,' he said quietly. 'Just chill and listen to me.'

'For fuck's sake, what are you playing at?' hissed Paxton.

'This can go one of three ways, Ben,' said Hickey. 'I can pull the trigger and blow your brains over the sink and we'll all live happily ever after. Except you, of course, because you'll be dead. Or you can cut my boss's throat with that knife, he bleeds to death, I pull the trigger and blow your brains over the sink.'

'Hickey . . .' warned Paxton.

'Now, there's a third way, Ben. You put down the knife, I take a step back, and we do what we came here to do, which is have a chat.'

'You came here with guns,' said Ben.

'Your mate attacked us with a knife,' said Hickey. 'He stabbed Vince there. We just came to talk.'

'You came here with guns,' repeated Ben, pressing the knife harder to Paxton's throat.

'And if we hadn't, we'd all be sitting in the hallway bleeding,' said Hickey. 'Now, drop the knife. I don't want to do anything melodramatic like counting to three, but trust me, Ben, I will put a bullet in your face.'

Sweat was pouring down Ben's face and he licked his lips. 'Maybe I let him go and you still shoot me?'

'Why?' said Hickey. 'I've nothing against you. My boss here still wants to talk about his drugs. So drop the knife and we can all go home.'

Ben was breathing shallowly, his chest rising and falling as his mind raced. Hickey waited, his eyes never leaving the man's face. Eventually the Algerian took the knife away from Paxton's throat. He held it to the side and dropped it on to the work surface. Paxton staggered across the kitchen, cursing.

Hickey slammed the gun against the side of Ben's head and grinned as the Algerian slumped to the floor. 'Twat,' he said.

Charlotte Button put down her cup of tea. 'You hit him?' she said. 'He did what you wanted and you still hit him?'

Dan Shepherd shrugged. 'I'm David Hickey, bouncer turned enforcer. It's what I do. If I hadn't hit him, I wouldn't have been in character.'

Button sighed. 'Spider, even an undercover SOCA agent has to follow some rules. You really can't go around hitting people willy-nilly.'

Shepherd grinned. 'Willy-nilly?'

'You know what I mean. I'm your boss, remember? I'm supposed to ensure that you at least come close to following approved procedure.'

'I just clipped him,' said Shepherd. 'I know what I'm doing.' He leant back in his chair and stretched. They were sitting in a third-floor office in Soho, one of several where Button met the undercover operatives who worked for the Serious Organised Crime Agency. Spring sunshine streamed in though the two skylights. One wall, to the left of the door, was covered with surveillance photographs of Peter Paxton and his crew. Shepherd featured in several, never far from Paxton's side.

'So what happened?'

Shepherd ran a hand over the stubble on his head. He didn't like cutting his hair so short, but it was part of Hickey's character. He'd be glad to get rid of the garish jewellery, too. 'Paxton had us haul them into the kitchen and tie them up. Then he found an iron and switched it on.'

'Spider, please, don't tell me you tortured them.'

'It didn't come to that,' said Shepherd. 'The one called Ben started to cry as soon as the little light went on. The drugs were in the loft. Twelve kilos of Afghan heroin. It was a trial run and it had gone exactly as planned, except they'd decided that as it was so easy they might as well cut out the middle man.'

'Where's the heroin now?'

'Still in the house,' said Shepherd. He glanced at his watch. 'Probably being picked up as we speak. Paxton didn't want to risk driving around with twelve kilos of smack in the Jag so he's sending some of his boys around to pick it up.'

'And the Algerians are still tied up in the kitchen?'

'No, we killed them and buried them in the New Forest.' Shepherd laughed when he saw the horror on Button's face. 'I'm joking, Charlie,' he said. 'Paxton's hard but he's not a psycho. So far as I know he's never killed anyone. He just explained how things were going to be and the Algerians agreed to it.'

'Encouraged by the red-hot iron, I suppose?'

'They were trying it on. Once Paxton showed them he meant business, they buckled. It won't happen again.'

'And Clarke?'

'Nothing serious,' said Shepherd. 'I took him to a tame doctor that works for Paxton and he put a few stitches in the wound and gave him an anti-tetanus shot. I think the injection hurt him more than the stabbing.' He picked up his cup of Starbucks coffee and sipped.

'Any idea when the next delivery will be coming over?'

'Paxton does everything on a need-to-know basis,' said Shepherd. 'Last night was the first time he mentioned the Eurostar. Seems that the Algerians in France have one of their guys working security and when he's on the night shift they can get the heroin into the toilet holding tanks. Getting the gear out of the Temple Mills depot is a piece of cake. All the security is going in. No one expects them to be bringing stuff out. It's the French end that's the key. They do their rotas at the end of each month so they have to wait until their man's working nights before they can arrange a delivery. The twelve kilos was a trial and I figure that the next shipments are going to be much bigger.'

'If I run the cleaning staff personnel records by you, can you pick out the three guys you roughed up?' She grinned. 'Of course you can, you and your total recall. I tell you, Spider, it would make my life so much easier if everyone on my team had a photographic memory.'

'Sure,' said Shepherd. 'And Paxton said they had family at the French end. That could be with Eurostar or the cleaning company, but cross-checking with their personnel records should net everyone.'

'Job well done,' said Button.

'When are you going to move against Paxton?' asked Shepherd.

'We'll give it a month or so,' said Button. 'We'll let you get clear and beef up the surveillance. I'll liaise with the French so that we can mop up their end, too. Win some Brownie points with Europol.'

'So I'm done?'

'Just come up with a good reason to part company with Paxton and we'll call it a day,' said Button. She nodded at the gold Breitling. 'Don't forget to return the watch,' she said, 'and the jewellery.'

'It's all a bit flash for me, anyway,' he said. 'So, now we've got Paxton sewn up, have you anything else lined up for me?'

'There's a few possibilities,' said Button.

'Something close to home would be good,' said Shepherd. 'It's been a while since I've spent time with Liam.'

'I'll see what I can do,' said Button, 'but I don't think Hereford's a hotbed of crime.'

'Sheep rustlers?'

Button arched an eyebrow. 'You know as well as I do that SOCA's charged with targeting the country's major drug-dealers, people-traffickers and hardcore criminals. And I don't think any villain worth his salt is going to base himself in the town that's home to the Special Air Service, do you?'

Shepherd grinned and raised his paper cup to her. 'It's always worth a try,' he said.

'On the subject of SOCA, we've a little housekeeping to do,' she said. 'To date you've effectively been on secondment. Over the next week or so we have to make the switch irrevocable.'

'Are you telling me I've been on probation?'

Button waved a hand dismissively. 'Virtually everyone who was involved in setting up SOCA was initially brought in on a temporary basis. We weren't sure whose faces would fit and who would want to stay. Now we're in the process of solidifying things.'

'Which means what?'

'Basically there's one more set of papers to sign and you become a fully fledged civil servant.'

'Lovely,' said Shepherd.

'The job remains the same but you will no longer be a police officer.'

'So what am I?'

'As I said, a civil servant.'

'So as I run after the bad guys waving my SIG-Sauer, I shout, 'Stop in the name of the civil service!, do I?'

'When was the last time you actually arrested someone, Spider?' she asked. 'That's not what you do. You work under cover, you gather evidence.'

'But I lose my rank, is that what you're saying? I'll no longer be a detective sergeant?'

'That's right. But your pay scale remains the same. You'll get more holiday entitlement, as it happens, and your pension will improve. It's no big deal. And you've got to have another psychological assessment but you were due one anyway.'

'Who'll be running through the canyons of my mind this time?'

'It's still Caroline Stockmann.'

Shepherd liked Stockmann and knew the interview wouldn't be a problem.

'How's your son?' asked Button.

'He's fine. Hereford's working out really well for him. We're just down the road from his grandparents and he's settled in at school. The only downside is me being away from home such a lot, but I wasn't there much when we lived in Ealing. At least now if I'm away his grandparents can keep an eye on him.'

'And the au pair's still there?'

'Katra? Yeah, three years now. She's practically family.'

Button looked amused and Shepherd pointed a warning finger at her. 'Don't go there.'

'Still nothing on the romance front, then?'

'Certainly not with Katra.' Shepherd laughed. 'Don't worry about me on that score.'

'I just like to make sure my people are happy.'

'I'm happy,' said Shepherd.

Button smiled. 'Then if you're happy, I'm happy.'

'Would you like more champagne, sir?' asked the stewardess, with a gleaming smile that was as cold as the bottle she was holding. She was a dyed blonde with too much makeup. British Airways selected its staff for the long-haul first-class cabin on seniority rather than sex appeal.

'Please,' said Noel Kinsella, holding up his glass.

Elizabeth put a hand on her husband's arm. 'Honey, do you think it's a good idea to arrive smelling of drink?'

'It's champagne,' said Kinsella, 'and it's only my third glass.' He gave her a peck on the cheek. 'One for the road,' he added.

Elizabeth sighed with annoyance. She was a teetotaller in a family where alcohol was either embraced at every opportunity as a long-lost friend or hated as much as a political opponent. There were no half measures with the Kennedys, and Elizabeth was firmly in the camp that believed alcohol was a vice with no redeeming qualities. She had hoped she'd be able to convince her husband to cut down his alcohol intake after they had married but she had been as successful at that as he had been at stopping her smoking.

She looked out of the window. There was nothing but thick cloud below them. Elizabeth wanted a cigarette, badly. She had brought nicotine chewing-gum with her but it had done little to stifle her craving for a little white tube between her fingers and a lungful of cool, fragrant smoke. She had often thought of starting an airline that offered only smoking flights. Non-smokers would be banned, and all the flight crew would smoke. She was sure she could fill every seat.

Elizabeth would have preferred to fly on an American airline, but the British police officers accompanying her husband had already booked tickets on the British flag-carrier. He had paid for upgrades for the cops and they were sitting at the rear of the first-class cabin. They were dressed in reasonable suits and their shoes were shined, but they clearly didn't belong in first class, so the dyed-blonde stewardess and her gay male colleague had virtually ignored them throughout the flight.

'Not long now,' said Kinsella. Two lawyers were sitting on the other side of the cabin, one a partner in the Boston firm that handled much of the legal work for the Kennedy family, the other a partner in a top London firm of criminal lawyers. They had brokered the deal that was bringing Kinsella back to the United Kingdom. As part of the deal, he would not be handcuffed and there would be no physical contact between him and the officers as they left the plane.

Officially, Kinsella was not flying back of his own accord, he had simply stopped fighting the extradition order that had been filed against him. It was a fine detail, but it had given him an edge when he was negotiating his return. It meant that he could fly first class to London where he would be arrested, but instead of being taken into custody he would be allowed to spend two nights in a five-star hotel before flying on to Belfast. He would be officially charged in Northern Ireland but would be immediately granted bail until his trial, which the British Government had agreed to fast-track. The two lawyers would ensure that the authorities stuck to their side of the deal.

The plane landed smoothly and taxied to its stand. The Kinsellas waited patiently for the steward to open the door and hand the passenger manifest to the ground staff. Then he smiled at the couple and waved for them to leave.

'Thank you for taking such good care of us,' said Elizabeth, with a smile. They stepped through the door, closely followed by the two policemen.

Two men in suits were standing in the gangway. 'Noel Marcus Kinsella?' said one. He had a Belfast accent, as did the two policemen who had flown over with them. The Northern Ireland police had no intention of allowing their English counterparts to steal their glory.

'Present and correct,' said Kinsella, brightly. He reached for Elizabeth's hand.

'Noel Marcus Kinsella,' said the man, 'I am charging you with the murder of Robert Carter on the twenty-eighth of August nineteen ninety-six. You do not have to say anything unless you wish to do so, but I must warn you that if you fail to mention any fact which you rely on in your defence in court, your failure to take this opportunity to mention it may be treated in court as supporting any relevant evidence against you. If you do wish to say anything, what you say may be given in evidence.'

'Heard and understood,' said Kinsella. 'Now, can we get to our hotel, please? I need a shower.'

The old man inhaled the steamy fragrance of the mint tea, then sipped. It was the first Monday of the month and, as he always did on the first Monday of the month, he was sitting on a large silk cushion in a palatial tent in the desert some twenty miles from Riyadh. He had driven there in a convoy of four-wheel-drive SUVs. When he had been younger he had made the journey on a camel, as befitting his Bedouin roots, but now he was in his eighties and had a swollen prostate so he had no choice other than to travel by car.

The old man was Othman bin Mahmuud al-Ahmed, and he was worth a little more than four hundred million pounds. By most standards Othman was rich, but he was a pauper compared with the men he served. The princes who ruled the Kingdom of Saudi Arabia measured their wealth in billions, and Othman had made his money by carrying out the tasks they regarded as beneath them. He was a facilitator, a middle man who helped to sell the oil that lay far beneath the dunes, and to acquire the weapons that kept the Kingdom's enemies at bay. He had bought some of the most expensive homes in the world for his royal clients, ordered jumbo jets with circular beds and Jacuzzis with gold-plated taps. Othman was semi-retired now, though one could never fully retire from the service of the Saudi royals. When they called, Othman would answer. It would be that way until he died.

Othman was a wealthy man, and he believed in helping those less fortunate. That was why, once a month, he journeyed into the desert, sat in a tent and made himself available to any citizen who wanted to speak to him. It was the Bedouin way.

Othman placed the glass on a gold-plated saucer and nodded at his manservant, Masood, at the tent's entrance. Masood was in his late sixties and had served Othman for a little more than forty years. Othman trusted him like no other. He was his assistant, his butler, his food-taster, though never his confidant. Othman trusted no man with his innermost thoughts. Masood pulled back the silk curtain and ushered in the next visitor. It was just before midday and Othman had spoken to twenty-six men already. Women were not permitted to address him directly, but it was permissible for a man to make a request on behalf of a woman, providing he was a blood relative. Othman would remain in the desert until he had seen every man who wanted an audience. Some wanted advice, some an introduction to further their business interests, some wanted money, some simply to pay their respects. Whatever they wanted, Othman would listen and, wherever possible, grant their requests.

Masood ushered in a dark-skinned man wearing a grubby *dishdasha*, his head swathed in a black and white checked *shumag* scarf. He looked at Othman, then averted his eyes. Masood nudged him and he walked over the rugs to the centre of the tent. 'Greetings, sir,' he mumbled. He rubbed his nose with the back of a wrist, then put his hands behind his back and stood awkwardly, like a schoolboy waiting to be punished.

'Sit, please,' said Othman, waving at a row of embroidered cushions.

The man sat cross-legged and put his hands on his knees, still reluctant to meet Othman's gaze.

Masood hovered at the man's shoulder and asked him if he wanted tea or water. The man shook his head. Masood went back to the tent's entrance.

Othman was used to people being uncomfortable in his presence. He was rich and powerful in a country where the rich and powerful held the power of life or death over lesser mortals. 'What do you need from me?' he asked quietly.

The man swallowed nervously. 'I bring you a message, sir, from your son.'

'I have many sons,' said Othman.

'From Abdal Jabbaar,' said the man.

Othman's breath caught in his throat. 'Abdal Jabbaar is dead,' he muttered.

'Yes, sir, I know. I spoke to him before he died.'

'Where?'

'I was in Guantánamo Bay. I was held by the Americans, as was your son.'

The man was mumbling and Othman strained to hear him. 'The Americans let you go?' he asked.

'After four years. They decided I was not a threat.'

'And are you a threat to them?'

The man looked up and smiled cruelly. 'I was not when

they took me to Cuba, but I am now,' he said. 'I hate the infidels and I will do whatever I can to eradicate them from the face of the earth. But first your son said I was to speak with you, and to tell you what they did to him.'

Othman studied the man in front of him with unblinking eyes. The other lowered his own, reluctant to meet Othman's baleful stare.

'What is your name?' asked Othman.

'I am Khalid Wazir.'

'Would you like a drink?' asked Othman, picking up the silver teapot. This time the man nodded. Othman poured mint tea into a glass and handed it to him. 'So, Khalid Wazir, I am listening. Do not be nervous, my friend. You have done me a great service in coming here. Tell me what my son said.'

'He was tortured by the Americans,' Wazir whispered. He sipped his tea, then placed the glass on a small wooden table inlaid with ivory.

'I assumed that,' said Othman. 'They said my son took his own life, but I know that he would never have done such a thing.'

'They tortured us all,' said Wazir. 'They are animals. They have no honour.' He sighed mournfully. 'Sir, I do not know how to tell you what I must.'

'My son is already dead. What else can you tell me that would be worse?' said Othman quietly.

Khalid Wazir took a deep breath, then laid a hand over his heart. 'Sir, your son wanted me to tell you that they killed his younger brother, your son Abdal Rahmaan.'

The old man frowned. 'Abdal Rahmaan died in a car crash,' he said.

Khalid Wazir shook his head. 'He was burnt alive by the Americans,' he said. 'Tortured and killed to put pressure on Abdal Jabbaar.'

The old man sat back in his seat. Abdal Rahmaan had been found in the burnt-out wreckage of his SUV in Qatar after the car had careered off the highway and slammed into an electricity pylon. That was what the police had told Othman and he had had no reason to doubt them. Until now. 'You are sure of this?'

'I can only tell you what your son told me,' said Khalid Wazir. He took a deep breath. 'There is more.'

'Tell me,' snapped Othman. His patience was wearing thin.

'Your daughter,' said Khalid Wazir. 'The infidels tortured your daughter, Kamilah.'

'That cannot be so,' said Othman, coldly.

'They assaulted her. They threatened to rape her when she was pregnant with your grandchild. They did this and showed Abdal Jabbaar what they were doing. They wanted information from Abdal Jabbaar so they killed Abdal Rahmaan and assaulted Kamilah. Your son wanted you to know this.'

'Did he tell you who did this to him? Did he give you their names?'

Khalid Wazir nodded. 'An American called Richard Yokely. And an English woman, Charlotte Button.'

Othman sat with his back ramrod straight. He forced himself to stay impassive though his instinct was to scream, curse and swear vengeance on those who had abused his family.

'I am sorry to bring you such news,' said Khalid Wazir.

Othman acknowledged the man's apology with a wave of his liver-spotted hand but said nothing. He had come to terms with the death of his two sons, and even accepted that Abdal Jabbaar had killed himself while in the custody of the Americans, but what Wazir had told him had shocked him to the core. The police in Qatar had shown him photographs of Abdal Rahmaan's burnt-out car and told him that no other vehicle had been involved, that it had been a simple accident, that Abdal Rahmaan had probably fallen asleep at the wheel. But that had been a lie. A deliberate lie. More than a lie – there had been a conspiracy. And if Abdal Rahmaan had been murdered, then perhaps Abdal Jabbaar had not killed himself. Perhaps he, too, had been murdered by the Americans.

He had not seen Kamilah for three months. She was living with her husband in Nice, in the South of France. Othman had held his granddaughter soon after she was born, and had never suspected that anything was wrong. He understood why. Kamilah's husband was a good man but he was a devout Muslim and would be unable to live with a wife who had been defiled by unbelievers. No matter how much he loved his wife, Kamilah's husband would shun her for ever. Othman's daughter had known this so had said nothing, preferring to hide her shame and suffer in silence.

Khalid Wazir was watching Othman nervously and Othman forced himself to smile. No doubt the man feared for his safety, that Othman would lash out at the bringer of bad news. But Othman bore him no ill will. It had taken courage to tell a father that two of his sons had been murdered, and Othman would reward him handsomely. What Khalid Wazir had told him was heart-breaking, but at least now Othman could take his revenge on those responsible. Othman made a small beckoning motion with his right hand. Masood padded over and bent down so that his ear was level with Othman's mouth. Othman whispered that he should give Khalid Wazir fifty thousand dollars from the ornate silver casket that stood on a low table to the left of the tent's entrance. Masood bowed and went to it as Othman continued to scrutinise Khalid Wazir. 'They tortured you, the Americans?' Othman asked.

'It was nothing compared to what they did to your sons.'

'They beat you?'

'In my case the abuse was mental more than physical. They would not let me sleep. I had to kneel with my hands on my head for hours at a time. They said they would keep me for ever unless I told them everything I knew about al-Qaeda.'

'And what do you know about the Base?' asked Othman. 'The Base' was the meaning of *al-Qaeda*, though the term was rarely used in the Western media. 'The Base' sounded too normal, too non-threatening, so they preferred to use the more sinister Arabic name.

'Nothing.' Wazir smiled bitterly. 'I was a mechanic, working in Philadelphia. My boss was Iraqi, an old friend of my father's, and he took me on when I arrived in the country. He worked me hard and paid me little, but I was there illegally so I could not complain. I was not political. I just wanted to make money to send back to my family. But my boss hated the Americans, even though he had lived there for twenty years. He was helping a group of fundamentalists who were planning an anthrax attack in New York, and he had me work on one of their vehicles. The group were arrested and they found my fingerprints on the truck. Men from Homeland Security came to my apartment in the middle of the night and three days later I was in Guantánamo Bay. They kept me there for four years. It was where I met your son.'

'And what will you do now?'

'I was deported to Iraq. I swore to your son that I would come to see you, but then I will return to my country and fight the infidel. I have many skills that will be useful.'

'My manservant will give you money,' said Othman. 'And you have my gratitude for ever. If there is anything you need in the future, you have only to ask.'

'I did not do this for money, sir,' said Wazir, but Othman silenced him with a languid wave. Wazir realised that to argue would cause offence, so he lowered his eyes and mumbled his thanks. He stood up, and as he left the tent, Masood handed him a bulky package containing brand new hundred-dollar bills.

Othman put a hand to his forehead. A headache was building. Masood was at his shoulder. 'Can I get you anything, sir?' he asked. He had obviously heard everything Wazir had said, but knew better than to admit as much to his employer.

Othman shook his head. 'How many are still waiting?' he asked.

'A dozen at most, sir,' said Masood. 'I shall send them away.'

'No,' said Othman. 'I shall see them.'

'Very well, sir,' said Masood, and padded over the rugs to the entrance.

Othman took a deep breath and let it out slowly. He had to be strong. He could not afford to show weakness in front of the men who wanted an audience with him. With wealth and power came responsibility. It was the Bedouin way.

Shepherd stopped his black BMW X3 in the road and switched off the engine. His other car, a Honda CRV, was parked in the driveway. Katra would have picked up Liam from school by now. Shepherd had been away from his son for just over a fortnight, and although he had tried to phone home every evening he hadn't always managed it. Being under cover meant working unsociable hours and as David Hickey didn't have children he could only use his personal phone when no one was within earshot.

He climbed out of the SUV and walked up the driveway to the cottage. Liam's bike was lying on the front lawn and Shepherd wheeled it to the back door. Liam was sitting at the kitchen table reading a football magazine and yelped when he heard the door open. 'Dad!' he yelled.

'Who were you expecting? Father Christmas?' Liam rushed over to him and hugged him. 'Have you got bigger while I was away?'

'It was only two weeks,' said Liam. He released his father and squinted up at his head. 'What happened to your hair?'

'I had to cut it,' said Shepherd.

'You look like a skinhead.'

'It'll grow,' said Shepherd.

Katra appeared from the kitchen in a blue tracksuit, her hair tied back in a ponytail. 'I was about to play football with Liam,' she said.

'I'll have a kick-about with him,' said Shepherd.

'Great, it'll give me time to make *mavzlji.*'

'What's that?'

'Dad, don't you know anything? *Mavzlji* are meatballs. Made from pigs' brains.'

Katra grinned. 'My grandmother used pigs' brains,' she said to Shepherd, 'but I use minced pork.' Her Slovenian accent had all but disappeared during the three years she had worked for Shepherd, but the hours she spent watching daytime soap operas meant she had picked up the Australian habit of ending every sentence as if it was a question.

'Glad to hear it,' said Shepherd, and ruffled his son's hair. 'Come on, let's see if you can get any past me.'

They went out into the garden and Liam picked up a muddy football. He dropped it at his feet then kicked it to Shepherd, who dribbled it across the lawn. The grass needed cutting. He hadn't mown it since they'd moved in. He kicked the ball back to his son. 'The garden's a mess, isn't it?' he said.

'Because Mum isn't here,' said Liam. 'She always looked after the garden.'

'Hey, I did a lot of digging in the old one, remember?'

'Only because Mum told you what to do,' said Liam. 'She decided where to plant things.' He kicked the ball hard and it sailed past Shepherd. He turned and jogged after it, retrieving it from an overgrown vegetable patch. Liam was right. Sue had designed their old garden in Ealing, and although he'd done the spadework and helped her carry bedding plants and fertiliser from the garden centre, it had been her vision. 'So how about you and me get to work here?' he asked.

'Do you know how?'

'How hard can it be? Anyway, we need a big lawn to play football on, right? And the trees are fine as they are. We just need plants and bushes and stuff. Maybe a rockery or two.'

Liam grinned. 'A rockery?'

'Your mum liked rockeries. Don't ask me why.' Shepherd kicked the ball back so Liam, who caught it on his chest, let it fall to the ground and trapped it with his right foot. 'You've been practising,' called Shepherd.

'I'm on the school team now,' said Liam. He flicked the ball into the air, headed it three times, then let it drop on to his right foot. There was a strip of plaster just below his knee.

'What happened?' asked Shepherd, pointing at it.

'I tripped,' said Liam. 'It's just a graze.' He kicked the ball, which whizzed past Shepherd and banged against the shed.

'Why didn't Katra call me?'

'I told her not to. Are we going to play?'

Shepherd went to Liam and put his hand on the boy's shoulder. 'Why did you tell her not to phone me?'

'I didn't want you to worry, Dad. It's only a graze. It's not like I needed stitches or anything.'

'I'm your dad, it's my job to worry,' said Shepherd.

'Yeah, but what could you have done? Would you have come home?'

Shepherd screwed up his face. His son had the knack of asking disconcerting questions. 'If you'd needed me, sure.' Shepherd could hear the lack of conviction in his voice and it was clear from Liam's face that he'd heard it too. 'But you're a big boy, right? You'll be eleven soon.'

'That's what I thought you'd say,' said Liam. 'That's why I told Katra not to call you.'

'I'm your dad, Liam. I care about you more than anyone else in the world.'

'I know.' He seemed unwilling to meet Shepherd's eye.

'Just because I'm away, it doesn't mean I'm not worried about you or that I'm not thinking about you.'

'Are you going away again?' asked Liam.

'Hopefully not for a while,' said Shepherd.

'You always say that,' said Liam, ruefully.

'And I always mean it,' said Shepherd. 'But sometimes there's work that needs doing and I have to do it.'

'Why can't someone else do it?'

'It's my job.'

'But you could get another job, couldn't you?'

Shepherd laughed. 'Like what?'

'You could work in a bank, like Granddad.'

'Liam, I was a soldier. Now I'm a policeman. Well, sort of a policeman. Anyway, guys like me, we can't work in an office.'

'Why not?'

'Because I'd be bored,' Shepherd said. It was the best answer he could come up with.

'So you do it because it's exciting, not because it's your job?'

'Everyone has to work,' said Shepherd. 'Everyone has to do something.'

'I just wish you weren't away such a lot,' said Liam.

'If I was a salesman I'd be away all the time. People have to travel for all sorts of jobs. Look at airline pilots. If I was a pilot, I'd never be here, would I?'

'At least people don't shoot at pilots,' said Liam, flatly.

'What?' said Shepherd.

'Nothing.'

'Who says I'm being shot at?' asked Shepherd. 'Have Gran and Granddad said something?'

'I just heard them talking, that's all, last time I was at their house.'

'And what did they say?'

'Nothing,' said Liam. 'Really, nothing.'

'They said I was shot at?'

Liam shrugged. 'That's what Mum used to say, too.'

Shepherd flopped down on to the grass. 'Sit,' he said. Slowly Liam sank down next to him, but turned his back. 'I help to catch criminals,' said Shepherd, 'but it's not like on the TV – the bad guys don't go around shooting the men who are trying to catch them. They honestly don't. They know that if they shoot someone, they'll go to prison for a long, long time.'

'Sometimes policemen get killed.'

'Not very often, Liam, and if I do my job properly, which I do, no one's going to get the chance to hurt me. I have partners, I have a boss, I have a whole lot of people watching out for me.'

'But you have a gun, right?'

Shepherd sighed. Yes, he had a gun. It was in the house, locked in a drawer in his wardrobe. A SIG-Sauer, his favourite weapon. It had always been a bone of contention with Sue, but Shepherd had argued that it was just a tool he needed to carry out his job effectively. She had always insisted that it be hidden from Liam, but when the boy was ten Shepherd had decided he was old enough to know about firearms. Most firearm accidents involving children arose from ignorance so he had shown the gun to Liam and explained how it worked, how dangerous it was, and that it was never, ever, to be taken from the locked drawer. 'I have a gun, yes.'

'Because you shoot people, right?'

'Liam, I don't go around shooting people.'

'Granddad says you do.'

'He said what?'

'He said you've shot people. Is that true, Dad? Have you shot people?'

'What did Granddad say to you?'

'Nothing. I was upstairs and he was talking to Gran.'

'And what did he say?'

'Nothing.'

'I just want to know what he was saying, Liam. You're not in any trouble. And neither is your granddad.'

Liam sighed. 'Gran said she wished you had a job that wasn't so dangerous because I'd already lost one parent and it was stupid of you to take risks when you were all I had left. Granddad said you were a hero and that you only shot people to save lives.'

Shepherd smiled ruefully. 'They're both right.'

Now Liam turned to him. 'So you have shot people, right?'

'Yes,' he said. 'But it's not something I want to talk about now. Maybe when you're older.'

'Why not now?'

'Because it's not easy to explain, Liam. And because you're too young to understand.'

'I'll be a teenager in two years.'

'And I can't tell you how much I'm looking forward to it.' He put his arm round his son. 'One day I'll talk it all through with you, I promise. Okay?'

'Okay,' said Liam.

'Some people like to talk about what they do,' said Shepherd. 'They like to tell war stories. I don't. A lot of what I've done is locked away, deep inside, like it's in a vault. And it's a big thing for me to open that vault. I did for your mum, and one day I will for you.'

'Dad, I understand. I'm not a kid.'

Shepherd laughed. 'Right,' he said. 'Now, shall we have another kick-about before we eat those cow brains?'

'Pig brains,' said Liam. 'I bet I can get six past you one after the other.'

Shepherd groaned. 'I bet you can, too.'

Joseph McFee blinked as the hood was pulled off his head. He was kneeling opposite a blindingly bright light that was shining into his face. He coughed and spat on the floor. A figure was standing in front of him. 'Who the fuck are you?' he asked. He strained against the duct tape that had been wrapped tightly round his wrists.

The figure walked to the lamp and twisted it so that it was shining at a framed photograph, on a metal table, of a man in his twenties, wearing the uniform of an RUC inspector. There was a half-smile on the subject's face, as if he was flirting with whoever had taken the shot. Recognition dawned. 'Robbie Carter,' McFee said. He knew then that there was no hope. 'You killed Adrian Dunne? He was a good man.'

The figure grabbed him by the scruff of his neck, dragging him to his feet.

'We served our time, all of us did,' said McFee. All he could hear was deep breathing. In and out, slow and controlled.

'Look, it was Dunne and Lynn killed the peeler. I didn't even have a gun. I broke down the door and I was there when it happened. That was what they said at the trial and it was the truth. I was there but it wasn't me who killed him.'

The sound of the gun was deafening in the confined space and McFee's left leg felt as though an iron bar had been slammed against it. He fell to the side and staggered, trying to regain his balance. He clamped his teeth together to stop himself screaming. 'I didn't kill him,' said McFee. He winced as pain lanced through his leg. 'I didn't even have a gun. I was there but I didn't kill him.'

The gun roared again and McFee's right leg collapsed. He pitched forward. He managed to turn his head just before he hit the floor so he didn't smash his face, but the fall had knocked the breath out of him.

He felt rather than heard footsteps as he gasped for breath. He could feel the blood pouring from his shattered knees and his ribs hurt with every breath he took. Not that the pain mattered. He knew that nothing mattered any more. He wanted to beg for his life but he knew there was nothing he could say that would prevent what was about to happen.

He began to pray. 'Our Father who art in Heaven, hallowed be thy name . . .' The gun barked again.

Shepherd heard the rat-tat-tat of an assault rifle being fired on automatic as he pushed open the door to the indoor range. The Major was standing with his back to the door and looked over his shoulder as Shepherd came towards him. 'Spider, good to see you,' he said. He lowered the weapon he'd just fired and shook hands.

Major Allan Gannon was well over six feet tall, with a strong chin and wide shoulders. His nose had been broken at least once. He was wearing camouflage fatigues with Converse sneakers, and a Rolex Submariner on his left wrist. A yellow foam plug nestled in each ear, protection against the deafening gunshots. The metal briefcase that contained the secure satellite phone nicknamed the Almighty stood against the wall. No matter where the Major went he was never far from it. The only people who had access to it were the Prime Minister, the Cabinet Office, and the chiefs of MI5 and MI6. No matter who called, it was never good news.

'Didn't expect to find you in Hereford,' said Shepherd.

'They try to keep me nailed to that desk, but I managed to tunnel out,' laughed the Major. 'I like the haircut. You joining the Marines?'

Shepherd ran his hand over his scalp. 'I was under cover with a gang of heavies who thought that short hair, tattoos and an earring meant you were hard. It'll grow back.'

The Major grinned. 'Yeah, I wish I was hard.' He showed Shepherd the weapon he had just fired. 'Seen one of these before?'

'It's the Heckler MP7, right? They came out just before I left the Regiment.'

The Major nodded. 'They call it a Multi-role Personal Defence Weapon, these days.'

'Better than the MP5?'

'I like it,' said the Major. 'It's got a 4.6-by-30-millimetre round, which packs the same punch as an assault rifle, and it'll cut right through Kevlar body armour at two hundred metres. But it handles like a .22 with hardly any recoil. It's like a rock during burst fire, even at nine hundred and fifty rounds a minute. NATO was getting fed up with bullets bouncing off body armour so they asked for a new weapon and Heckler came up with this.' He put it on a table and picked up a second weapon, thinner and longer than the MP7 with a smaller hand-grip. 'We're doing a compare and contrast with this,' he said. 'Heckler's UMP. Universale Maschinenpistole.'

'*Ja, mein Führer,*' said Shepherd, clicking his heels and bowing. 'Ve used it ven ve invaded Poland, *ja?*'

Gannon handed him the UMP. 'Now, this one was specifically designed to replace the MP5. It fires from a closed bolt, like the MP5, but is designed for bigger cartridges.

Mainly polymer construction, it's a full pound lighter than the MP5. It comes in three versions. This one is the UMP45 which uses the .45 ACP cartridge. Lots of stopping power.'

'Which is all well and good if you hit the target,' said Shepherd, 'but I wouldn't want bullets like that whizzing around where there's a risk of collateral damage.'

'Sure, but you have to take into account that, these days, the bad guys all wear body armour,' said the Major. 'Even the old double-tap to the chest with an MP5 comes up short if the guy's got a Kevlar vest. The clever thing about the UMP is that all three versions are the same basic design and can be converted to any of the other calibres by switching the bolt, barrel and magazine. So you can have the nine-by-nineteen-millimetre Parabellum if you prefer it, but you have the option of converting it to take the .45 or the .40 Smith & Wesson cartridge.'

Shepherd hefted the UMP. It weighed about five pounds, with its twenty-five-round magazine, and didn't look much different from the MP5 he'd used during his time with the SAS.

'So, how's business?' asked the Major.

'Same old,' said Shepherd. 'Drugs, mainly. That's SOCA's bread and butter.'

'Don't you feel you're wasting your time putting drug-dealers away? They're supplying a need, and presumably for every one you put behind bars there's another waiting to take his place, right?'

'I just do what I'm told,' said Shepherd. He sighted at one of the targets down the range, the weapon's stock fitting snugly against his shoulder.

'You've got better things to do than arrest drug-dealers,' said Gannon. 'You should come and work for the Increment. Get involved in anti-terrorism. Do something that makes a difference.' The Increment was the Government's best-kept secret, and the Major ran it. It consisted of a group of highly trained special-forces soldiers who were used on operations considered too dangerous for Britain's intelligence agencies. The Major was able to draw on all the resources of the Special Air Service and the Special Boat Service, plus any other experts who might be needed.

'I'm too old to be an action man,' said Shepherd.

'You're almost ten years younger than me,' said the Major, 'and it's not all jumping out of planes and firing from the hip.' He indicated a box of earplugs on the table.

'I'm happy with SOCA,' Shepherd said. 'It's challenging, and I get to spend time with Liam too.' He popped plugs into his ears and worked his jaw as they expanded to fill his ear canals.

'And the lovely Miss Button?'

'Mrs Button,' said Shepherd. 'Married with child.'

'Don't get too attached,' said the Major.

'What do you mean?'

The Major picked up the MP7 and fired a short burst at the terrorist target twenty-five yards away. The tang of cordite in the enclosed space made Shepherd's eyes water. The Major grinned at the tight grouping in the centre of the dummy's head. 'We had some MI5 hotshots down for weapons training last week,' he said. 'They weren't a bad crowd, as it turned out, but they sure as hell couldn't hold their booze. We took them on a pub crawl and I had a very interesting chat with a young lady who works in Five's surveillance department.'

'I bet you did,' said Shepherd. He aimed the UMP at the target next to the Major's and pulled the trigger. The weapon's relatively slow rate of fire and the large-calibre rounds meant he had to keep a tight grip as it kicked. Even before he'd finished he knew that several of his shots had gone wide. He grimaced as he put the gun back on the table. 'Give me the MP5 any day,' he said.

The Major slapped him on the back. 'If that's any indication of your marksmanship, you'd better stick with an MP3,' he said. 'Or, better still, an iPod.' He handed the MP7 to Shepherd and bowed theatrically towards the targets. 'Pray try again, m'lord,' he said, in his best Jeeves impersonation.

Shepherd raised the weapon to his shoulder. He slipped his finger inside the trigger guard. The weapon had a similar safety feature to the Glock pistol – the trigger was in three sections of which the middle had to be pulled first before the outer sections would move. It helped prevent an accidental discharge. It wasn't a feature that Shepherd appreciated. It made the trigger less sensitive and Shepherd believed that a man who could accidentally fire a weapon shouldn't be handling one in the first place. In all his years as an SAS trooper and undercover cop he'd never once fired without meaning to. He loosed a quick burst and smiled at the almost total lack of recoil. There was none of the kicking and bucking he associated with the UMP yet a tight cluster of holes had appeared above the terrorist's heart. 'Nice,' he said.

'And the rounds have enough velocity so that once they've punched through body armour they start tumbling,' said the Major. 'The ammunition is pretty much exclusive to the gun, the bullet is made of hardened steel and it's smaller than a nine-millimetre so you can get loads of them in a magazine. It's a real man-stopper. The German Army's already using it and the Ministry of Defence police here have already signed up for it.'

'It's a good gun,' said Shepherd. 'I just hope the bad guys don't start using it.' He handed it back. 'What did you hear about Charlie?' he asked.

The major raised his eyebrows. 'What makes you think I heard anything about the lovely Mrs Button?'

'Because I'm a cop and you're transparent,' said Shepherd.

Gannon laughed. 'Fair point,' he said. 'Seems that Charlie's a bit of a hero with MI5. And they reckon she'll be back there before long.'

'Office gossip or something more substantial?'

'Substantial gossip, from what I understand. The way my little songbird told it, Charlie was one of several MI5 high-flyers who were seconded to SOCA at its inception. The spooks were worried that SOCA might get ideas above its station, so they wanted their own people on board from the get-go. But it was never a permanent attachment, and my source is guessing that before long she'll be back in the fold.'

'There'll be lots of movement back and forth between SOCA and the other agencies,' said Shepherd.

'She's a spook,' said the Major. 'Graduate entry, dyed-in-the-wool MI5. What I'm saying is, don't nail your colours to her mast because, come the day, she'll sail off into the sunset.'

'Leaving me high and dry? You do love your metaphors, don't you?'

'In your line of work, your boss means everything,' said the Major.

'I've changed bosses before,' said Shepherd.

'But this is different,' said the Major. 'She's not with SOCA because she wants to put criminals away. She's there because MI5 sent her. And when they click their fingers, she'll be back. You want a boss who's committed, not one who's plotting her career path.'

'I hear you,' said Shepherd.

'I'm just watching your back, Spider, same as always.'

'And I wouldn't have it any other way,' said Shepherd. 'Now, do you want to put the targets back to fifty yards and see who'd be better off with the iPod?'

The Judge fiddled with the papers in front of him, then peered across the crowded court at the man in the dock, who stared back at him, head held high. The Judge had a pair of reading glasses perched on the end of his nose and looked over the top of them as he addressed the man.

'Noel Marcus Kinsella, you have pleaded guilty to the callous murder of Inspector Robert Carter, a man who was murdered on the orders of the Provisional wing of the Irish Republican Army, for no other reason than that he was a serving police officer.'

Kinsella folded his arms and stood with his legs shoulder-width apart.

The Judge spoke slowly. The regular court reporters had perfect shorthand but he knew that most of those in his court were from the British media and usually depended on electronic recording equipment, which was banned in courtrooms, and he didn't want to be misquoted.

'I therefore sentence you to life imprisonment with a recommendation that you serve a minimum of sixteen years.' He leant back in his seat. 'But, as we both know, my recommendation counts for nothing, and neither does the sentence I have imposed on you.' He gazed coldly at Kinsella. 'Under the terms of the Good Friday Agreement I have no doubt that you will not serve a single day in prison for the brutal murder of a brave young police officer. While I, like most of the population, are grateful for what the Peace Process has achieved, I have to say that some issues concern me greatly. The murder of Robert Carter is one such. Mr Carter was doing his job, protecting both sides of the community. He was a good father and a loving husband. You were part of a group who decided to murder him, to shoot him in the knees and then the head in front of his wife and young child. You have shown no remorse, and you have made it clear that you are pleading guilty for no other reason than to expedite the process so that you can gain your freedom.'

The Judge took a deep breath as if steadying himself. 'Get on with it!' shouted a man in the public gallery.

The Judge ignored the interruption. 'Under the terms of the Good Friday Agreement, a minimum of two years must be served before early release can be considered. But it has been made clear to me that, in your case, you will be freed under the Royal Prerogative of Mercy, which means that you will serve no time.' The Judge scowled at Kinsella. 'There is a certain irony in that, considering that you showed Mr Carter not one iota of mercy.'

The Judge lifted a glass of water to his lips and drank slowly, his eyes continuing to burn into Kinsella's. He put down the glass, then dabbed his lips with a handkerchief before he went on. 'The court system is charged with deciding guilt or innocence,' he said slowly, 'but we are also charged with apportioning punishment. The murder of a brave young police officer should not go unpunished. Yet that is what is happening here. You have pleaded guilty, but there is no doubt in my mind that you feel no guilt. You deserve to be punished for what you did that evening in nineteen ninety-six, but that will not happen, which disgusts me today. Justice is not being served, but political expediency is.' He paused again. 'Take him down,' he said, shaking his head in disgust.

Two uniformed prison officers reached for Kinsella, who shook them away. 'You're not to touch me,' he said. He looked at his two lawyers.

'Take him down, but do not restrain him,' said the Judge.

The British lawyer stood up. 'Your Honour, in view of the fact that Mr Kinsella will almost certainly be released later this afternoon, could he simply not walk free from the court now?' he said, in an upper-class English accent.

The Judge scowled at him. 'Mr Kinsella can sit in a cell until the paperwork arrives,' he said. 'If it was up to me he'd rot in Hell.'

Kinsella grinned at the Judge. 'Thank you, your Honour,' he said. 'You have a nice day, now.' He went down the stairs leading to the cells below the court, followed by the two prison officers.

There were loud cheers from the public gallery and two young men at the front unfurled an Irish flag. Two burly bailiffs moved to grab it but the Judge waved them back. There was nothing to be gained from confronting the demonstrators. He left the room by his private entrance. He had a bottle of malt whisky in his office and intended to make full use of it.

Othman bin Mahmuud al-Ahmed removed the leather hood from the falcon's head and studied its inquisitive jet black eyes as he made soft shushing sounds. The few seconds after the hood had been removed were always tense. The bird needed reassurance and to hear the voice of its master. The Saker falcon was beautiful, one of the old man's favourites. It had a wingspan of more than a metre but he barely felt its weight as it gripped his arm with its curved talons. The Saker generally hunted rodents but the falconer had been training it to take birds in flight and it had proved an able pupil. It cocked its head, then opened its beak and called, 'Kiy-ee, kiy-ee.' Othman and the falcon stood in the shade of a large yellow and red umbrella held aloft by Masood.

'Yes, pretty one,' said the old man. 'It is time to hunt. Time to kill.' He peered out over the desert dunes. Two white Range Rovers stood to his left, with his falconer, Sandy Macgregor. The old man had met Macgregor while he was staying at the prestigious Gleneagles Hotel in Scotland, and had hired him shortly afterwards. Now Macgregor earned a six-figure salary and a range of expatriate privileges, including a luxurious five-bedroom villa, business-class flights home for himself and his family, and a place at a top international school for his twelve-year-old son. Half a dozen other falcons waited on block perches attached to the rear of one of the Range Rovers. They were still hooded and cocked their heads as they listened intently, knowing that one of their number was about to be flown and that soon it would be their turn. Two of Othman's bodyguards waited beside them, big men in safari jackets, their heads wrapped in red and white checked *shumag* scarves, their eyes shielded with impenetrable wraparound Oakley sunglasses. Both men were Americans, former Delta Force soldiers. Othman had no love for America or Americans but, like the Saudi Royal Family, he had come to appreciate that Delta Force produced bodyguards second to none.

He rubbed the falcon's brown chest feathers. It arched its neck, spread its wings and called again, 'Kiy-ee, kiy-ee.' It was a female, almost six years old. Females generally made better hunters than males. They were larger, had keener eyesight and were better suited temperamentally to the task. They were patient: a male would rush in and waste its energy chasing anything that moved, but the females watched and waited until sure of making a kill. It was one of the few instances in male-dominated Saudi life when the male was regarded as inferior to the female.

Macgregor only gave the falcon water once a week. The bird took enough liquid otherwise from the blood of its prey. All the birds were weighed twice a day, first thing in the morning and last thing at night. The key to keeping a falcon alert was to make sure it wasn't too well fed. Overfeeding led to laziness, but underfeeding made it resentful and testy. The trick was to keep it just hungry enough to make it a determined hunter. The Saker hunted every day under Macgregor's watchful eye, and the old man flew it several times a week, as he did all his hunting birds. The falcons were trained in the cool air of the early evening, but hunted best in the hours between sunrise and midday. Othman had been driven out into the desert as the sun was edging over the horizon, smearing the black sky with a reddish glow. Macgregor had prepared the birds as the sun had climbed higher and now, an hour into the day, a slight breeze was blowing from the west, ruffling the falcon's feathers.

Macgregor lowered his binoculars. 'Two o'clock, sir,' he called. 'About four hundred metres.'

Othman turned towards the two o'clock position. A small bird was flapping purposefully, heading towards the town in the distance. The old man raised his arm in the direction of the prey and pushed his gloved hand forward. As the falcon spread its wings, the old man opened his fingers wide, releasing the jesses. The falcon climbed into the air. The old man shielded his eyes with his gloved hand.

The falcon was heading directly for its prey. The Saker did not kill by dropping from a great height, it built up speed and attacked from behind and to the side, ripping at the victim's throat with its talons and following it to the ground to finish the kill with its beak. As Othman watched it gain on the small bird, he held his breath, eyes burning fiercely. 'Go on, pretty one,' he muttered. 'Kill for me.'

The falcon hit the bird hard, then veered to the left as the shattered ball of feathers tumbled to the ground. It cried in triumph as it glided in a full circle, then landed on its prey and began to feed.

Macgregor hurried across the sand to retrieve the falcon before it ate too much.

Othman heard an engine buzz in the distance, sounding like an angry wasp. He narrowed his eyes. A quad bike with large tyres was heading his way, spurts of sand spraying up behind it. Othman had been expecting its driver. His name was Muhammad Aslam – Servant of the Kind One. It was an appropriate name, Othman knew, because Muhammad Aslam was a fixer. Not a fixer in the way that Othman himself acted as a facilitator, organising multi-million-dollar deals and overseeing complex financial transactions. Muhammad Aslam operated at the other end of the spectrum, arranging violence for those who did not want to get their hands dirty. He could make bad things happen – at a price – his ability to do that enhanced by his employment with al-Shurta, the Saudi public security police.

Othman's two bodyguards reached for their handguns but Othman nodded at Masood, who called that the visitor was expected. The men took their hands from their weapons but kept their eyes on the quad bike as it slowed and came to a standstill close to the Range Rovers.

As Muhammad Aslam climbed off it, a bodyguard went over and patted him down, then motioned for him to join Othman. Aslam was forty-two years old, but two decades with the Saudi police had aged him. There were dark patches under his eyes, deep wrinkles across his forehead and at either side of his mouth, and he had a badly trimmed drooping grey moustache. He was wearing a red baseball cap and sunglasses, both of which he removed as he approached. He bowed his head as he greeted Othman.

'Let us go to the shade,' said Othman. 'The sun is fierce today.'

They walked together to a large marquee that had been set up some distance away from the Range Rovers. Inside, a jug of iced mint tea, another of iced water, and a plate of fruit had been set out on a table, with three chairs. Aslam waited until Othman was seated, then sat down himself. Masood poured tea for them, then backed out of the marquee, leaving them to talk alone.

Othman pushed the plate of fruit towards Aslam, who nodded his thanks and took an orange segment. 'I need your help,' said Othman.

'Whatever you need, I am here,' said Aslam. He bit into the orange and sucked noisily.

'I need a man who can hunt,' said Othman. 'I need a man who can hunt and kill.'

'There are many such men in the world,' said Aslam.

'My sons have been killed,' said the old man. 'I want revenge. It was the infidels who killed them, and I want them killed by a Muslim. They used their religion against my sons, so I will use Islam against them.'

'I can find you such a man,' said Aslam. '*Inshallah.*' God willing.

'The infidels who killed my sons made sure they suffered, so I want them to suffer in the same way. I want them killed by hand, I want them to bleed and to scream. I want them to hear the names of my beloved sons as they die.'

'It shall be done, I swear,' said Aslam.

'Money is no object,' said Othman. 'I shall pay whatever I must, but I want it done quickly. I am an old man and I do not know how much time I have left.'

'You have a long and fruitful life ahead of you, I am sure,' said Aslam.

A slight smile creased Othman's weathered face. 'Do not flatter me, my friend,' he said. 'I am too old for sweet words.'

'I did not mean to offend,' said Aslam. 'I shall carry out your wishes immediately.'

Othman nodded. 'I thank you for that. Let me know your fee and I shall have the money transferred to your account.'

'Do you wish updates on my progress?'

'I require only to know that the man and the woman are dead, that they died in pain, with the names of my sons in their ears.'

Aslam stood up, bowed, then walked back through the sand towards his quad bike. One of the bodyguards went with him.

Macgregor came into the marquee with the falcon. Othman held out his gloved hand, palm down, and the bird hopped on to it. He caught the jesses between his thumb and first finger, and with his other hand he stroked the falcon's chest feathers. 'So, sweet thing,' he whispered, 'are you ready to kill again?'

The bird returned the old man's cold stare for several seconds, then it arched its neck and cried to the sky.

Shepherd finished his coffee, folded his copy of the *Daily Mail*, and stood up. He had been sitting in the coffee shop for a quarter of an hour. He hadn't seen Charlotte Button go into the office so he assumed she was already there. He went outside, waited for a gap in the traffic and jogged across the road. The door that led to the offices on the upper floors was between a butcher's and a florist's. There were three brass nameplates and an entryphone with three buttons. Shepherd pressed the middle one and waved up at the CCTV camera that monitored the entrance.

The door buzzed and he pushed it open. Button hadn't closed the door to the office and she smiled as he came up the stairs. She was wearing a red suit, the skirt cut just above the knee, and red high heels. 'You could have at least brought me a tea,' she said. You were in the coffee shop for fifteen minutes, weren't you? Doing the *Daily Mail* crossword?'

'The Sudoku, actually,' said Shepherd, 'so I guess that means you weren't looking over my shoulder. Anyway, I was just checking I was clean. I wouldn't want to blow a perfectly good SOCA safe-house.' He followed her into the office, unable to stop himself admiring her legs. Button often wore jeans or other trousers so they were rarely on display. She had very good ones, he decided. Firm and shapely, the ankles smaller than his wrists.

'I've got a meeting at SOCA headquarters this afternoon,' she said, 'and flashing a bit of skin tends to cut me a lot of slack.'

'If my legs were as good as yours, I'd be flashing them too,' said Shepherd.

'Why, thank you, kind sir.'

The office was lined with filing cabinets and volumes on tax law. There were four desks, one in each corner of the room, and a door. Button went through it and sat on a high-backed executive chair behind a large oak desk. 'Everything okay?' she asked.

Shepherd took one of the two wooden chairs on his side of the desk. 'Raring to go,' he said.

'I'm glad your hair's growing back because we'll be making use of your roguish good looks,' she said, as she opened a manila file and passed a photograph across the table.

'You are joking, I hope,' said Shepherd, as he scrutinised the photograph. It was a head-and-shoulders shot, ten inches by eight, of a woman in her mid-thirties with shoulder-length wavy red hair and freckles across her nose. She was laughing and there was a sparkle in her green eyes. 'Elaine Carter,' said Button.

'Pretty,' said Shepherd.

'Possible serial killer,' said Button.

'Ah,' said Shepherd. 'I thought serial killers were all middle-aged white males.'

'That's if you believe in profiling,' said Button. 'Elaine here is a special case.' She passed over another photograph, of a man lying face down on a terracotta tiled floor, a pool of blood around his head. 'Her husband was Robbie Carter, an RUC Special Branch officer. An inspector.'

Shepherd looked at the photograph. The hair at the back of the man's head was matted with blood. 'She killed her husband?' he asked.

'Spider, your psychic skills leave a lot to be desired. We'll get on a lot quicker if you let me tell you what we know and you make the occasional grunt.'

Shepherd looked more closely at the photograph of the dead man. There were smaller pools of blood around his knees.

'Robbie Carter was shot by an IRA execution squad in nineteen ninety-six,' continued Button. 'They gunned him down in front of his wife and young son.' She slid five photographs out of the file and spread them in front of Shepherd, like a poker player displaying a winning hand. She tapped the photograph on the far left. 'Adrian Dunne. He was caught fleeing a punishment shooting a year after Carter was killed. He'd used the same gun as he had for the Carter killing and was sent down for life. Released under the Good Friday Agreement.' She took another photograph and placed it on top of the first. It was a crime-scene shot. The body in it was naked and lying face down. There were gunshot wounds to the man's head and knees. 'Dunne was killed two weeks ago.'

She ran a red-painted fingernail down the photograph next to the one of Dunne. This man was the oldest of the five, with thinning grey hair and the ruddy cheeks of someone who had spent a lot of time outdoors. 'Joseph McFee. Left the Provos once the Peace Process got rolling and is thought to have joined the Real IRA. He didn't actually shoot Carter, and no evidence was presented that suggested he was carrying a gun, but he got life as well, plus additional life sentences for killing two British soldiers and three other policemen. He was released two months after Dunne.'

'Is it just me or is the world going crazy?' asked Shepherd. 'He murders two soldiers and four coppers and we let him out?'

'It was part of the Peace Process,' said Button. 'That was the deal.'

'Then the deal sucks, as my son would say. What we're saying is that if you murder a drug-dealer you'll spend twenty years plus behind bars. Kill a copper or a soldier and they'll let you out early.'

'You won't hear any arguments from me on that score,' said Button. She took a photograph from the file and laid it over the head-and-shoulders picture of McFee. It was from a crime scene, an almost exact match of the first. 'McFee was shot last week.'

She paused to make sure she had his undivided attention. 'Both men, McFee and Dunne, were shot with the same gun. Robbie Carter's service revolver.'

Shepherd quirked an eyebrow. 'Open and shut, then?'

'If it was, they wouldn't have called us in,' said Button. 'Carter's gun was never found. His wife said she had no idea where it was and there was a suggestion that the killers took it with them.'

'Is that possible?'

Button shrugged. 'Elaine Carter didn't mention the gun being taken at the time but she was pretty forthcoming with other details. In fact, it was her recollections that helped put the execution squad behind bars. So we're assuming that the gun wasn't taken at the time. The rifling on the bullets used in both killings is an exact match to those on record for Carter's gun. A Smith and Wesson .357 Magnum.'

'Nice gun,' said Shepherd. 'Not regular police issue, though. Back in the nineties the RUC were using the nine-millimetre Smith & Wesson 5904.'

'Back then Special Branch were allowed a degree of flexibility in their choice of handgun,' said Button. 'The Magnum would be a man-stopper, I gather.'

'It would do a lot of damage, that's for sure,' said Shepherd.

'All guns issued to officers are test-fired at the PSNI's Weapons and Explosives Research Centre and they keep a ballistic report on file along with a sample casing and an expended round,' said Button. 'WERC gave our technical people their samples and the report and, as I said, the bullets are a match. So, now we've got two of Carter's killers dead, and three still alive. For the time being, at least.' She pointed at the photograph in the middle. 'This is Gerry Lynn. A hard man, is Mr Lynn. He's the one who shot Carter in the legs. They went in to kill Carter, so the shots to the knee seem to have been nothing more than badness on Lynn's part. Ballistics showed that his wasn't a killing shot. He was released after serving three years, again under the Good Friday Agreement.' Shepherd looked expectantly at the file, but Button shook her head. 'Mr Lynn is very much alive, but is obviously a little jittery.'

'Under police protection?'

Button chuckled. 'Far too macho to let the police take care of him,' she said. 'The IRA have him under wraps. He's been their golden boy since the Northern Bank robbery in December two thousand and four.'

It had been Ireland's biggest ever raid. A group of men had kidnapped bank employees and got away with twenty-six million pounds, which, by all accounts, had swelled the coffers of the IRA. 'Lynn was involved in that?'

'That's the intel the RUC had, but it was never proved.'

'They never found the bulk of the money, either,' said Shepherd.

'It's been laundered by now,' said Button. 'And if Lynn kept any, it's well hidden.' She tapped the photograph second from the right. 'The driver, Willie McEvoy, was the first to be caught and was sentenced to life. Released six years ago under the Good Friday Agreement. Now he's a drug-dealer in East Belfast. Heroin, cocaine, cannabis, you name it, Mr McEvoy can supply it. He's been refusing police protection, no doubt because he's afraid it'll cramp his style.'

Shepherd picked up the fifth photograph. 'This one I know, of course,' he said.

'Ah, yes, he's quite the celebrity,' said Button. 'Noel Kinsella. He fired one shot in the Carter house, which missed. Bullet ricocheted off the floor and smacked into a kitchen cabinet. Once Lynn and Dunne were taken into custody, Kinsella did a runner. He was located in the States and the authorities started extradition proceedings but even after Nine Eleven the Americans were loath to do anything to offend the Irish-American lobby so they entered a legal limbo. Then Kinsella had a change of heart, stopped opposing extradition and agreed to fly to the UK.'

'Because he knew that under the Good Friday Agreement he wouldn't do any time?'

'Exactly,' said Button. 'He pleaded guilty, showed no remorse, was sentenced to life by a very angry judge, and was out on the streets by teatime. The thing that set alarm bells ringing was that the killing started after he agreed to come back and face the music.'

'The last straw, is that what you mean?'

'At least the others served some time, even if only a few years. But it was all over the papers that Kinsella was coming back into the welcoming arms of Sinn Fein and that he wouldn't be doing any time. There's even talk of a role for him in the Northern Ireland Assembly.'

'Is that possible?' asked Shepherd.

'The way things are going, you can't rule it out,' said Button. 'It's *Alice in Wonderland* territory.'

'Two murders don't necessarily mean there'll be more,' said Shepherd.

'Two murders with Robbie Carter's gun can't be coincidence.'

'If it's the widow, good luck to her,' said Shepherd.

'That's a gut reaction,' said Button.

'They killed her husband in cold blood and walk out after a few years,' said Shepherd. 'That's not justice.'

'It's not about justice, it's about bringing an end to the IRA's armed struggle,' said Button.

'The Government did a deal with terrorists,' said Shepherd. 'Lay down your arms and we'll let your killers go free.' He pointed at the photograph of Carter. 'They shot him in 'ninety-six, right? The IRA called a ceasefire in 'ninety-four. Then, because things weren't going their way, they called off the ceasefire and were killing again. When the Government caved in they announced that the ceasefire was on again.'

'He was unlucky, that's for sure.'

'Luck had nothing to do with it,' said Shepherd. 'The IRA shot him like a dog. I tell you, if they'd killed someone I loved I doubt I'd stand by and let bygones be bygones.'

'I never took you for a vigilante,' said Button.

'When it's personal, all bets are off,' said Shepherd. He studied the photograph of Noel Kinsella. 'This is recent?'

'Taken a year ago at one of his extradition hearings.'

Kinsella was in his early thirties, good-looking with a strong chin, piercing blue eyes and jet black hair slicked back with gel. 'Is your interest because you want to put the wife away, or because you want to protect Kinsella? Him being married to a Kennedy and all.'

'A very minor Kennedy,' said Button.

'I seem to remember that Ted was at the wedding,' said Shepherd.

'I wouldn't read too much into the connection,' said Button. 'The issue is more about making sure that no harm comes to someone who was extradited from the States. I know that Kinsella effectively returned of his own accord but our government went to a lot of trouble to get him back, and if anything should happen to him, it'll make it that much harder to extradite anyone else.'

'So it's more about protecting IRA killers than it is about catching whoever's knocking them off?'

'Two men have died,' said Button. 'Let's not forget that.'

'Three, if you count Robbie Carter, and from my perspective, he was worth a dozen of them. Here's a question for
you, Charlie. Let's suppose Elaine Carter's been killing these
guys and let's say we put her away. How long will she get?'

'That's for the court to decide, Spider.'

'Premeditated murder? Three shots including one in the
back of the head? She'll get life. And for her life will mean
life. There'll be no early release, no Good Friday Agreement
to put her back on the streets.'

'No one ever said life was fair,' said Button.

'So why did the case end up on your desk?' asked Shepherd.

'What do you mean?'

'You know what I mean,' said Shepherd, sitting back in
his chair and linking his fingers behind his head. 'Has SOCA
decided to target her, or has someone in government decided
they want to protect the husband of a minor Kennedy?'

'Two murders have been committed, Spider. That puts it
within our brief.'

'No argument there. But we're not in at the request of the
Northern Irish police, are we?'

'They won't know you're on the ground, that's true.'

'And your old firm? MI5?'

'This is a SOCA operation. We won't be clearing it with
anyone else.'

'Which means when I pop up with my English accent
everyone and anyone could be checking up on me.'

'Which is why your legend will be watertight.'

'Like the proverbial duck's arse?'

'I'll be watching your back, Spider.'

'I know that, Charlie,' said Shepherd. 'That's never an
issue.' He ran his finger through his hair. 'I've done some
dirty jobs, but putting away the widow of a dead cop has to
rank pretty much at the top of the list.'

'If she's doing it, she's a serial killer. You can empathise
with her, you can sympathise, but if she's a killer we have to
stop her.'

'Even if she's killing killers? Killing the scum that murdered her man? Would you kill to avenge your husband, Charlie?'

'That's not the sort of question you can ask a person, it really isn't. I'm not a killer, Spider. I've never killed anyone.'

'Well, I have. In combat and in the line of duty. And if someone ever killed someone close to me, I wouldn't hesitate. I really wouldn't.'

Button held up her hands. 'I hear what you're saying. But what you or I might or might not do is hypothetical. Here in the real world two men are dead and it's our job to find out who killed them.' She reached into her handbag and passed a packet of Marlboro across the table. 'You'll need to start smoking,' she said.

'Why?'

'She's a smoker. Forty a day. In my experience, smokers tend to trust other smokers.'

'That sounds like the voice of experience.'

Button nodded. 'I started when I was a teenager. Only gave up a couple of years ago.' She gestured at the packet. 'That's her brand. Should help you break the ice, if nothing else.'

Shepherd picked up the pack. 'You're serious?'

'You're not local, Spider. You'll need all the help you can get to gain her confidence.'

'And offering her a cigarette will get me in, will it?'

'Trust me. It'll help.'

'It's beautiful,' said Elizabeth, looking up at the grey stone walls of Belfast Castle. 'But I thought it would be more . . . castley.'

'Castley?' said Kinsella. 'What do you mean?' They were standing in the grounds by a fountain. Beyond the castle they could see the wooded slope of Cave Hill. The building's window frames, guttering and downpipes had been painted pink. Two big men in dark suits, Kinsella's police bodyguards, waited near the stairs that led down from the car park to the gardens.

'More like a castle, you know,' said Elizabeth. 'With a moat, turrets and slits for archers.'

Kinsella laughed and hugged her. 'It's not a real castle,' he said. 'It's more of a baronial mansion. It was built in eighteen seventy as part of the British occupation,' he said. 'It's a clone of Balmoral, the Queen's Scottish home.'

'Where's your romance?' she said, putting her arms round his waist and kissing his cheek. 'Have you seen the white cat yet?'

'The what?'

'The white cat. There's a legend that the castle will only prosper so long as there's a white cat living there.'

'You've been reading those guidebooks again.'

'I want to learn about your country's history,' she said. 'If things work out the way we hope, I might be Ireland's first lady one day.'

'You're an ambitious wee thing, aren't you?'

'We want the same thing, honey, and you know it.' Elizabeth stiffened. 'Noel, there are three men coming this way.'

Kinsella smiled as he recognised the man in the middle of the group. 'It's okay, sweetheart. He's Gerry Lynn, an old friend.'

Kinsella's minders moved to intercept them but Kinsella told them it was okay, he knew who they were.

Gerry Lynn strode across the grass, his long coat flapping behind him. It had been more than a decade since Kinsella had seen him and he had put on weight. His hair was grey and thinning, but he had the same flint-hard eyes. 'On the tourist trail, are you?' he asked.

'Elizabeth wanted to see the castle,' said Kinsella. 'Figured it'd be easier to meet here. My minders prefer me to stay in at night.'

The two men hugged. Kinsella frowned as something hard dug into his chest. He stepped back and patted Lynn above the heart. 'What the hell's that, Gerry?'

Lynn undid two of his shirt buttons to reveal a white

bulletproof vest. 'I'm not taking any chances, lad, and if I were you I'd do the same.' He glanced at the two men shadowing Kinsella. They were in their early thirties, both a little overweight. Their jackets were unbuttoned and their eyes were constantly sweeping the area. 'Bring them with you, did you, from across the water?'

'Special Branch,' said Kinsella. 'RUC.'

Lynn chuckled. 'The RUC's long gone,' he said. 'It's the Police Service of Northern Ireland now. And there's no more Special Branch. It's called the Intelligence Branch, which is an oxymoron if ever there was one.'

'Leopards and spots comes to mind,' said Kinsella.

'Nah, they're changing,' said Lynn. 'There's more Catholics joining and they're accountable now.'

'Are you going to introduce me?' asked Elizabeth. She smiled at Lynn. 'You'll have to forgive my husband, he doesn't have much in the way of social graces.'

Lynn held out his hand. 'Gerry Lynn. Pleased to meet you.'

They shook hands. 'You're wearing a bulletproof vest?' asked Elizabeth.

'It's nothing,' said Kinsella, hastily.

'A bulletproof vest isn't nothing,' said his wife. 'What's going on, Noel?'

'Nothing. It's fine.'

'You keep saying it's nothing but he's wearing a bulletproof vest and he says you should wear one, too.'

'I was joking, love,' said Lynn.

'Please don't "love" me, Mr Lynn,' said Elizabeth, frostily. She turned to her husband. 'We need to talk, honey.'

'We will, baby,' said Kinsella. 'Let me have a chat with Gerry first.'

Elizabeth glared at him. He tried to kiss her but she moved away. 'I'm serious, Noel,' she said.

'So am I, baby. You visit the antiques shop while Gerry and I have coffee and a chat.'

'Noel . . .'

Kinsella kissed her on the cheek. 'Baby, come on now, I have to talk to Gerry.' Elizabeth looked as if she wanted to argue, but then she walked away from him. 'Elizabeth!' Kinsella caught up with her and they went to the side of the castle where there was an entrance to the antiques shop and a tea-room.

'Ten minutes,' said Elizabeth.

'Sure,' said Kinsella.

Elizabeth picked up a framed watercolour of the castle as Kinsella and Lynn went through to the tea-room, their minders following.

Kinsella's eyes were on the men who had arrived with Lynn. One was in his late forties, short and stocky with unkempt red hair, the other tall and lanky, in his late twenties. They were dressed casually in leather jackets, jeans and training shoes. 'They're not cops, are they?'

Lynn chuckled. 'No.'

'What's with the vest, Gerry? Do you seriously think someone's going to shoot you in broad daylight? Those days are gone.'

'You think?' said Lynn. 'You know yourself it doesn't matter whether it's day or night. Someone's shooting and everyone gets their head down. We did as many shootings in the day as we did at night.'

'Speak for yourself, Gerry. I was involved in just the one.'

'Aye – and then you ran off to America with your tail between your legs.' He put up his hands as anger flashed across Kinsella's face. 'I meant nothing by that, Noel.'

'When they pulled in McEvoy I knew it was only a matter of time before they'd be knocking on my door,' said Kinsella.

'You were a Volunteer, Noel. You should have stood your ground. We were fighting a war and in a war there are casualties.'

'There was no way I was going to spend the rest of my life in jail,' said Kinsella.

'Well, now, luckily it never came to that,' said Lynn. 'And

look at you, guilty of murder but not a day behind bars. Who says fortune favours the brave?' Kinsella's face darkened and Lynn patted him on the back. 'I'm only messing, Noel.'

They sat at a quiet table. Lynn despatched one of his bodyguards to get two coffees. 'What did they tell you?'

'Who?'

'The cops. What did they tell you about Adrian and Joe?'

Kinsella's minder was out of earshot at a table where he could keep an eye on the entrance. 'Same as they told you, I suppose, that they were dead and that until they find out who's responsible I should be protected.'

'Did they tell you how they were killed?'

'Shot.'

Lynn grinned triumphantly. 'The lying bastards.'

'They weren't shot?'

'They were shot, all right, but it's the way they were shot that matters. They didn't tell me, they haven't told the media, and they're treating you like a mushroom, too.' He leant close to Kinsella. 'They were shot in the knees, and in the back of the head. Does the significance of that hit home, now?'

'Carter,' said Kinsella.

'Carter,' repeated Lynn.

'Why didn't they tell me?'

'They're not saying. Scared of bad publicity, maybe. Or copycat killers. But I've got a source in the cops who says they were definitely shot in the head and knees.'

'Shit,' said Kinsella.

'Yeah, shit,' said Lynn. 'If I were you, I'd lose your police minders and let the boys take care of you.'

'Are you serious?'

'You can't trust the cops,' said Lynn. 'For all we know, it could be cops doing it.'

Kinsella shook his head. 'Can't do that, Gerry. It wouldn't look good.'

The bodyguard returned with cappuccinos. He put the cups on the table and rejoined his colleague.

'I'm going to be offered a role in the Assembly,' said Kinsella. 'That's why I came back. They've got big things planned for me, Gerry. Big things.'

'Because of your wife?'

'It's sod all to do with Elizabeth. It's me they want. The Assembly's the future, Gerry. It's the way to a united Ireland.'

'And that means turning your back on your old friends, does it?'

'It means aligning myself with Sinn Fein rather than the IRA,' said Kinsella.

'Be careful who you turn your back on, Noel,' said Lynn.

'What's that supposed to mean?' asked Kinsella.

Lynn stood up and clapped him on the shoulder. 'Just be careful, that's all.' He walked out of the coffee shop, flanked by his bodyguards.

Hassan Salih settled back in the buttery leather seat of the white Rolls-Royce and looked out over the waters of the Persian Gulf.

'There are drinks in the cabinet in front of you, sir,' said the driver.

'I'm fine,' said Salih. 'Where are you from?'

'Bangladesh, sir,' said the driver. 'You are here on business or holiday?'

'Business,' said Salih. He stared at the back of the driver's head. Like most of the countries in the Middle East, at least those with oil, the locals brought in overseas workers to do the jobs they felt were beneath them.

'You have stayed at the Burj Al Arab before, sir?'

'I'm not staying, just visiting,' said Salih, 'but it will be my first visit. And this is my first time in a Rolls-Royce.'

'All the hotel's cars are Roll-Royces,' said the driver, 'and every suite has its own butler.'

'Amazing,' said Salih.

'The Burj Al Arab is the only seven-star hotel in the world.'

'I heard that,' said Salih.

'And it is the most beautiful,' said the driver. 'It was designed to represent the shape of a dhow.'

The hotel was ahead of them, a thousand-feet-high steel and glass structure on an island some three hundred metres offshore. It gleamed in the harsh sunlight, and to Salih it looked more like a curved blade than a ship. The Rolls turned to the right and headed over a causeway. Uniformed flunkeys were already waiting as it glided to a halt. Salih climbed out, and explained that he had no luggage and would be attending a meeting in one of the suites. A bellboy escorted him to the reception desk and handed him over to a blonde woman with Slavic cheekbones who took him up in the lift to the fifteenth floor, where she passed him on to a Bangladeshi butler. The man knocked discreetly and stood aside to let him in.

An Arab man in his early forties was sitting on a sprawling sofa. He was wearing an expensive dark blue suit and black patent-leather shoes that glinted in the sunlight streaming through the floor-to-ceiling windows that overlooked the sea. The man did not get to his feet, merely indicated the second sofa. 'Please sit,' he said, in accented English. 'Do you want anything to drink?' He stroked his greying moustache as he studied Salih.

'I'm fine,' said Salih. His own English was perfect. He had spent two years as a postgraduate student in California and was a frequent visitor to the United Kingdom. He had worked hard to lose his accent. The man dismissed the butler as Salih sat down. 'You have my money?' asked Salih.

'Of course,' said the man. A black leather attaché case stood beside the sofa. Salih picked it up and clicked open the two locks. Inside he found bundles of hundred-dollar bills. American dollars. The only kind worth having. 'I do not as a rule fly to meet a man I do not know,' said Salih.

'The fact that I sent you a first-class ticket and ten thousand dollars, along with a promise of the hundred thousand you have there, persuaded you, I suppose,' said the man.

Salih took out one of the bundles and riffled through it. Then he selected a note and held it up to the light.

'Do not worry, they are genuine,' said the man. 'I would not have gone to all this trouble to give you counterfeit notes.'

Salih put the note back into the bundle and closed the briefcase. 'We agreed that the hundred thousand dollars buys you one hour of my time,' he said. 'I'm listening.'

'I have need of your skills. A man and a woman. The man is American, the woman is British.'

'And how did you hear of me?'

'Your reputation is second to none.'

'Really?' said Salih. 'The fact that you are a senior officer of the al-Shurta wouldn't have had anything to do with you getting in touch with me?'

The man's smile tightened a fraction.

'You think I wouldn't have checked you out?' said Salih. 'Your name is Muhammad Aslam and your office is on the fifth floor of the police headquarters building in Riyadh. You have three wives and are blessed with sixteen children.'

'I am impressed,' said Aslam.

'Your youngest son was born on April the sixteenth. He weighed a little over six pounds.' He smiled. 'I could go on, but I'd only be showing off, wouldn't I? I hope my point is taken. As I said, I would not have flown here to meet someone I didn't know.'

'If you hadn't checked me out, you wouldn't have been the man I want,' said Aslam.

Salih patted the briefcase. 'Is this personal money, or are you acting as an intermediary?'

'So far as you are concerned, I am the client. But, of course, I am acting on behalf of a person who wishes to remain insulated from such matters.'

'Is he a member of the Royal Family?'

'Would that be a problem?'

'I do not trust the royals,' said Salih. 'They have a habit

of distancing themselves by removing those who have served them.'

'The person I am acting for is not royal,' said Aslam, 'but he is a Saudi.'

'And the targets, they are in the Kingdom?'

'No. The woman is in England, the American moves around. Neither will be in Saudi Arabia.'

'Are there any special requests?'

'There are,' said Aslam. 'They must be killed by hand. With violence.'

'So this is for revenge?'

'Very much so.'

'Up close and personal, as they say.'

'They must die in pain,' agreed Aslam. 'Is that a problem?'

Salih smiled. 'It is a challenge,' he said. 'But challenges must be paid for.'

'And your fee would be?'

Salih's smile widened. 'It will depend on the targets,' he said.

'The American works for the Government. Former CIA, now in one of the greyer areas of Homeland Security. The woman is a police officer in England.'

'Not civilians, then,' said Salih.

'Civilians are cheaper?'

'Of course, because they are easier to deal with. I will require two million dollars each. Plus all expenses, which will be considerable.'

'How considerable?'

'I will need a quarter of a million dollars in advance. That will be non-refundable, whatever the outcome.'

'Agreed.'

'I will make my preparations, and before I go ahead I will require fifty per cent of my fee, the rest to be paid once the job is done.'

'Also agreed,' said Aslam. 'There is something you must do when you kill them.'

'I am listening,' said Salih.

'When they die, they must be told that they are dying because of what they did to Abdal Jabbaar bin Othman al-Ahmed and to his brother Abdal Rahmaan. Those must be the last words they hear as they die. Do you understand?'

'I understand,' Salih said. He paused briefly. Then, 'Why did you come to me?' he asked.

'Because you are a Muslim,' said Aslam, meeting his gaze. 'They must be killed by a Muslim.' Salih nodded slowly. 'And because you are very good at what you do. You have never been caught and, as far as I am aware, you have never failed.'

'Not once,' said Salih.

'You are able to move freely between countries and you are, above all else, a professional. So, you are the perfect choice. Now, is there anything you require from me that will assist you?'

'Just the money,' said Salih.

'I can supply you with passports and visas if required.'

'I have my own sources.'

'Of course.' Aslam took an envelope from his jacket pocket and stood up to hand it to Salih. 'I do not have photographs, unfortunately, but I have accurate descriptions of both parties, full names and some personal details.'

'That will be enough,' said Salih, taking the envelope. He dropped it on top of the money and clicked the locks of the attaché case. 'We shall not meet again,' he said. 'Unless my fee is not forthcoming, of course.'

Muhammad Aslam chuckled. 'I heard you had a sense of humour,' he said.

'You heard wrong.'

Shepherd pulled up in front of the industrial unit and parked the Audi A6 next to Charlotte Button's Lexus. The unit was on the outskirts of Liverpool on an industrial estate close to the M57. The car hadn't been Shepherd's choice. It had been delivered to his home in Hereford as part of his legend and he regretted having to leave his SUV behind. He was Jamie Pierce, a website designer and computer geek, who was relocating from Bristol to Belfast and who would have no need of an SUV. Along with the car he'd been given a file containing the Jamie Pierce legend, which he'd committed to memory. He was single, had never married and had no children. A man who was more comfortable with computers than with people. One of the hardest things about being under cover was remembering the personal details of his legend and blanking out his own past. In the real world he had a ten-year-old son, and a wife who'd died in a senseless traffic accident, but while he was under cover he had to push them to the back of his mind. Shepherd hated having to pretend that his family had never existed, no matter how necessary it was.

Two other vehicles were parked outside the unit, a fluorescent green VW Beetle and a black Jeep Cherokee with wire wheels. Shepherd didn't know who owned the Beetle but the Cherokee belonged to Amar Singh, a technician who had worked for the Metropolitan Police but transferred to SOCA at the same time as Shepherd. He climbed out of the car and pushed open the door into the unit. Button and Singh were deep in conversation. A woman with curly blonde hair in a long green dress with a cardigan draped over her shoulders was standing by a pile of furniture with a clipboard. They all looked up as Shepherd walked across the concrete floor. Singh flashed him a thumbs-up. 'Spider, welcome,' said Button. 'This is Jenny Lock, our dresser.'

Shepherd shook hands with Lock. 'You were at Five with Charlie?' he asked.

'I'm freelance,' she said. 'I go where the money is.' She was in her mid-thirties, pretty with flawless skin and long eyelashes.

'Charlie keeps telling me there's no money at SOCA,' said Shepherd.

'Only when I see your expense claims,' said Button. She

glanced at the furniture and cardboard boxes. 'I wanted Jenny to go through everything before it gets delivered to Belfast.'

'Fine by me,' said Shepherd.

'What time's your sailing?' asked Button.

'Plenty of time,' said Shepherd. 'It leaves at ten thirty so I should get to the port just after nine.'

'We've got the removal firm booked on the morning ferry,' said Lock, 'so it should be with you early afternoon tomorrow.' She handed him the clipboard. As a dresser, her job was to provide the accessories that went with his legend. Shepherd inspected the furniture and electrical equipment. There was a Dell computer and monitor in their original boxes, along with a printer and a Sony laptop. 'We've put lots of work-related info on to the hard drives, and set you up with an email address that's got work-related correspondence. We'll be sending you stuff every day, and I suggest you reply whenever you can. Neither of the computers are secure, of course, so stay in character with anything you send.'

'Of course,' said Shepherd.

'A lot of Elaine Carter's friends are police and police wives, so there's a chance you'll be checked out,' said Button.

'You think someone'll get into my computers?'

'Wouldn't you?' said Button. 'Given the chance? You know how protective cops can be of their own. And not just the cops. Let's not forget you're an Englishman in Belfast. MI5 is still very much active in the province so anyone with an English accent will attract attention. The IRA have disarmed but they're still active, while the UDF, UVF and the rest of the Unionist boys will be looking at you. Belfast has changed since the Peace Process gained momentum, but both sides are still gathering intelligence.'

'My legend better be watertight, then.'

'It's rock solid,' said Button. 'I've set up designated phone numbers for three former employers on your CV and we've put motoring offences on the PNC. We've flagged your details on the computer so if anyone looks at you we'll know straight

away. We've used a safe-house in Bristol as your former
address and we've backdated utility accounts, council-tax
payments and the electoral roll. We even put you on a local
GP's list. I'll give you all the details before you leave.'

'And the car's kosher?'

'You've had it since new, and it ties in with the speeding
offences. We've got backdated parking tickets. We'll leave the
British plates on.' She nodded at Singh. 'Amar has rigged
up a special mobile for you.'

Singh handed Shepherd a new model Nokia. 'Stun gun?'
asked Shepherd.

'Infinity transmitter,' said Singh. 'Everything it picks up is
sent through the phone system to my receiver, whether or
not the phone is switched on.' Singh grinned. 'So be careful
what you say.'

'How do I switch it off?'

'You don't,' said Singh.

'What if I take out the battery?'

Singh sighed. 'Yes, obviously, if you remove the power
source, it won't be able to transmit.'

'I wouldn't advise that, Spider,' said Button. 'We can track
you through the phone, too. It's got GPS. We'll need to know
where you are.'

'I'm not sure I want you eavesdropping on my every word.'

'If you get close to her, if you win her over, she might give
herself away at any time. We've got the house covered but
we need to have you wired when you're outside. I decided
the phone was better than you wiring yourself up.'

'You've got the house covered?'

'I was coming to that,' said Button. 'Amar went in two
weeks ago, posing as a surveyor. All the rooms are wired for
sound.'

'What?'

'There's a microphone in every electrical socket,' Singh
told him.

'So every time I burp or fart, it'll be recorded?' said Shepherd.

'The on-off switch on the socket turns the microphone on and off too, so you'll have some privacy,' said Singh.

Shepherd gestured at the door. 'Can I have a word, Charlie?'

'Of course,' she said, and they went outside. She waited until he'd closed the door, then asked, 'Is there a problem?'

'I didn't realise this was going to be so personal,' he said. 'Everything I say and do, I'll be watched.'

'No cameras, Spider, but yes, someone will be listening. How else are we going to get evidence against her?'

'Usually we wait till I'm in, and then I'm wired up.'

'Same principle here.'

Shepherd shook his head. 'This is different.'

'Not shy, are you? Is that the problem?'

'It's not a problem,' said Shepherd. 'I'm just not happy about everything I say and do being on the record. Being under cover means telling lies, and I don't want that coming back to haunt me.'

'We all know you have to do what you have to do,' said Button. 'Anything not relevant will be deleted, you have my word.'

'Will I be expected to give evidence in court?'

'Not if I can help it,' said Button. 'The last thing we want is to have her on trial. There'll be a lot of sympathy for her, after what the IRA did to her husband. If she goes on trial, it'll stir up a whole lot of bad feeling.'

'So you expect her to plead guilty?'

'If you get her confessing on tape, and if you get the gun, I don't see that she'll have much choice.'

'Yeah? Any chance of her cutting a deal under the Good Friday Agreement? Like the bastards who shot her husband?'

Button flashed him a warning look. 'Spider . . .'

'Her husband was a cop, Charlie. A cop doing a difficult job. They shot him in cold blood and the Government released them as part of a political settlement. I don't think there's much that's political about shooting a man in front of his wife and child, do you?'

'It doesn't matter what I think, Spider. I've as much sympathy for Elaine Carter as you, believe me, but if she's killing, she has to be stopped. Between you and me, the powers-that-be'll probably do a deal, a reduced sentence in exchange for a guilty plea.'

'It's a shitty world, Charlie.' He sighed.

'You're preaching to the converted,' said Button. 'Look at it this way. Better you're the one rather than some hard-arsed cop with an axe to grind. At least you can empathise.'

Shepherd took out a packet of Marlboro and popped one into his mouth. He offered them to Button but she declined. He lit the cigarette and blew smoke into the air.

'How are you getting on with those?' asked Button.

'At least I can inhale without coughing now. I just hope I don't get addicted before the job's over.' Button was looking longingly at the cigarette and he offered her the packet again.

She wrinkled her nose, then sighed and took one. 'I suppose it doesn't count if I didn't buy it,' she said.

'One won't hurt you,' said Shepherd. He lit it for her.

Button inhaled deeply, held the smoke in her lungs, then blew it out. 'Disgusting habit,' she said.

Tears sprang to Willie McEvoy's eyes and he blinked them away, not wanting to die like a crying baby. 'There's half a kilo of cocaine upstairs,' he said, 'and money. There's thirty grand under the bed. It's yours. Take it.'

The barrel of a gun was pushed against the back of his neck. He heard the click-click-click of the hammer drawn back.

'Look, if I'm on your turf, I'll leave,' said McEvoy, his voice trembling. 'I'll up and go. I'll leave Belfast. There's no need to do anything stupid, okay?'

McEvoy stared at the wall in front of him. There was a small wooden cross with a figure of Jesus next to a framed photograph of the Pope. 'Please, Jesus, don't let me die like this,' he whispered. 'I'll do anything, anything, just don't let me die.'

McEvoy heard a rustle and a gloved hand reached over his shoulder, holding a photograph. McEvoy recognised the face in the picture and his heart sank. Robert Carter, in his RUC uniform and cap. McEvoy had been hoping he was being robbed, that all he had to do was to give up his money or his drugs and he'd escape with a beating or, at worst, a bullet in the leg. Now he knew this wasn't about drugs or money.

Tears rolled down his cheeks. 'I only drove the car,' he said. 'That's all I did. I drove the sodding car. I didn't even have a gun, they said that at my trial. I didn't even have a gun.' McEvoy put his hands up to his face and sobbed. He knew what had happened to Adrian Dunne and Joseph McFee. 'I've got money in the bank and I own three apartments in the city. Two apartments in Liverpool. More than a million quid's worth. I'll get the money for you tomorrow and I'll sign the apartments over to you.'

The gloved hand took the photograph away from his face.

'I did my time,' said McEvoy. 'I didn't shoot him. I didn't have a gun. I drove the car. I waited and I drove them away. That's all.' McEvoy felt a warm wetness spread round his groin and smelt his own urine. He'd pissed himself. He was crying like a baby and he'd pissed himself. Anger flared through his system and he lowered his hands, his tear-filled eyes blazing with hatred. He clenched his hands into fists. 'I'm not going to die like this,' he said. 'Fuck you, I'm not going to . . .'

The gun barked and McEvoy felt a searing pain in his left leg, as if he'd been hit with a hammer. He staggered to the right and almost immediately there was a second bang and his right leg buckled. McEvoy screamed. He lurched forward, arms flailing. His knees felt as if they were being pierced by red-hot pokers and the strength drained from his legs. 'This isn't fair . . .' he said. He didn't hear the shot that blasted through the back of his skull and tore through his face, spraying his brains and blood across the wall in front of him.

* * *

It took Shepherd less than twenty minutes to drive to the ferry terminal. He was directed to one of the lines of cars waiting to board, and an hour later he was sitting in the cafeteria eating an egg-mayonnaise sandwich and drinking coffee as the ferry headed across the Irish Sea. The Norfolkline ship took just over eight hours to make the crossing and he had booked a cabin so that he could get some sleep. His fellow passengers were a mixed bag. There were middle-aged motorcyclists in black leathers, families with children, and groups of workmen travelling with the tools of their trade.

Shepherd studied a Belfast street map as he ate. He had been to Belfast three times in the past when he had worked for Superintendent Sam Hargrove's police undercover unit, twice to infiltrate drugs gangs and once as back-up for a local Irish cop who had been trying to penetrate a counterfeit-currency ring. He had missed out on the IRA years, when members of the SAS put their lives on the line working under cover in Northern Ireland. It had been a dirty war, with casualties on both sides. There had been successes and failures, and war stories were still told in the bars and pubs of Hereford by the guys who had been through it.

Shepherd had come up against paramilitaries from both sides during his time in Belfast, but only as members of criminal gangs. As both sides downgraded their terrorist activities, the men with the guns found other ways to fill their time, from drug-dealing to armed robbery. Going up against criminal gangs in the city had been tough, not least because Shepherd's English accent marked him as an outsider. The city's criminal fraternity had split along tribal lines, but he'd been surprised to find that his nationality had never been held against him. The anger and hostility seemed to be directed between Catholics and Protestants, and as an Englishman he was deemed almost superfluous to the conflict. They were hard men, though, and most had started out throwing stones and petrol bombs at armoured Land Rovers before graduating to shootings, punishment beatings and, eventually, sectarian murder. That was the big difference for Shepherd. Most of the criminals he dealt with in mainland Britain were hard men, but few had seen a dead body and the vast majority had never killed anyone. But Belfast was brimful of men who had been trained to kill and who had taken lives for no other reason than that the victim was of the wrong religion. He was interested to see how the city had changed following the historic agreement for power-sharing.

He headed for his cabin at just after midnight and went straight to sleep. He woke at five thirty, shaved and washed, then went back to the cafeteria for coffee. At just before six the captain announced over the loudspeaker system that they were arriving in Belfast and Shepherd went down to the vehicle deck and sat in his Audi.

There were no checks as he drove off the ferry. There was little traffic on the roads and he was soon on a dual-carriageway on the outskirts of Belfast. He drove up into the Castlereagh Hills and turned on to Castlemore Avenue. The first houses he passed were detached, but then he came to a neat row of semis. He slowed and checked the numbers. His house was on the right, a neatly tended garden in front with a wrought-iron gate. He stopped the car, opened the gate, then drove up to the garage door. It was just before eight o'clock.

A white VW Golf was parked outside the garage attached to Elaine Carter's house, but no tell-tale movement of the curtains on the ground or upper floor. Shepherd guessed she was probably still in bed. He looked at the house that would be his home for the next few weeks. The windows hadn't been cleaned for a while but the white-painted wooden frames were in good condition, as was the front door.

He took out the keys Button had given him and unlocked the front door, which opened into a small hallway. Two rooms led off to the right, a front room with a brick fireplace and a dining room with a single bare bulb hanging from a ceiling rose. Upstairs there were three bedrooms. The one at the front was the largest, with built-in wardrobes. The window gave over the city, and in the distance he saw the giant yellow cranes of the Harland and Wolff shipyards, which had built the ill-fated *Titanic*, and beyond the urban sprawl, the Belfast hills. The sky was cloudless and the sun glinted on the cars driving through the city streets below.

There was a small shower room off the bedroom, and a bathroom off the landing. The two other rooms overlooked the back garden.

Shepherd went downstairs. There was no furniture in the house, but most rooms were carpeted. He went into the kitchen. Cheap wooden units, a twenty-year-old fridge and a gas cooker that didn't appear to have been cleaned for a few years. Worn lino with a tile effect covered the floor and there was a table with a Formica top in one corner. He opened the fridge. Inside, he found a plastic-wrapped piece of mouldy cheese and a can of beer. He flicked on the switch at the socket and the fridge buzzed.

Shepherd sat at the table. He looked at his wristwatch, a Casio with a miniature calculator keyboard under the digital display. It was the watch of a computer nerd, part of his cover. The removal van was due that afternoon and he had to stay in the house until then. He rested his head against the wall. 'Home, sweet home,' he muttered to himself.

Othman bin Mahmuud al-Ahmed sipped his sweet tea and consulted his diamond-encrusted gold Rolex. He had a full thirty minutes before he was due downstairs. He had taken a suite at the Al Faisaliah, one of Riyadh's top five-star hotels, even though his palatial villa was only an hour's drive away. The hotel was hosting a three-day defence exhibition and conference, and although he was semi-retired he liked to maintain the contacts he had built up over the years. All the major defence companies had set up shop, showcasing the latest communications and surveillance technologies.

The British were there, of course, the Americans and the French, wearing fake smiles and five-thousand-dollar suits. The Russians were still trying to sell their post-Cold War junk, shamed by the Japanese and their state-of-the-art electronics. Othman was especially interested in meeting the Chinese. They had come a long way in recent years, and had moved from copying Western technologies to developing their own cutting-edge equipment. They already had a fighter jet on the market and Othman was sure that within the next twenty years they would be rivalling the Americans in arms sales. Othman planned to bring a few Chinese up to his suite for drinks, then to the lounge above the restaurant at the top of the hotel to sample his private stock of Havana cigars. A telephone rang and his lips thinned in annoyance.

His manservant picked up the receiver, listened, then placed his hand over the mouthpiece. 'It is Muhammad Aslam,' he said.

Othman put his teacup on to the silver tray in front of him, then stood up slowly, his knees cracking like dry twigs as they always did when he stayed in one position for too long. Stiff joints were one of the many penalties of age. He went to his manservant and took the phone from him. Masood padded discreetly away as Othman put the receiver to his ear. 'What you asked has been arranged,' said Aslam.

'He is a Muslim?'

'From Palestine. He is a professional.'

'How long will it take?' asked Othman.

'I have told him we would like matters expedited as quickly as possible, but the nature of the targets is the limiting factor.'

'And the cost?'

'There will be expenses, of course,' said Aslam. 'I have agreed four hundred thousand dollars in advance. And the fee is five million dollars. He will require half once he has made his preparations. That will be non-refundable.'

'That is standard practice?'

'At this level, yes,' said Aslam. 'Once he is in play the only thing that will stop him is his own death or capture.'

'And he was clear on the details? The manner in which it is to happen? And what must be said?'

'I explained everything.'

'I shall transfer the funds to your account tomorrow,' said Othman. He replaced the receiver and went back to his chair. He doubted that the assassin had asked for five million dollars, but Aslam was acting as middle man and middle men always took their percentage. That was how Othman had made his fortune, so he did not grudge another man his share. Besides, Othman didn't care how much it cost. All that mattered was that the man and woman who had murdered his sons should die in agony, knowing why they had been killed.

The bell rang and Shepherd opened the front door to find two men in blue overalls and a Pickfords van parked outside. A third man was unlocking the back of the vehicle.

'Mr Pierce?' said the oldest of the three. He was holding a metal clipboard.

'That's right,' said Shepherd.

'I'm George, from Pickfords,' he said. 'If you show me which rooms are which, we'll get started. Don't suppose the kettle's on, is it? I'm parched.'

Shepherd grinned. 'Tea or coffee?'

'Coffee, unless it's instant,' said George. 'Mutt and Jeff here will drink anything.'

The young man raised a hand. 'I'm Jeff,' he said, 'and he' – pointing at their companion – 'isn't really called Mutt.'

Shepherd took George around the house, then went to the kitchen and made four cups of filtered coffee. The removers worked quickly and efficiently. Even with a ten-minute break, they took just two hours to unload the van, open the cardboard boxes and set out the furniture. As Shepherd was signing the receipt, a white VW Golf turned into the driveway next door. Shepherd slipped George three twenty-pound notes, then waved at Elaine Carter as she climbed out of her car.

She looked prettier than she had in the photograph Button had shown him. Her hair was dark red rather than ginger and she was wearing makeup that emphasised her high cheek-bones and full lips.

Shepherd stepped over the line of shrubs that separated his garden from hers. 'Hi,' he said, holding out his hand. 'I'm Jamie Pierce. I guess I'm your new neighbour.'

She was wearing a dark blue overcoat with the collar turned up and carrying a leather attaché case. She transferred the case to her left hand and shook his. 'Elaine,' she said. 'Elaine Carter. You're English, huh?'

'I'm afraid so,' said Shepherd. 'Is that a problem?'

'Of course not,' she said. 'You don't want to believe all the bad press Belfast gets.'

'Hey, I've heard nothing but good,' said Shepherd. 'That's why I was happy to move here.'

Elaine gestured at the house. 'Did you buy it, or are you renting?'

'It's mine,' said Shepherd. 'Or, at least, it will be in thirty years.'

'It'll be a great investment.'

'Are you an estate agent?' said Shepherd.

'Independent financial adviser,' said Elaine. 'Pensions, insurance, investments.' She grinned. 'Mortgages, too. Pity you didn't talk to me first. There are some good deals to be had just now.'

Shepherd rubbed his chin. 'Maybe we should talk about it some time,' he said. 'I'm self-employed and everyone tells me I should get a pension.'

'The sooner the better,' said Elaine. 'Let's have a chat once you're settled in.'

Jeff tooted the horn of the Pickfords van as it rumbled off down the road. George seemed disgruntled and Shepherd guessed that the tip hadn't been big enough.

'Got everything you need?' asked Elaine.

'An Aston Martin would be nice,' said Shepherd.

Elaine laughed. She had a pretty laugh, Shepherd decided, and definitely not the laugh of a hardened killer. 'I meant bread or milk. The basics,' she said. 'Anyway, the Audi's a nice enough motor.'

'It's a business expense,' said Shepherd.

'You drove it here?'

'Sure, the ferry's easy enough.'

'I know – I drive to the UK when I have meetings over there. I'm afraid of flying, believe it or not.'

'Have you got time for a coffee?'

'I've some calls to make. Maybe tomorrow. What time do you get back from work?'

Shepherd grinned at the house. 'I work from home,' he said. 'This is my office.'

'Tomorrow then,' said Elaine. She flashed him a smile, showing toothpaste-commercial teeth. 'Welcome to the neighbourhood.'

There were more than five hundred people in the queue that ran back and forth between the taped barriers. A dozen immigration officers stood behind podiums, their faces blank as they matched passport photographs to faces and quizzed the holders on their reasons for wanting to enter the United Kingdom. The air-conditioning was struggling to cope and people were fanning themselves with magazines or wiping their brows with handkerchiefs. Children were crying and businessmen with briefcases muttered under their breath. Most waited patiently, though. They came from countries where every bureaucratic function took ten times longer than was truly necessary.

Hassan Salih strode towards the EU nationals line. Ahead, a group of Indian women in brightly coloured saris clutched British passports and chattered in Urdu. The line moved quickly. There were no questions, no interrogations, just a quick look at the passport, a swipe through a terminal and a curt nod. Salih was travelling on a French passport under a Moroccan name. The passport was genuine, as was the photograph. It had been applied for under the name of a French Moroccan labourer who was about Salih's age. Salih had paid the man ten thousand Euros to apply for the passport and then killed him and dropped him from a motorboat some twenty miles off the coast near Marseille, the body weighed down with a length of anchor chain.

There were just two immigration officers dealing with the EU line, compared with more than a dozen handling the non-EU visitors. Anyone with an EU passport had automatic right of entry into the United Kingdom. No visas were necessary, no forms had to be filled in, and there were no questions to be answered. Provided the passport was valid, and provided the face of the person holding it matched the photograph inside, entry was guaranteed. It was a major weakness in the country's border controls, Salih knew, and one that he was more than happy to take advantage of.

Salih had his story well prepared, but it would only take a few careful questions for a suspicious immigration officer to realise that he wasn't French. There would be no questions. There never were. If the passport was genuine, the holder could not be refused entry. And Europe had allowed itself to become so multi-racial that there was no way of telling a person's nationality from their appearance. Salih could spot an Egyptian at fifty feet, could list half a dozen differences between a Saudi and an Iraqi, could recognise a Palestinian among fifty Jordanians. But there was no way of telling if someone was British by looking at them. The British had granted citizenship to every race and creed on Earth, everyone from Bosnian war criminals to Jamaican drug-dealers, and once granted it was virtually impossible to revoke. The French, too, had been eager to offer citizenship to anyone who wanted it. The line moved forward. Behind Salih were a Pakistani couple and three small children. The husband was clutching five British passports.

One of the immigration officers was a middle-aged Chinese woman with thick-lensed spectacles, the other a young man barely out of his twenties, with a neatly trimmed goatee beard. Both smiled politely as they handed back passports. The famous British politeness.

The Indian women continued to chatter in their own language as their passports were checked. The immigration officers didn't speak to them. Salih shuffled forward. When it was his turn he handed over his passport with a smile and kept his head up. The Chinese woman studied the photograph, then looked up at him. Salih maintained eye contact. She scrutinised his face for a couple of seconds, then returned to the photograph. She pursed her lips and flicked through the passport. There were only a couple of visa stamps, one for South Africa and another for Dubai. She ran the bar code inside the cover through the reader on her terminal. A copy of the passport picture flashed up on the screen. She closed the passport and handed it back to him. 'Have a nice day,' she said.

'You too,' said Salih. He headed down to Baggage Reclaim, then straight out through the green channel. He only ever flew with hand luggage. Everything he needed he could buy.

The arrivals area of Heathrow's Terminal Three belonged more to a third-world country than the capital of the United Kingdom. It was packed with people waiting to greet passengers and the authorities made no attempt to keep the walkways clear. Africans, Indians and Arabs were pushing, shoving and shouting. Salih had to ask half a dozen times for people to move so that he could get through, and most did so grudgingly. He emerged to find a line of drivers, men in dark suits, holding signs with the names of their clients. Most were Afro-Caribbean or East Asian. Salih ignored them and walked out of the terminal building to where the black cabs waited.

Shepherd sat at his kitchen table sipping a mug of coffee and reading the *Belfast Telegraph*. It was the strangest undercover operation he'd ever been on. Usually he was tasked with infiltrating gangs which meant hanging around pubs and bars, putting himself about and making his presence felt. Often it was a matter of working his way up the food chain, targeting a low-level villain, befriending him, then using him to get close to the target. But Elaine Carter was a different proposition. She was a woman and he was a man, and if he came on too strong he'd scare her off.

He finished his coffee, put the mug into the sink, then went down the hallway to the sitting room. Elaine's VW was parked in the driveway. He didn't want to appear too keen so he'd ruled out approaching her. She was a financial adviser and he'd made it clear that he'd like advice. All he could do now was wait for her to take the bait.

He switched on the television. There was no cable, just the regular terrestrial channels, and nothing but mindless daytime chat-shows to watch. He paced up and down, swinging his arms back and forth, feeling like a caged animal. He went back into the hallway and picked up the phone book, flicked through it, looking for local gyms, then realised that that wasn't an option. He had to be in the house, close to Elaine.

He went back into the kitchen and picked up the paper again. This was worse than being in prison – at least there he'd have people to interact with. He switched on the kettle but almost immediately switched it off again. He didn't want another coffee. He wanted something to do. The garden was a mess. The lawn was overgrown and the flowerbeds were filled with weeds. He could start work on it. It would give him something to do, and it was a good way of reminding his neighbour that he was there.

His mobile phone rang. It was Button. 'Willie McEvoy's dead,' she said.

'Same MO?'

'I'm afraid so,' said Button. 'Two might possibly be coincidence but three means we've got a serial killer.'

'Well, Elaine Carter was at home last night, so far as I know. Her car was parked in the driveway.'

'McEvoy was shot the night before last. The body was only discovered this morning.'

'Same gun?'

'The bullets are being checked as we speak. I've had them sent to our technical people in London to compare with the test-fired round we got from the Weapons and Explosives Research Centre. But they were the same calibre, for sure.'

'Makes a loud noise, the .357,' said Shepherd. 'And you can't silence a revolver.'

'McEvoy's house is in Short Strand in East Belfast and Short Strand isn't the sort of area where people dial nine-nine-nine when they hear gunshots,' she said. 'The police still aren't trusted.'

'And I suppose nobody saw anything.'

'Deaf, dumb and blind,' said Button. 'You've got to remember that for years the Catholic population regarded the RUC as the enforcers of the Protestant administration. If they had a problem that needed policing, they'd go to the paramilitaries. That's not going to change overnight.'

Shepherd's doorbell rang. 'I think Elaine's a-calling,' he said.

'That was quick,' said Button.

'I met her when I moved in. She's coming to sell me insurance.'

'Good luck,' she said. 'Remember, we'll be listening to every word.'

Shepherd ended the call and went to answer the front door. It was Elaine Carter. She was dressed casually in jeans and a pink sweater over a white shirt, carrying her briefcase in her left hand and a bottle of Moët et Chandon in her right. Under her left arm she had a spiral-bound notebook. 'Moving-in present,' she said, offering him the champagne.

'Thanks,' he said. 'If I had orange juice I'd offer you a Buck's Fizz, but as I haven't, I can't.'

'It's a bit early for me and I'll be driving this afternoon, so I'll settle for coffee.'

Shepherd took her through to the kitchen, switched on the kettle and put the champagne in the fridge next to a bottle of milk.

'Settling in okay?' she asked. She sat at the table and put her briefcase beside her chair.

'I was just realising how much work I've got to do on this house,' he said.

'The previous owners were quite old,' she said. 'The husband was in his eighties and his wife was bed-bound for the last couple of years so they weren't able to do much in the way of DIY.'

'The garden's a mess, too.'

'You should have seen it ten years ago,' said Elaine. 'Madge kept it lovely. She used to win prizes for her roses. Then she got Alzheimer's and her husband spent all his time taking care of her so it just went downhill.'

'Are they still alive?'

'She died three years ago and he's in a home. Who did you buy it from?'

'My solicitor handled everything,' said Shepherd. The kettle boiled and he poured water into a cafetière and put it, with a jug of milk and a bowl of sugar, on the table next to a large glass ashtray.

'You smoke?' she asked.

'I'm afraid so,' said Shepherd. He picked up a packet of Marlboro and a disposable lighter and sat down opposite. 'But I can wait.'

Elaine smiled. 'I smoke, too,' she said, 'and that's my brand.'

'Thank God for that, I'm dying for a cigarette,' said Shepherd. He offered her the packet, took one for himself and lit both.

Elaine laughed. 'It feels almost illegal these days, doesn't it?'

'You ever tried to give up?'

'A few times. You?'

'My grandfather smoked his whole life and died in his

sleep at eighty-seven,' he said. 'Cigarettes and coffee are my staples while I'm working. I don't think I could get through the day without them.'

'What is it you do?'

'Website design. I specialise in purchasing systems, encouraging people to buy on-line. Boring.' He pushed down the plunger of the cafetière and poured the coffee. 'You said you were scared of flying. Were you serious?'

'I'm afraid so,' she said. 'I know it's totally irrational, I know that flying is pretty much the safest way of travelling, but there's something about being in a metal tube thirty thousand feet above the ground that just seems so . . . unnatural.'

'I do have trouble with the concept of metal being lighter than air, but they seem to work,' said Shepherd. 'Have you ever flown?'

'Never,' said Elaine.

'That must make holidays difficult.'

'Ireland's a beautiful country,' she said, 'and there's the ferry to the UK. You came over from Liverpool, right? On the Norfolkline?'

Shepherd nodded.

'I do business in Liverpool and Manchester and I use the Norfolkline every few months. I get the overnight ferry, then do a day's work and take the night ferry back. If I need to get to London I go to Dublin and get Stena Line or Irish Ferries to Holyhead and drive from there. It's less than twelve hours door to door and I get to use my own car. If I want to go to France I take the ferry to the UK, and Eurotunnel gets me to the Continent. I took the *QE2* to the States a few years ago. Really, it's no biggie. And I tell myself I'm doing my bit for global warming by not flying.'

'Have you tried hypnosis or tablets?'

'Everything,' said Elaine. She held up her cigarette. 'I think there's more chance of me giving up smoking than getting me on a plane.' She sipped her coffee. 'Do you know many people here in Belfast?'

'There's a couple of guys who work from an office in the city, sales, mainly, but with email and the phone, there's no need for us to meet in person. Most of the office staff are in London and I'm lucky if I see them once in three months.'

'That sounds a bit sad,' said Elaine.

'It's the way of the world,' said Shepherd. 'My work is mainly computer-based and it doesn't really matter where that computer is.'

'So why did you move here?' she asked, tapping her cigarette into the ashtray.

'We've quite a big customer base in the city and they like to see a human being from time to time. I was flying in about once a week and we decided it made more sense for me to set up here, for a while at least.'

'No family?' She opened her notebook and clicked a black Parker ballpoint pen. 'I'll make a few notes.'

'Just little old me.'

'Are you employed by a company?'

'I work mainly for one firm, but I'm effectively freelance,' said Shepherd.

'So you're self-employed?'

Shepherd nodded.

'And how much would you earn in a year?'

'It varies, depending on the contracts we get. Between sixty and eighty thousand, I guess.'

Elaine swung her briefcase on to the table and clicked open the locks. 'This isn't a sales pitch,' she said, 'but I've a few brochures you should read, about pensions and the like.' She handed him some printed leaflets. 'What about investments?' she said.

Shepherd shrugged. 'This house, I guess,' he said. 'Some cash in the bank.' He stubbed out his cigarette.

'Pension plan?'

'Nope.'

'ISAs?'

'I've no idea what they are. Sorry.'

'So you probably don't have a PEP tucked away?'

'No idea what a PEP is, either.'

'Don't worry, that's why I'm here to help,' she said. 'Shares? Unit trusts?'

'Nope. Nope.'

'Insurance?'

Shepherd held up his hands. 'I'm hopeless, aren't I?'

'You're like most people,' she said. 'You're too busy earning your money to think about investing it.' She handed him more leaflets. 'I can suggest a range of tax-free investments that you should think about. The big one for you is your pension. Have a look at those and see if anything interests you.'

'Elaine, retirement is years away,' said Shepherd, 'and I'll probably die in harness anyway.'

She took a final drag at her cigarette and put it out, then picked up her pen again. 'That's where you're wrong,' she said, scribbling in her notebook. 'Sixty is the new forty, these days. You want to retire at – what? Fifty-five? Sixty? You could live to be eighty or ninety. How are you going to fund all the things you want to do after you've retired?'

'Good question,' said Shepherd. 'I guess I'd always assumed the state pension would kick in.'

Elaine shook her head. 'It will probably be all but history by then. But if you start saving now, you'll have a decent nest egg put by for when you do retire. And with the tax you get back from the Government, the sooner you start the better.' She tapped the leaflets. 'Read, digest, and we'll discuss.'

'Yes, ma'am,' said Shepherd. 'I had a teacher like you once.'

'You obviously need a little discipline,' she said. She finished her coffee and put down the mug. 'I've given you enough to think about.' She peered at her watch, a stainless-steel Cartier. 'Plus I've got to be in Londonderry this afternoon.'

Shepherd stood up and showed her out. He wasn't sure how he should say goodbye. A handshake seemed too formal but he didn't feel he knew her well enough to kiss her cheek.

She was on her way down the path when she turned back. 'What do you do for fun, Jamie?'

'Television, the Internet, the regular stuff.'

'Do you play pool?'

'I've been known to pick up a cue. Why?'

'Tonight's my pool night and there's a bunch of us going to Laverys in Bradbury Place. Come along – I'll introduce you to some people. We're normally there from about eight.'

'I might just do that,' said Shepherd. 'So long as you promise not to hustle me.'

The sky overhead was clear of clouds but there was a chill in the air and Salih turned up the collar of his overcoat as he walked along Swain's Lane towards Highgate Cemetery. A middle-aged woman in a fleece jacket and a bobble hat asked if he was there for the funeral. Salih nodded, and she pointed up the path that led through the Victorian burial ground. Salih thanked her. The cemetery was packed with tombs and monuments, most of them overgrown with brambles and ivy. Tree roots pushed their way between the stones and moss obscured the names and dates of the long-dead.

The path wound to the left and Salih followed it. There were stone angels with spreading wings, massive crosses, and tombs as big as garden sheds, built to stand for centuries, in an attempt to keep alive the memory of the dead. It was a waste of time, Salih knew. A generation or two at most, then virtually everyone who lived was forgotten. Testament to that, most of the graves were untended. Only rarely were people remembered and then it was for their deeds. The greater the deed, the longer the memory. It didn't matter whether that deed was good or bad. The great dictators of the world were remembered just as vividly as the great peacemakers. But most people lived, died and were forgotten. That was the way the world worked, and Salih had no plans to fight it. He didn't want to be remembered. He wanted to live his life, take his pleasures where he could, and prepare himself for whatever lay beyond.

He saw Viktor Merkulov on a wooden bench fifty feet or so from a small crowd of mourners that had gathered round four sombre men in dark suits who were lowering a mahogany coffin into the ground. Merkulov had the physique of a weightlifter that had gone to seed. His square face was topped with thinning hair and a pig-like nose with large flared nostrils. His shoulders strained against his black Burberry trenchcoat. Salih slowed and checked that no one had followed him up the path, then went to sit beside Merkulov. 'Who died?' he asked.

'A man,' said Merkulov. He nodded at a thirty-something woman with shoulder-length dyed-blonde hair who was dabbing her eyes with a lace handkerchief. 'That's the widow. The teenager by her side is the son.' A boy with a crew-cut and pimply skin, wearing an ill-fitting pinstriped suit, stood beside her. He was staring at the coffin, his jaw muscles straining as he forced himself not to cry.

'Did you know him?'

'He was just a man.' Merkulov lit a small, dark cigar, cupping his hand against the wind until he got it to draw.

'Why do you like funerals so much?' asked Salih.

'I don't like funerals,' said Merkulov. 'I like burials. I like to see the coffins being lowered into the cold, damp earth. It makes me realise how lucky I am to be alive.'

'It doesn't worry you that one day it'll be you?'

Merkulov chuckled. 'I'll be cremated, my friend, and my ashes will be scattered over Manchester United's pitch.'

'You want footballers to run over you?'

'Hallowed ground,' said Merkulov. 'And what about you? You'll be in Heaven with forty-two virgins, will you?'

'*Inshallah*,' said Salih. 'God willing. And it's seventy-two virgins, not forty-two.'

'You really believe in your religion, don't you?'

'Without religion, what is there? Without religion we're animals.'

'And you believe in God?'

'I believe there is no God but Allah and that Muhammad was his messenger. What about you? You are a believer?'

'After what I've seen? The things I've done? There is no God, my friend, but if there is I'll be sent straight to Hell.'

'Then what's the point of life?'

'Procreation,' said Merkulov. 'Children. They are the part of us that lives on.'

'Our deeds live on, too,' said Salih. 'What we do will be remembered. For a while at least.'

The widow scattered a handful of earth over the coffin, then leant against the boy, tears running down her cheeks. The priest bent to mumble words of comfort, and the boy put his arm round his mother.

'For a while, maybe,' said Merkulov. 'But children bring the only sort of immortality that truly exists. That's why you Muslims are allowed to have more than one wife and why your leaders keep telling you to have children.'

Salih didn't want to argue with the Russian, especially about religion. Merkulov was an infidel, an unbeliever, lower than the animals in the field. He was something to be used, in the same way that oxen were used to toil in the fields. Before the fall of the Soviet Union, Viktor Merkulov had worked for the KGB, the Komitet Gosudarstvennoi Bezopasnosti. He had been a high-ranking officer with the Seventh Directorate, responsible for the surveillance of foreigners and Soviet citizens. When the KGB was transformed into the Sluzhba Vneshney Razvedki, the Foreign Intelligence Service, Merkulov transferred to the new organisation but soon realised that his surveillance and intelligence skills were much in demand for the country's booming private sector, especially the criminal fraternity. He went freelance and was soon reaping the benefits, buying apartments in Moscow, Paris, London and New York and amassing a small fortune in Swiss bank accounts. Salih had used him several times in the past and trusted him.

'So, how can I help you, my friend?' asked Merkulov,

settling back on the bench as he watched the mourners taking turns to sprinkle soil on to the coffin. He blew out a tight plume of bluish smoke.

'I am looking for two people,' said Salih. 'An English woman and an American man. The woman is Charlotte Button. She is based in London but I can't find her on any electoral roll and her phone number is not listed. In the past she worked for MI5, I'm told.'

'A spy?' said Merkulov. He smiled. 'Not a name I recognise.'

'A former spy,' said Salih. 'She is involved in law enforcement now, but I need to know where she is working.'

'And the man?'

'Richard Yokely. Former CIA, now something shady within Homeland Security.'

'Now that is a name that rings a bell,' said Merkulov. 'He is a dangerous man. A very dangerous man.'

'Whereas I am a pussycat, of course,' said Salih.

'You are what you are, old friend,' said Merkulov, 'and I am what I am. But Yokely is in a league of his own. If you are planning to take him on, I would suggest you are well prepared.'

'That's why I've come to you, Viktor. And that's why I'll pay you well. He is former CIA, then?'

'He cut his teeth in South America,' said Merkulov. 'He was never active in Russia, but in recent years he has worked in Africa, Afghanistan and Iraq.'

'Doing what?'

'Information retrieval, I think they call it these days. Torturer-in-chief, you might say. He has been flying the world with the rendition programme, taking terrorist suspects to places where torture is still permitted. He is a frequent visitor to the Ukraine, for instance.'

'Where you have contacts, I am sure.'

Merkulov smiled. 'I have contacts everywhere, my friend. As do you. Yokely was with the Intelligence and Security

Command, also known as the Tactical Concept Activity, a black ops group that was run from somewhere deep within the Pentagon. And he left them to join Grey Fox.'

Salih raised his eyebrows. 'Ah,' he said.

'You've heard of Grey Fox?'

'A presidential assassination squad,' said Salih. 'Government-sanctioned killers.'

'Off the top of my head I'm not sure if he's still with Grey Fox, but it gives you an indication of the calibre of the man,' said Merkulov.

'I'll need photographs, and I'll pay whatever it takes to get an itinerary.'

'I shall do what I can,' said the Russian. 'But with a man like Yokely, I shall have to tread carefully.'

Salih smiled. 'You and me both,' he said. 'Payment on your usual terms?'

'One of the few things in life that does not change,' said Merkulov.

Salih took an envelope from his jacket pocket and handed it to the Russian. Merkulov slid it into his pocket without opening it. He did not check the contents. He knew that the ten-thousand-pound retainer would be in used notes, as usual.

'Are you staying?' asked Salih, as he stood up.

'I like to hear the soil thudding on the coffin,' said Merkulov. 'It sounds like closure.'

'I'm surprised you don't dance on the grave after they've finished.'

The Russian frowned. 'Why would I do that?' he asked, confused.

'It doesn't matter,' said Salih, and walked away.

Shepherd arrived at Laverys at a quarter past eight. He'd changed into faded jeans and a dark blue blazer over a white polo shirt. Laverys was a traditional Irish bar with a red and black frontage. There were stairs on the left that led up to the third-floor pool bar. A sign on the door warned that there was a dress code – no baseball caps or tracksuit bottoms. He pushed open the door and went in. A Chuck Berry song was blaring out from the speakers on the walls, and everything was painted black – the walls, floors and ceiling – and the bar to the left was staffed by young men in black shirts. He bought himself a Jameson's and soda then leant against the bar to look about him.

The third floor was a labyrinth of small rooms filled with pool tables. Most of the clientele were young men in sweat-shirts and jeans who would probably have been more comfort-able in baseball caps and tracksuit bottoms. He saw Elaine in a room facing the bar, leaning over a table and showing several inches of cleavage through a pale blue silk shirt. She played the shot, then straightened. When she spotted him, she waved him over.

There were three tables in the room, and two fruit machines. Elaine was playing against a man in his late forties, tall with broad shoulders, a strong chin and bright blue eyes. Shepherd knew immediately that he was a police officer, and a senior one at that. He had a policeman's watchful eyes, and a confident way of standing that suggested he could take pretty much anything that was thrown at him. Shepherd and he made eye contact and Shepherd went into grey-man mode, dropping his shoulders, glancing at the floor and tugging at the sleeve of his blazer.

'Jamie, good to see you,' said Elaine, air-kissing him on both cheeks. He caught a hint of her perfume. 'This is an old friend, John.'

'Less of the "old", please, Elaine,' said the man. He held out his hand. 'John Maplethorpe.'

'Jamie Pierce.' Shepherd shook hands with Maplethorpe, firm but not too firmly, and averted his eyes. He didn't want Maplethorpe to gain the impression that Jamie Pierce was an alpha male or in any way a threat to him.

A couple in their early thirties were playing at the next table. Elaine introduced them as Kevin and Rosalyn

Brimacombe. The man was also a policeman and he studied Shepherd carefully as they shook hands.

Elaine pointed out another two couples at the third table, all friends of hers, and another couple sitting on a red and blue plastic-covered bench seat. Shepherd saw that all of the men and one woman were cops. They were friendly and polite, but he could feel them taking his measure.

'Not working at Holywood, are you?' asked Maplethorpe.

Elaine wagged a finger at him.

'Holywood?' said Shepherd, playing the innocent.

'It's John's little joke,' said Elaine. 'Holywood is where MI5 has its headquarters. Palace Barracks.'

'You think I'm James Bond?' said Shepherd. 'I wish.'

'Jamie's a website designer,' said Elaine. 'He's the neighbour I was telling you about.'

'Sorry, Jamie, I'm only messing with you,' said Maplethorpe. 'But it's fair to say there are a lot more English accents around here than there used to be.'

'What is it you do?' asked Shepherd.

'I'm a policeman for my sins,' said Maplethorpe.

'Interesting times, I suppose,' said Shepherd.

'If by interesting you mean the end of a great tradition of policing, I suppose so,' said Maplethorpe.

'Steady, John. He's a civilian, remember.'

Maplethorpe bent over the table and played his shot. He blinked several times as if he was having trouble focusing his eyes, but then he hit the white hard and a ball cannoned into a corner pocket. 'You play, Jamie?' he asked.

'I used to, but I'm probably a bit rusty,' said Shepherd.

Maplethorpe potted the black and Elaine patted him on the back. 'It'd be nice if you let me win from time to time,' she said. 'Go on, Jamie, give him a game.'

Elaine watched as they played. Shepherd was a reasonable player, but Maplethorpe was much better and within three minutes he was potting the black again. 'You're good,' said Shepherd.

'A misspent youth,' Maplethorpe told him. 'Rack 'em up again and we'll have another game.'

They played pool until just after eleven. Then Elaine said she was going home and asked Shepherd if he was driving. 'I knew I'd be drinking so I left the car at home,' he said.

She grinned. 'I knew I wouldn't so my car's outside. Come on, I'll give you a lift.'

They left the bar, walking through a group of smokers huddled round the doorway. 'How do you know so many policemen?' asked Shepherd.

'Didn't I tell you? I was married to one.'

'What happened?'

'He died,' said Elaine.

'I'm sorry,' said Shepherd. 'I didn't know.'

'Of course you didn't,' she said. 'Anyway, it was a long time ago.'

'John's a good guy.'

'He used to work with Robbie, my husband.'

'What does he do with the police?'

'He's a detective superintendent.'

'That's high up, isn't it?'

'He's an important guy, right enough, but he's handed in his notice. He's not happy with the way the job's going.'

'Bit young to retire, isn't he?'

'He'll find something. There's a lot of private security companies and the like setting up here now.'

A figure stepped in front of them, a man in his late twenties, the hood of his sweatshirt pulled over his forehead. 'Got a cigarette?' he asked.

Elaine stopped and reached into her bag. 'Sure,' she said.

Two more men rushed up behind them, trainers slapping on the pavement, hoods up. The first man pulled a revolver from his pocket. 'Give me your wallet,' he hissed at Shepherd.

Shepherd stepped in front of Elaine, putting himself between her and the gun. 'Stay cool,' he said quietly.

Elaine screamed as another man pulled a flick-knife and

pressed the chrome stud to eject the blade. He held it to her throat. 'Yer feckin' money,' he shouted.

Shepherd took out his wallet and gave it to the man with the gun. 'Just stay cool,' he said. 'No one's going to give you any hassle. Take the money and go.'

'Your phone,' said the man, putting the wallet into the pocket of his jeans.

'You don't want my phone,' said Shepherd. 'It's a piece of shit and it's password-protected.'

Elaine was panting, her eyes wide with fear.

'Yer fuckin' phone,' said the man with the gun. He pointed the revolver at Shepherd's face but his hands were shaking.

'Okay,' said Shepherd. He took the phone slowly from his jacket pocket and handed it over.

The man holding a knife to Elaine's throat nodded at her bag. 'Her money too. And her phone.'

The third grabbed the bag and rooted through it until he found what he wanted. He threw the bag into the road, then jumped away, still brandishing the knife.

'You say anything to the peelers and you're dead!' shouted the man with the gun. 'We're with the Provos.' He ran, with the other two after him.

Shepherd put his arms around Elaine. 'Are you okay?' he asked. 'Did he hurt you?'

'I'm fine,' she said. 'Bastards.'

Shepherd took a deep breath. 'The important thing is that we're okay.'

'Scrotes like that make me sick,' said Elaine. 'They've all come out of the woodwork since the Troubles ended. In the bad old days the paramilitaries kept them under control. Muggers, housebreakers and joyriders got one warning and then a kneecapping.'

'You sound like you think that was a good thing,' said Shepherd. He retrieved her bag from the road, dusted it down and gave it to her.

'We've just been robbed at gun and knifepoint. Damn right

I think it was a good thing,' she said. She pointed down the road. 'My car's there. At least we weren't carjacked.'

They walked together to the Golf and she drove them home. As she pulled up in her driveway, she offered Shepherd a nightcap. She unlocked the front door and the burglar alarm beeped. He stood behind her as she tapped in the four-digit code to deactivate it. He didn't have to make a conscious effort to remember the number. His photographic memory worked effortlessly. Whatever he saw, whatever he heard, he never forgot. Shepherd had seen a television documentary once in which a psychologist had explained that the human brain recorded everything, but not everyone could recall what was stored in it. Most were only able to remember a fraction of the information in their brain, but Shepherd had had total recall since he was a toddler.

'We should call the police,' said Elaine. 'They probably won't catch them but at least we should make a report.'

'There's no point,' said Shepherd. 'They'll have taken the money and ditched the wallet and purse by now. We should just count ourselves lucky we weren't hurt.'

'I suppose so,' said Elaine. 'But I'm going to block my phone and stop my credit cards right away.'

Shepherd followed her into the kitchen and sat down at the table as she switched on the kettle.

'I've got to use the loo,' she said.

'More information than I needed,' said Shepherd.

She laughed and went upstairs. Over by the fridge there was a metal box with a stencilled picture of a bunch of keys on the front. Shepherd went over to it and opened it. Half a dozen different keys hung on hooks inside. He ran his finger along them. There was a car key on a VW key fob and a rusting steel key that looked as if it belonged to the shed at the bottom of the garden. One was a brass key which looked as if it fitted the kitchen door. A ring with two keys looked like a spare set for the front door. He took them off the hook. One was a Yale, the other for a deadlock. Taking them was a gamble but, assuming they were a spare set, there was a good chance that Elaine wouldn't notice they were missing. He slipped them into his pocket, closed the box and sat down again.

When Elaine came back he was smoking. He held up the cigarette. 'Hope you don't mind.'

'Go ahead,' said Elaine. 'That's one of the pains about going out these days – you can't smoke anywhere.'

'They'll be fining you for smoking in your own home before long,' said Shepherd. His stomach was turning somersaults. She had welcomed him as a neighbour, invited him into her social circle, brought him into her home, and the first thing he had done was steal her keys. There were times when he hated what he did for a living, and this was one of those times.

As soon as he got home, Shepherd retrieved his personal mobile from the bedside table and phoned Charlotte Button. 'Are you okay?' asked Button. 'We were listening in on your phone and we heard what happened. It was over so quickly we didn't have time to do anything.'

'It put the wind up Elaine but it was okay. Just muggers.'

'With a gun?'

'One had a gun, the other a knife. Said they were Provos but that was bollocks. Do you have a fix on the phone?'

'A house in a street off the Falls Road,' said Button. 'Do you want us to send the local cops around and pick them up?'

'I don't want to raise red flags,' said Shepherd. 'The cops might wonder how you got the location, and then they might start looking at me. I'd rather sort it out myself.'

'Spider, I don't want you blowing an investigation just because you fancy a bit of rough-and-tumble.'

'It'll be fine. And I could do with the exercise.'

'Do you need back-up?'

'Charlie, if Elaine hadn't been with me I'd have sorted it out then and there,' said Shepherd. 'I can handle it.'

Button gave him the address.

Shepherd went out and got into his Audi. He drove to West Belfast and parked in a quiet road about a hundred yards from the address Button had given him.

The house was in a two-storey brick terrace with a slate roof. At the end of the street a gable wall had been painted with a hooded terrorist holding a Kalashnikov rifle in front of the Irish tricolour. Shepherd looked up and down the street, but there was no one around. He put his finger on the doorbell and kept it there.

He heard a buzzing from inside the house and after a minute the lights went on upstairs. There were heavy foot-steps on the stairs, then the light went on in the hallway and the door opened. 'Who the feck is that?' asked a man's voice.

Shepherd took his finger off the bell, stepped back and kicked the door. The wood splintered and it crashed open, slamming the man against the wall. Shepherd stepped inside. The man was standing with his back to the wall, holding his bleeding right hand. He was wearing boxer shorts with red hearts on then and a grubby T-shirt. Shepherd recognised him as the man who had pulled the knife on Elaine and hit him in the solar plexus, then chopped him on the back of the neck as he slumped forward, gasping for breath. The man fell to the ground and curled up into a foetal ball. Shepherd closed the front door, kicked him hard in the kidneys, then hurried up the stairs.

A bedroom door was open and the light was on. The duvet had been thrown aside. The door to the front bedroom was closed. Shepherd flung it open. There was enough light coming in from the street for him to see a man in pyjama bottoms groping under his bed. A girl pulled the duvet around her as Shepherd walked purposefully into the room.

The man cursed and his hand appeared from under the bed holding a gun. Shepherd hit the gun away with his right hand, grabbed the man's throat with the left and smashed his head against the wall, then did it a second time and slapped him, left, right, and left again. Blood splattered across the wall. The woman whimpered but Shephered ignored her. 'Where's my wallet?' he asked. 'And where's my phone?' He grasped the man's nose and twisted it until he heard the cartilage crack.

'Kitchen,' said the man, blood pouring from his nostrils.

Shepherd hauled him off the bed by the hair and out on to the landing. He pointed at the crying girl. 'Keep quiet and you'll be fine.' He shut the door.

The man was scrabbling on his hands and knees but Shepherd kept a tight grip on his hair. He dragged him to the top of the stairs, then kicked him. The man thumped down like a dead weight, leaving smears of blood on the wall. Shepherd hurried after him, then shoved him in to the kitchen. The two mobile phones were on the kitchen table, with Shepherd's wallet and Elaine's purse. Shepherd threw the man against the fridge, punched him in the stomach, and opened his wallet. The credit cards were still there but the money had gone. He bent down, took a handful of hair and pulled the mugger to his feet. 'Where's the money?' he growled.

The man pointed to a drawer and Shepherd opened it. Inside, he found several hundred pounds and a plastic bag of little white tablets. Shepherd stuffed the cash into the pockets of his jeans, then kneed the man in the groin. 'If I ever see you again, I'll kill you. Do you understand?' he hissed.

The man nodded.

Shepherd kicked him in the ribs. 'I can't hear you,' he said.

'I understand,' said the man. The lower part of his face was covered with blood.

Shepherd sneered at him. 'You really with the Provos?'

'Yeah.' He coughed and moaned.

'Haven't you heard? You're supposed to have laid down

your arms,' said Shepherd. He stamped on the man's right hand with the heel of his shoe and heard the fingers crack.

He went back into the hallway. The man who had opened the door was groaning. Shepherd stepped over him and walked out into the street.

The Jamie Pierce mobile rang as he headed for his Audi. It was Button. 'Winning friends and influencing people, Spider?' she asked.

'All sorted,' said Shepherd.

Salih's mobile phone vibrated in his top pocket and he fished it out. It was Viktor Merkulov. The Russian wanted to meet so Salih arranged to see him in an hour at Porter's restaurant in the heart of Covent Garden.

Salih arrived on time but the Russian was already at a corner table and half-way through a bottle of red wine. Salih knew it was one of the Russian's favourite restaurants. It served traditional English food, fish and chips, steak and kidney pudding, with tourists making up most of its clientele. The tables were far enough apart for privacy and a tail would be easy to spot, but the food was why Merkulov had wanted to meet there. He waved his glass at Salih. 'I knew you wouldn't want wine so I started without you,' he said, as Salih sat down.

Salih took a menu from a pretty Polish waitress and poured himself a glass of mineral water.

'I'm having the steak and kidney – the pudding, not the pie,' said Merkulov. 'With mushy peas, of course.'

'You are nothing if not predictable,' said Salih.

'If you find something you like, stick with it, my friend,' said the Russian. He sipped his wine and dabbed his lips with a napkin. Salih ordered fishcakes and chips. 'I have pictures for you,' Merkulov went on, 'of them both.'

'Excellent,' said Salih.

'The woman joined MI5 from university,' said the Russian. 'A double first from Cambridge. She was with the International Counter-terrorism Branch. Two years in Belfast when the IRA was still active. Then she moved to the Joint Terrorism Analysis Centre where she was regarded as a high-flyer. She was never involved with counter-espionage so she didn't cross my path. As a serving MI5 officer she had the lowest of profiles. I have a birth certificate but little in the way of personal details, I'm afraid.'

'No current address?'

'She doesn't appear on any electoral roll. It could be that she's married, that Button is her maiden name and every-thing is in her husband's. But even if that's not so, MI5 would have sanitised everything. I did the check anyway. She is not registered with a general practitioner under her name and there are no credit cards for a woman of that name and general characteristics.'

Salih sipped his water. He had hoped for more but the Russian was right. If she worked for the security service her masters would protect her as a matter of course.

'Last year she left MI5 to join the newly formed Serious Organised Crime Agency.'

'Interesting,' said Salih. 'Intelligence agents don't change horse mid-career.'

'SOCA needed staff, and the traditional police are too set in their ways,' said Merkulov. 'They recruited from MI5, MI6 and various private-sector agencies. Button had run under-cover operatives for MI5 so they approached her to run SOCA's undercover unit.'

'SOCA works throughout the UK, right?'

'Country-wide,' said the Russian. 'The undercover unit mounts its own investigations but also accepts assignments from individual forces.'

'Tell me about SOCA,' said Salih.

'Just under four and a half thousand employees. It was set up in 2006 when the British Government merged the National Crime Squad, the National Criminal Intelligence Service, the investigative sections of Customs and Excise and the Immigration Service.'

'Do we know where she's working at the moment?'

'No. The problem is that SOCA is so new I have few contacts within it. I hope to rectify that over the next few months. I can tell you that she isn't based at SOCA head-quarters. In fact, she doesn't appear to operate out of a permanent base and seems to have no ancillary staff reporting directly to her. I'm sorry I can't be of more help.'

Salih sipped his water and carefully placed his glass on the table. 'And the American?'

'I have photographs, and the contents of his SVR file, which is substantial. Unfortunately, it's also light on personal infor-mation. His details were cleansed during his time with the CIA so there's nothing of his early life on file. No birth certificate, no education or service record. There is a good chance that Richard Yokely isn't his real name. We know what he has done, and we know where he has been but, like all of the men who work for black operations, we have no real idea of who he is.'

'Do you know his present location?'

The Russian looked pained. 'I'm afraid not, my friend. Yokely flies in and out of countries without documentation and, like Button, he has no permanent base. We see him visiting embassies around the world, and there are photo-graphs of him on rendition flights to Egypt, the Ukraine and Pakistan. He is a frequent visitor to Guantánamo Bay, of course. And to Iraq and Afghanistan.'

'What about locating him? How would I go about doing that?'

'We could put the word out, but frankly, my friend, I am loath to do that. A man like Yokely will have contacts around the world and he would soon know that someone was on his trail. It would be the same if someone started asking ques-tions about me. It would not be long before I received a phone call tipping me off.'

'So we would know where he is, but he would know that we're looking for him?'

'Exactly.'

'What about his phone?'

'He uses disposable Sim cards or secure satellite phones,' said the Russian.

'Would you be able to get me a current number?'

'At a price. Do you want to contact him?'

'It's a possibility. See what you can do.'

The waitress brought their food and the two men waited until she'd gone before continuing their conversation.

'I'm sorry I haven't been more helpful,' said Merkulov.

Salih knew that the Russian's professional pride had been dented. 'If it was easy, Viktor, anyone would be able to do what we do.' He speared a chip with his fork. 'Obviously I want you to keep a watching brief. And there'll be a bonus on anything you can get for me.'

Merkulov picked up his glass and clinked it against Salih's. 'Always a pleasure to deal with a professional,' he said.

Shepherd drove into the city centre and parked his Audi in a multi-storey car park. He found a locksmith in a side road off Great Victoria Street and handed over the two keys he'd taken from Elaine's kitchen. The elderly man behind the counter copied them while he waited.

When he got back to his house, Elaine's car had gone. He parked in front of his garage and switched off his engine. It was late afternoon. He took out his mobile phone and called Elaine. When she answered she was obviously driving. 'I hope you're on hands-free,' he said.

'Hi, Jamie. Yeah, I'm fine.'

'Just wondered if we could have a chat this afternoon about the stuff you gave me.'

'I'd love to,' said Elaine, 'but I'm off to see a client now and probably won't be back until six.'

'Maybe tomorrow, then,' said Shepherd. 'Drive carefully.' He cut the connection. It was just after four o'clock. He climbed out and walked across the grass to her front door, checking that no one was watching. He took the newly cut keys from his pocket and let himself in. The burglar alarm beeped softly. He shut the door, went down the hallway and tapped in the four-digit security code. The beeping stopped. Shepherd took a deep breath. What he was doing was totally illegal and he knew that in entering her house without a search warrant he risked blowing the whole operation, but he also knew that he wasn't going to get anywhere by taking Elaine Carter out for an occasional drink.

He went into the kitchen and replaced the keys he'd taken. He knew he shouldn't stay in the house for more than thirty minutes, in case she returned early. Where would she hide a gun? He kept his own weapon in a locked drawer, but Elaine would have to be more circumspect because she could never be sure that the police wouldn't turn up with a search warrant. He smiled to himself. That, of course, assumed she was guilty and was using her husband's service revolver to murder his killers. If she didn't have the gun, he could search the house until kingdom come and not find anything. He looked at the key box and wondered whether he should start with the garden shed. He decided against it. Elaine had been married to a cop so she'd know how cops think. The shed was one of the first places they'd look. Garden sheds were also vulnerable to break-ins, so if she had it she'd be more likely to hide it in the house. People tended to conceal guns in the same sort of places that drug-dealers hid their wares – under floorboards, behind skirting, in toilet cisterns and water tanks, in the back of stereos and televisions. Or buried in the back garden. Shepherd realised he was wasting time. He would do it methodically and search one room at a time.

Charlotte Button's mobile rang and she picked it up off the bedside table. It was her husband. 'Graham, I'm sorry I didn't call earlier,' she said. 'I was rushed off my feet.'

'Where are you?' he asked.

'Belfast. I'm staying at the Europa but use the mobile because I'm not in the room much.'

'It's a good thing I trust you because you're behaving like an unfaithful wife,' said Pickering, but she could tell he was joking.

'I wish I had time for a lover,' she said. 'It's been non-stop the last few days.'

'All for the greater good, I'm sure,' said Pickering, with a touch of irony. 'Zoë phoned yesterday. She's lost her mobile.'

'What? She's only had it a couple of months.'

'I'm just the messenger, darling,' said Pickering. 'She made a reversed-charge call from the school to my office, bless her, and asked if you'd call her back. I did try her mobile number but it's not ringing.'

'I'll phone the school tomorrow,' said Button. 'Did she sound okay?'

'Same as usual,' said Pickering. 'Getting information out of her is like getting blood from a stone.' He chuckled drily. 'Just like her mother.'

'What about you? Everything okay?'

'Only just got home and I'm knackered,' said Pickering. 'There's a small chain in Ascot that we might be able to buy if we can get the financing lined up.'

'Well done you,' said Button.

'It's not a done deal yet, darling. I've got to get my ducks in a row and there's a lot of ducks. But if I can pull it off we'll be twenty per cent bigger in one fell swoop.'

'Fingers crossed, and we'll celebrate when I get back,' said Button.

'Which will be when, do you think?'

'A couple of days. Maybe three. Love you.'

'Love you too.'

She ended the call. Suddenly she missed him, and thought about calling him back to tell him that she really did love him and that she was so glad she was sharing her life with him. She realised just as quickly that if she did he'd think something was wrong. She'd make it up to him when she got home. She had some very sexy underwear in the bottom drawer of her dressing-table that she'd bought on a whim from Agent Provocateur a few months ago. It was still in its wrapper, a black and red lacy bra, sheer matching panties and black suspenders with silk roses. It was time to give it all a trial run. She was sure it would make him feel a lot better than a phone call.

The sunlight glinted on the massive golden dome atop the mosque. It was quite a sight, and distinctly out of place in Regent's Park, thought Salih, as he strolled across the grass towards it. The hundred-and-forty-foot-high minaret was the tallest structure around and the mosque dominated the area. He had taken the Tube to Baker Street station and the mosque was just a short walk away.

The building was less impressive close up, drab, seventies-style concrete that had been pitted and darkened by the capital's pollution. Salih walked through the courtyard, slipped off his shoes and went into the main prayer hall. It was Friday, the main Muslim day of worship, and the hall was crowded but not full. Men were standing, bowing and kneeling on the red carpet, which had been woven in a pattern of a thousand prayer mats, all facing Mecca. The favoured places were closest to the wall nearest Mecca, and it was there that the men wearing traditional Muslim dress prayed, their heads covered. Towards the back of the hall they were more casually dressed, many in jeans and sweatshirts.

Above them was the dome he had seen from outside, the inside decorated with brightly coloured mosaics. A huge chandelier hung from the centre, and around the dome's edge there were inscriptions from the Koran.

There were no women in the prayer hall, of course. They were prohibited from praying with the men and banished to a gallery upstairs. It was the way of Islam, Salih knew, but he disagreed with the way that the sexes were segregated. He had never been married, but one day he hoped to have a wife and when he did he would not force her to cover

herself from head to foot when she went outside. Salih considered himself a good Muslim and he had read the Koran
many times, but he knew that most religious leaders had
twisted the words of the Holy Book for their own ends.

Salih began to pray. Like all good Muslims he prayed five
times a day, though more often than not he didn't go to a
mosque to communicate with God. As he prayed, he looked
around and eventually spotted the man he had come to see.
His name was Hakeem and, like Salih, he was Palestinian.
Hakeem's family had been killed by the Israelis and he had
fled to Europe, first to France and then to Britain where he
had applied for asylum. Hakeem had been less than truthful
with the Bangladeshi lawyer who had handled his applica-
tion and with the Home Office panels he had appeared
before. While it was true that his wife and two sons had been
killed when Israeli soldiers stormed his house in Gaza, it was
because Hakeem was a skilled bombmaker who had sent
more than a dozen suicide-bombers to kill civilians in Tel
Aviv. Four years after he had arrived in London, Hakeem
was granted British citizenship.

As Hakeem got to his feet and headed out, Salih caught
his eye. Hakeem hurried over and the two men embraced
like the old friends they were. Hakeem kissed Salih on both
cheeks. 'Finally you come to England,' he said, squeezing
Salih's shoulders. 'I can show you the sights.'

'I'm here for work, not pleasure,' said Salih.

'You said you needed my help and, as always, I am here
for you,' said Hakeem. 'Nothing is too much trouble for the
man who saved my life. Come, let me buy you a drink and
we can talk.'

Hakeem put his arm around Salih's shoulders and they left
the prayer hall. 'Have you been here before?' asked Hakeem.

'London, or the mosque?'

'The mosque.' Salih shook his head. 'Quite a coup,' said
Hakeem. 'It was designed by an Englishman – can you believe
that? King Faisal of Saudi Arabia put up a third of the cost.

I don't think he could believe his luck – can you imagine the Saudis agreeing to build a cathedral in one of their royal parks?' He laughed. 'The British, they think they are so magnanimous, but in reality they are stupid. They think so little of their heritage that they throw it away.'

'They see being multicultural as a strength,' said Salih.

'It is a weakness,' said Hakeem. He slapped his chest. 'I have a British passport, but I am a Muslim first.' He waved at the men filing out of the prayer hall. 'Every single man here would say the same. That is what the British will never understand. Our religion is what defines us. It makes us what we are. What do they have? A hollow church that bends with the wind, that allows abortion, adultery and men to lie down with men. Up to fifty thousand Muslims come here to pray during the Eids, and there isn't a church in the country that can boast that. Islam is growing stronger by the week as their religion withers and dies.'

They walked to a café close by a bookshop that specialised in Muslim publications. Hakeem ordered two glasses of fruit juice and the two men took a quiet table where they couldn't be overheard. 'So how can I help you?' asked Hakeem. 'What is it you need from me?'

Salih lowered his voice to a whisper. 'I need two men. Two men who can be trusted.'

'To do what?'

'To kill.'

Hakeem sipped his juice. 'Who is to be killed?'

'A woman.'

'An infidel?'

'A Muslim. A young girl. But it has to be done, and it has to be done with violence.'

'The men who help you, will they be at risk?'

Salih shook his head. 'Everything will be planned to the last detail.'

'I have two young men who are eager to prove themselves. They will need to be told a story, of course.'

'Of course.'

'They would have to think that what they are doing is for the *jihad*.'

'I will make sure of it,' said Salih.

Hakeem glanced around the room, but no one was paying them any attention. 'Their names are Mazur and Tariq. British-born, they were brought up as Muslims but became fundamentalist three years ago. They have spent time in Pakistan and were selected for special training.'

'Special training?'

'They were considered *shahids*,' said Hakeem. 'And I think it would have not taken much to persuade them to take the final step. They are both committed. The fire burns inside them already. It just needs to be fanned.'

Salih nodded. The *shahids* were happy to die for Islam as martyrs, the front-line warriors of the *jihad*. They believed that if they died serving Allah, they would be rewarded with a place in Heaven, alongside seventy of their relatives. And Heaven for the *shahids* meant an eternity of sex with seventy-two black-eyed virgins and eighty thousand servants to take care of them. Salih didn't believe in the seventy-two virgins – in fact, he was dubious about Heaven as a concept – but the *shahids* believed, which was what made them so dangerous. A man who truly believed in a glorious afterlife would have no hesitation in crashing an airliner or blowing up a Tube train, providing that the last words on his lips were *Allahu Akbar*. God is great.

'Do they worship here?' asked Salih.

'They used to go to the Finsbury Park mosque,' he said. 'They were selected and groomed by Abu Hamza himself.'

Salih knew of the hook-handed preacher who had taken control of the inner-city place of worship and turned it into an al-Qaeda training camp. 'They must not look like fundamentalists,' he said.

'They shaved off their beards when they came back from Pakistan, and they wear Western clothing,' said Hakeem. 'We moved them away from Finsbury Park when Abu Hamza became a publicity junkie.'

The British authorities had tolerated Abu Hamza's brand of racial hatred for years, but eventually their patience had worn thin. He had been sent to prison, convicted of inciting murder and racial hatred, but not before he had despatched hundreds of British Muslims to training camps in Pakistan and Afghanistan. 'They are below the official radar?' asked Salih.

'They are what the authorities here call "invisibles". They can travel freely in and out of Britain, yet they have dual citizenship so they arrive in Pakistan as nationals and can stay there as long as they like. I heard of them and suggested that they return to London. They can make a bigger impact here.' He lowered his voice again. 'We are trying to get them into Heathrow,' he said. 'We already have two of our people working on the security staff at Terminal Three. Now we are trying to get Mazur and Tariq on the baggage-handling staff. The British are so politically correct that they aren't even allowed to question why so many Muslims are applying to work at the airports. But the day will come when we have everything in place and you will see an event to rival Nine Eleven in the United States.' He raised his glass in salute. 'And while I give my life to Allah, what are you doing? Creating havoc for money?'

'If I create havoc, I'm not doing my job properly,' said Salih.

'But you do what you do for your own ends,' said Hakeem. 'Where is the glory in that?'

'There is no glory,' agreed Salih.

'But there is money?'

'Oh, yes,' said Salih. 'There is money.' He reached into his jacket pocket and handed over a bulky envelope. 'This is for your expenses.'

Hakeem weighed it in his hand.

'Ten thousand pounds,' said Salih. 'That is for the introduction. There will be another forty thousand if the two men are suitable.'

'I shall use it wisely,' said Hakeem.

'I am sure you will,' said Salih.

As soon as Charlotte Button had had breakfast, over the *Irish Times* and the *Independent,* she phoned Culford School and asked to speak to her daughter. She had to wait almost ten minutes before Zoë came to the phone. 'Hi, Mum.'

'Zoë, I'm sorry I didn't call you yesterday but I didn't get back until late. Daddy says you lost your phone.'

'It wasn't lost, it was stolen,' said Zoë.

'Have you told the school?'

Zoë's sigh was loaded with sarcasm. 'Of course,' she said.

'And will they tell the police?'

'Mum, it's a phone. The police don't care about phones.'

'I'll need a police report to make a claim on our insurance,' said Button.

'I don't think the school likes to call in the police. They handle things themselves.'

'Oh, so they'll find it for you, will they?'

'Mum, please. Just send me a new phone, okay? Dad said you would.'

'And did Dad say why he couldn't do it?'

'He said he was busy.'

'And I'm not?' Zoë sighed again. Button pictured the contempt in her daughter's eyes, and the way her lips had pressed into a tight line. 'I'm sorry, honey. I'll get you a phone and send it to you.'

'A Sony-Ericsson, okay?'

'What's a Sony-Ericsson?'

'It's a phone. Everyone here has one.'

'I thought Nokias were the phones to have.'

'Oh, Mum, Nokias are so yesterday. The new Sony-Ericsson is savage.'

'Savage? That's good, right?'

'Yes, Mum, that's good.'

'Okay. Is everything else all right?'

'Fine,' said Zoë. 'Look, I have to go. Love you.'

'Love you,' said Button, but the line was already dead.

She sat on the bed tapping the phone against the side of her head. Zoë was thirteen and had boarded at the school since she was eleven. It had been Graham's idea, but Button hadn't needed much persuading. They both had careers, and the only other options would have been a live-in au pair or turning Zoë into a latch-key kid. They had agreed that boarding-school was a better solution, and Zoë had been surprisingly agreeable. It had made her more independent, and she was thriving in the hothouse academic environment, but with that had come a coldness that often brought tears to Button's eyes. She wasn't sure if it was normal teenage rebellion or because Zoë had been sent away from home, but either way it was painful.

She tossed the phone on to the bed. Zoë was their only child and there had been complications that made it unlikely they'd have more. Not that she and Graham had planned a big family. Zoë had been an accident, a happy one but an accident nevertheless, and neither Button nor her husband had ever put her in front of their careers. They loved Zoë, of course, but Graham wanted to build his business and Button had always been determined to get to the top of her profession. And to do that she had had to make sacrifices. Button didn't regret the decision they'd made, but that didn't make Zoë's coldness any easier to bear.

She picked up the phone and pressed redial, then cancelled the call. Zoë had lessons to go to, and she wouldn't appreciate being dragged back to the phone. In any case, what could she say to her? That she loved her? That she missed her? That she wished she was there to give her a hug? She caught sight of herself in the mirror above the dressing-table and flinched. She looked scared.

She stood up and stared out of the window over the city. It was impossible to have everything, no matter what the glossy women's magazines said. You couldn't have a successful career, a fulfilling sex life and an adoring family. You had to make choices, and more often than not those choices led to sacrifices. No one had forced her to send Zoë to boarding-school, just as no one had forced her to join MI5 or SOCA. Suddenly she craved a cigarette, and laughed. Once a smoker, always a smoker.

Salih watched the two men from across the restaurant. They were young Pakistanis, with glossy gelled hair, dark brown skin and black eyes. They looked like a couple of male models, tall with broad shoulders and tight stomachs. He toyed with his coffee cup and wondered why two such good-looking young men would consider blowing themselves into a thousand pieces. They were British-born, which meant they had access to the country's health and education systems, they lived in a country where the police didn't shoot rubber bullets or worse into crowds, where civilians weren't dragged off the streets and searched or roughed up, where soldiers couldn't kill children and receive nothing worse than a reprimand.

Salih had been born in Israeli-occupied Gaza, where children died because hospitals lacked equipment and medicine, where schools had no textbooks, where two-thirds of the population had no jobs and where most families lived on less than ten dollars a month. Salih understood why so many Palestinians wanted to take up arms against the Israelis, and why so many were prepared to give up their own lives. But Mazur and Tariq weren't Palestinians. They hadn't grown up under the heel of an occupying power. They were free men in a free country, which was what made their decision to give up everything for Allah so mystifying.

The slightly taller of the two, who was sporting a small gold earring in his left ear, laughed at something the other had said, showing perfect white teeth. A waiter brought them cups of coffee and a hookah pipe, which he lit for them. The guy with the earring took the first smoke, then handed the mouthpiece to his friend. They were early. Salih had told them to be in the café at midday, but it was only half past eleven.

Salih toyed with the almond croissant on his plate. He preferred to work alone but there were times when he needed assistance and this was such an occasion. One person alone could not do what he had planned. There had to be three, which meant he needed Mazur and Tariq. He took out his mobile phone and called the number Hakeem had given him. A few seconds later an Asian pop tune sounded from the taller man's pocket. He fished in his jacket and pressed his phone to his ear. 'I am here,' said Salih.

The man frowned. 'What?'

'Across the room.'

The man looked round and Salih held up his coffee cup, then cut the connection. The man said something to his friend and they both looked in Salih's direction. Salih sipped his coffee, then put down his cup and beckoned them over.

'You are Hassan?' asked the taller of the two.

Salih held up the mobile phone and smiled.

'Of course it is. He called you, didn't he?' said the other man. He held out his hand. 'I am Mazur.'

Salih shook it. 'Yes, I am Hassan. Please sit.' Salih took the tall man's hand. 'You are Tariq?'

'I am.'

He had a tight grip and his nails had been neatly trimmed. Salih could smell expensive cologne. Tariq sat down opposite Salih, and Mazur on Salih's right.

The waiter brought over the hookah. Salih caught the fragrance of green apples from the smouldering tobacco. 'May I?' he asked.

'Of course,' said Tariq.

Salih drew the fragrant smoke into his mouth, then blew it out and sighed. 'That's good,' he said. He handed the pipe back to Tariq.

'Hakeem said you needed help,' said Tariq.

Salih kept his voice low. 'There is something I need doing, and I need the services of men who are prepared to do whatever it takes to serve Allah.'

'That's us,' said Mazur.

'You were trained in Pakistan?'

Both men nodded.

'Do you mind telling me why?'

'We learnt what we could in London, through the Internet and books, but we needed real training,' said Tariq. 'We had to know how to use weapons and explosives.'

'But why did you want such training?' pressed Salih.

'To fight for Islam,' said Mazur.

'But you're British,' said Salih.

'We're Muslims first,' said Tariq, 'Pakistanis second, British third. If we don't stand and fight as Muslims, the infidels will crush us.' His eyes were burning with the intensity of a zealot.

'What started you on this journey?' he asked. 'Nine Eleven?'

Mazur nodded, but Tariq shook his head. 'I realised long ago that Muslims were in danger of being exterminated from the face of the earth,' he said. 'Look at what happened in Kosovo, in Palestine, in Chechnya. When I was a kid Abu Hamza came to our mosque to give a talk and collect funds. I had never heard a man who spoke like him. Afterwards he said he recognised something in me and that when I was ready I should seek him out at the Finsbury Park mosque. As soon as I was old enough I went to see him and that was when I learnt about *jihad*, that Muslims have to fight our oppressors until we have established a true Islamic state.'

'It was Nine Eleven that changed me,' said Mazur. 'It was the way the Americans reacted. The Saudis flew the planes into the World Trade Center, but the Americans were too cowardly to attack them. Instead they attacked the Muslims in Afghanistan and then in Iraq. What did Afghanistan have to do with the attacks on the World Trade Center? Nothing. And the Iraqis? Saddam Hussein hated al-Qaeda. Hated bin Laden.'

'It's true,' agreed Tariq. 'And then what did the Americans do? They picked up Muslims around the world and took them to Cuba to interrogate and torture them. The Americans are on a crusade, a crusade to destroy all Muslims. We have to defend ourselves, we have to meet violence with violence.' Tariq had a movie-star smile, but there was no doubting his sincerity.

Salih understood why the two men had become such hard-line fundamentalists. It had all been part of al-Qaeda's grand plan. Until the moment that the four planes had been hijacked in the United States, most Western countries had given little thought to the Muslim populations in their midst. Muslims and Christians were getting on just fine, but Islamic funda-mentalists knew that peaceful coexistence was a threat to their religion. Religions spread best when fired by funda-mentalism, and fundamentalists need someone to struggle against. It was the backlash after Nine Eleven that had fired Muslims like Tariq and Mazur and thousands more like them. The man with the beard and the Kalashnikov had known exactly what he was doing when he attacked the World Trade Center and the Pentagon. He had no interest in the men, women and children who had died. Neither did he care about the damage to the buildings. What he wanted was for the West to lash out at Muslims, and he had succeeded. The West had gone to war with Afghanistan and Iraq, and Muslims round the world had united to rise up in protest.

Salih had watched the second airliner smash into the World Trade Center live on CNN as he sat in a hotel room in Zurich. He had been paid a quarter of a million dollars to kill an Iraqi biochemist who was planning to defect to America with details of Saddam Hussein's biological-warfare programme. Salih had watched the towers collapse and had realised then that the world had changed for ever – and changed for the worse.

Salih was a Muslim but he wasn't a fundamentalist. He hated the Israelis but he hated them because of what they had done to his country, not because of their religion. Salih killed for money, not for his beliefs. He did it coldly and dispassionately. But men like Tariq and Mazur would kill because they were angry and because they hated non-Muslims. And because they believed that if they died for Allah, they would go to Heaven. That was what made them so dangerous.

Salih sipped his coffee. 'I need your total obedience,' he said. 'Whatever I ask you to do, you must do without question.'

Mazur and Tariq looked at each other, then nodded. 'Hakeem said we can trust you,' said Tariq.

'It's not about trust,' said Salih. 'It's about obedience. If I do not have that, we should part company now.'

'We shall obey you,' said Mazur. 'Whatever you ask, we shall do.'

Salih stared at them for several seconds, then he nodded slowly. 'There is a girl that has to die,' he said quietly. 'She betrayed two of our men in Pakistan, and because of that one of the men is dead and another is being held by the Americans.'

'Bitch,' said Tariq, venomously.

'She has to be killed, and she has to be killed with violence,' said Salih. 'Are you prepared to do that?'

Mazur swallowed nervously. 'I am,' he said, his voice a hoarse croak.

Tariq nodded enthusiastically. 'I am too,' he said.

'There is one more thing,' said Salih.

Mazur and Tariq leant forward, eager to hear more.

Shepherd woke up just after eight. He shaved, showered, pulled on a pair of jeans and a polo shirt, then went downstairs. He cooked himself eggs and bacon, made a cup of coffee and read the *Belfast Telegraph* as he ate. A packet of Marlboro lay on the table in front of him but at no point did he consider lighting up. The cigarettes were a prop, nothing more. He couldn't go more than a few hours without a cup of coffee, but he had never craved nicotine.

He washed up, then looked out of the sitting-room window. Elaine's driveway was empty. He sat down to watch daytime television with the sound low so that he would hear her return. At just after midday he made himself another cup of coffee and gazed out of the sitting-room window as he drank it. The driveway was still empty. When he'd finished his coffee he washed his mug, then paced round the kitchen. He hated doing nothing. At least if he was penetrating a criminal gang he could hang out with villains. He felt like a dog that had been locked in the house while his master was at work and could see why it might chew the furniture.

He'd taken a risk in searching Elaine's house, and he'd only gone through the rooms on the ground floor before he'd called it quits. But he knew, too, that the only way to find out whether or not she had a gun was to be proactive. He opened the front door. There wasn't a car or a pedestrian in sight. Everyone was either at work or in front of the television. Shepherd closed the door behind him and went to Elaine's front door. He pressed the bell and heard it buzz in the hallway. He pressed it again, for longer this time, but there was no response. Her car wasn't in the driveway but the garage door was down. Perhaps it was inside.

He stood back. All the curtains were drawn at the upstairs windows. He took the keys out of his pocket and inserted the first in the lock. As he turned it he heard a car driving up the road. He pulled out the key, palmed it, pressed the doorbell and took a pace back. He heard the car slow and pressed the bell again.

A horn beeped twice and he looked over his shoulder. It was Elaine in her white VW Golf. He waved with his left hand as he slipped the key into his back pocket. His heart was pounding. If she'd been a minute later she'd have caught him red-handed and the whole operation would have been blown.

She pulled up in the driveway and climbed out of the Golf. 'Hi, Jamie, what's up?' she called.

'You'll never guess what happened,' he said. 'I've got your phone and your purse.'

'You have not,' she said.

'A couple of cops came round this morning. They stopped a car and the guys in it did a runner, but they left behind half a dozen stolen mobile phones, your purse and my wallet.'

'I don't believe it,' she said.

'Sometimes you get lucky,' said Shepherd. 'Put the kettle on and I'll bring your stuff round.'

Tariq looked down at the girl. She had been bound and gagged with strips of insulation tape. 'She's awake,' he said. 'She's pretending to be unconscious.'

Salih walked over and stood next to him. He kicked the girl's side and her eyes opened. She stared up at the two men in horror. 'Good,' said Salih. 'We can begin.'

Mazur was sitting on the sofa, drinking a can of orange Fanta. 'Why don't we wear masks?' he asked.

'Because the people in Pakistan who want this done want it done by Muslims,' said Salih. 'Don't worry, once I've shown them the picture I'll delete it.'

'It's okay, Mazur,' said Tariq. 'If it wasn't okay, Hakeem wouldn't have asked us to do this.'

Mazur drained his can and dropped it into a black plastic bag. He stood up. 'I'm ready,' he said.

The girl was lying on a large sheet of clear plastic. There would be blood. A lot of blood. Salih had rented the serviced apartment for a month. It was close to Paddington station and its two main attractions were that it had a varnished hardwood floor and that it could be accessed from a lift in the underground car park.

Salih picked up his mobile phone. 'You know what you have to do,' he said. 'Untie her, but keep the gag in place because there are other people in the building. Strip off her clothes.' He handed Tariq a carving knife. 'Then you slit her throat.'

The girl bucked and writhed on the floor but she was helpless. The Valium injection Salih had given her when they had abducted her had worn off. It was important that she was conscious when she died, that she was fighting for her life. In an ideal world he'd have taken the gag off but he couldn't risk her screams being heard.

Salih stood back and raised his phone. He pressed the button to start its video camera, the signal that Tariq and Mazur should begin.

Shepherd sipped his coffee. He was sitting on the black leather sofa in Elaine's front room. She'd put an Oasis CD on her stereo before making them both coffee and putting out a plate of Jaffa Cakes. She sat down next to him. 'Everything's there,' she said, closing her purse. 'Even the money. There's not a quid missing.' A big-screen Panasonic plasma television hung on the wall in front of them, with Bang and Olufsen tower speakers at either side. A book-case had been built into the wall and on it was a framed photograph of Elaine and Robbie Carter on their wedding day. He had worn his RUC uniform, and she was in a white dress. There was only one other photograph on show, of Elaine and Robbie on a sofa with a small boy lying across their laps, grinning. It was in a silver frame on the mantelpiece.

'He was a good-looking man,' said Shepherd, nodding at the wedding photograph.

Elaine smiled fondly. 'There must have been fifty cops there, it would have been a great day to carry out a robbery in the city.'

'He died, you said.'

'He was shot by the IRA,' she said quietly. She reached for her packet of Marlboro and lit one, then passed the pack to Shepherd.

'Oh, my God,' said Shepherd, hating his fake sincerity. 'That's awful.'

'It was a long time ago.'

'What happened?' he asked, then added hurriedly, 'I'm sorry. That was a stupid thing to ask.' He lit a cigarette and inhaled deeply.

'It's all right, Jamie. It was a long time ago. There were five of them and they burst into the house one night and shot him.'

'Elaine, no! That's terrible.'

'It's what it was like back then. It was a war.'

'And you saw it happen?'

'It was in the kitchen.'

'Did they catch them?'

'They caught four of them. They were sent to prison but they were all released under the Belfast Agreement.'

'You mean the Good Friday Agreement?'

Elaine sighed. 'Depends which side of the divide you're on,' she said. 'The Catholics call it the Good Friday Agreement.'

'Because of the religious overtones, I suppose.'

'Or because they want to make it seem like their own agreement,' she said bitterly. 'Anyway, whatever you call it, the politicians decided to set free the paramilitaries. All four walked free. The fifth had run away to America.'

'I'm sorry, Elaine.'

'It happened. I got over it.'

'I don't see how you could ever get over something like that,' said Shepherd.

'It's the old cliché. Time heals all wounds.'

Shepherd sipped his coffee. He knew he had to ask about her son. It was an obvious question for Jamie Pierce to ask, but he hated intruding into her personal grief. 'Where's your son now?'

Elaine forced a smile. 'He died too. A few years ago. Leukaemia.'

'Elaine . . .'

'Please don't say you're sorry, Jamie. I've had all the sympathy I need over the years.'

'What a nightmare for you. What a bloody nightmare.'

'I've had more than my share of bad luck.' Elaine held up her cigarette. 'That's why I've got no fear of these things. The one thing I've learnt is that people die whether or not they smoke.'

'Why didn't you move?' he asked. 'How could you stay here after that?'

'It was our home,' she said quietly. She looked at her watch. 'Anyway, I've got calls to make before everyone goes home for the day, so I'm going to have to kick you out.'

Shepherd finished his coffee and stubbed out his cigarette. 'Next time the coffee's on me,' he said.

'I'll hold you to that.'

Shepherd went back to his house, feeling guiltier than he'd ever felt in his life. He liked Elaine Carter, he liked her a lot, and despised himself for lying to her.

Frank Khan hated shopping. And he especially hated shopping with his wife. On the rare occasions that he ventured into a shopping mall or a department store, he did so knowing exactly what he wanted and how much he was prepared to pay. But his wife had a totally different approach. Shopping was a hobby, perhaps even a sport, a recreational activity to be relished and, if possible, shared. It was his day off and he had no good reason to refuse when she asked him to go with her to the local shopping mall. He had been working late for the last couple of weeks so he had decided that a shopping trip would get him into her good books, but within an hour he was bored and wanted to go home.

'What do you think?' said his wife, holding up a green dress that shimmered under the overhead fluorescent lights.

'How much is it?' She inspected the price tag and winced.

'I think I'd better wait outside,' said Khan. 'I need a cigarette.'

He walked out of the shop and lit one, inhaled deeply and blew a smoke-ring.

'Women love to shop, don't they?' said a voice. An Asian man in his thirties was standing next to him. He was good-looking, with skin the colour of polished teak and amused dark brown eyes. He was wearing a long black cashmere coat over a suit and tie and his hands were in his pockets. 'They'd shop all day if they could.'

Khan smiled. 'If it was an Olympic sport, we men wouldn't stand a chance. Is your wife inside?'

'I'm not married, Chief Superintendent,' said the man.

Khan frowned. 'I'm sorry, do I know you?'

'We almost met at your niece's funeral,' said the man. 'The Saffron Hill Cemetery.'

'Ah,' said Khan. 'You were a friend of Sara's?'

'Not exactly,' said the man. 'I know you, of course. Chief Superintendent Frank Khan, one of the highest-ranking Muslim police officers in the country. A role model for all British-born Muslims. You must be very proud.' Khan took another drag on his cigarette and squinted at the man through narrowed eyes. 'Except, of course, Frank isn't your given name, is it?' continued the man. 'That would be Farook. But I suppose you changed it to make life easier, didn't you?'

'They called me Frank at school.'

'Because Farook was too alien? Too different? And you wanted to blend?'

Khan moved a little away from him. 'Really, I have to go,' he said. 'It's been nice meeting you.'

'You were close to Sara, weren't you?' said the man. 'I could see at the funeral how upset you were. It was such a terrible death.'

'Yes,' agreed Khan. 'Such a waste.' He looked pointedly at his watch.

'A terrible death, but not necessarily a waste,' said the man. 'At least something can be gained from a terrible death. And if something can be gained, there is no waste.'

Khan dropped his cigarette on to the pavement and ground it out with his heel. 'Who are you? What do you want?'

The man smiled, showing perfect white teeth. 'You can call me Hassan. My name isn't important. But that doesn't mean what I have to say to you isn't of the utmost importance.'

'Forgive me, but I must find my wife.'

Khan started to walk back into the shop but Hassan gripped his elbow. Khan tried to pull away but the man's fingers dug into his arm like steel claws. Hassan was still smiling, but his eyes were ice cold. He put his mouth close to the policeman's ear. 'I'm going to show you something, Chief Superintendent,' he whispered. 'Something that will upset you. But for your sake and for your wife's sake, you must remain calm.'

'What are you talking about?' said Khan.

'Take a good look at the man who is standing behind your wife over there,' said Hassan.

Khan's frown deepened. She was talking to a middle-aged saleswoman and holding up the green dress. Behind her stood a tall, good-looking Asian man with gelled hair and a gold earring. He was wearing a shiny leather jacket with the collar turned up.

'You see him?' said Hassan. 'The man in the leather jacket with his hands in his pockets?'

'Yes, I see him,' said Khan. 'What's this about?'

'I want you to look at this,' said Hassan, taking a mobile phone from his coat pocket. 'It will upset you, but you must keep calm because the man who is standing behind your wife has a knife in his pocket and if you react badly he will stab her in the throat, then run off to the street where a motorcycle is waiting to spirit him away.'

Khan's jaw dropped.

'Smile, Chief Superintendent. Smile as if you haven't a care in the world.' Hassan held up the mobile phone, the screen facing Khan. His thumb pressed a button and a jerky video began to play.

Khan bent closer to the screen. A woman in jeans and a T-shirt was lying on her back on a floor. Her mouth was taped so all he could hear were grunts. An Asian man grabbed her arms and pinned them to her sides. Khan's stomach lurched as he realised it was his niece, Sara. A second Asian man unfastened her jeans and pulled them down her legs. He tossed them to the side, then ripped off her panties. Sara was kicking out but the first man was holding her tight. The man who had ripped off her panties looked into the camera and Khan caught his breath. It was the man now standing behind his wife in the shop.

'Keep smiling,' said Hassan, 'as if you haven't a care in the world.'

Khan stared at the screen in horror. The man who was holding Sara let go of one wrist and the second man pulled off her shirt. Sara was tiring. Although she was still struggling there was no strength in her movements.

The camera moved closer as a knife cut through her brassiere. Her full breasts fell free and Khan wanted to look away but he couldn't take his eyes off the screen. She was naked now and he could see the tape round her mouth pulsing as she breathed.

The first man grabbed Sara's hair, grinned at the camera and raised the knife. It flashed downwards and blood spurted across her throat. Khan gasped.

Sara thrashed around for a few seconds, then went still. Blood formed a pool round her body. For the first time Khan realised she had been lying on a sheet of plastic.

The man put away the phone and shrugged. 'Stay calm,' he said. 'We don't want to hurt you or your wife.'

'Who are you?' said Khan.

'I told you. You can call me Hassan.' His thumb flashed over the phone's keyboard.

'You killed her?'

'Actually, the man standing behind your wife killed her. Then we took her to the alley where her body was found.

There is nothing to connect us to her murder. Trust me on that. Nothing other than the video on this phone. And I have just deleted it.'

Khan's wife was still deep in conversation with the saleswoman, and behind her stood the man from the video, his hands deep in his pockets. Khan's mind was spinning. He'd just seen a video of his niece being brutally murdered, and the man who'd done it was standing behind his wife. He knew that as a police officer he should run over and grab the killer, pin him to the ground and arrest him for the murder of a pretty young girl who had never done anyone any harm. Dear, sweet Sara. He clamped his teeth together.

'I know what you're thinking, Chief Superintendent,' said Hassan. 'You're thinking that you should be acting like a policeman. Calling for back-up. Pressing charges against me for the murder of your niece. That was your first impulse and, of course, it's understandable. But I'm sure you realise now that the reason I went to Sara's funeral was so that I could follow you home. I know where you live, Chief Superintendent. I have stood outside your house and watched your son and daughter go to school. I have watched your wife go shopping. I have watched you come home at night. And the man who killed your niece is just as capable of killing your wife and your children. So take a deep breath, stay calm and try to smile.'

'What do you want?' whispered Khan.

'What I want, Chief Superintendent, is for you to stop acting like a policeman and to start acting like a Muslim.'

Salih and Tariq walked down the street to the multi-storey car park where Salih had left his rented Ford Mondeo.

'Who was he?' asked Tariq.

'That doesn't concern you,' said Salih.

'You showed him the video you took of the girl we killed.'

'Tariq, I told you at the start. You obey me without question.'

'I have obeyed. I have done everything you asked. But I would like to do more. I would like to learn from you.'

Salih frowned. 'I'm not seeking an apprentice.'

'Then let me help you,' said Tariq.

'I don't need help,' said Salih. Tariq seemed about to say something, but instead he bit his lower lip. The two men walked in silence to the car park. Salih didn't say anything until they were sitting inside the car. 'You can tell no one what you have done,' he said.

'That's a given,' said Tariq. 'I killed a girl. Why would I tell anybody?'

Salih ran his hands round the steering-wheel. 'What about Mazur? Is he okay about what we did?'

'He believed Hakeem, that we were carrying out *jihad*. He wasn't happy about killing a girl but he believes it was necessary for the greater good.'

'And you, Tariq? What do you believe?'

Tariq flashed his gleaming white teeth but didn't say anything.

'Your smile doesn't impress me,' said Salih, flatly.

'I didn't mean to offend you,' he said.

'Why did you ask me who that man was, the man I spoke to?'

'Because you told us the video was to show people in Pakistan. You didn't say we'd be showing it to someone in England. And it was clear from the look on the man's face that he knew the girl.'

Salih exhaled slowly.

'It was a mistake to ask you, and for that I apologise,' said Tariq.

'It's complicated, and I have been less than honest with you,' said Salih.

'Hakeem said that in helping you we would be helping the struggle against the infidel.'

'That is true,' said Salih.

'Can you explain to me why killing the girl helps us hurt

the infidel?' Salih's eyes narrowed, and Tariq held up his hands. 'I'm sorry, I've offended you again.'

'What do you want from me?' asked Salih.

'I want to help. And to learn.'

'To learn what?'

The fire was back in Tariq's eyes. 'I have never seen a man like you before, even in Afghanistan. We trained there in a camp, they taught us to kill, and yet even the men who taught me were not like you.' The words tumbled out and Tariq took a deep breath to calm himself. 'It was easy for them because they were fighting in the hills and they could shoot at the enemy with their Kalashnikovs and RPGs. In Pakistan they taught us how to make bombs, but bombs are an easy way of killing people. What you do, it's more . . .' Tariq struggled to find the right word. 'It's more intelligent. More considered. The way we abducted and killed that girl, it was perfect. You had every step planned. We were never in danger of being caught. You told us what we had to do, we did it, and it was perfect.'

'It has to be that way,' said Salih. 'There can be no margin for error.'

'That's what I want to do,' said Tariq.

'You want to kill people? Then you should become a *shahid*.'

'I want to kill specific people,' said Tariq. 'Blowing up civilians is a waste of time unless you do it regularly. People forget. The Tube is as crowded now as it ever was. It's almost as if the bombs have been forgotten.'

A housewife walked by, pushing a supermarket trolley laden with carrier-bags. Tariq stopped speaking until she was putting her shopping into the boot of her car.

'Abu Hamza told me that all unbelievers should die. It says so in the Koran. But I want to kill the people at the top. The politicians and the generals. And I want to target them, I want the world to see them beg for forgiveness before I take their lives. I want to behead them and show their beheadings on the Internet. Can you imagine the effect of that? To

see the Foreign Secretary or the Prime Minister himself killed
on video?'

'You're setting your sights high,' said Salih.

'That's what we have to do,' said Tariq. 'Nine Eleven was
a grand statement. So were the Madrid bombings and the
suicide-bombers on the Tube here. But now the brothers at
the mosque are talking about putting bombs in shopping
malls and nightclubs. I tell them it's pointless. If you kill
nobodies, people forget. We have to aim high. We have to
make it more personal. And I think that by working with you
I can learn how to do that. You have the skills I need. And
I can help you.'

'I work alone,' said Salih.

'With respect, that's not true,' said Tariq. 'You needed my
help with the girl. You might need it again.' He lowered his
voice. 'I have killed for you, Hassan. I have proved my loyalty.
You know you can trust me.'

Salih smiled. 'If I didn't think I could trust you, I would
have killed you already.' His eyes bored into Tariq's. 'Very
well,' he said. 'This is what you must do. Get yourself another
phone and buy a pay-as-you-go Sim card. Once you have
it, send me a text. How reliable is your memory?'

'It's good.'

Salih told Tariq his mobile-phone number and made him
repeat it five times. 'Do not store my number in your phone.
Keep it only in your head. Do not use that phone to contact
anyone else. Anyone. You use it only for me. Do you understand?'

'I understand.'

'At some point in the future I may call on you again.'

Tariq grinned. 'Excellent,' he said. 'You won't regret it.'

'I hope the same goes for you,' said Salih, and started the
car.

Khan finished cleaning his teeth and went into the bedroom.
His wife was already in bed, reading one of the trashy novels

she loved. Khan had often wondered why a woman who was such a romantic at heart had decided to marry a man whose career involved dealing with the scum of the earth. There was precious little romance in the life of a police officer.

'You look tired,' said his wife, her eyes still on her book.

'I'm okay,' he said. It was a lie. He was far from okay. A man had threatened him, and Khan had no idea how to deal with it. His first instinct was to inform his superiors but if he did there was no guarantee that his family would be protected. He knew that was one of the big lies – that the police could protect the public. They couldn't. They could solve crimes, they could control public order, they could hand out speeding tickets, but they didn't have the power to stop bad things happening. If Hassan wanted to kill Khan and his family, he would succeed.

'Draw the curtains, honey,' said his wife.

Khan went to the window. A man was standing in the street below, his hands in his pockets. Khan was short-sighted and he couldn't make out the man's features. He could see tanned skin and his glossy black hair glinted under the street-lights.

'What's wrong, honey?' asked his wife, from the bed.

'Nothing,' said Khan. He hurried to his bedside table and put on his glasses.

'What on earth are you doing?' said his wife, sitting up.

When Khan got back to the window, the man had gone. He hadn't seen his face but he was sure it had been Hassan, and that he had been sending him a clear message. Hassan could reach him, no matter where he was. Tears of frustration welled in his eyes and he took off his glasses. 'I thought somebody was breaking into a car,' he said.

'Always the policeman,' said his wife. She patted the bed. 'Come here.' Khan sat on the bed and put his glasses back on the bedside table. He sighed. 'Bad day at the office?' asked his wife, and began to massage his shoulders.

'You could say that,' he said.

'A good night's sleep cures a lot of ills,' she said, and kissed his neck.

Khan forced a smile, but inside he was more scared than he'd ever been. He knew there was no hiding from a man like Hassan. Khan either did what Hassan wanted, or his family would die.

Shepherd looked down from the bedroom window. Elaine had driven off in her VW at just after nine o'clock that morning and it was now close to midday. He went downstairs, switched on the television, went into the kitchen and turned on the kettle. Then he saw the four dirty mugs in the sink and realised he'd probably had enough caffeine that morning. The view from the kitchen window reminded him of the state of the garden. He needed something to occupy him so he might as well tidy it, he thought.

He'd found the key to the garden shed in a drawer in the kitchen shortly after he'd moved in. Now he unlocked the door. Inside he found an old petrol mower, a selection of rusty garden tools, a green plastic watering-can and stacks of chipped terracotta flower-pots. Earwigs scuttled away from the daylight and there were curtains of cobwebs in the corners of the sloping roof.

His mobile rang and he took it out of his back pocket and looked at the display. It was Button. 'Everything okay?' she asked.

'Just thinking about doing a little gardening,' he said. 'She's gone out, not sure when she'll be back.'

'You're getting closer, aren't you?'

'Softly, softly,' said Shepherd. 'But, yes, I'm getting closer.'

'I've had the results on the bullets they took out of Willie McEvoy. They came from Carter's service revolver, same as the ones that killed Dunne and McFee. We're going to have to up the ante, Spider. We've kept a lid on this so far but eventually someone'll talk.'

'I can't push her too hard, Charlie.'

'We need to find that gun.'

'I'm working on it.'

Shepherd ended the call and pulled out the mower. He unscrewed the cap on the fuel tank. It was empty. He went back into the shed and rooted around for a petrol can. Among the spades and forks he found a pole with a metal hook at the end. It wasn't a garden implement he had ever seen before. He pulled it out. There was a dark red centipede on the handle, which he shook off. It scurried under the shed. Shepherd held up the pole and stared at it, wondering what it was. Then he smiled.

Charlotte Button handed over her SOCA credentials to a bored uniformed sergeant. She flashed the man a smile, 'I have a two o'clock appointment with Chief Superintendent Khan,' she said.

The sergeant noted her details on a clipboard and handed back her ID card. 'I'll phone his office,' he said. 'Visitors have to be escorted upstairs, I'm afraid.'

'Not a problem,' said Button. She sat on an orange plastic chair and put her briefcase on the floor beside her. The waiting area smelled of stale sweat and there were grubby fingermarks on the walls. A poster offered an amnesty on all knives handed in before the end of the year. Another informed victims of domestic violence that they could phone the police for help. An old lady was standing at the counter, telling a young blonde policewoman that her next-door neighbour's dog was barking all night and keeping her awake. Button wanted a cigarette so she took a stick of chewing-gum from her handbag to stifle the cravings. She looked for a bin to throw the wrapper in but there wasn't one so she put it into her coat pocket. The old lady was crying now and dabbing her eyes with a lace handkerchief.

A door opened and a woman in her late twenties, wearing a dark skirt and blazer, smiled at Button. 'Can you come with me, please?' she asked, holding the door open. She handed Button a plastic tag with VISITOR on it and a bar code. Button clipped it to her coat. 'You're not carrying a weapon by any chance, are you?' asked the woman.

'Good Lord, no,' said Button.

'I'm sorry, I have to ask,' said the woman. 'We get all types in here, and everyone has to go through the security. Sorry.' Button put her handbag and mobile phone on a conveyor belt that passed through an X-ray machine, followed the secretary through a metal detector, picked up her things, then walked to the lift. They went up to the sixth floor.

Khan had a corner office, as befitted his rank. The woman showed Button in straight away. He was wearing his uniform and stood up when he saw her. She had never met the chief superintendent but she had seen him on television many times, usually touted as one of the top Muslim police officers in the country. He was a big man with wide shoulders and a bulging stomach that strained at his jacket. His heavy jowls overhung his starched shirt collar. He strode round his desk, his arm outstretched, and his stubby fingers grasped Button's hand. 'Thank you so much for coming, Ms Button,' he said.

Button smiled. 'Charlotte, please,' she said. Her eyes flashed across Khan's desk. There was a framed photograph of the chief superintendent with his wife, son and daughter, a clear plastic in-tray filled with correspondence, a brass paperweight in the shape of a cat, and a large mug with a picture of the Eiffel Tower on the side filled with pens. A computer terminal stood on a side table and on the wall behind it hung framed photographs of Khan meeting the great and the good – shaking hands with Ken Livingstone, the Mayor of London; looking solemn with two bearded mullahs; with his arm around David Beckham; standing next to the commissioner of the Metropolitan Police; sharing a podium with Tony Blair; and being presented with a certificate by an earnest-looking man in a dog-collar. By the door there were several framed certificates, including an honorary degree from Leeds University.

'Please, sit down,' said Khan. He showed Button to a black leather corner unit by the window. 'Tea, coffee?'

'Tea would be lovely,' said Button, taking off her coat. 'Anything but Earl Grey.'

The chief superintendent smiled at his secretary. 'Iced tea, please, Anita,' he said, and sat down as she left the office. 'Have you been to Leicester before?' he asked.

'My first time,' said Button. 'It's hardly a hotbed of crime.'

'We have our moments,' said Khan, 'but I know what you mean. I doubt there are many villains on our patch that SOCA would consider targeting.'

'But you have something for us now, I gather.'

'Possibly,' said Khan. 'But I wanted to talk it through with you before making an official request for your undercover unit.' He smiled but not with his eyes. 'I was one of those who expressed reservations about SOCA when it was first mooted,' he said. 'There was a fear that you'd cherry-pick the high-profile cases and leave us under-resourced to cope with the rising levels of street crime.'

'The powers-that-be saw us as a resource that all forces across the country could draw on,' said Button.

'A British FBI, they were calling it,' said Khan, 'and in the States there's constant friction between the federal and state agencies.'

'There's a world of difference between the FBI and SOCA,' she told him. 'Funding for one.'

'Policing is all about money,' agreed Khan. 'I'm more of a resource manager than a thief-catcher these days.'

'Well, anything I can do to help.'

'There's something I'm not quite clear about. Where were you before you joined SOCA?'

'MI5.'

Khan nodded thoughtfully. 'And how is SOCA working out for you?'

'It's challenging,' she said, 'but I was never particularly

deskbound during my time with Five. I ran agents and spent a lot of time in the field.'

'Would I be right in saying you joined MI5 from university?'

'Yes.'

'Fast-track?'

'I'm afraid so.'

'Nothing to be ashamed of,' said Khan. 'I was fast-tracked. The force wanted more ethnic minorities among its officers. I suppose MI5 needed more women.'

Button raised an eyebrow. 'I prefer to think I was selected on merit,' she said.

'Of course, of course,' said Khan, quickly, 'but you know what I mean. Fast-tracking allows an organisation to be realigned where necessary.'

'Actually, there are more women on the staff of MI5 than men, and the last two Director Generals have been women. The glass ceiling was broken in the intelligence services a long time ago.'

'Well, we've still some way to go,' said Khan. 'So, tell me, what else did you do when you were with Five?'

'I was in the National Security Advice Centre, working on serious crime investigations. After Nine Eleven I was moved to the International Counter-terrorism Branch, and when SOCA was formed, I was approached to head up the undercover unit.'

'And you're juggling a family as well as a career?'

Button frowned. 'This is starting to feel like a job interview.'

Khan's belly jiggled as he chuckled but his eyes were still hard. 'I'm sorry if I appear to be prying, Charlotte. It's just that I like to know who I'm dealing with, especially when the matter is somewhat sensitive.' He waved at the photograph of his family on the desk. 'Family means everything to me,' he said, 'but I've had to sacrifice a lot to get to where I am today.'

'You have to make time,' agreed Button. 'I'm lucky, my husband is very supportive, and our daughter loves boarding-school. It's not quite Hogwarts, but that whole Harry Potter thing has made it so much easier to send them away.'

'Your husband also works for the intelligence services?'

Button shook her head. 'He's an estate agent. That's how I met him. He sold me my first apartment. I don't want to be rude, Chief Superintendent, but I have to be in Belfast this afternoon.'

'A case?'

'I'm running an operation there, yes. What is it you need doing?'

Khan opened his mouth to speak, but there was a knock at the door and Anita appeared with a tray. Khan waited until she had put it in front of him and left the room. 'I have a problem, Charlotte. A very sensitive problem that will need a very sensitive touch.' Khan leant forward. 'Racism has always been a problem within the police, both in the way they deal with the public but also in the way they deal with each other. I believe, Charlotte, that several officers at the very top of this force are racist. And I need you to expose them.'

'Racist in what way?'

'In the worst possible way,' said Khan. 'Racist comments, blocking the promotion of officers from ethnic minorities, backpedalling on cases in which minorities are the victims.'

Button looked pained. 'I'm sorry, Chief Superintendent, but that's really not within my remit,' she said. 'We're tasked with investigating major crimes, drugs, people-trafficking.'

'Racism *is* a major crime,' said Khan, sternly. 'It's something I take very seriously indeed.'

'As do I, Chief Superintendent, but in order for me to commit resources, the case has to be within our remit.'

'I need an officer to be under cover in our headquarters here. I can't use anyone from our force, obviously, which is why I thought SOCA would be the ideal solution.'

'Have you considered approaching the Met and asking them to second an officer?'

Khan sighed and sat back. 'I had, but the nature of the investigation is such that there might be . . . ramifications. It might result in the dismissal of officers at a very senior level, and men like that have friendships that reach across geographical boundaries.'

'I think what you're suggesting is highly unlikely,' said Button. 'Police investigate their own all the time.'

'But generally not at such a high level,' said Khan. 'Look, I understand your reservations about initiating such an investigation, but is there anything I can do to persuade you to help me?'

'I don't see how I can, Chief Superintendent. I'm sorry.'

Khan nodded. 'Okay,' he said. 'Let me give it some more thought.' He stood up and offered his hand. 'Thank you for coming to see me, anyway. I'm sure you've a lot on your plate at the moment.' He showed her to the door. As he held it open he raised a finger. 'Oh, do you have a card with a direct line, just in case I need to pick your brains?'

'I don't work from an office,' said Button. She reached into her bag and pulled out a purse. 'But I have a mobile.' She fished out a business card and handed it to him.

'Good luck in Belfast,' said Khan, and closed the door behind her.

Khan sat at his desk for the best part of an hour, staring blankly at a file in front of him. Eventually he sighed and stood up. He took his overcoat off the hook on the back of his door. 'I'm heading out for a while, Anita,' he said to his secretary.

'Do you need your car?' she asked.

'I'll walk,' he said. 'I'll be back before three.'

Khan took the lift to the ground floor, went through the metal detector and out into the street. Half a dozen civilian workers were clustered around the entrance, smoking and chatting. He lit a cigarette and strode away from the building.

He hated himself for what he was doing but he had no choice. Hassan knew where he lived and Khan had no doubt that he would wreak terrible vengeance on his family if he didn't do what he wanted. He had thought long and hard after Hassan had approached him, considering his options late into the night as he drank endless cups of coffee and smoked his way through two packets of cigarettes. If he went to his bosses and told them what had happened they could put him under police protection. But what would that mean? For the rest of his life he and his family would be virtual prisoners. His children's education would be ruined, his family would lose their friends, his career would stall. Everything he had worked for, all the sacrifices he had made, would have been for nothing.

There were two phone boxes a short walk from his office but he passed them, deep in thought. He cursed under his breath. He should have listened to his parents and become a doctor. They had always wanted him to study medicine, but even as a teenager he had known he wasn't cut out to be a medic. He didn't want to be around sick people, he wanted to catch criminals. He wanted the uniform, the squad cars and the comradeship. He'd studied law at university, but only because he knew that a law degree would get him on to the police fast-track promotion scheme. He'd made inspector within five years, superintendent five years later, and eventually even his parents had accepted that he'd made the right choice. He was doing well in a job he loved, and all the signs were that he was destined for even greater things. He knew he was already spoken of as the first Asian police commissioner, and all he had to do was keep climbing the slippery pole, seizing opportunities as they presented themselves and ensuring he didn't make any stupid mistakes. He chose his public appearances carefully and had two tame journalists, both Asian, one on a redtop tabloid, the other on a worthy broadsheet, who could be relied on to write puff pieces as needed.

He had planned his career perfectly, he had forged useful friendships and distanced himself from anyone who might have held him back, and now it was all to be wrecked because of a man called Hassan. A man who would kill an innocent girl to gain power over another human being. Hassan was pure evil, and Khan knew that even a high-ranking police officer was powerless in the face of such a man. He had dealt with hundreds of criminals over the years – thieves, drug-dealers, conmen, thugs and murderers – but he had never been confronted before by a man like Hassan. Khan knew that if he didn't do what Hassan wanted, he would kill Khan's family. He was as sure of that as he was that there was nothing the police could do to protect them. There was no way to hide from a man like Hassan.

He reached another phone box and stopped, checked that no one he knew was around, then took Button's business card from his wallet, pushed a pound coin into the slot and tapped out the number Hassan had given him. The phone went straight to voicemail.

Khan cleared his throat. He was about to cross a line, and once he had crossed it there would be no going back. He closed his eyes. Images of Sara being murdered flashed through his mind and he shuddered. He had to protect his wife and family. They were all that mattered. If others had to be sacrificed so that his family were safe, so be it. 'She lives in Surrey,' he said. He cleared his throat again. 'She's married with one child. The daughter is at boarding-school. Her husband is an estate agent, close to where they live. She's working on a case at the moment in Belfast and will be back and forth between London and Northern Ireland over the next couple of weeks.' Khan took a deep breath and exhaled through clenched teeth. 'Her mobile number . . .' He hesi-tated. Hassan hadn't said why he wanted information about Charlotte Button, but Khan knew there could be only one reason. He wanted her dead. He said a silent prayer, but knew that wouldn't help. He closed his eyes and continued to talk into the phone, his voice a hushed whisper.

★   ★   ★

Shepherd went upstairs with the wooden pole where, on the landing ceiling, he found a hatch with a small brass ring between the two back bedrooms. He reached up with the pole, inserted the hook and pulled. As the hatch opened, a folding aluminium ladder came into view. Shepherd used the hook to draw it down, then climbed up it.

At the top he stepped into an attic and flicked a light switch. There were wooden beams running the length of the area and foam insulation had been sprayed into the gaps between the beams. A stack of cardboard boxes stood just inside the trapdoor. Shepherd opened one. It was full of women's clothing. The old man who had lived there before him must have put it up here after his wife had died.

Shepherd sat back on his heels and picked up a blue woollen cardigan with cream buttons. After Sue had died, he couldn't bring himself to take her clothes out of the wardrobe for four months. Then he had put them into black bags and left them in the spare bedroom at their house in Ealing. It wasn't until Katra had arrived that he had thrown them out. He knew exactly how the old man had felt. He put the cardigan back into the box and closed it.

A brick wall divided his half of the attic from Elaine's, with a plastic water tank at one end. He walked carefully across the beams to the dividing wall and banged it with the flat of his hand. He had hoped it would be plaster board that he could cut through it, but it was bricks.

He returned to the trapdoor, went down the aluminium ladder, folded it up and closed the hatch. He took the pole downstairs and went to the sitting room. Elaine's driveway was still empty. He took out his mobile and called her. 'Hey, where are you?' he asked.

'Bangor,' she said. 'I've a few calls to make here. Why, what's up?'

'I saw a guy in your back garden,' said Shepherd. 'Teenager, I think, prowling around. He was heading for the shed but when he saw me he bolted. I had a quick look around and there were no windows broken or anything so he was probably just trying his luck.'

'The burglar alarm's usually enough of a deterrent,' said Elaine. 'They see the box and go off in search of a house that's less trouble.'

'Like mine?' said Shepherd.

Elaine laughed. 'I'm afraid so,' she said. 'You should get an alarm, too. Thanks for keeping an eye on things for me, Jamie.'

'It's the neighbourly thing to do,' he said.

Salih walked out of Maida Vale Tube station and crossed Elgin Avenue. Viktor Merkulov was sitting outside a Starbucks café, sipping a *latte*. He was wearing a cashmere overcoat and a fur hat, and a pair of black leather gloves lay on the table in front of him. Salih smiled. The man dressed like a Russian cliché.

Merkulov waved as he walked over. 'Come, my friend, sit down, what would you like to drink?'

'Why are you sitting outside?' asked Salih. 'It's freezing.' He already knew that the Russian had chosen Maida Vale for their meeting because it was a short walk from St John's Wood where he owned a three-bedroom penthouse apartment with views over Lord's cricket ground.

'This?' laughed Merkulov. 'This is nothing. I can tell you have never been to Siberia.'

Salih sat down. 'No coffee for me,' he said.

'Tea, then,' said Merkulov, standing up.

'Tea,' agreed Salih. 'No milk. No sugar.'

The Russian went inside to fetch it. Salih shivered and folded his arms. He was wearing a reefer jacket over an Aran sweater but the wind chilled him. An elderly woman walked past with a Jack Russell on a tartan lead. She looked at him suspiciously and he smiled amiably. 'Good afternoon,' he said. 'Lovely dog.'

The woman's jaw dropped, then her face creased into a

smile. 'Thank you,' she said, and hurried off. Salih's smile tightened as he watched her go. All Muslims were regarded with suspicion in London, following the bombings on the Tube system. It didn't matter that the terrorist attacks were the work of a very small minority of Islamic fundamentalists, every brown face was treated as a potential threat.

Merkulov returned with a mug of tea and two chocolate muffins. He put the tea in front of Salih, then sat down heavily and held out the plate.

'I always worry about eating with former KGB people,' Salih said. 'I feel I should be checking everything with a Geiger counter.'

Merkulov scowled. 'Just because a Russian dissident gets radiation poisoning, everyone blames us,' he said. He took a bite from a muffin and continued to speak with his mouth full. 'Do you really think that if Putin wanted someone dead, he couldn't arrange to have it look like an accident? There are experts who can make any death look like an accident. Look at what happened to Princess Diana.' Muffin crumbs splattered across the table and he wiped his mouth with the back of his hand.

Salih grinned. 'You're not taking credit for what happened to Diana, are you?'

'Of course it wasn't the KGB, we had no reason to harm her. But the British Establishment, now that's a different matter.'

Salih slid a folded piece of paper across the table. 'I need someone to track this mobile phone for me. Can you do that?'

'It belongs to the American or to the woman?'

'The woman,' said Salih. 'She might be in Northern Ireland.'

'Do you know which phone company she's with? Vodaphone, T-Mobile? Orange?'

'All I have is the number,' said Salih. 'I need to know where she is.'

'That's easy,' said the Russian. 'Do you know what make of phone she has?' Salih shook his head.

'Some of the new models have GPS capability, which means we can pin her down to a few metres in real time. If not, we'll know which transmitter she's near. In the city that could be a hundred feet or so.'

'And would you be able to get a list of calls, incoming and outgoing?'

The Russian pulled a face. 'All things are possible, my friend. For a price.'

'And get me the locations of the numbers?'

'The landlines, of course. It is harder to get the locations of mobiles.'

Salih took a brown envelope from inside his jacket and slid it across the table. 'Ten thousand pounds on account,' he said.

Merkulov picked up the envelope. 'It will take me a day or two at most.'

'I want to know by tonight,' said Salih. 'I will pay what-ever it takes.'

'This is why I'd never feed you a radioactive soda,' said Merkulov, tapping the envelope on Salih's shoulder. 'You are too valuable a customer.'

Shepherd checked that no one was on the pavement, then used his keys to open Elaine's front door. He was carrying the pole he'd found in his garden shed. He closed the door behind him and tapped the four-digit code into the keypad on the burglar-alarm console.

On his last surreptitious visit to Elaine's house he'd searched the ground floor. He still had to do the bedrooms but he decided that the attic was a better bet. He used the pole to open the hatch and pull down the folding stairs, then went up and switched on the light. The layout was a mirror image of his own attic, with the water tank in the far corner, next to the dividing wall with his own property. Half a dozen cardboard boxes had been stacked against the tank, and there was a wooden cabin trunk with a combination lock. Shepherd had a quick look through the boxes but they contained junk – old lamps, toys, ornaments, several children's annuals and some schoolbooks, scuffed handbags and winter coats.

Shepherd reclosed the cardboard boxes and knelt beside the trunk and examined the combination lock. A three-digit number would open it, which meant there were a thousand possible combinations. Assuming it would take two seconds to try each number, he could do all thousand in two thousand seconds, which was just over half an hour. He had time but . . . He closed his eyes and went to the file Button had shown him, mentally flicking through the numbers that meant something to Elaine. He tried her birthdate, month and day, then day and month. No joy. He tried her husband's birthday. Her wedding anniversary wouldn't work because it fell on 3 May, which meant two digits. Would she have used the date her husband had been killed – 28 August? He tried eight-two-eight and two-eight-eight but neither worked. Her son, maybe. Little Timmy. He tried his birthday, month followed by year, then year followed by month. The lock clicked open.

Inside the trunk he found three photograph albums, two with a green fake leather binding, the third bound in white leather. He took out the first and flicked through it. There were photographs of Elaine as a baby, as a child and as a young woman. She had been a pretty toddler with long, curly red hair.

The second album contained pictures of her with her husband, mostly holiday snaps. Several had been taken on beaches, and in every image they were holding each other. They had clearly been a close couple. Half-way through the album she was pregnant, then she and her husband were holding a baby. Shepherd felt dirty as he rooted through Elaine's memories. He had no right to be handling her possessions, prying into her personal life.

The third album, the white one, was filled with wedding pictures. The first was familiar – he had seen it on the bookcase in the sitting room. The second was a group photograph of everyone at the wedding, more than a hundred people. John Maplethorpe was standing next to Robbie Carter.

In the middle of the album he found a photograph of Carter with five men and, again, Maplethorpe was standing next to him. He must have been best man, Shepherd thought, and the others were ushers. There were pictures of Elaine with her parents, Carter with his parents, Elaine with the bridesmaids, the couple inside the church and in the churchyard. Shepherd had a similar album of his own wedding. Like Elaine, he kept it in the attic. He couldn't throw it away, but neither could he bear to open it.

Under the third album he found five framed photographs. Two had been taken at the wedding – in one Robbie was holding her under a cherry tree in full blossom, and in the other he and Maplethorpe were both planting a kiss on her cheek. The other three were of Timmy as a baby in his mother's arms, as a toddler, grinning at the camera, and in his school uniform.

Underneath the photographs lay a small bubble-wrapped package, which Shepherd opened carefully. Inside he found a stainless-steel Omega watch and a gold wedding band on a thin gold chain. They had obviously belonged to her husband and for some time at least she had worn the ring round her neck. Shepherd felt like a grave robber. Elaine had loved her man with all her heart, and he knew he had no right to root through her possessions. He kept Sue's jewellery in a box in his wardrobe, next to his gun and ammunition, and knew how he'd feel if a stranger ever touched it. He rewrapped the watch and the ring, then put them on top of the framed photographs.

He turned back to the trunk and took out several newspapers, all from 1996, with Robbie Carter's photograph on the front pages. Underneath them were two hardback journals with the RUC crest on the front. Shepherd flicked through them – lists of dates and times, people Carter had met and places he'd been to. In notes of meetings with informers he had used codewords in place of names. He scanned a few entries but they were innocuous.

A red wool scarf came next, but when Shepherd picked it up his eyes widened. A box of ammunition lay beneath it, .357 rounds made by an American company, PMC. He opened it. Inside, there were spaces for fifty bullets. Shepherd quickly counted those that remained. Twenty-six. Two dozen were missing. He took one out and slipped it into his pocket.

The doorbell buzzed and Shepherd froze. Instinctively he switched off the light even though there was no chance of it being seen from the outside. His heart pounded, even though he knew there was nothing to worry about. Elaine would hardly be ringing her own doorbell.

He replaced the contents of the trunk, taking care to put them in the position he'd found them. He relocked it and went down the ladder, pushed it back into place and closed the trapdoor. Then he crept into the bedroom. A dark saloon car was driving away from the house.

He hurried downstairs, reset the burglar alarm, went outside and locked the front door. He hadn't found a gun but the ammunition was worrying. Why would Elaine keep it if she didn't have a gun? There was something else too. The Omega watch had been ticking. It was a self-winding model, which meant that after a day or two in the trunk it would have stopped. It had been rewound or even worn in the past couple of days.

Hassan Salih thrust his hands deep into the pockets of his overcoat. A cold wind blew down the Thames, rippling the muddy brown waters. On the south side of the river the giant London Eye turned slowly, giving the tourists in its capsules the best view of the city. The sky was cloudless, as blue as it was above Salih's native Palestine, but the temperature was at least thirty degrees lower.

Salih glanced over his shoulder, but he was already sure he wasn't being followed. London was a great place to hide. He had read somewhere that a third of its inhabitants had been born overseas. It was a city of foreigners, a city of strangers. There was no such thing as a typical Londoner any more, so no one stuck out.

The Russian was sitting on a wooden bench that overlooked the river. He blew smoke as Salih sat down next to him and gestured at the giant wheel with his cigar. 'It has to be the mother of all targets, doesn't it?' he said. Salih assumed that the question was rhetorical so he said nothing. 'I mean, its full name is the British Airways London Eye, so blowing it up would be on a par with bringing down a 747. And you'd probably kill as many people.'

'Are you planning a terrorist atrocity?' asked Salih. 'I didn't think it was your style.'

'Nor my area of expertise,' said the Russian. 'I leave that sort of thing to your kinsfolk. But what do you think? Four suicide-bombers? Blow up individual pods? Or a massed attack at the bottom to see if you could bring down the entire structure. Can you imagine what it would look like? One big bang and the wheel slams into the Thames. Everyone on it would be killed, guaranteed. And such an image! That's what al-Qaeda wants – images. They didn't care about the three thousand or so who died in the Twin Towers. They wanted that image of the buildings on fire, then collapsing. Same with the attacks on the Tube. It's a symbol of the city, and their attacks are all about symbolism.' He blew smoke, then jabbed his cigar towards the giant wheel. 'And over there, my friend, is one hell of a symbol.'

'I've no interest in terrorist attacks or symbolism,' said Salih. 'The only symbols I care about are those found on banknotes.'

The Russian guffawed and slapped Salih's knee. 'We are

alike in that respect, my friend.' He took out a leather cigar case and offered it to Salih, who shook his head. 'You don't smoke?' asked Merkulov.

'A hookah pipe sometimes,' said Salih. 'I like my smoke sweet and fragrant.'

Merkulov put the cigar case back inside his coat. His hand reappeared with a gleaming white envelope, which he gave to Salih. 'She's in Belfast,' he said. 'At least, she was this morning. She's moving backwards and forwards between Northern Ireland and London. She visits Glasgow every two weeks.'

Salih opened the envelope and took out three computer printouts. One was a list of phone calls made and received with the date and time of each. The second showed the location of the mobile when the calls had been made and received. The third was a list of landline locations.

A group of Japanese tourists walked past, heading for a booth that offered boat trips along the river. 'And what about getting the locations of the mobile numbers she's been communicating with?' asked Salih.

Merkulov grimaced. 'That's tough and expensive. If you want that done you'll have to tell me which numbers to check and we'll do them one by one.'

Salih studied the list. 'She's been calling one mobile number a lot while she's in Belfast. Can you get me a list of calls made and received from that phone? Say, another five thousand pounds?'

'You don't need locations?'

'Just the numbers at this stage.'

'Then five will be okay,' said the Russian.

Salih handed him an envelope. 'Here's twenty on account.'

The Russian put it into his pocket. 'It is always a pleasure to do business with a professional like yourself,' he said. 'Be careful, old friend. I wouldn't want to lose such a good customer.' He grunted as he stood up and blew a cloud of blue-grey smoke towards the Thames. Then he walked off in the direction of the Houses of Parliament.

Salih watched him go. The Russian's legs moved awkwardly as if he was having problems with his hips. Merkulov was in his late sixties, but he was in a business where age was no barrier to success. All that mattered was the quality of the information he traded. Salih's profession was much more age-dependent: his survival depended on his fitness and performance. He reckoned he had another five years ahead of him, ten at most. By the time he was forty he would be either retired or dead.

He crossed his legs and watched a tourist boat battle upstream, dozens of cameras clicking as a bored woman in a red anorak held a microphone to her lips and detailed the buildings that lined the banks. It would be a challenge to go up against a man like Yokely. It wasn't the first time Salih had been paid to kill another assassin and he doubted it would be the last. It was a job like any other. The problem lay in getting close to the man, who moved between countries leaving virtually no trace. But if Yokely was close to Button, perhaps that was his weakness. If Salih killed the woman, Yokely would attend the funeral. Once he was in the open, he would be vulnerable.

Salih stood up and headed for Embankment Tube station.

Jonas Filbin tossed a briquette of peat on to the fire and prodded it with a brass poker, then settled back in his over-stuffed leather armchair. 'They'll be banning this before long, I'm sure,' he said. 'The Government's legislating all the pleasures out of life. Either that or taxing them to death.'

'Aye, you can't beat a real fire,' said Gerry Lynn, swirling his whiskey around the glass. He was sitting on a leather sofa with Michael Kelly, one of his IRA minders. Kelly was a few years younger than Lynn, with a mop of red hair that defied all attempts to comb it into shape. He had taken off his jacket to reveal a shoulder holster with a large automatic under his left armpit. He was drinking a mug of sweet tea. He wouldn't touch alcohol when he was working. The other minder, Mark

Nugent, was in his late twenties and deferred constantly to him. Nugent had been on defensive driving courses and was a crack shot, though he had only ever fired on the range. The IRA had announced its 1994 ceasefire as Nugent had turned thirteen. Although he had been through the organisation's training programme, he had missed the opportunity to put those skills into action against the British.

The four men were in a farmhouse in north County Dublin, a large rambling grey-stone building amid acres of potato fields. It had been in Filbin's family for six generations and he had moved there from Belfast after his release from prison following the Good Friday Agreement. Filbin's elder sister was upstairs in bed.

Filbin and Lynn had shared a cell in Long Kesh for almost eighteen months and had been released on the same sunny July morning. Filbin had served just six years for the murders of two policemen and the attempted murder of two soldiers. He had refused to recognise the British court that tried him and had been given four life sentences but like Flynn had been released early under the Good Friday Agreement. Filbin was in his sixties with a farmer's ruddy complexion and watery brown eyes.

'And how's Sean MacManus, these days?' asked Lynn.

'Still in Portlaoise, and not a happy bunny,' said Filbin.

'Aye, well, that's what you get if you leave your fingerprints on a gun,' said Lynn. Portlaoise was the most secure prison in Europe, guarded twenty-four hours a day by the Irish Defence Forces. It was also one of the oldest, and bleakest, gaols in Ireland and was where the Irish Government kept its terrorist prisoners. MacManus was a member of Continuity IRA, which, unlike the Provisionals, had been granted no favours under the Good Friday Agreement. He would rot in jail for the kidnap and murder of two Gardai officers.

'Aye, but you can see the irony in the situation, I'm sure,' said Filbin.

'The irony?' repeated Lynn. He sipped his whiskey.

'Well, we're Irish, and he's Irish. We killed coppers, he killed coppers. He gets sent down, we get sent down. But he's sleeping on a pissy mattress and getting an hour of fresh air a day, and here's you and me drinking whiskey and raising our glasses to a job well done.'

Lynn grinned. 'Aye, there's irony there.'

'But did you ever think, when we were in Long Kesh, that we'd be out so soon, free and clear?'

'For the first couple of years I was sure I'd die behind bars,' said Lynn. 'But remember in 1998, when Mo Mowlam turned up to talk to Mad Dog and that nutter Stone? That's when I knew things were going to happen and the Brits wanted rid. Sure enough, three months later the Good Friday Agreement's signed and we had our tickets out.' He raised his glass. 'Here's to Martin and Gerry, God bless 'em. There were those that doubted them, but the boys came through.'

Filbin raised his glass. '*Tiocfaidh ar la!*'

'*Tiocfaidh ar la*? Our day will come? Our day has come, Jonas. It's here and now.'

'And there's the irony,' said Filbin, kicking off his boots and wriggling his toes. 'We're getting what we wanted, what we fought and killed for, and the likes of Sean are still eating prison food.'

'He backed the wrong horse,' said Lynn. 'Continuity and Real IRA are pariahs now and always will be. There's no going back for them. And no going forward. The War on Terror has made sure of that. All terrorists are tarred with the same brush, these days. I tell you, Jonas, the Good Lord was smiling down on us. If we'd still been at war come Nine Eleven the Provos would have been smashed, no question.'

'Aye, timing's everything,' agreed Filbin. He poured more whiskey into their glasses. 'So what's it like now, Belfast?'

'Boom town,' said Lynn. 'If I didn't already own a couple of houses, I wouldn't be able to afford one. It's gone crazy. We've got tourists photographing themselves in front of the Peace Wall and coach trips down the Falls Road.'

'And the cops?'

'None too happy with their new name and the fact that Sinn Fein are scrutinising their every move, but fuck 'em, hey?'

'Aye to that,' said Filbin. 'Do you think it was the cops that did for your boys?'

Lynn sighed. 'Who the fuck knows? The Brits swear blind it wasn't, but how the hell would they know? If it was rogue cops they'd hardly broadcast what they were doing.'

'The SAS settling scores?'

'That'd be more likely in Joe's case because he had a few run-ins with them. I dare say they wouldn't mind giving me the old double-tap too, but Willie McEvoy was a wheel man and never shot anyone, let alone a Sass-man. In any case, the Sass are too busy in Afghanistan and Iraq, these days.'

'Well, it won't be the spooks because they can't move these days without some parliamentary sub-committee or another breathing down their necks,' said Filbin. 'And they've got bigger things to worry about than settling old scores.'

'Who would have thought London could be more dangerous than Belfast? Bombs on the Tube, nutters trying to get bombs on planes, buying job lots of fertiliser and planning to blow up shopping malls.'

'Bloody amateurs,' said Filbin.

'They're on a learning curve, same as we were in the seventies and eighties,' said Lynn. 'And they've got the advantage that they're happy enough to blow themselves to kingdom come as well. We'd never have got guys prepared to kill themselves for the cause, but the ragheads are queuing up to be martyrs.'

Filbin grinned mischievously. 'That's because they've got seventy-two virgins waiting for them in Heaven.'

Lynn laughed. 'Yeah, that was always a problem for us. We could never have found seventy-two virgins in Belfast.'

Filbin drank some whiskey. 'I went to school with Joe

McFee. Threw my first petrol bomb and did my first kneecapping with him. He didn't deserve to die like that, shot like
an animal.' A faraway look came into his eyes. 'Who'd do
that, huh? You're right about the spooks, though. MI5 and
MI6 aren't allowed to kill anyone. The cops and the army
might have scores to settle, but the spooks are too cerebral
for that. University graduates one and all.'

Lynn cupped his glass in both hands. 'It could be the
Prods, getting in a last hurrah,' he said. 'I wouldn't put it
past them. They're laying down their arms, so they say, but
they're not decommissioning and there's some mad bastards
who won't listen to their leadership anyway.'

'So what's the plan?' asked Filbin.

'I keep looking over my shoulder,' said Lynn, and patted
his chest, 'and I'm wearing a vest, though I'm not sure how
much good it'll do because McFee, Dunne and McEvoy were
all shot in the back of the head.'

'And the knees, right?'

'Yeah.'

'Which is how the RUC Special Branch guy died, isn't it?
I'm assuming that's not a coincidence.'

Lynn's eyes narrowed. 'What big ears you've got, Grandma.
The cops haven't revealed the details, just that they were
shot.'

'I might be a farmer these days but I've still got friends
in the North. I'm told that Joe and the guys were killed the
same way Robbie Carter died.'

'That's what I've heard, yeah.'

'Then it's as obvious as the nose on your face. Someone's
taking revenge for what you did to him. Family or friend.
Has to be.'

'The cops say they're looking at that, but they won't tell
me what they've got, if anything. I made a few enquiries
myself. Carter's parents are old, he's got a brother in Canada
and his widow's got no connection with paramilitaries. Neither
has her family.'

'So that just leaves the whole of Special Branch.' Filbin scowled.

'We killed Carter in 1996,' said Lynn. 'I know revenge is a dish best served cold but waiting this long is ridiculous.' He grinned at Kelly and Nugent. 'Anyway, with these guys babysitting me, no one's going to get near me.'

Kelly lifted his mug of tea in salute. 'That's the plan, anyway,' he said.

'What about Noel Kinsella?' asked Filbin. 'Who's taking care of him?'

'He's thrown in his lot with the Brits,' said Lynn, contemptuously. 'He's got the cops watching over him – and the spooks as well, from what I hear. Lying low in London until they get the killer.'

'Is it right he's been promised something in the new Assembly?'

'Apparently.'

'And that he's married well?'

Lynn chuckled. 'A Kennedy.'

'Well indeed, then,' said Filbin.

'It's a love match, I'm told.'

'There's only one person Noel Kinsella loves and that's himself,' said Filbin. 'Between you and me, I never really trusted him. Always out for what he could get.'

'He's destined for better things now,' said Lynn. 'In his own mind, anyway.' He paused. 'I'd better be going.'

'Stay the night, Gerry. There's a spare bed.'

'We can be back home in a couple of hours,' said Lynn. 'It's motorway and there'll be no traffic this time of night.' He drained his glass. 'It was good to see you, Jonas.'

Filbin hugged him. 'You be careful, yeah?' He kissed Lynn on the cheek.

Kelly and Nugent pushed themselves out of their chairs and shook his hand. 'You take care of this man now,' he said.

Kelly and Nugent walked with Lynn to their Lexus. Nugent climbed into the driving seat and Lynn sat next to him. Kelly

walked to the barred metal gate at the entrance to the courtyard and opened it.

Nugent drove slowly across the cattle grid and waited while
Kelly closed the gate and climbed into the back.

'Right, boys, don't spare the horses.'

Nugent headed slowly down the gravelled track that led
to the main road. As they left the farm, he flipped on the
full headlights, their powerful beam flooding the track ahead.
A fox hurried away, its tail low, and an owl soared into the
darkness.

'He's real old-school, Jonas, isn't he?' said Nugent.

'Careful what you say. He's not much older than me,' said
Lynn.

'I meant politically,' said Nugent.

'He wasn't over the moon about power-sharing, but Jonas
is a realist. That's the way it's got to be if we're going to win
the long war.'

'What's going on up there?' asked Kelly, peering out of
the side window.

Lynn squinted through the windscreen. A Land Rover was
in the ditch to the left of the track, its bonnet up.

Nugent slowed the Lexus. 'An accident?'

'Ignore it, man,' said Kelly. 'Just put your foot down and
get us past it.'

'I don't see anyone, do you?'

'Mark, put your bloody foot down!' said Lynn.

'We're in the South here, nothing's going—'

'Do as he says, Mark,' said Kelly, from the back seat. 'Get
us out of here.'

As Nugent opened his mouth to reply, his face exploded
in a shower of blood and skull fragments that splattered
across the dashboard and windscreen. A second shot shattered the rear window and Kelly slumped forward, blood
pouring from his throat. Lynn grabbed the steering-wheel
and lifted his right leg over Nugent's left, trying to get his
foot to the accelerator. The engine roared but the car didn't

move. A third shot rang out, and for a moment Lynn thought he'd been hit, but there was no pain. He fumbled for the gear lever, screaming in frustration.

The passenger door was pulled open and the barrel of a gun was pressed to the side of his head. Lynn raised his hands. 'I'm not armed,' he said.

Salih sat in his hotel room and studied the map of the United Kingdom that he'd spread out across the double bed. He had spent an hour in Borders in Oxford Street and had purchased *A–Z* street directories that covered all the areas that appeared in the list of landline locations the Russian had given him. He sipped a glass of Evian water and eyed the circles he had marked on the map. Most were dotted in and around London and were either police stations or government offices. None of the numbers belonged to private residences. Charlotte Button had made two calls to Leicester, to the police headquarters building where Khan worked. She had made several to Glasgow numbers and two to Belfast. Over the past fortnight she'd made fifty-three calls to landlines and twice as many to mobiles. She'd spent most of this week in Belfast.

Salih inserted a new pay-as-you-go Sim card into his phone and called the Belfast number. The Europa Hotel. He cut the connection and smiled to himself. There was a good chance that Charlotte Button was staying at the Europa, though he doubted she would be using her own name. Belfast was as good a place as any to kill her, but hotels were public places and Salih would need time to kill her in the way that Muhammad Aslam had stipulated.

He walked around the bed, looking down at the map. One of the landlines was located in Culford School at Bury St Edmunds in Suffolk. Salih had Googled the name and discovered that it took boys and girls as boarders. It was a place for the rich to educate their children away from home. Khan had said Button had a daughter, and that the daughter had been sent to boarding-school. Now Salih knew where she was, and if he got the daughter, he'd get the mother, guaranteed. Salih had no reservations about killing women or children. People were people, no matter their age or sex, and Salih's profession was to kill. But the boarding-school was a long shot. If the child was there, it might be weeks before her mother visited.

Salih sat on the bed and studied the map again. At some point Button must have phoned her home. There were two numbers, in Berkshire and Surrey, to the south-west of London. Merkulov had supplied addresses for both. One was in the centre of Windsor, the other a village called Virginia Water in Windsor Great Park, about eight miles from Heathrow.

Salih had a small Dell laptop on the dressing-table, connected to the hotel's Wi-Fi network. He had an account with www.192.com, which he had opened when he was in Dubai. It allowed him access to a huge database, including phone directories and electoral rolls. Salih had been surprised to discover how much information about its citizens the British Government was prepared to make available to anyone with computer access, but he was more than happy to take advantage of it.

He had already entered 'Charlotte Button' in the website's search engine and come up with nothing, country-wide. This time he simply entered 'Charlotte' and the address in Windsor. It came up blank. He tried with just the address but the search engine insisted on a name or a description of a business. Salih sat back and flipped through his notepad. Khan had said that the woman's husband was an estate agent. He tapped in 'estate agent' and hit the search button. In less than a second the website gave him the name of an estate agent at the address. Salih smiled. Sometimes information was hard to come by; sometimes it was like plucking apples from trees. Now he knew where the husband worked.

He cleared the search engine and entered the Virginia Water address with the name 'Charlotte'. He hit the search button and, almost immediately, the address popped up with two names above it. Charlotte Pickering and Graham Pickering. Salih muttered a prayer, thanking Allah for all his works. Charlotte Pickering was almost certainly Charlotte Button.

'Got you,' he muttered.

Shepherd was stretched out on the sofa watching an episode of *Midsomer Murders* when his mobile rang. It was Button. 'We've got a problem, Spider.'

Shepherd squinted at the digital display on his wristwatch. It was just after three thirty in the afternoon. 'I'm listening.'

'Gerry Lynn was murdered last night near Dublin.'

'Shit.'

'Shit is right. Now, tell me you've got Elaine Carter under surveillance.'

'No can do, Charlie. She's not at home and I haven't seen her all day.'

'Where are you?'

'Home.'

'I'm coming round.'

'I'm not sure that's a good idea.'

'She's not there, you said.'

'I know but—'

'Stay put, Spider. I'll be there within the hour.' The line went dead.

Shepherd made himself a mug of coffee and went on watching Inspector Barnaby. Like most television shows *Midsomer Murders* bore almost no relation to reality. Two polite middle-class detectives were knocking on the doors of well-kept cottages asking questions over cups of tea and cucumber sandwiches. In the real world ninety per cent of murders were solved within the first hour or so of the victims' deaths. More often than not a family member or business acquaintance had killed them, and the motive boiled down to anger brought on by money, revenge or sex, with drugs or alcohol fuelling it. Usually there was no real detective work involved. It wasn't easy to take a life and most people who killed were immediately stricken with remorse. They'd stay with the body until the police came or walk into a police station and confess. Those who tried to cover their tracks were usually caught because a few simple questions asked of the deceased's nearest and dearest would throw up the names of any suspects. Then it was simply a matter of nailing down where they had been at the time of death. Rarely was there any mystery to be solved.

One of the nice middle-class detectives was about to reveal who the murderer was when Shepherd's doorbell rang. He muted the television's sound and went to open the front door.

Button was wearing a fawn belted raincoat over a dark suit and carrying a Prada bag. She walked past him and down the hall to the kitchen. 'Got any wine?' she asked. 'I need a drink.'

'Red or white?'

'I don't care what colour it is.' She took off her coat, threw it over a chair and sat at the kitchen table. She put her head in her hands.

Shepherd opened the fridge and took out a bottle of Frascati. Button groaned when she saw the label. 'Is that all you've got?'

'There's champagne,' said Shepherd. 'Elaine gave it to me. But I like Frascati. It's crisp, clean, and you can drink it with anything.'

Button laughed. 'Just pour it, Spider.'

'So what happened?' asked Shepherd, as he uncorked the wine.

'The Garda Siochana called it in last night,' said Button. 'They found the bodies on a farm in County Dublin.'

'Bodies?'

'Lynn and his two IRA minders. The guy who owned the farm, Jonas Filbin, was in gaol with Lynn and was released under the Good Friday Agreement at about the same time. He moved south and took over the family farm. Lynn and his minders had left and were heading back to Belfast. There was a Land Rover in a ditch on the road outside. Looks like they stopped to see what was going on and the minders were shot through the car windows. Lynn either got out or was forced out and was walked into a field. A bullet in each knee and one in the back of the head. Filbin heard the shots but the Garda took their time getting to the scene and the killer was long gone.'

'Killer or killers? One woman taking out three men?'

'Don't get sexist on me, Spider. You're starting to sound like your dinosaur of a colleague Jimmy Sharpe.' There was a packet of Marlboro on the table and she reached for it, then plainly had second thoughts. 'He sends his regards, by the way.'

'I can't see Elaine Carter taking on three IRA killers in a shoot-out,' Shepherd said. He pushed the cigarettes towards her.

Button picked up the packet and took one out. Shepherd lit it for her. 'The driver was shot in the back of the head, the guy in the back seat took a double-tap to the chest and didn't even have his hand on his gun,' she said. 'Lynn wasn't armed. It was hardly a shoot-out.'

Shepherd nodded thoughtfully. 'I don't want to get all forensic on you, but if this happened in a field, there must have been footprints.'

'It happened in Ireland, and they're not as forensically minded as we are,' said Button. 'Half a dozen of the Garda's finest were trampling around before anyone thought to cordon off the area.'

'But the same gun was used?'

'They're going to check the bullets and will send us the results, but they're insisting on doing the work themselves. The murders took place on Irish soil so we've got no claim on the evidence. But the way Lynn was shot makes it a fairly safe bet that it's the same killer. Now, talk me through this. When did you last see her?'

'Yesterday evening.'

'So she'd gone when you got up this morning?'

'Yes.'

'But she could have left last night?' She looked around for an ashtray.

Shepherd retrieved one from the draining-board and put it in front of her. 'Her car's still in the driveway,' he said. 'She either walked or called a cab, and before you ask I didn't see a cab.'

Button put her still-burning cigarette into the ashtray and ran her hands through her hair. 'This is one hell of a screw-up, Spider.' She smiled apologetically. 'I'm not saying it's your fault – I'm not saying it's anyone's fault – but the shit has really hit the fan. We were tasked with monitoring the single suspect in a multiple-murder case and now it looks as if she's killed again.'

'Assuming it's her.'

'It's a hell of a coincidence, isn't it? The one day she's not here Gerry Lynn's blown away. A shot in each leg and one to the head. Same way her husband died.'

'She travels a lot, so it's not unusual for her to be away,' said Shepherd. 'She's always driving to see clients.'

'But her car's still here.' She picked up her cigarette and drew deeply on it.

'Maybe she took the train. Look, we still don't know she's the killer, Charlie. And nothing she's said or done has suggested to me that she is.'

'Except that you can't account for her whereabouts last night when Lynn was being marched into a field and executed.'

Shepherd held up his hands. 'Hey, you know as well as I do that you can't have effective surveillance one-on-one,' he said. 'If you'd wanted her watched every minute you should have put multiple teams on her. There's only me here, and even if I sat by the window all day I've still got to sleep.'

'I said I'm not blaming you, just trying to work out where we go from here.'

'She'll be back. I'll talk to her, sound her out.'

'You're getting closer to her?' She picked up the cigarette, took a drag and blew smoke.

He considered her question. 'I think so,' he said, 'but probably not close enough for her to tell me she's shot and killed six men.' He took a deep breath. 'There's something I should tell you,' he said. 'I had a look around her house today.'

Button's eyes narrowed. 'You broke in?' She stubbed out the cigarette.

'I had keys. I did a pretty thorough search and there's no gun. But I did find some ammunition in the attic.'

'First of all, if she went to kill Lynn then, it's pretty bloody obvious that she'd have taken the gun with her,' said Button. 'Second of all, what the hell did you think you were doing? You can't break into a suspect's house without a warrant, you know that. If you had found anything it wouldn't have been admissible. Damn it, Spider, you could have blown the whole case.'

'First of all we don't have a case,' said Shepherd. 'Second of all I already said I didn't break in. I had keys. And third of all, if I had found a gun I sure as hell wouldn't have done anything with it. But at least we would have known it was there.'

'And if you'd been caught?'

'That's hypothetical,' said Shepherd. 'I wasn't caught. And there was nothing in the house to suggest that Elaine Carter is a serial killer or a mass murderer.' He went to the kitchen cabinet above the fridge and came back with the round he'd taken from the box in Elaine's attic. 'Except this.' He gave the bullet to her and splashed more wine into her glass. 'You're right, of course. It was the wrong call. I just wanted to push things along. And maybe I didn't find the gun because she had it with her. But there was a box of those rounds in an old trunk along with some papers and photographs.'

Button weighed the cartridge in her palm. 'It's a .357, same as Carter's service revolver, right?' She put it on the table by her glass.

'That's what it looks like,' said Shepherd. 'PMC .357 Magnum 158-grain semi-jacketed rounds. They'd be my ammo of choice for the gun he had.'

'PMC?'

'That's the manufacturer's name,' said Shepherd. 'One of the firms that supplied rounds to the RUC. It was an old box. The manufacturer's date was two years before Robbie Carter was killed, so they almost certainly belonged to him. The box originally contained fifty and there were twenty-six left. Twenty-five after I took that one. Your forensic boys should be able to tell if it's similar to the rounds that were used to shoot his killers.'

'That'll be a help, but it's no proof that she's the killer even if the rounds are the same. If they are RUC issue we can assume that dozens if not hundreds of officers had the same ammunition.'

'Maybe not,' said Shepherd. 'Remember, most RUC officers were issued with nine-millimetre Smith & Wessons. But I take your point. Without the gun we don't have proof. So, where does that leave us?'

'The words "shit", "creek" and "paddle" spring to mind,' said Button. 'The powers-that-be are going to be looking for someone to blame for this.'

'Me, you mean?'

'I was thinking me, actually. It's my operation.'

'You're still assuming Elaine's the killer,' said Shepherd, 'and we don't know that.'

'Proving a negative is going to be next to impossible,' she said. 'We either prove she's killed these six men, or that it's the work of someone else. It doesn't get us anywhere to say that we don't think she did it.'

Shepherd sipped his wine. 'There is a bright side,' he said. 'At least it was Lynn and not Kinsella who was killed. Lynn was a nasty piece of work and I doubt there'll be many tears shed for him.'

'I'll be sure to tell the Home Secretary so when I'm next

in his office,' said Button. She raised her glass to him. 'Here's to my short and eventful career with the Serious Organised Crime Agency,' she said. 'I need another cigarette.'

The widow was quite beautiful, thought Viktor Merkulov, as he watched her at the graveside. She was in her late twenties and her knee-length black coat was open to reveal a low-cut dress that showed off an impressive pair of breasts. Her long blonde hair glistened in the afternoon sun and her nails were painted blood red. She was wearing a pair of Gucci sunglasses, but every now and again she would glance towards a good-looking man at the edge of the crowd of mourners. He was a few years older and elegantly dressed, the suit almost certainly Armani and the shoes Italian, handmade. Merkulov was sure he was the woman's lover. There were no children around, and no one old enough to be the deceased's parents. Merkulov didn't know who the dead man was, but he was fairly sure that the widow wouldn't miss him.

The widow had arrived at the cemetery in an expensive Mercedes sports car, the man in the Armani suit a few minutes later in a yellow Ferrari. Most of the mourners were men in their forties, probably work colleagues – bankers or stockbrokers. Merkulov knew that if he'd attended the service he would have learnt something about the man they were burying, but he had no interest in eulogies. He cared only about the burial.

The priest was saying whatever it was that priests said at funerals. The widow reached up to rub her left eye with the back of her hand but Merkulov knew she wasn't crying. In fact, no one was shedding tears. There were sombre faces and clasped hands, but no tears.

A man in a fawn raincoat sat down next to him. 'You've always had a thing for funerals, haven't you, Viktor?' He spoke with an American accent.

He was watching the mourners so Merkulov could see

only his profile. He had short gun-metal grey hair and thin lips. He crossed his legs at the ankles. He was wearing black leather shoes with tassels and bright red socks. 'Do I know you?' asked Merkulov.

'We've never met,' said the man. 'But I know you. And you seem to think you know me.' He turned with an easy smile on his face. 'Richard Yokely,' he said. 'Nice to meet you at last. I've followed your career with interest over the years.'

Merkulov glanced over his shoulder. A man in his early thirties was standing a few paces away, his hands deep in the pockets of a black overcoat. He had a thick scar above his lips and he returned Merkulov's stare with hard eyes.

'Yes,' said Yokely. 'He's with me.' He nodded to Merkulov's right. 'Him too.'

Another big man was positioned some twenty paces away, wearing a matching overcoat. Like the other, his hands were in his pockets.

'We're professionals, you and I, aren't we, Viktor?' said Yokely.

'I suppose so,' said Merkulov. If he had been in Russia he'd have been carrying a gun, probably two, but in Britain the penalties for being caught with a weapon were too severe to take the risk. They had outlawed most knives, and even a baseball bat was classed as a weapon unless it was accompanied by a ball.

'Professionals in a world of amateurs,' said Yokely. 'We're a dying breed.' He smiled. 'Some of us dying quicker than others, of course.'

'What is going to happen?' said Merkulov.

'To the world?' said Yokely.

'To me.'

Yokely patted his back. 'Are you carrying any sort of weapon?' he asked.

'Sadly, no.'

Yokely laughed. 'Viktor, even if you had a submachine-gun under your coat, it wouldn't do any good with my two colleagues there.'

Merkulov sighed. 'I knew it was a mistake to look for you.'

'But you were paid well?'

'Of course.'

'So you took a risk. I can understand that. You have bills to pay, and there's no pension at the end of your career, is there?'

'Can I make a phone call before . . .' He left the sentence hanging.

'Before what, Viktor?'

'Before you kill me.'

'Let's talk first,' said Yokely. He waved at the cemetery gates. 'We've a van outside, Viktor, a blue Transit. You and I will walk together to it. When we get close the back doors will open and you will get in. You will lie face down on the floor.'

The Russian nodded.

'My men are armed, and if you try to run they will shoot you. They won't shoot to kill so, one way or another, you will get into the van. And we won't be taking you to hospital so you'll only be putting yourself through a lot of unnecessary pain.'

Merkulov stood up and shrugged. 'I am too old to run,' he said.

Yokely put his arm around Merkulov's shoulders. 'You and me both,' he said.

They walked together to the cemetery gates. Yokely's companions followed.

Charlotte Button looked at her cigarette. 'Filthy habit,' she said. 'How come you're not smoking?'

'I smoke when she's around, but that's it.'

'You don't get a craving?'

'I guess I don't have an addictive personality.'

She raised an eyebrow. 'You mean I have?'

Shepherd chuckled and poured more wine into her glass. 'Most people could give up if they set their minds to it.'

Button took a long drag on her cigarette, then blew smoke at him. 'At times,' she said, 'you're a patronising prick.'

'Thank you, ma'am,' said Shepherd. The doorbell rang, startling them. 'Shit,' he said. 'That must be her.'

Button put down her cigarette. 'Okay, I'm your sister, my name's Rachel,' she said calmly. She picked up the bullet and slipped it into her bag. 'I live in Cambridge, I'm a pharmaceuticals sales rep and I'm in Belfast pitching a new drug to GPs. I'm married with no children. I haven't seen you since Christmas when you came to our house for dinner. My husband's name is Clive. Got it?'

'Got it,' he said. 'Just one thing, are you my older sister or younger?'

'Answer the door, baby brother.' She picked up her cigarette.

Shepherd hurried down the hallway. Outside, Elaine Carter was holding a potted plant. 'Belated housewarming gift,' she said.

'Thank you,' he said. 'But you already gave me a bottle of champagne, remember?'

'Actually there was a buy-one-get-one-free at the Spar,' she said, 'but it's the thought that counts.'

'Come in and have a drink,' he said. 'And say hello to my sister.'

'Your sister? I didn't know you had one.'

'My brother lacks the basic social skills, I'm afraid,' said Button, from the kitchen door. 'I blame our parents, but they did a good enough job with me.' She held out her hand. 'Rachel,' she said. 'I'm the brains of the family.'

Elaine laughed. 'I'm so glad to meet you,' she said. 'Jamie never talks about his family.'

'He's ashamed of us,' said Button.

'Leave it out, sis,' said Shepherd. 'Do you want some wine?' he asked Elaine. 'You'll have to be quick before Rachel finishes the bottle.'

'You know he drinks Frascati?' said Button. Shepherd followed Elaine into the kitchen and put the plant into the sink. Button poured wine for her and the three sat down.

Button clinked her glass against Elaine's. 'Any friend of Jamie's . . . has my sympathy.'

'She's been drinking, as you can tell,' said Shepherd. 'I went round earlier to see if you fancied joining us but you weren't there.'

'Up to my eyes in work,' said Elaine. 'So, where do you live, Rachel?'

'Cambridge. I'm in Belfast for a couple of days on business.'

'Have you been here before?'

'I'm over every few months. I'm a pharmaceuticals rep and our company keeps increasing the size of my territory. What about you?'

'Financial adviser,' said Elaine.

Button laughed. 'You should take a look at Jamie's finances,' she said. 'He's forever in the red.'

'I'm working on it,' she said. She sipped some wine. 'What was he like as a kid?'

'A bit of a nerd, I'm afraid. Always had his nose buried in a book.'

'That's so not true,' said Shepherd.

'And he played with dolls.'

Shepherd glared at her. 'Action Man wasn't a doll,' he said. 'He was an action figure.'

Button winked. 'Still sensitive about it, as you can see. What about you, Elaine? Got any brothers?'

'Three sisters,' said Elaine.

'I didn't know that,' said Shepherd.

'You never asked,' said Elaine.

'Typical man,' said Button. 'If you're not talking about them, they're not interested. Are they all in Belfast?'

'The two elder ones, Kathy and Joyce. Eight kids between them. Our youngest sister, Sally, lives in London. Got married last year.'

'And why did nobody snap you up?' Button asked.

'Sis!' exclaimed Shepherd. He knew exactly what she was doing and that he had to play his part.

'What?' said Button.

'It's okay, Jamie,' said Elaine, taking his hand.

'What's okay?' asked Button, feigning confusion.

'Elaine's husband was murdered.'

Button's hand flew to her mouth. 'I'm so sorry,' she said to Elaine. 'I had no idea.'

'Of course you didn't,' said Elaine. 'Really, it's okay.'

'Murdered? Wow!'

'Sis . . .' said Shepherd.

'Jamie, it was a long time ago,' said Elaine. 'You don't have to walk on eggshells.' She smiled at Button. 'He was killed by the IRA.'

'Elaine, how terrible. I'm so, so sorry. You must have been devastated.'

'They did it in front of me and our son. So, yes, devastated would be about right.'

'You have a son?'

'Sis, do you have to interrogate her like this?'

'I'm just asking, Jamie. Now what have I said?'

'Elaine's son died,' said Shepherd, quietly.

He knew Button was faking her reaction, but she was entirely convincing. 'Oh, my God,' she said. 'Did they kill him too?'

'Leukaemia,' Elaine said.

'Oh, God, that's awful. A friend of mine had leukaemia at university. She had chemo, her hair fell out and she was sick for months. She had a bone-marrow transplant and that's what saved her.'

'We looked everywhere for a donor but no one in the family was suitable,' said Elaine, 'so they went through all databases world-wide but still couldn't get a match.'

'I'm so sorry, Elaine,' said Button. 'Jamie was right, me and my big mouth.' Tears were welling in her eyes.

Elaine rushed over to her. 'It's okay, it's okay,' she said, putting her arms around Button and hugging her.

'I'm so sorry,' repeated Button, and looked over Elaine's

shoulder straight into Shepherd's eyes. The tears were fake too, Shepherd realised. Charlotte Button was one cool customer.

'You weren't to know,' said Elaine. She kissed Button's cheek, then sat down next to her. Shepherd passed across her wine glass. 'It's great to meet your family,' she told him, and touched Button's glass with her own. 'It helps to put him in context.'

'That's a good thing, is it?' asked Shepherd.

'You were a bit of a man of mystery,' said Elaine.

Button pushed back her sleeve and gasped at the time. 'I'd better be going,' she said.

'You're not staying here?' asked Elaine.

'I'm at the Hyatt,' said Button.

'You're letting your own sister stay at a hotel, Jamie?' Elaine remonstrated. 'Shame on you.'

'It's my choice,' said Button.

'I don't have a bed in the spare room yet,' said Shepherd.

'You can stay with me,' said Elaine.

'Maybe next time,' said Button. 'The room's paid for now so I might as well use it. And I'm off early in the morning.' To Shepherd, she said, 'Can you call me a cab?'

'You're a cab,' said Shepherd, straight-faced.

Button grimaced at Elaine. 'I had to put up with jokes like that all the time I was a kid.'

Shepherd called a local minicab company, who promised him a car within ten minutes.

'Just time for another bottle, then,' said Button.

Merkulov shivered. He was naked and cold. His bare feet were flat on the concrete and his hands were crossed over his groin. They hadn't tied him to the chair but there was no need. There were three of them and it had been decades since Merkulov had been anything but mediocre at hand-to-hand combat. He was a thinker, not a fighter, whereas the two men that had accompanied Yokely were muscular and looked as if they could kill with their bare hands. They had taken off their overcoats and were standing behind Yokely, their arms folded across their chests. They wore heavy cotton shirts, dark jeans and workboots.

Yokely was still wearing his coat, though he had unbuttoned it. 'Sorry about the smell, Viktor,' he said, 'but pigs will be pigs.'

There was a grunt to Merkulov's right and he flinched. In a pen, half a dozen adult pigs were shoving their noses into a metal trough. There were ten pens in the barn, separated by metal bars with peeling paint. The air stank of urine and faeces.

'Pigs are actually very clean animals, left to their own devices,' said the American. 'It's only because we humans lock them into cells that they live in their own filth. They're actually closer to us than monkeys. Genetically, there's little difference.' He walked over to the pens and looked down at the feeding animals. 'I've never really understood why Muslims hate them so much. Pig kidneys have been implanted in humans, and pig hearts have been used to support failing human ones.' He looked over his shoulder at Merkulov. 'So, who is your client, Viktor? Who has been paying for information about me?'

'His name is Hassan Salih.' Merkulov knew there was no point in lying to him. They had taken his shoes and clothes, and two long machetes, a pair of industrial bolt-cutters and a carving knife had been placed on a wooden table near the entrance to the barn. His life was in the American's hands and if he wasn't completely honest with him the two men with hard eyes would kill Merkulov and feed him to the pigs.

'And who is this Hassan Salih?' asked Yokely.

'An assassin.'

'From?'

'Palestine.'

Yokely folded his arms. 'And he paid you for information about me?'

The Russian nodded.

'Did he want information about anyone else?' asked Yokely.

'Just you,' said the Russian.

'That is the last lie you will ever tell me, Viktor. Do you understand? Pigs will eat anything. I'm sure you know that.'

'I understand,' said the Russian.

'Would it help you if I got them to remove a finger? Or a toe? Or an ear? To show how serious I am? Would that help convince you, Viktor?' Yokely gestured at the two men and they went to the table, their boots crunching on the concrete floor.

'A woman called Charlotte Button,' said Merkulov, hurriedly. 'She used to work for MI5 and now she works for the Serious Organised Crime Agency.'

'And what were you able to tell him?'

'Not much,' said Merkulov. 'No address, no family details. But he had a mobile phone number and I was able to check that out for him. He wanted to know where she was.'

'And where is she?'

'Belfast, London and Glasgow, mostly.'

'He's using her phone to track her?'

'That's right.'

'Anyone else?'

'He wanted me to check a number she's been calling while she was in Belfast. He wanted a list of calls made to and received by that phone.'

'Did you find out whose it was?'

'Someone called Daniel Shepherd. The bill goes to a house in Hereford.'

Yokely's jaw tightened and Merkulov realised he had said something significant. He began to speak faster, knowing that the information he had was the only thing keeping him alive. 'The phone is in Belfast most of the time. There are calls to Button's, to the landline at the address in Hereford and other mobile numbers. I haven't given the information to Salih yet. I could hold off if you wanted me to. I could tell him I've got to go back to Russia.'

'The number in Hereford? You've checked it out?' Yokely's brow was furrowed and he pursed his lips.

'Not yet. I'm still working on it. But it's a landline so I'll be able to find out who lives there.'

The American held up a hand to silence him. 'Did you track my phone?' he asked eventually.

Merkulov shook his head. 'No.'

'I'm glad to hear that,' said Yokely. 'Now, here's the million-dollar question, Viktor. Who is paying this Salih?'

'I don't know,' said Merkulov. 'I really do not know. But money is no object to whoever it is. Everything I ask for, Salih pays.'

'And you have worked for him before?'

'I have supplied him with information, yes.'

'And we can assume that he intends to assassinate me and Charlotte Button?'

'Yes.'

'It's not a name I've heard before.'

'He keeps a low profile.'

'Even so, I know most of the men who kill for money. The serious players, anyway.'

'Hassan Salih is a serious player,' said Merkulov, 'but he uses many names. I'm not even sure that Salih is his real name.'

Yokely picked up a chair and placed it in front of the Russian, then sat down facing him so that their knees were just inches apart. 'But you don't know who wants me dead?'

Merkulov smiled thinly. 'From what I've heard, a lot of people would like you dead.'

Yokely chuckled and patted the Russian's knee. 'You're right, of course. But most of those who would wish me harm don't have the resources to hire a man like this Salih.' The American folded his arms. 'How does this end, Viktor? How do we play it?'

The Russian glanced anxiously at the two men behind Yokely. One was holding a machete now and the other was tapping a pair of bolt-cutters against his leg.

'This Salih, there's no way he can kill me, Viktor,' said

Yokely. 'I know that for a fact. Do you know why I know that for a fact?'

Merkulov shook his head.

'Because I'm going to die a very old man. Every fortune-teller I've ever been to has told me so. Everyone who has read my palm has said I have a lifeline that goes on for ever.' Yokely splayed the fingers of his right hand and held it out to the Russian. 'Do you read palms?'

'I'm afraid not,' said Merkulov.

Yokely stared at it. 'Long, long lifeline,' he said, almost to himself. 'No accidents, no illness, just my three score and ten plus a healthy bonus. Probably die in my sleep.' He grinned at the Russian. 'So, hand on heart, I can tell you I'm absolutely one hundred per cent certain that this Salih will do me no harm.'

'You are a lucky man, Mr Yokely.'

'Yes,' said Yokely. 'I am. And what about you, Viktor? Are you lucky?'

'Until today I thought I was. But apparently I was over-optimistic.'

'It's good to see you haven't lost your sense of humour,' said Yokely, clapping. He folded his arms again and stared at the Russian for a full minute. At first Merkulov held his eyes, but eventually dropped his own to the muddy concrete.

'I'm in two minds as to what I should do, Viktor,' said Yokely, eventually. 'Part of me wants to watch these guys cut you up and feed you to the pigs. But part of me thinks that you could be useful to me.'

'It is a dilemma,' agreed the Russian.

'I would like to know who's paying Salih,' said Yokely, 'and wants me dead. Seems to me that you might be able to find out.'

'I could do that for you, yes.'

'But can I trust you? That's the question.'

'I could give you my word.'

Yokely chuckled. 'I'm not sure that your word would be enough,' he said. 'And I'm not the type to issue threats. They always seem such a waste of time. Like bluffing in poker. Do you play poker, Viktor?'

'No.'

'I used to, but I wasn't that great a player because I refused to bluff,' said Yokely. 'I figured, what's the point? You either have the best hand or you don't. If you don't have a good hand you might as well fold at the start. Thing is, you can't play like that for long because once your opponents realise that you never bluff, they fold whenever you want to bet. So you can't win. Now, life, that's different. If people know you never bluff, they have to take you seriously. They have to believe you will do what you say you will. And a threat is a sort of bluff, isn't it? If I threaten you and don't follow through, then it weakens me. You can see that, can't you?'

'Yes,' said Merkulov.

'You know what I can do to you, don't you, Viktor? And that I can get to you anywhere in the world? Even in Russia? There's quite a few guys in Moscow owe me favours. And I can get Mr Putin on the phone if I really want to. So there's no hiding-place, not really.'

'I will help you,' said Merkulov. 'I will get you the information you want.'

Yokely reached into his trouser pocket and took out a pound coin. 'Heads or tails, Viktor?'

'What?'

'Heads or tails?'

Merkulov swallowed nervously. 'Heads.'

Yokely tossed the coin high into the air, watched it rise and fall, caught it with his right hand and slapped it on to the back of the left. He slid away his hand to reveal that the coin was heads up. 'You see, Viktor? It's your lucky day, after all.' Yokely turned to the men behind him. 'Give Mr Merkulov his clothes. He'll be working with us for a while.'

★   ★   ★

Shepherd walked Button out to the waiting minicab. 'Well, she's all primed,' said Button. 'If you can't get her to open up after that, you never will.'

'Were those tears real?'

'I can empathise with someone losing a child, Spider. I'm a mother, remember?'

'You were good in there,' said Shepherd.

'Surprised?' She shivered.

'Frankly, yes. I've never seen you in an undercover role before.'

'I didn't sit at a desk when I was at MI5. Do you think they'd have allowed me to head up SOCA's undercover unit if I didn't know what I was doing?'

'I was trying to pay you a compliment.'

'Well, you failed miserably,' she said. 'Now, give me a brotherly peck on the cheek and I'll be out of here. She might be watching.'

She turned her cheek and Shepherd brushed it with his lips. 'Take care, yeah?'

'Always,' she said. 'Don't forget that the microphones are on.' She climbed into the back of the minicab and he waved as the car drove off.

Shepherd went back into the house. Elaine was pouring more wine into her glass. 'Do you want to sit in the front room?' said Shepherd. 'The sofas are more comfortable than those wooden chairs.'

'Sure,' said Elaine. She got to her feet unsteadily with her glass. Shepherd picked up the bottle and they went into the sitting room. 'It's funny being in your house because it's a mirror image of mine,' she said, dropping into one of the sofas. The television was still on, the sound muted. A news programme. Three men in suits were being grilled by an overweight presenter with thinning hair.

Elaine half watched the screen as she sipped her wine. 'I had the BBC asking me a couple of years ago if I'd meet the men who killed Robbie. Can you believe that?' She slipped off her shoes and drew her legs underneath her.

'Journalists are parasites, most of them,' said Shepherd. 'They don't care about the people they write about, or the effect their stories have on them.'

'It wasn't just journalists. That black archbishop was part of it – Desmond Tutu. They were making a series where they were bringing together people from both sides and getting them to talk while he sat there and looked all sympathetic. I told them to go screw themselves.'

'Who exactly did they want you to talk to?' asked Shepherd.

'We never got that far,' said Elaine, 'but I didn't want to talk to any of them. There's not one of the bastards expressed any regret for what they did. What was I supposed to do? Forgive and forget, shake the hands of the men who blew Robbie's brains across the kitchen floor?' She swigged her wine. 'Fuck them – fuck them all. I hope they rot in hell for what they did to Robbie and Timmy.'

She was close to being drunk, Shepherd could see. And the microphones Amar Singh had planted would be recording every word. Her defences were down, so all he had to do was let her talk. With the right nudges she might incriminate herself.

'What do you mean?' he asked. 'You said they didn't hurt Timmy, that he died of leukaemia.'

Elaine had another swig. There were tears in her eyes. 'Yes, Timmy got leukaemia. Bad leukaemia.' She forced a smile, 'It's funny – isn't it? – but that's what they say. Good leukaemia and bad leukaemia. Good leukaemia has a high cure rate, bad leukaemia . . . doesn't. They tried chemo and they wanted to try radiation but they needed a bone-marrow donor. After they'd looked at all our relatives and searched all the data-bases without sucess, they told me Robbie would probably have been a match. So when those bastards killed Robbie, they killed Timmy too.'

Shepherd reached over and took her free hand. 'I'm sorry.'

'You don't have to say that,' said Elaine.

'I'm sorry for the hurt you're feeling. I can understand why you feel the way you do.'

'How?' said Elaine, pulling away her hand. 'You never lost a wife, you never held a newborn baby in your arms, knowing he was part of you, that you were totally responsible for him, then watched him die in a hospital bed, begging you to stop the pain.'

Shepherd did know what it was like to have a spouse snatched away, to know that the person you loved most in the world was gone for ever. But he couldn't tell Elaine because to her he was Jamie Pierce and Jamie Pierce had never married and didn't have children.

'I'm sorry, Jamie, I didn't mean to snap,' she said.

'I'm amazed you're as calm as you are,' said Shepherd. 'I don't think I'd cope half as well as you if I was married and someone shot my wife.'

'What would you do?'

Shepherd pretended to consider the question, but he already knew what he was going to say. 'I'd hunt them down and kill them,' he said slowly. 'No question about it.'

Elaine smiled. 'And how would you do that? You're a website designer.'

'I'd do whatever I had to,' said Shepherd. 'Pay someone.'

'A hitman? Now, where in God's name would you find a hitman?' She was still smiling at him.

'This is Belfast, Elaine. There's no shortage of killers here. You know that better than anyone. I'd find someone who'd do it and pay them whatever they wanted.'

Elaine shook her head. 'It's not as easy as that.'

'Or I'd do it myself,' he said.

'And where would you get a gun?'

'Gun, knife – I'd strangle them with my bare hands. I don't know. I'm sure I'd do something, but I guess it's all hypothetical.'

'For you,' she said. 'For me . . .' She sighed. 'The anger and the hatred eat away at you, so you have to deal with them as best you can. I know some women who lost their men who have forgiven and moved on with their lives, but there's no way I can forgive the men who killed Robbie. They killed him as if they were killing a dog, Jamie. They forced their way into our house and shot him in front of me, then walked out as if it was the most natural thing in the world. How can men act like that? How can they sit down and plan to kill a husband and father? Killing in a war I can understand, or losing your temper and lashing out, but planning to murder a man in front of his wife and child? How can a human being do it?'

'I don't know.'

'And then the British Government lets them go. They say it's okay to let the evil bastards back on to the streets because the IRA has given up violence. But what about Robbie and Timmy? Am I going to get them back?'

'It's a nightmare, I know.'

'No, you wake up from a nightmare. This is my life, Jamie. You know Noel Kinsella, the one who ran off to the United States? He came back and pleaded guilty to murdering my husband and served not one day in prison. Not one day. Even the judge said that was wrong. Tell me, Jamie, what sort of world do we live in where you can murder a man and not be punished?'

'I don't know.'

'You and me both,' she said. She gulped some more wine and refilled her glass. 'You're not trying to get me drunk, are you?' she asked.

'Now, why would I want to do that?'

'To have your wicked way with me.' She laughed.

'Great! So I'd have to get you drunk to stand a chance with you, would I?'

Elaine stopped laughing. 'Are you flirting with me, Jamie?'

Shepherd held her eyes for a few seconds, then grinned and shook his head.

'I like your sister,' said Elaine.

'Yeah, she's a sweetie,' said Shepherd.

'She doesn't look much like you.'

'She takes after our mum. I'm like Dad.'

A face flashed up on the television screen. Shepherd recognised it immediately. Gerry Lynn. Elaine saw his reaction and looked at the screen. 'That's Lynn, one of the bastards who shot Robbie,' she said.

Shepherd reached for the remote control and turned up the sound.

The picture of Lynn was replaced by a video shot of forensic investigators in disposable white suits on a rutted track standing round a Lexus. The back window had been shot out. The camera panned to the right where more white-suited figures were working in a muddy field.

A female reporter with a Scottish accent was explaining that three men had been shot dead on a farm outside Dublin and that the killings followed a series of sectarian shootings, but that sources within the Police Service of Northern Ireland did not believe that the Peace Process was breaking down.

Elaine listened intently. 'Good riddance,' she said quietly. She was staring at the screen with undiluted hatred.

The video was replaced with a studio set. The female presenter was a pale-faced blonde with straight hair and penetrating eyes. She was interviewing a senior police officer. She grilled him as if she believed he personally had pulled the trigger and barely gave him the opportunity to answer her rapid-fire questions. She suggested that the police had been slow to investigate the previous killings and that some members of the Republican movement believed the police were unconcerned about the murders because the victims were convicted killers. The officer explained patiently that the killings were being investigated but that without witnesses or forensic evidence there would be no quick resolution. The presenter interrupted him to ask if he thought there was a connection with the death of Joseph McFee. The officer started to tell her that it was one avenue being investigated but before he could finish she was saying she had spoken to Republicans who feared that the police were involved in some way with the killings. At this the officer was lost for words.

The camera cut away to another presenter who read out the latest crime figures from an autocue. Shepherd muted the sound again.

Elaine gulped more wine, then refilled her glass again. 'They didn't even mention Robbie,' she said. 'Lynn murdered Robbie and they didn't even mention it.'

'I guess they think Lynn's the story now,' said Shepherd. 'That's what journalists do, they look for the angle.'

'It's like they don't care about the real victims. They want to make it look as if Lynn's the hero in this.'

'They weren't making him out to be a hero,' said Shepherd. 'But his murder is the news story.'

Elaine pointed at the screen. 'You heard what that silly cow was suggesting,' she said. 'She was making it sound like the police killed Lynn.'

'Maybe they did,' said Shepherd. 'Maybe there are cops who resent the fact that so many of the men they put away are back on the streets.'

'That's crazy,' said Elaine. 'The police don't do that.' Her eyes blazed and Shepherd stayed quiet. He didn't want to antagonise her. 'You don't understand what it's like to be a cop, Jamie. Living with Robbie, I got to see just how their hands are tied. Everything's geared to protect the criminals.' She waved her glass at the television. 'The media too – they're always on the side of the villains. Do they care that Lynn shot my husband in front of me and my little boy? That Lynn and his IRA bastard friends blew Robbie's brains out for no other reason than that he worked for the RUC?'

'I'm sorry,' said Shepherd again.

'You don't have to keep saying you're sorry,' she said. 'It's not your problem. It's never been your problem.'

Shepherd sipped some wine.

'I'm glad Lynn's dead,' she said. 'And I'm glad McFee's dead. Whoever killed them should get a medal.'

'What about the others?' asked Shepherd.

'The others?'

'The ones with Lynn and McFee? How many were there?'

'Three,' said Elaine. 'Adrian Dunne, Willie McEvoy and Noel Kinsella.'

'Has anything happened to them?'

'Nothing they didn't deserve,' she said.

'They're dead?'

'Adrian Dunne was shot a couple of months ago, Willie McEvoy too. Kinsella's still around. He ran away to the States and the Americans refused to extradite him. He came back last month but because of the Belfast Agreement he didn't serve a day.'

'What are the odds of that?' asked Shepherd.

'Odds of what?'

'Elaine, come on. Out of the five men who killed your husband, four are dead.'

'The killings are still going on, Peace Process or not,' said Elaine. 'Now it's old scores being settled or gangsters fighting over drugs.'

'But four out of five? Haven't the police questioned you?'

Elaine laughed. 'You think I've been behaving like some crazed vigilante?'

'Of course not,' said Shepherd. 'But I would have thought the police might wonder if there's a connection.'

Elaine was astonished. 'I can't believe you'd say that, Jamie.'

'I'm not suggesting anything, I'm just saying, cops are cops, wouldn't they think that you might be involved?'

'Involved in what way?' she said defensively.

'I don't know. But you above all people would want them dead, wouldn't you?'

'There's a world of difference between wanting someone dead and killing them.'

'Of course there is. If it was me, I'd want the men responsible dead.' He thought of Amar Singh and Charlotte Button listening to this. And recording everything that was said.

Elaine's eyes were brimming with tears. 'I lost my husband,' she said, her voice shaking. 'I lost my husband and I lost my son. Yes, the men who ruined my family deserve to suffer and die. But do you think I want to spend the rest of my life behind bars?'

'Elaine, I didn't say *I* thought you did anything. I said the police might think that.'

She put down her glass and got to her feet, a little unsteadily. 'I'm going home.'

'Elaine, please, don't be angry.'

She glared at him. 'Why? Are you frightened I might shoot you?'

'Don't be silly,' said Shepherd.

'Oh – so first I'm a vigilante, and now I'm silly, am I?' She swayed a little. 'I'm going home.'

'Elaine, come on, let me make you a coffee.'

'Now you're saying I'm drunk? I'm not drunk, Jamie. I'm not drunk, I'm not silly and I'm not a murderer.' She brushed past him and hurried down the hallway, keeping her left hand on the wall to help her balance. Shepherd hurried after her but she got to the front door ahead of him and let herself out.

'Elaine!' he called, but she was already running across the lawn to her house.

Shepherd closed the front door and swore under his breath. He went into the sitting room and peered through the window. Elaine was trying to insert her key into the lock. It took her several attempts and then she was stumbling inside and slamming the door behind her.

His mobile phone rang. It was Button. 'You pushed too hard, Spider,' she said.

'I know. It got away from me, I'm sorry.'

'Is it retrievable?'

'I think so. She was a bit drunk, and that's probably why she reacted the way she did. I'll let her sleep on it and see how she feels tomorrow. I don't think it's her, Charlie. I really don't.'

'You found bullets in her attic. And, from what I heard, there's a lot of anger there. Anger and hatred.'

'But she's not a killer.'

'And you say that based on what?'

Shepherd rubbed the back of his neck. 'On the basis that it takes one to know one,' he said quietly.

'Elizabeth, you're worrying about nothing,' said Kinsella. 'And keep your voice down. I don't want the Rottweilers to think we're arguing.'

'We *are* arguing, honey,' said Elizabeth, frostily. 'A friend of yours has been killed and you don't seem the least bit concerned.'

'I hardly knew the guy,' said Kinsella.

'Concerned about us,' snapped his wife. 'Us! You and me! I don't give a shit about him, it's you and me I'm worried about.'

'That's what we've got the Rottweilers for,' said Kinsella. 'They're not going to let anything happen to me. To us. They can't afford to.'

'Your friend Lynn had bodyguards, too, remember?'

'He had a couple of IRA heavies, nothing like the protection we've got.'

Elizabeth sighed. 'You don't get it, do you? I can't live like this, Noel. I'm sorry, but I can't.'

'Your family has always had bodyguards. And with good reason. Don't give me grief over this.'

'Look, it doesn't matter how many bodyguards you have or how good the security is. If someone wants to kill you . . .' She trailed off.

Kinsella put his arms around her and kissed her on the top of the head. 'I'm sorry, baby,' he said.

'I didn't know it would be like this,' she said.

'Neither did I,' said Kinsella.

'I thought we could settle down, have children, make a life here.'

'We can, baby. We can.'

'But not like this.'

'What do you want me to do?'

'I just want them to catch whoever it is.'

'You and me both,' said Kinsella. He kissed her again. 'Let me see what I can do.'

'I want to go home.'

'This is home,' said Kinsella.

'My home,' she said. 'I want to go back to the States.'

Hassan Salih parked his hire car in the King Edward Court car park in the centre of Windsor. He locked it and headed for Windsor's main shopping street. The sun was shining and it seemed that every second person was a tourist holding a street map or guidebook. Peascod Street was pedestrianised, lined with shops and building-society offices. Large black tubs containing well-tended trees were dotted along the pavement and baskets of brightly coloured flowers hung from the street-lamps. A group of Etonians sat on a curved metal bench eating ice-cream, their black tailcoats and pinstriped trousers a throwback to an earlier age when the British had an empire and the school's alumni ran it. An American woman in stretch trousers pointed a digital camera at them and asked if she could take their photograph. They agreed and posed good-naturedly, and before long half a dozen tourists were clustered in front of them, clicking cameras.

At the top of Peascod Street a black statue of Queen Victoria, holding an orb, gazed severely at the throngs. The sweeping castle, for which Windsor was famous, lowered over her. The royal standard was flying from the solitary flagpole at the top of the main tower, indicating that the sovereign was in residence.

The estate agent's was between a coffee shop and a bookstore, glossy photographs of properties for sale and rent in the window. Salih was wearing a dark grey suit he'd bought from a tailor in London's Savile Row, with a white cotton shirt and nondescript tie. He was carrying a leather briefcase he'd found in Harrods. He had paid for all his purchases with cash.

There were six desks in the office. Two were unoccupied and a middle-aged woman sat at the one by the door. Salih assumed she was the secretary. A glossy magazine was propped up on her keyboard and she was talking into a headset. Young women sat at two more desks, a blonde with a ponytail and a dyed blonde with pink streaks. Both wore heavy mascara, blue eye-shadow and garish nail polish. The only man in the office was in his early forties with black hair that was greying at the temples. He was wearing a blue pinstriped suit but had hung the jacket over the back of his chair and rolled up his shirtsleeves. There was a small brass plaque on his desk with his name – Graham Pickering. He was talking animatedly into his phone, his left hand jabbing the air.

Salih waited until Pickering had replaced the receiver, then pushed open the door and went in. The secretary was still talking on her headset and pointed at a chair by the window. Salih ignored her and strode over to Pickering. 'How do you do?' he said, and extended his hand. Pickering shook it. 'I'm looking to buy a house in the area, ideally detached with a garden. I have a twelve-year-old son who likes cricket.' Salih sat down and put the briefcase on his lap.

'And what sort of budget do you have?' asked Pickering.

Salih shrugged, as if money was of no concern to him. 'Three million. Four, perhaps.'

Pickering grinned. 'I'm not sure we could run to a cricket pitch, but we could certainly get you a decent-sized garden for that. Close to Windsor?'

'Please,' said Salih. 'Somewhere with character.'

Pickering stood up and went to a filing cabinet, pulled open a drawer and searched through a row of pale green files. 'I've a selection of properties in that price range,' he said. 'Why don't you have a look through them and let me know which ones you want to view?'

'Excellent,' said Salih. 'Windsor's a lovely town. We thought our son might go to Eton.'

'It's a great school,' said Pickering.

'Do you have children?'

'A daughter.'

'Does she go to Eton?'

Pickering laughed. 'It's for boys,' he said. 'Our daughter is away at another boarding-school.'

There was a pine-framed photograph on Pickering's desk. Salih turned it to face him. It was a family group – Pickering with a dark-haired woman in her mid-thirties and a girl with her mother's dark brown eyes. 'You have a lovely family,' he said. The woman was a few years younger here than she had been in the photograph Merkulov had given him.

'Thank you,' said Pickering. He went back to his desk and passed Salih a handful of printed brochures. He pointed to one. 'This is a little above your budget but it's quite special. There's a heated pool and an amazing snooker room.' He opened a drawer and gave Salih a typed form. 'If you put down your contact details, I'll send you anything new that comes on to the market. Where are you based?'

'Dubai,' said Salih, 'but I have an office in London.' He took out his wallet and gave Pickering a newly printed business card. 'The mobile is the best number to use but you can send any information you have to the address there.' It was an office in Mayfair that would collect any mail and divert phone calls to his pay-as-you-go mobile.

'Excellent, Mr Hassan,' Pickering said. 'I'll jot down the details and we'll get them on to the computer.' He began to fill in the form.

'What about you? Where do you live?' asked Salih, casually.

'A village called Virginia Water,' said Pickering. 'Nice area, but I don't know that there's much available at the moment. There's a lot of competition for houses in this area just now. Russian buyers have been snapping up anything that comes on to the market and they've got money to burn. There are two very good American schools locally so we get a lot of Americans too. We've an office there so I'll find out if anything's come on to the books in the last few days. There might be something on the Wentworth estate. Beautiful homes, and they have access to the golf course. Do you play?'

'Not well,' said Salih. 'What about your house? Could I persuade you to sell?'

Pickering looked up. 'Without seeing it?'

'I'm sure you've got good taste,' said Salih. 'And I'm sure that as you're in the business you'll have chosen well.'

Pickering chuckled. 'I do have a beautiful home, it's true,' he said, 'but if I were ever to think of selling it, my wife would kill me.' He returned to the form.

Salih nodded at the framed photograph. 'She doesn't look dangerous,' he said.

'Appearances can be deceptive,' said Pickering. He laughed. 'I'm joking, of course,' he said. 'At least, I think I am.'

Salih put the brochures into his briefcase, stood up and shook Pickering's hand. He smiled to himself as he left. He had everything he needed. He knew where Charlotte Button lived, where her husband worked and where her daughter went to school. Now it was just a matter of time.

Shepherd pressed Elaine's doorbell and took a step back. He was holding a bunch of flowers he'd bought at a local filling station. He waited for a minute or so, then pressed the bell again, for longer this time. Maybe she was in the shower. He glimpsed movement at the bedroom window, and cursed under his breath. She wasn't in the shower, she was ignoring him. He'd hoped that after a night's sleep she'd have calmed down but now it seemed it wasn't going to be as easy as that. He decided against kneeling down and shouting through the letterbox or leaving the flowers at the door. Better to try later. He hoped he hadn't blown the investigation.

★　★　★

Richard Yokely flashed his embassy ID at the marine standing guard at the door to the Secure Communications Room. The soldier's hands tightened around his M-4 carbine. 'I'm sorry, sir, but beverages aren't permitted inside,' he said.

Yokely held up his Starbucks cup. 'My *latte* isn't exactly a security threat, son.'

The marine looked even more uncomfortable. 'I'm sorry, sir. There have been spillages in the past so beverages are now not permitted inside.'

'If I were to promise to be careful with mine, would you let me take it in?'

'Sir, I'm just following the rules, Sir.' The marine's voice had gone down an octave.

Yokely put his face close to the soldier's. 'And what if I were to tell you that generally rules don't apply to me? And that if you continue to be an officious prick I'll have you transferred to the Iraqi desert where you'll spend the rest of your military career picking up body parts? What would you say then?'

The marine's jaw tightened. 'Sir, I'd have to say that beverages are not allowed in the Secure Communications Room, Sir.'

Yokely's face broke into a grin. 'Good for you, son,' he said. 'Don't you ever be intimidated by a big swinging dick because he's got the power of life and death over you.' He patted the marine's arm. 'Without rules, where would we be? Living like savages, right? That's why we're in the war against terror, to preserve the rules that make our world such a joyous place to live.' He handed the cup to the marine. 'Hold on to that until I come out, will you?'

Yokely swiped his ID through the card reader. The lock clicked and he went into the windowless room. The concrete walls were double-layered and between the layers a network of wires blocked all radio frequencies. The only communication between the room in the basement of the American embassy and the outside world was through the shielded wires that led from the two computer terminals and the half-dozen phones, most of which were dedicated lines to offices in the United States.

Yokely swiped his ID through a terminal and typed in a six-digit identifying number. A Homeland Security logo filled the screen. Yokely moved the cursor to click a button marked 'Video Conferencing', then tapped in the number of a secure terminal in Washington DC. Thirty seconds later he was looking at Karl Traynor, a senior analyst with the Financial Crimes Enforcement Network. Traynor was in his early forties, with slicked-back hair and was wearing one of his trademark tweed jackets with leather patches on the elbows. He was tapping at his computer keyboard. 'Testing, testing, one-two-three,' he said.

'Karl, how's Washington?' said Yokely. He pressed a button on his keyboard and one of the plasma screens on the wall opposite the door flickered into life to show a larger-than-life image of the analyst.

'Threatening to snow,' said Traynor. 'How's London?'

'Spring has sprung,' said Yokely. 'The birds are singing, and all's well with the world. Well, except for the three hundred home-grown terrorist groups that are actively working to bring about mayhem and destruction.'

'I can never get a decent steak there,' said Traynor.

'Then you're not trying,' said Yokely.

'Aren't all their cows mad or something?'

'Mad or not, they make great steaks. I need a favour or three, if you've got the time.'

'FinCen is here to serve,' said Traynor. 'Your wish is my command.' FinCen collected data under the Bank Secrecy Act and worked with law-enforcement agencies and Financial Intelligence Units around the world to follow money trails that led, hopefully, to the paymasters of terrorism. Much of the agency's work was the checking of suspicious-activity reports filed by the country's banks and financial institutions, which were now running at almost three-quarters of a million annually. The vast majority of SARs were false positives and only a very small percentage led to investigations. But once a positive lead had been generated, Traynor and his team were put on the case, following the money trail with the tail-wagging enthusiasm of bloodhounds after an escaped convict. FinCen also had access to the eleven million financial transactions that went through some eight thousand banks in two hundred countries using the SWIFT network. The agency's supercomputers allowed it to sift through the raw data like prospectors panning for gold.

'I need someone looked at,' said Yokely. 'He uses a number of aliases, but in the UK he's known as Hassan Salih. He's a Palestinian, but is very well travelled. Other names he has used include Shafquat Husain, Asif Iqbal and Majid Jasim.' Yokely spelled out each name and Traynor wrote them down. 'I need to know about any large financial transactions he has made over the past twelve months.'

'Large being?'

'Six figures and above.'

Traynor chuckled. 'Richard, I know they tell you that size isn't everything but six figures is not large. Six figures, no matter what the currency, is a drop in the ocean. I don't even get out of bed for six figures.'

'Remind me again what the total cost of Nine Eleven was,' said Yokely, drily. 'A few hours' flight training, a dozen box-cutters and nineteen first-class tickets, I seem to remember.'

'Actually, we've been able to track half a million dollars that was used to fund Nine Eleven,' said Traynor, 'but I take your point. So, this Hassan Salih is al-Qaeda?'

'Almost certainly not,' said Yokely, 'but it's quite possible that he's worked for al-Qaeda members on a freelance basis. A hired gun, you might say. Can you ID any accounts he has?'

'Sure. Give me a day, yeah. You can do me a favour in return. Two, as it happens. Chocolate HobNobs. Two packets.'

'Can't you get them in Washington?'

'If I could, would I be asking you? Plain, not milk.'

'Your cookies will be in the post.' Yokely jabbed at a button on the console and the screen went blank. He tapped out a second number. There was a buzz of static, then the screen flickered into life again. This time a balding man in his late forties was grinning at Yokely and waving a bottle of Jack Daniel's. Dean Hepburn was a senior analyst with the National Security Agency. He was based at the NSA's headquarters in Forte Meade, Maryland, known to the forty thousand or so men and women who worked there as Crypto City. It was practically a small town of fifty buildings half-way between Washington and Baltimore, hidden from prying eyes by acres of woodland. 'Dean, how are the wife and kids?' asked Yokely.

'Bleeding me dry,' said Hepburn, swinging his feet on to his desk. 'How goes the fight between good and evil?'

'Never ending,' said Yokely. 'I need a favour.'

Hepburn grinned. 'Ask and you shall receive. I'm here to do your bidding, O Master.' He raised his glass in salute and took a long slug of his whiskey.

'If I give you a UK cellphone number, can you give me details of all traffic through it and positioning?'

'Does the pope shit in the woods? I was hoping you might want something that would challenge me.' Yokely knew that what he was asking Hepburn to do wasn't remotely challenging for an organisation with the resources of the NSA. It had listening stations around the world, which monitored all phone and Internet traffic and passed it to the analysts at Forte Meade and their multi-billion-dollar supercomputers, which sifted through millions of daily calls and transmissions looking for key words or voices. Anything suspicious was passed to human experts for analysis. The NSA was a key weapon in the fight against terrorism, identifying and locating targets, then sending on the information to the CIA.

Yokely told Hepburn the number Merkulov had given him. 'The phone belongs to a Palestinian who uses a number of names,' said Yokely. 'The one I have is Hassan Salih but that doesn't count for anything. He's in the UK at the moment, but there might be a Belfast connection. I need to know every call he makes and receives, and a location. I also need you to get a voice print next time he makes a call and run it through the computers. See if you can get a match.'

'You think this guy's active?'

'Oh, he's very active, I'm just not sure in what field. That's why I'd like you to keep it off the books for now, until I know for sure what he's up to.'

'I hear and obey,' said Hepburn.

'I'd appreciate an SMS on my cellphone anytime you get anything,' said Yokely. 'I might be under some time pressure here.'

Hepburn raised his glass. 'See you in Crypto City some time,' he said.

'You can bank on it,' said Yokely. He winked and ended the conference call. He swiped his ID card through the reader to get out of the secure room. The marine was still holding the cup of coffee. Yokely took it from him. 'Thanks, son,' he said cheerfully. 'All's well with the world and we can sleep easy in our beds tonight.'

'Sir, glad to hear it, Sir,' said the marine, stone-faced.

'You and me both, son,' said Yokely.

Shepherd was lying on the sofa reading the *Belfast Telegraph* when his doorbell rang.

He found Elaine, wearing dark glasses, outside. 'I'm sorry,' she said.

'Sorry for what?' he asked, genuinely confused. The flowers he'd bought for her by way of apology were on the coffee-table in the sitting room.

'Snapping at you. I drank too much wine. Sorry.'

Shepherd put his hand on his heart. 'Elaine, I was ringing your bell this morning to apologise for the way I behaved. It should be me saying sorry.'

'I was drunk,' she repeated.

'And I was an arsehole,' he said.

'I'm sorry I didn't open the door when you rang,' she said. She gestured at her sunglasses. 'I did some more drinking when I got home and my eyes look like the proverbial piss-holes.'

'Can we stop apologising to each other?' said Shepherd.

'Only if you let me buy you lunch,' said Elaine.

'Sure,' said Shepherd. 'When?'

'Now, of course. Or do you have a better offer?'

Shepherd laughed. 'My better offer is thawing in the sink before I microwave it.'

'Come on, then,' said Elaine.

She drove into the city centre and down a side road Shepherd didn't know. She parked with two wheels on the pavement and switched off the engine. On his left Shepherd saw a line of metal railings, and on his right a brick building, whose lower windows were covered with mesh screens similar to the ones he'd seen protecting armoured cars in Iraq. 'Where are we?' he said.

'What's wrong?'

Shepherd's pulse raced. They were alone in the street and he couldn't even hear traffic in the distance. 'Nothing,' he said.

She slid a hand round his neck and moved her face closer to his. 'You're not still thinking I'm a mad woman out for revenge, are you?'

He could see his face reflected in the lenses of her sunglasses. 'Of course not.'

She kissed his cheek. 'Good,' she said. 'Come on, I'm starving.'

They got out of the car, and she pushed open a red door that led into a fish-and-chip shop that looked as if it hadn't been decorated since the fifties. From behind the counter a middle-aged man peered over the top of a pair of reading glasses and waved a spatula at them. 'Elaine, love, how are you?'

'Hungry,' said Elaine. 'How's the haddock?'

'The cod's better. Sit yourself down and I'll get you something special.'

Shepherd followed her to the seating area – three lines of wooden booths. He sat down opposite her on a hard wooden bench. A glass salt cellar and a bottle of vinegar stood between them on the table. 'I've been coming here since before I was born,' said Elaine. 'My mum used to have cravings for the batter when she was pregnant. My dad used to bring her in and she'd peel the batter off the fish and eat it. I still come with my parents once a month.'

The walls were lined with wood panels and the room was bright with utilitarian fluorescent lights. A fan heater had been screwed to one wall close to the ceiling. A printed sign read optimistically 'WE DO NOT ACCEPT £50 OR £100 NOTES'. Another sign offered garlic mayo, pepper sauce and sweet chilli sauce for fifty pence a portion. A woman in her sixties, wearing a padded anorak over a black and white checked apron, came with the food, two oval plates piled high with battered cod and chips. She put down a handful of sachets of ketchup on the table. 'I know you like your tomato sauce, Elaine,' she said. 'Mugs of tea?'

'Lovely, thanks.' Elaine picked up her knife and fork and grinned at Shepherd. 'Tuck in, and tell me it's not the best fish and chips you've ever tasted.'

'I'm still getting over the image of your mother picking off the batter,' said Shepherd.

'The fish wasn't wasted. My dad took it home,' she said.

Shepherd cut off a piece of fish and popped it into his mouth. The batter was crisp and the fish perfectly cooked. 'Excellent,' he said. As he chewed, a large man in a brown trenchcoat appeared in the doorway. John Maplethorpe waved and came over to them.

'You're not following me, are you, John?' asked Elaine, standing up to kiss him on both cheeks.

Maplethorpe nodded at Shepherd over her shoulder. 'Now,

why would I be doing that?' he said. 'What's with the movie-star shades?'

'Hangover,' she said. 'Join us.'

'I'll just have a mug of tea, but I won't eat,' said Maplethorpe, squeezing on to the bench seat next to her. 'Good to see you again, Jamie,' he said.

'And you,' responded Shepherd.

'I saw Elaine's car outside so I thought I'd stop by for a chat. This place hasn't changed in . . . how many years?'

'More than I can remember,' said Elaine. 'John, Robbie and I used to come in at least once a week for lunch, if I could drag them out of the office.'

Maplethorpe patted his expanding waistline. 'Those were the days when we used to burn off the calories as fast we ate them,' he said. 'Now they go straight to my gut and stay there.'

'Speak for yourself,' said Elaine. 'I'm still wearing the same size jeans as I was back then.'

The waitress came back to their table, notebook in hand, and looked disappointed when Maplethorpe only ordered a mug of tea. 'Tell you what, bring me cod and chips as well,' he said, 'but make it a small one.' As she walked away, Maplethorpe rested his arms on the table and interlinked his chunky fingers. 'You heard what happened to Gerry Lynn?' he asked Elaine.

'Good bloody riddance,' she said.

'Here's to that,' said Maplethorpe.

'Do they know who did it?' she asked.

Shepherd sipped his tea as he watched Elaine carefully. The question seemed genuine.

'It happened in the South so the Irish cops are handling it, which probably means they'll never find out,' said Maplethorpe. 'The Garda are the original Keystone Cops,' he said to Shepherd.

'We saw it on the news,' said Shepherd.

The waitress returned with Maplethorpe's fish and chips

and a mug of tea. Maplethorpe groaned when he saw the size of the fish, which was several inches longer than the plate. 'It's put the wind up Noel Kinsella, I can tell you that much,' he said. He speared a chip on his fork and stuffed it into his mouth.

'Good. Maybe he'll go back to the States with his bitch of a wife.'

'Funny you should say that,' said Maplethorpe. 'According to the guys babysitting him, she wants to get the hell out of Belfast.'

'Please tell me you're not protecting that slimy bastard,' said Elaine.

'Not me personally, but the Intelligence Branch is,' said Maplethorpe.

Elaine put down her knife and fork. 'Noel Kinsella murdered my husband, and now his former colleagues are protecting him?'

'No one looking after Kinsella had worked with Robbie,' he said. 'None of them were with Special Branch back then.'

'What about you, John? What if they asked you to body-guard him? Would you?'

'Like hell I would,' said Maplethorpe. 'But I'm leaving anyway so there's nothing they can do to me.'

'John, this is so bloody unfair. That bastard got away scot-free and now you're protecting him.'

'It's not me, Elaine. It's the system.'

'Why can't the British police look after him? It's the Brits who've sold out to the terrorists.' She flashed Shepherd an apologetic look. 'No offence, Jamie.'

'None taken,' he said. 'I agree with you. The British Government set Kinsella free, so he's their problem. This wouldn't have arisen if they'd put him behind bars where he belonged.'

'Here's to that,' said Maplethorpe. 'Anyway, I just wanted you to know that he's leaving Belfast so we won't be seeing him on television or in the bloody papers. They're heading off to London later this week and the word is that they'll be going back to the States. Good riddance to them both, I say.'

'I don't understand that Kennedy woman,' said Elaine. 'How could she marry Kinsella, knowing he was a murderer?'

'The Americans have always looked at the IRA through rose-tinted glasses,' said Maplethorpe. 'To her they're probably twinkly-eyed freedom-fighters sitting by peat fires playing their fiddles when they're not fighting the evil British occupiers. They've never really understood what's been going on here.'

'He's a murderer, John. It doesn't matter why he did it. He killed Robbie.'

'I know, I know,' said Maplethorpe. He took out a bottle of painkillers and swallowed two.

'Are you okay, John?' asked Elaine.

'Just a headache,' said Maplethorpe. 'Stress brings it on.'

'Why London?' asked Elaine.

'She doesn't feel safe in Belfast, but doesn't want to appear to be running away with her tail between her legs. So, they'll spend a few weeks in London. If we don't catch the killer, they'll go back to Boston.'

'And in the meantime the cops are bodyguarding them?'

'It's been made clear that if anything happens to the Kinsellas, heads will roll.' Maplethorpe grinned. 'Just hope it doesn't happen before I leave – wouldn't want them to have an excuse to slash my pension.' He gestured at Shepherd with his knife. 'How are you settling in, Jamie?'

'Fine,' said Shepherd.

'We should have another game of pool.'

'I'll look forward to it.'

Richard Yokely stretched out his legs and waved at Karl Traynor on the large plasma screen. The other man was sitting at a desk in the Washington secure room sipping from a mug. 'They let you have coffee in there, Karl?' he asked jealously.

'Sure. Can't function without a caffeine injection, you know that.'

'They won't let me have it in here,' said Yokely.

'Ah, well, rules are rules,' said Traynor. He pushed his spectacles up his nose. 'Are you ready?'

'I am.'

'Two weeks ago Hassan Salih received a payment of a quarter of a million dollars from an account at the Mashreq Bank in Dubai. It belongs to one Muhammad Aslam. The money was transferred to an account at the DBS Bank in Singapore in the name of Majid Jasim, which was one of the names you gave me. Yesterday a further two million dollars were transferred by the same route.'

'Do you know who Muhammad Aslam is?'

'Sadly not. He's not on our watch list and he's not on the list of Specially Designated Nationals. All we get from the SWIFT download are names, account numbers and amounts. We can follow the money, but we're not in a position as yet to get the personal details of the account holders. We can apply through the Financial Action Task Force, but it takes time.'

Yokely made a note of the name on his pad.

'Now, large deposits were made into Muhammad Aslam's account in Dubai shortly before he made the two transfers to Singapore. Four hundred thousand dollars went in two days before he sent the quarter of a million to Singapore, and two and a half million the day before the two million was sent to the Majid Jasim account. Both transfers came from the Gulf International Bank in Riyadh, a personal account belonging to one Othman bin Mahmuud al-Ahmed.'

'Ah,' said Yokely.

'You know the name?' asked Traynor.

'Oh, yes,' said Yokely. 'He's a very important man, is Othman. A very big wheel.'

'We know of him, of course. He's a fixer for several of the Saudi princes so we have to give him clearances from time to time. The way I read it is that the money is coming from Othman and that Muhammad Aslam is acting as a middle man, taking his commission before he passes the funds on.' Traynor glanced at his watch. 'I've got a Treasury meeting in fifteen minutes. Is there anything else you need from me?'

'How much is in the Dubai account at the moment?' asked Yokely.

'There's the six hundred and fifty thousand dollars' difference between what went in and what went to Singapore, plus a few hundred thousand that was already there. So, just short of a million bucks. If you want I can talk to the Office of Foreign Assets Control and get the account frozen. And I could have Aslam put on the SDN list. It might be a bit harder going against Othman as he has political connections here in Washington.'

The list of Specially Designated Nationals was one of the big guns in the OFAC armoury. Once on the list, a person's assets were blocked and all Americans prohibited from dealing with them. Anyone on the list became a virtual pariah, their travel options were limited and any businesses they were connected to withered and died. 'For the moment we'll just give them enough rope to hang themselves,' said Yokely. 'If we start freezing assets they'll know that we know. But keep a watching brief, please, Karl, and update me on any further transfers. What happened to the money in the Singapore account?'

'It's not been touched. At the moment there's a little over five million US dollars in it. I've had a look at transactions over the past five years. From time to time money is paid in from mainly Middle Eastern accounts, then transferred to Switzerland, the Cayman Islands and the British Virgin Islands. Various names to those accounts, but most of them are the aliases you gave me.'

'Thanks, Karl. Do me another favour, will you? Run a worldwide search for those aliases and pin down every account he has. At some point in the future we'll freeze them.

And check for withdrawals over the past month. I'm pretty sure Salih is in London, but it'd be helpful to have confirmation.'

'What about my HobNobs?'

'I FedExed them yesterday,' said Yokely.

Traynor flashed him a thumbs-up and the screen went blank. Yokely sat back in his chair and linked his fingers behind his head. 'So, Othman bin Mahmuud al-Ahmed, you want me dead, do you?' he whispered. 'Well, you've thrown the dice. Let's see how they land.'

Shepherd was using a pair of shears to hack away at the hedge in the back garden when his mobile phone beeped. He looked at the screen. It was a text message from a number he didn't recognise. 'KELLY'S CELLAR. 6 P.M.' He frowned. Only the people he'd met in Belfast and Charlotte Button had his number. Mentally he ran through the phone numbers he knew, but there was no match. He called it back, but the phone had been switched off. There was an outside chance that the message had been sent to the wrong number, but Shepherd doubted it. It was just after three o'clock now so he had plenty of time. He finished the hedge, then went upstairs to shower and change.

He drove into the city centre and parked in a multi-storey close to Royal Avenue, then spent ten minutes walking round the shops in Royal Avenue, the City Hall behind him, checking reflections in shop windows. Kelly's Cellar was down Bank Street to his left, but he carried on walking. A group of Hari Krishna devotees were jumping up and down, banging drums, clashing cymbals and chanting, watched by a group of Goth teenagers with black hair, pale faces and pierced noses. He went into a Virgin Megastore and wandered among the rows of CDs and DVDs for fifteen minutes until he was sure he wasn't being followed, then left and headed back to the bar.

The Goths were still staring at the Hari Krishna group as Shepherd walked by. One of the girls had a safety-pin through her ear and a silver ring in one nostril. Shepherd realised self-mutilation wasn't something that he found the least bit attractive. He wondered what he'd do if Liam ever decided to dress in black with white makeup, mascara and assorted body piercings or started to bang a drum and chant. His boy was only ten, but time flew and he wasn't looking forward to the rebellious teenage years.

Kelly's Cellar was a traditional two-storey black and white pub with a slate roof. It would perhaps have been more at home on a windswept moor, surrounded by bleating sheep, but now it was hemmed in by a branch of Tesco and a red-brick shopping centre. He took a last glance over his shoulder and pushed open the black wooden door. There was a long bar to his right and a line of wooden tables at which old men in thick coats were drinking pints of Guinness, newspapers open at the sports pages. Four women with pinched faces and cheap clothes were cackling together like witches and drinking halves of bitter.

Shepherd scanned the faces as he went to the bar but there was no one he recognised. A red-haired man in a stained T-shirt and jeans asked what he wanted to drink and he ordered a Jameson's and ice. 'Can I buy you a drink, you Brit bastard?' said a man behind him, in a poor imitation of a Northern Irish accent.

Shepherd spun around. His eyes widened. Richard Yokely was the last person he'd expected to see in a Belfast pub. The American grinned but Shepherd held up a hand to silence him. He got out his mobile phone, took off the back and removed the battery.

'Someone listening in, are they?' said Yokely.

'What the hell are you doing here?' said Shepherd. 'Since when has Belfast been your turf?' He put the phone and the battery back into his pocket.

'I'm a quarter Irish, didn't I tell you?' said Yokely, clapping Shepherd on the back. 'Well, two-eighths, actually. A great-grandmother on my mother's side was from Donegal and a great-grandfather on my father's was from Warrenpoint.' He ordered a pint of Guinness.

'So, you're here to revisit your roots, O'Yokely, is that it?'

'Nothing so mundane, I'm afraid,' said Yokely, in his regular Southern drawl. He was wearing a long tweed coat over a brown wool suit and brown leather shoes with tassels. He stuck out his hand and Shepherd shook it. The chunky class ring on Yokely's right ring finger bit into his palm.

Yokely paid for their drinks and they went to a corner table. He sipped his Guinness and wiped a line of white foam from his upper lip. 'Never tastes the same outside of Ireland,' he said. 'They do a great steak and Guinness pie upstairs, with diddly-diddly music if you're lucky.'

'How did you get my number, Richard? It's a pay-as-you-go and it's only been valid for the past week or so.'

'A long story.'

'I'll give you my home number and a pay-as-you-go you can call,' said Shepherd, 'but I'd rather you didn't contact me on operational phones in future.'

Yokely flashed him a mock salute. 'Message received and understood.'

'I'm serious,' said Shepherd. 'For all you knew I might have been surrounded by armed crack-dealers when you sent me that SMS.'

'Actually, I knew exactly where you were and what you were doing,' said Yokely. 'And you've got more to worry about than drug-dealers, believe me.'

'You should also be aware that everything said in the vicinity of that operational phone is recorded,' said Shepherd.

'Got it.'

'And what do you mean, I've got more to worry about than drug-dealers? Why do you always talk in riddles? What's going on?'

'Smile, Spider,' said Yokely. 'We're just a couple of tourists shooting the breeze. That's why I chose this place.' He sipped his Guinness, then wiped his upper lip on his sleeve. 'We're just a Yank and a Brit on the tourist trail. This place was built fifty years before the founding fathers signed our Constitution, did you know that? We don't have anything this old back in the States. Did you know the United Irishmen planned the 1798 Rising here? It's a real piece of history.'

'Funny how the world changes, isn't it?' said Shepherd. 'Terrorists become folk heroes, providing they get what they want and enough time passes.'

'Don't tell me you're becoming cynical in your old age.'

'My job is to put murderers behind bars,' said Shepherd. 'You can see why I'd be frustrated when my government decides to set them free early for political reasons.'

'Is that why you're here?' asked Yokely. 'To put murderers behind bars?'

Shepherd narrowed his eyes suspiciously. 'Do you know why I'm here?'

Yokely raised his glass. 'Yes,' he said.

'Do you know everything I do?'

'Pretty much.' The American grinned.

'You know we have laws against stalking,' said Shepherd.

'So sue me. Anyway, you should be thinking of me more as a guardian angel than a stalker.'

'That's why you're here, is it?' said Shepherd. 'To protect me?'

'Spider, I just wanted to get in touch without going through the lovely Charlie,' Yokely said. 'I needed a chat, man to man.'

'She's already warned me about going behind her back,' said Shepherd.

'Behind her back, over her head, between her legs, she can't dictate who you speak to in your own time.'

'Strictly speaking, I'm on SOCA time and Charlie's my boss.'

Yokely reached inside his jacket pocket and gave him a photograph of two men in traditional Arab dress: flowing white robes, headdresses and sandals. One was in his sixties or seventies, the other in his thirties. There was a strong facial resemblance so Shepherd figured they were father and son. The two men were sitting at a café table, glasses of tea in front of them. The older man was smoking a cigarette and looking at the other with amusement. Shepherd stared at the faces. He hadn't seen either man before.

'The old guy is Othman bin Mahmuud al-Ahmed,' said Yokely. 'He made a fortune acting as a middle man for the Saudi Royal Family. Weapons, ships, property investments. Semi-retired, these days, but he still has incredible contacts across the Arab world. And probably a few senators in his pocket. We know of two MPs who live well above their means thanks to Othman's generosity and he was a regular visitor to Number Ten during the Thatcher years.'

Shepherd handed back the photograph and Yokely slid it inside his jacket.

'Othman wants Charlie dead,' said the American, flatly.

'Shit,' said Shepherd.

'He has deep pockets and he knows people. Generally speaking, what Othman wants, Othman gets.'

'You've told Charlie, right?'

'No,' said Yokely. 'And I'm not planning to.'

'What?'

'The sort of people Othman will send to kill her aren't going to be put off by a couple of uniforms standing outside her front door,' said Yokely.

'You can't play with her life like this,' hissed Shepherd.

'Hear me out,' said Yokely. 'The other man in the photo-graph is Abdal Jabbaar bin Othman al-Ahmed. British citizen, don't you know?' he said, in a passable upper-class English accent. 'Courtesy of his dad's money, of course. Eton-educated, followed by a spell at the London School of Economics. Now dead. And the father blames Charlie.'

'Because?'

'Because he's a vindictive shit who needs to blame someone,' said Yokely. 'Abdal Jabbaar was behind some of the biggest al-Qaeda atrocities in recent years, including the

London Tube bombings and the attack on the Eurostar. He killed himself three months ago in a prison in the Ukraine. Good riddance to bad rubbish, as they say. He was responsible for the deaths of several hundred civilians and I for one would happily dance on his grave.'

'So how did he die?'

'Suicide, I'm told.' Shepherd cocked an eyebrow and Yokely put up his hands. 'Cross my heart, Spider. He slashed his wrists.'

'So why does he blame Charlie?'

'She interrogated him a while back, before we shipped him off to Guantánamo Bay.' He smiled without warmth. 'It was a robust interrogation.'

'If you sent him to Guantánamo Bay, what the hell was he doing in the Ukraine?'

'We needed to be more forceful with our interrogation, and the Ukrainians are more . . .'

'Forceful?' Shepherd filled in.

'I was going to say flexible,' said Yokely.

'So flexible that he killed himself?'

'He wasn't being tortured, Spider.'

'I'm guessing that depends on your definition of torture,' said Shepherd. 'Why was Charlie involved in his interrogation?'

'Her language skills. She's fluent in Arabic. Plus she's a woman. Plus we had to do it on the hoof. We were under time constraints.'

'So you were involved?'

'We had him in the American embassy. He was behind the bombs on the Eurostar but we didn't know what the target was.'

Shepherd drained his glass and put it on the table. 'Can I take a shot in the dark here and venture a guess that you're on Othman's hit list, too?'

'I was coming to that,' he said.

'I'm sure you were.'

'The old man has taken it into his head that Charlie and I were responsible for the death of his sons and put a price on our heads. But Charlie's the reason I'm talking to you. I'm a big boy, I can take care of myself.' He pointed at Shepherd's empty glass. 'Another?'

'Sons?' said Shepherd. 'You said "son" before. Singular.'

'Abdal Jabbaar killed himself in the Ukraine. His brother died while Charlie and I were interrogating Abdal Jabbaar.'

'Under what circumstances?' asked Shepherd.

Yokely smiled tightly. 'That's classified.'

'But two of this man's sons are dead? And he blames you?'

'He blames the two of us,' said Yokely. 'Now, do you want another drink?'

'It's my round,' said Shepherd.

When he got back to the table, Yokely was whispering into his mobile phone. He cut the connection as Shepherd sat down.

'So, here's the scoop. The information I have is that Othman bin Mahmuud al-Ahmed has hired a Palestinian to kill us both. Me and Charlie. His name is Hassan Salih but that means nothing. He uses lots of different aliases.'

'Picture?'

'If I had one, you'd have it. This guy has stayed off our radar. He's a real pro.'

'But you're not worried?'

'Not for myself, Spider. I'm always on the move, I have no family to speak of, no real base. And I'm well protected by virtue of what I do. Charlie's a whole different ball-game.'

'You have to tell her,' said Shepherd.

'And if I do, what then? She and her family go into hiding. Her kid gets pulled out of school. Her career is put on hold. For how long? The killer just waits. Eventually she goes back to work and so does he.'

'I get the feeling you have a plan.'

'We know there's a contract on her so we watch her.'

'Without telling her?'

'It's the only way, Spider. And you know people, right, people who can keep an eye on her?'

'She's a former spook. She'll spot a tail a mile off.'

'So tell them to be careful. Keep their distance. I'll arrange full-on electronic surveillance and every professional killer we know will be red-flagged.'

Shepherd sipped his whiskey. 'You're using her as bait.'

'We're protecting her.'

'You're using her as bait to catch a killer who's also got you on his hit-list.'

'You say tomato, I say potato. If I didn't think it was the only way to go, I wouldn't be here.' He sipped his Guinness. 'There's something else you should know.'

'I'm listening.'

'Salih has been tracking Button's mobile. The one she uses to talk to you.'

'So he's got my number?'

'I thought you should know.'

Shepherd's jaw clenched. 'Richard, if he knows my mobile number and he has the right contacts, he can get my call lists. Which means he gets all the numbers I've been in contact with.'

'I'm afraid so.'

'Which means he'll have my home phone number.'

'You can change your Sim card,' said the American.

'That's locking the stable door and you know it,' said Shepherd. 'Besides, I can't go changing my number mid-operation.'

'There's no reason to suggest that he's interested in you,' said Yokely. 'I just wanted to be straight with you.'

Shepherd massaged the bridge of his nose. 'Let's just say we get the guy,' he said. 'The father will hire someone else. If he's as rich as you say, he can keep paying until the job's done.'

'I'll take care of the father,' said Yokely.

'Meaning what?'

'Meaning I'll take care of him. Sooner rather than later. It's just a matter of choosing the time and the place.'

'You're going to kill him?'

'I'll neutralise the threat,' said the American. He raised his glass in salute.

'Tomato, potato,' said Shepherd.

Salih stood in the shadows of a spreading willow as he watched the narrow-boat go by. It was on the Regent's Canal, heading to Camden Town, packed with revellers dancing to a four-piece jazz band. The musicians were good, riffing on a Duke Ellington classic, and Salih was tapping his foot in time to the tune. It was a little after nine o'clock, and the moon was almost full, the sky so clear that Salih could see the craters on its surface. He turned up the collar of his coat and walked to the basin where the narrow-boats could turn around a small man-made island.

The Russian was waiting there, smoking one of his small, foul-smelling cigars. 'How are you, old friend?' asked Merkulov.

'Everything is good,' Salih said.

Merkulov hugged him, then the two men started to walk along the towpath, their feet crunching on the gravel. 'She was in Belfast today,' said Merkulov. He took an envelope from his coat pocket and handed it to Salih. 'There's a list of her recent calls.'

Salih pocketed the envelope. 'What about the number she keeps calling in Belfast?'

'It's in there too. It's a pay-as-you-go, so it could belong to anyone. But I checked the numbers called from it and one is the home number of a SOCA officer, a man called Daniel Shepherd. The address is in Hereford, near the Welsh border. Either whoever has that phone is calling Shepherd, or Shepherd is calling his home.'

Salih frowned. 'Hereford is where the SAS is based, right?'

'Yes.'

Salih nodded slowly. 'So this man is possibly former special forces, now working for Charlotte Button in Belfast?'

'That's an assumption, but probably valid.'

'Can you get me information on him?'

'I still have no reliable contact in SOCA, but I do know several former SAS officers. I can check him out through them. But it will be expensive.'

'How much?' said Salih.

'It's not a question of how much I pay them,' said Merkulov. 'If they give me information on Shepherd and something happens to him, they'll be gunning for me. I can check him out, that's easy enough, but I'll need your assurance that you won't do anything drastic to him.'

'Drastic?' repeated Salih, with amused eyes.

'You know what I mean. If I check him out for you and a couple of days later there's a bullet in his skull my life will be over.'

'He's not my target, Viktor. You know that.'

'I'm sorry if I sound paranoid, old friend, but one doesn't fool around with the SAS.'

'How much would you want – to check out this Shepherd?'

'Twenty thousand pounds should cover it,' said Merkulov.

'Agreed,' said Salih.

'Whoever's paying you has money to burn,' said Merkulov.

'Money is no object,' said Salih.

'Why does he want Yokely and Button so badly?' said Merkulov. He finished his cigar and flicked the butt into the canal. It spun through the air in a shower of sparks, then plopped into the water.

'I don't care why people hire me,' said Salih. 'All I care is that they pay. You're the same. Money is our only master. Nothing else matters.'

Merkulov nodded. 'They take revenge seriously, the Arabs,' he said.

Salih smiled. 'I did not say my client was an Arab.'

'No, I assumed . . .'

Salih cut him short. 'The American. Do you know where he is?'

Ahead, a man in a black nylon bomber jacket was walking an aggressive Dobermann. He yanked on the dog's chain and swore as he walked past them. His head was shaven and a tattoo of a cobweb ran across his neck. He glared at Salih and Merkulov, as if he blamed them for his dog's misbehaviour.

'I am working on it,' said Merkulov, 'but he is difficult to track. He is able to move between countries without leaving any record of his passing.'

'That is why I pay you so much,' said Salih. 'If it was easy, I'd phone Directory Enquiries.'

'I know where he isn't,' said Merkulov. 'He isn't in the Ukraine or anywhere in the former Soviet bloc. And my contacts across Asia are sure he isn't there.'

'That still leaves a big chunk of the world, Viktor.'

'As I said, I'm working on it. Have you a deadline on this?'

'Generally my clients would rather I fulfilled my obligations sooner rather than later,' said Salih. 'How could we get a number for him?'

'Let me think about it,' said the Russian. 'Is it possible that he is in regular contact with Button?'

'I don't know,' said Salih. 'She's SOCA and he's American black operations. I doubt they would do much together.'

'They must have done something for your client to want them both dead.'

'Just because he wants them both taken care of doesn't mean they're connected,' said Salih.

'You don't know?'

'I didn't ask,' said Salih.

'It might be an idea to call him,' said Merkulov. 'Find out if there's a connection.' He gestured at the pocket into which Salih had put the envelope. 'It might even be that Yokely is one of the numbers on that list. If we think he is in regular contact with her, we'd have a better chance of finding him.'

Salih stopped walking and put his hands into his pockets. The man with the Dobermann disappeared around a bend in the canal. Salih looked over his shoulder. There was no one on the path behind them.

'Is that man over there one of yours?' said Salih, with a nod across the canal. The knife dropped from his sleeve as he brought his hand out of his coat pocket and slid easily into Salih's open palm. He grabbed Merkulov's hair with his left hand and pulled back the man's head to expose the throat.

Merkulov began to shout, but the knife slashed through his windpipe, reducing the sound to a watery gurgle. Arterial blood spurted in an arc from the Russian's neck as Salih pushed him into the canal. The body slapped into the water, Merkulov's legs thrashed for a few seconds, then stilled. Salih took a handkerchief from his pocket, wiped the knife clean, then dropped it into the depths.

He took one final look around, then walked away along the towpath. Part of him wished he'd been able to confront the Russian, to tell him that he knew he'd betrayed him and see the despair in the man's eyes before he'd taken his life, but he was nothing if not professional. Only amateurs gave in to the urge to explain to their victims. Only amateurs made their killings personal. Merkulov had betrayed Salih, so Salih had killed him. It had been inconvenient, but it hadn't been personal. The Russian wasn't the only intelligence source in London. Salih knew of three others, and he would have no problem in finding someone to get him the information he needed. He whistled softly as he walked, then smiled. It was the tune the jazz band had been playing. He took his mobile phone from his pocket and removed the Sim card. He broke it in half and tossed it into the canal.

Shepherd sat down at his computer, went on-line and booked a return flight from Belfast to Birmingham with British Midland for the next day. He didn't want Button to know he was leaving Belfast so he picked up one of his spare mobiles with a pay-as-you-go Sim card and went into the garden to phone Martin O'Brien. He had served with the Irish Rangers, Ireland's equivalent of the SAS, then set up his own VIP protection company. Shepherd had known him for more than twelve years and there were few men he trusted more.

Shepherd's luck was in because O'Brien was in the UK and agreed to meet him at Birmingham airport. Shepherd told him what he needed and O'Brien agreed to help, no questions asked.

As Shepherd ended the call, he saw Elaine Carter at her bedroom window. She was wearing pink pyjamas and waved. He waved back. Then she blew him a kiss. Shepherd grinned and returned it.

Salih lay on the bed and stared at the ceiling blankly. He clasped his hands together and steepled his fingers. He had spent the best part of the night pacing round the hotel room, trying to marshal his thoughts, and soon it would be time for his morning prayers. He didn't want to pray just yet because he had still to plan his course of action. He had been successful in the past because he never took risks. Everything he did was planned in advance, and for every action he took there was a fallback position in case something went wrong.

The Russian had been trying to set him up, of that Salih was sure. He had known Merkulov for more than five years and in all that time the Russian had never once asked for details of a client. Such details were unnecessary. Merkulov supplied information and it made no difference who was paying for that information. That the Russian had been asking questions about Salih's client had set alarm bells ringing, but when Merkulov had suggested Salih phone his client, he had known without a shadow of doubt that he had been betrayed. He had felt no remorse about killing Merkulov. If their positions had been reversed, the Russian would just as quickly have killed him.

Merkulov had betrayed Salih, which meant that someone knew Salih was in England and that he was being paid to kill Richard Yokely and Charlotte Button. The question was, who had Merkulov betrayed him to? Not the police, surely, because they would have arrested the Russian and charged him with conspiracy to murder. Perhaps it was the security services, MI5 or MI6. Or the American.

The Russian had wanted Salih to phone his client, which suggested that whoever turned him had access to phone-monitoring technology. Again, that pointed to the security services, or Yokely. Now that he had destroyed the Sim card, they couldn't track his phone or identify its position. He had already fitted a new Sim card from a shop in Edgware Road.

Salih ran through everything that Merkulov had known about him. He had known his name, and several aliases he had used in the past. He had known the pay-as-you-go phone number Salih had been using. And he had known who Salih's targets were. It wasn't much. Merkulov didn't know what passport Salih was travelling on or where he was staying. He didn't know what car he was driving or where he planned to go.

There had been no one watching them at the canal, Salih was sure. If there had been, they would surely have tried to prevent him killing Merkulov. After Salih had left the canal he had walked to Warwick Avenue Tube station, caught a Bakerloo Line train to the Circle Line, and had spent two hours going round it. He hadn't been followed, he was sure. No one knew where he was, and without the phone they had no idea where he would go next. That suggested the security services weren't on his case, because if they had turned the Russian they would almost certainly have had a surveillance team in place. That left the American.

The big question, though, was when the Russian had been turned. Yokely would certainly have access to mobile-phone tracking capabilities, so he would know exactly where Salih had been. Salih had used the mobile in his hotel, so as soon as he had left the Underground he had checked out, having first wiped the room clean of all fingerprints. Then he had registered at the Hilton close to Paddington station, a large, impersonal hotel frequented mainly by business travellers.

His trip to Windsor worried Salih, though. If Yokely had tracked his phone he would know that Salih had been in the vicinity of the office where Charlotte Button's husband worked. Did that matter? Salih sighed. Maybe not. Yokely would already know that Button was his target, so he hadn't learnt anything new in discovering he had been to Windsor.

Salih closed his eyes and took several deep breaths. The downside was that Yokely knew he was a target, and that Salih had been paid to kill him. And he would know that Salih had also been paid to kill Charlotte Button. That wasn't the end of the world. Salih had killed men before who knew they were targets, men who had surrounded themselves with armed bodyguards and hidden behind fortified walls. Anyone could be reached. It just took planning and patience. That Yokely knew he was being hunted made Salih's job harder, but not impossible.

The one thing Salih didn't understand was why Merkulov had given him the information about the SOCA agent in Belfast. The man called Daniel Shepherd. Anything that the Russian had said to Salih, and everything he had given him, must have been cleared by Yokely. That meant Yokely wanted Salih to know who Shepherd was and where he lived. It felt like a trap, but why set a trap when Yokely would have known that Salih was meeting Merkulov at the canal? Merkulov had made it clear he was having trouble getting information out of SOCA, yet he appeared to have had no problem in identifying Shepherd's landline. That suggested Yokely had fed him information. But why? Did Yokely know Shepherd?

Salih had been considering killing someone close to Button as a way of bringing her out into the open. Her husband was a possibility, as was her daughter, and now the man called Daniel Shepherd was an option. If Shepherd was her agent, she would surely attend his funeral. Was Yokely presenting Shepherd as a target? Salih sat up and shook his head, trying to clear his thoughts. Did that mean Yokely wanted Button dead? Was he clearing the way for Salih in the hope that he would be satisfied with just the one hit? That made no sense, no sense at all.

The possibility had occurred to Salih that Yokely wanted the Russian dead and had sent Merkulov to the meeting knowing that Salih would kill him. That would explain why no one had been at the canal watching him. But it didn't explain why the Russian had given Salih the phone records and the address. Salih rubbed his temples. Maybe he was thinking too much. Maybe Yokely didn't care about Daniel Shepherd. Maybe he didn't even know who he was. Maybe Yokely assumed that Salih was naïve or stupid and had sent Merkulov to pump him for information. Salih lay down again. Was he overthinking the situation? Was he starting to get paranoid, seeing death in shadows when they were only shadows, nothing more? Surely if Yokely knew that Salih was trying to kill him, he would have had Salih arrested or worse. Salih and Merkulov had conspired to commit murder, and in England that carried the same sentence as perpetration of the act. So what was Yokely after? Did he want to know who had taken out the contract on him? Was that why he had sent Merkulov to the meeting?

Salih's mind whirled and he tried to relax, to allow his subconscious to get to work on the puzzle. His instincts had stood him in good stead in the past and he knew they would do so again. He closed his eyes and concentrated on breathing deeply. Yokely was a professional, a man used to running black operations for the American Government. If he wanted Salih dead, he would have him killed without a moment's hesitation. So, the fact that Salih was still alive suggested that Yokely did not know he had been paid to kill him. So the American had not turned Merkulov. But if not Yokely, then who? Or had it all been a terrible mistake? Had the Russian simply been too inquisitive? Had Salih simply misread his curiosity? If he had, then, far from being a trap, the Daniel Shepherd details might be an opportunity he could make good use of.

Salih rolled off the bed and padded into the bathroom. First he would cleanse himself. Then he would pray. And then he would phone Tariq.

Shepherd caught an early-morning flight from George Best Belfast City airport to Birmingham. The British Midland flight was packed and the woman in the seat in front of him reclined it as soon as the wheels left the runway. Shepherd closed his eyes and tried to think pleasant thoughts until the plane landed. He had only a Nike gym bag with him so he walked straight from the plane to the arrivals area where Martin O'Brien was waiting for him, his shaven head glistening under the overhead lights. He grinned and the two men hugged. 'How's Belfast?' asked the Irishman.

'It's changed,' said Shepherd. 'You wouldn't recognise it. No one's shooting at you, for a start.'

'Yeah,' agreed O'Brien. 'A few years ago whoever would have thought that Belfast would be the safe place to go?'

'Crime rate's on the up. Before, they used to search them on the way into the shops. Now they search them on the way out.' They walked together to the car park. Shepherd peered at O'Brien's stomach. 'Are you losing weight?'

'I'm in training,' said O'Brien. 'I'm doing the Marathon des Sables next year.'

'Get the hell out of here,' said Shepherd. The Marathon des Sables was the toughest footrace in the world, a hundred and fifty miles across the desert in North Africa, run over six days with all supplies carried in a rucksack. It was equivalent to five and a half regular marathons with temperatures up to a hundred and twenty degrees.

'I needed the challenge,' said O'Brien.

'You're mad,' said Shepherd.

'You should do it with me,' said O'Brien. 'You still run, don't you?'

'I run, sure, but the Marathon des Sables isn't about running. It's about punishing yourself.'

'It's fifty per cent mental,' said O'Brien. 'If you think you can do it, you can.'

'Yes, Grasshopper. But that doesn't mean that if you believe you can fly you can jump off a tall building without there being consequences.' He slapped O'Brien's back. 'Seriously, though, I admire you. How old are you now?'

'Screw you, Spider.'

Hereford was just under fifty miles from Birmingham airport and O'Brien's Mercedes made good time. It was a little before six when they pulled up in front of the White Hart and he switched off the engine. 'I've got two guys for you to meet,' said O'Brien. 'They left the Regiment a couple of years back and spend most of their time in Iraq now, working for Blackwater. Serious money. Jack was a demolitions expert, and Billy was a linguist, fluent in seven languages including Arabic and Farsi.'

'I can't afford Iraq wages, Martin.'

'They both have places in Hereford and they're killing time before they head out to Baghdad again. They're happy to do it as a favour. Plus I told them you're a cop and that you'll take care of any parking tickets, speeding fines and the like.'

'And get them off the odd murder charge?'

'Can you do that?' asked O'Brien.

'No, I bloody well can't,' said Shepherd.

'They're good guys,' said O'Brien, climbing out of the Mercedes. 'Regiment wasn't happy about them leaving but there's not much they can do when security companies are paying five times what the army offers.'

He took Shepherd through a back door into the pub where three men in their sixties were sitting on stools at the bar. They glanced across as O'Brien and Shepherd walked in, then returned to their conversation. The barman had the look of a former sergeant major with bulging forearms and world-weary eyes. He nodded at O'Brien, who nodded back.

A man in his early thirties was sitting at a corner table, two half-finished pints of bitter in front of him. When he saw O'Brien he stood up. He was a couple of inches taller than Shepherd and a few pounds lighter, with broad shoulders and wavy brown hair that didn't appear to have been combed in a few days. He was wearing a grey sports jacket over faded blue jeans.

'Spider, this is Jack Bradford.' Bradford was also wearing the Rolex Submariner with the black bezel favoured by SAS troopers.

'Thanks for agreeing to this,' said Shepherd.

'Pleasure,' said Bradford.

'Where's Billy?' asked O'Brien.

Bradford gestured at the men's room. 'Taking a leak. Bladder like a marble, my brother.'

'What are you drinking?'

Bradford asked for another pint of bitter and Shepherd for a Jameson's with soda and ice. 'Billy'll have a pint, too,' said Bradford.

O'Brien went to the bar and Shepherd sat down. Bradford took out a pack of Silk Cut and stuck one into his mouth. 'Smoke?' he asked.

'No,' said Shepherd. 'Yes,' he corrected himself. He grinned awkwardly. 'It's a long story.'

'Giving up?'

'Just starting,' said Shepherd. He took one of Bradford's cigarettes and Bradford lit it for him with a battered Zippo. 'Martin says you're working in Iraq.'

'Yeah, bloody madhouse it is too. American contractors riding around like cowboys, armed to the teeth and acting like they're in the movies. I tell you, you've more chance of being shot by a trigger-happy Yank than you have of being blown up by an insurgent.'

'What are you doing out there?'

'Security,' said Bradford. 'Escorting clients to and from the airport, making sure that their homes and workplaces are secure. Babysitting basically. But it pays well.'

'Yeah, Martin was saying.'

'He said you were out there a while back, when Geordie Mitchell got killed.'

'Yeah. It was a mess. Did you know him?'

'Knew of him, but never met him.'

'He was a good guy,' said Shepherd. 'Sniper killed him. Wrong place, wrong time.' He rubbed his shoulder. A sniper had shot him, too, while he was with the SAS in Afghanistan. Like Geordie, he'd been in the wrong place at the wrong time, but unlike Geordie, the sniper's bullet hadn't killed him and he'd been helicoptered to an army hospital before he'd bled to death. Geordie had been hit in the head and had died instantly.

As O'Brien returned with a tray of drinks, the door to the men's room opened and Billy Bradford walked out. Shepherd did a double-take. The brothers were twins. O'Brien laughed. 'They're something, aren't they?'

Shepherd introduced himself and Billy sat down beside his brother. Other than their clothing, the two men were identical. Billy wore black jeans and a leather bomber jacket. 'Martin neglected to tell me you were twins,' said Shepherd.

'We had a lot of fun with them in the Regiment,' said O'Brien. He tapped Jack's arm. 'Remember those Yanks, the hard-as-nails Navy Seals?'

Jack laughed. 'They never sussed us, did they?'

O'Brien grinned at Shepherd. 'These Navy Seals came to Hereford for some joint training exercises. All muscle and not much up top, truth be told. They were so bloody gung-ho it was laughable. Every exercise was a competition and teamwork went out of the window. Anyway, they kept asking us what the hardest SAS endurance test was. So we told them.'

'The Fan Dance?'

'Exactly,' said O'Brien. 'The Fan Dance.'

Pen y Fan was the tallest peak in the Brecon Beacons, where the SAS put its recruits through selection training. It was a shade under three thousand feet up to its stony exposed plateau and the Fan Dance involved running up to the top fully loaded with kit and rifle, running down the other side, then back up and down again. It was a killer exercise that would test the fittest soldier.

'Anyways, they nagged and nagged to go on the Fan Dance, and said they wanted to go up against our fittest guy.' O'Brien's grin widened. 'We told them that was Jack. They reported at the bottom of Pen y Fan, nice and early. Jack was there with full endurance kit, an eighty-pound bergen, and his rifle, bright-eyed and bushy-tailed. The eighty-pound kit got the Seals hot and bothered because it's about twice the weight of theirs. Jack said no problem because he'd been eating his spinach. That pissed off the Seals so they started stuffing rocks into their bergens to make up the weight.' O'Brien took a long pull on his pint. 'So, we got them started and they went haring up the hill like the proverbial bats. Jack brought up the rear, taking it nice and slow. As soon as the Seals were out of sight, Jack came back down.'

'Because Billy was already at the summit,' said Shepherd.

O'Brien made a gun of his hand and pointed it at Shepherd. 'Got it in one,' he said. 'Billy'd been jumping up and down to work up a sweat, so he was panting like crazy when the Seals came charging up. They couldn't believe it. So they went hurtling down the far side, doing that strange grunting thing they do. Hoooh-hah!'

'Hoooh-hah!' echoed Jack and Billy.

'By this time we'd put Jack on a motorbike and taken him by road to the far side of the hill. When they got there he waved and asked them what'd kept them.' O'Brien slapped the table with the flat of his hand. 'Now they were fighting mad. Sweating like pigs, aching all over, they turned around and went storming back up the hill. They got to the top in record time and, of course, Billy was there to meet them, sitting on a rock and having a brew.'

'I offered them a cup but they said something very disrespectful about my mother and went hurtling down the hill,' said Billy. 'Hoooh-hah!'

'They broke pretty much every record for the Fan Dance, but when they got to the bottom and found Jack stretched out on a lounger with a cocktail in his hand, they still didn't get it. We never heard any more cracks about how superfit they were, and they went back to the States still scratching their heads.'

The four men laughed and drained their glasses. O'Brien went to the bar and returned with fresh drinks. 'Okay, here's the story,' said Shepherd. 'I've been told that a Palestinian hitman's got hold of my personal details. I don't have a photograph or a description, just a name, Hassan Salih, which means nothing. He uses a whole raft of names.'

'Raghead?' said Billy.

'Palestinian,' said Shepherd, 'but he has passports for all sorts of nationalities. Salih is a hitman, one of the best. He knows where I live and there's an outside chance that he might come looking for me.'

'There's a contract out on you?' asked Jack.

Shepherd shook his head. 'There's a contract out on the woman I work for, but while he's been sniffing around her he's come up with my details.'

'I've got to be honest. I don't see it'll be hard to spot a raghead in Hereford,' said Jack.

'I sure hope not,' said Shepherd, 'but I'd feel a lot happier if you two guys would babysit my boy until it's all sorted.'

'Not a problem,' said Jack.

'Plus he's got a very sexy au pair,' said O'Brien.

Billy raised an eyebrow. 'Has he now?'

'Katra,' said Shepherd. 'She's Slovenian.'

'And as fit as a butcher's dog,' said O'Brien.

'This gets better by the minute,' said Jack. 'Is she single?'

'Please don't take away my au pair,' said Shepherd. 'My home would fall apart without her. How are you guys fixed for guns?'

'Not a problem,' said Jack.

'It's an outside chance that anything will happen, but if it does the guy's a pro and he'll be tooled up.'

'We'll be carrying,' said Billy.

'Silencers would be a good idea,' said Shepherd. 'We've got neighbours.'

'No hand grenades, then,' said Jack, with a straight face.

The men had another round of drinks, then drove to Shepherd's house. Shepherd went with O'Brien while the Bradford twins followed in their black Range Rover.

Liam was in the kitchen eating fish fingers and chips when Shepherd opened the front door. 'Dad!' he shouted, and hurtled down the hallway to hug his father. Shepherd picked him up and swung him around. Liam screwed up his face. 'You smell of smoke.'

'I'm sorry about that.'

'Are you smoking?'

'I have to, for a while. It's part of my cover.'

'Smoking gives you cancer.'

'I know,' said Shepherd. 'Have you been behaving?'

'Sure,' said Liam.

'That's good, because I've a present for you in the car.'

'What is it?' asked Liam, excitedly.

Shepherd put him down. 'Say hello to your uncle Martin first.'

'Hi, Uncle Martin,' said Liam. 'Are you staying, Dad? Can we go fishing tomorrow?'

Shepherd ruffled his son's hair. 'Flying visit, Liam, I'm sorry.'

Liam's face fell. 'It's always a flying visit. When are you coming home?'

'Just a few more days.'

'You always say that, and it never is,' said Liam. A crafty smile lit his face. 'Can I have a dog?'

'What?'

'A dog. Can we get a dog? That way when you're not here I can play with it.'

'Maybe,' said Shepherd. 'Hang on, what are you saying? If you get a dog, you won't miss me so much.'

'I'll still miss you. But I'll have something to play with. What sort can I have? A red setter?'

'We'll see,' said Shepherd.

'But I am definitely getting a dog?'

'You're starting to nag me now,' said Shepherd.

'I won't nag if I know I'm getting a dog.'

'Liam . . .'

'Is that a yes? Yes, I'm getting a dog?'

O'Brien grinned. 'At times like this I'm glad I don't have kids,' he said.

'You can have this one if you want,' said Shepherd.

'Dad!' Liam protested.

'I'm joking,' said Shepherd, and introduced the brothers. 'This is Jack, and this Billy.'

Liam's mouth fell open. 'Wow, you're twins!'

They faked astonishment. 'We are?' said Billy.

'No way,' said Jack. 'I'm much better-looking.'

'You're the same,' said Liam. 'That's so cool.'

'Billy and Jack are going to be staying here for a few days,' said Shepherd. 'Just until I get back. Where's Katra?'

They heard footsteps and looked up to see her coming down the stairs in baggy grey cargo pants and a Nike sweat-shirt. Her hair was tied back in a ponytail. She frowned when she saw the four men, but then her face brightened. 'Dan!' she said. 'We weren't expecting you today.'

'It's a flying visit,' said Liam.

'Do you all want coffee?' asked Katra, and smiled when she recognised O'Brien. 'Oh, hi, Martin,' she said. 'Long time no see.'

O'Brien winked at her. Then Katra did a double-take. 'They're twins,' Liam explained. 'Jack and Billy.'

'I'm Jack,' said Billy.

'I'm Billy,' said Jack.

'Leave the girl alone,' warned O'Brien, 'and drop the Tweedledum and Tweedledee routine.' He grinned at Katra and cuffed Billy. 'He's Billy.'

'How can you tell them apart?' asked Katra.

'Billy's the ugly one,' O'Brien told her.

'Ignore them,' said Shepherd. 'Can you make us coffee while I show Billy and Jack around the house? Liam, finish your dinner.'

Katra headed for the kitchen with Liam in tow. Billy and Jack watched her go.

'Slovenian, huh?' said Billy.

'Pretty,' said Jack.

'Guys, please don't even think about it,' said Shepherd.

Richard Yokely had set his cellphone to silent but it vibrated in his pocket to let him know he had received an SMS. He took it out and flipped it open. The message was from Dean Hepburn at the NSA. 'Phone dead. Last location Little Venice, London.'

Yokely closed his phone and cursed. So Salih had either removed the Sim card in his phone or destroyed it. Either way Yokely no longer had any way of tracking him.

Salih stopped his rented Ford Mondeo under the railway bridge. A train rattled overhead and pigeons scattered. It was eleven o'clock and he was on time, but the road was deserted. Salih disliked tardiness. There was no excuse for it.

The man he was there to meet was a Yardie thug called Coates. His nickname was 'Fur'. Fur Coates. A stupid pun. Salih couldn't understand the cavalier way the blacks treated their names, as if one's name was a joke, something to be laughed at. Names like Ice T, P. Diddy and Snoop Doggy Dogg'. As far as Salih was concerned, names were chosen by parents, they were special, they had meaning, and they were not to be toyed with. Coates was a drug-dealer who also sold guns. Salih had not met him before but the man had sold several to Hakeem, good weapons at a fair price.

A large black Mercedes with gold wheel rims drove up behind the Mondeo and halted next to him. Throbbing rap music vibrated through Salih's seat. The tinted window rolled down and Salih winced as the music assaulted his eardrums. The driver had sunglasses pushed back on his head and a thick gold chain round his bull neck. He was holding the steering-wheel with two giant hands, each encrusted with chunky gold rings. A younger man was in the passenger seat, his eyes hidden behind wraparound sunglasses, lanky dread-locks hanging around his shoulders. The driver jabbed a finger at Salih, then motioned that he should follow the Mercedes. The window rolled up and the Mercedes drove off.

They went through the streets of Harlesden, past littered pavements and uncared-for houses, past shops with steel shutters down, walls covered with graffiti and tatty hip-hop posters. A police car rushed in the opposite direction, siren wailing.

The Mercedes made a left turn and Salih followed. They drove past an off-licence with barred windows and a book-maker's with posters offering odds on Liverpool's next European Cup game. A group of black teenagers in hooded sweatshirts and gleaming white training shoes looked envi-ously at the Mercedes, then glared at the Mondeo with undis-guised contempt. One made a gun with his hand and pointed it at Salih as he went by.

The Mercedes slowed, then drove down a narrow, unlit alley between two rows of terraced houses. It stopped and Salih parked a few yards behind it. He climbed out of his car. The passenger of the Mercedes walked over to him. 'I'm gonna need to pat you down,' he said, tossing his dreadlocks.

Salih held out his arms to the sides. 'Go ahead,' he said.

The man patted down his arms. 'If I already had a gun, why would I want to buy one?' asked Salih.

'You might want to rip us off,' said Dreadlocks. 'Can't trust anyone these days. You a friend of Hakeem?'

'Yes,' said Salih.

'He's one crazy Arab,' said Dreadlocks, running his hands carefully up and down Salih's legs. 'One day I'm gonna pick up the *Sun* and read that he's blown up a bus or something. You al-Qaeda?'

'No, I'm not al-Qaeda.'

'That Nine Eleven was something, wasn't it?'

'I suppose,' said Salih.

Dreadlocks straightened. 'The black man should learn from you Arabs. No one listens to us, no one cares about the shit in our lives, but everyone's bending down to make life better for you guys. Why? 'Cos they're scared of you. And they're not scared of us. You got the right attitude.' He turned to the Mercedes. 'He's clean, Fur,' he shouted.

Coates popped the boot of the Mercedes and got out. He was a big man, well over six feet six inches tall, with muscled calves that suggested hours in the gym coupled with active steroid use. He cracked his knuckles as he walked, bow-legged, towards Salih.

'You're Coates?' asked Salih.

'That's my name. Don't wear it out.' Coates opened the boot wide. There were three holdalls and a cardboard box inside. 'Hakeem said you wanted a handgun. Untraceable.'

'A Glock, if you have one.'

'Glock 17, if you want it. But it's not cheap.'

'I don't want a cheap weapon, I want a reliable one,' said Salih. 'And I want one that hasn't been used.'

'You've come to the right man,' said Coates. He unzipped the middle holdall. 'I know everything there is to know about guns,' he said. 'Everything and anything.'

'Is that right?' said Salih.

'Ain't nothin' I don't know about firepower,' said Coates, pulling a Glock from the holdall and handing it to Salih.

Salih took the gun and examined it. 'You told Hakeem he

could take a Glock on to an aeroplane because it's made of plastic,' he said.

'That's right,' said Coates. 'You can walk right through a metal detector. Damn thing won't beep or shit.'

'You are wrong,' said Salih. 'Only forty per cent of the Glock is plastic and there are more than enough metal parts to set off a detector. There's the slide and the barrel, and that's before you take into account the ammunition.'

Coates pulled a face as if he had a bad taste in his mouth. 'Seventeen nine-millimetre rounds in the clip,' he said.

'That much is true,' said Salih. 'That's why they call it the Glock 17.' He checked the action of the gun. 'Do you have the suppressor?'

Coates frowned. 'Say what?'

'The silencer,' said Salih, patiently. 'Hakeem should have told you that I wanted a silencer.' Salih ejected the magazine. It was full. He slotted it back into the butt.

'Yeah, man, 'course,' said Coates. He reached into the holdall and pulled out a bulbous metal suppressor, which was almost as long as the gun itself.

Salih took it and screwed it into the barrel of the Glock.

'It's good, yeah?' said Coates.

'It's adequate,' said Salih. 'How much?'

'The gun, the silencer and the seventeen in the clip, seven hundred.'

'Has it been fired?'

'No way, man,' said Coates.

'You are sure?'

'Sure I'm sure,' said Coates.

Salih pointed the gun at the Yardie and pulled the trigger. It made a sound like a balloon bursting. Coates took a step back and his mouth opened in surprise. Blood trickled down his shirt. 'It has now,' said Salih. He pulled the trigger again and the second bullet ripped into the man's chest. As Coates slumped, blood frothing from between his lips, Salih used his left hand to push him into the boot. Dreadlocks was fumbling for something inside his jacket, his mouth opening and closing in panic. Salih shot him twice in the head. Coates was thrashing around in the boot of the car and Salih put another two bullets into his head. He tucked the gun into his belt, lifted Dreadlocks in with Coates and slammed the boot.

Hakeem had been keen to tell Salih about Coates when Salih had asked him about local gun suppliers. Coates sold good guns at fair prices, but he talked too much. Hakeem had heard that Coates had been telling his Yardie friends he'd been selling guns to Muslims, and Hakeem did not want that fact broadcast. He wanted Coates silenced, and Salih was more than happy enough to help. The street at the end of the alley was deserted. High overhead a jetliner flew towards Heathrow. Salih headed back to his car, unscrewing the still-warm silencer from the barrel of the Glock.

Liam was in the garden, kicking a football against the back of the house. Shepherd went out and handed him a Carphone Warehouse carrier-bag. 'I forgot to give you your present,' he said.

'What is it?'

'Why don't you look?' said Shepherd.

Liam opened the bag. 'A Nokia!'

'It's the N73 music edition with a one-gigabyte memory chip,' said Shepherd. 'I've no idea what that means but the girl who sold it to me said it was what all the kids wanted, these days.'

'Thanks, Dad!'

'I've put my number in it so you can call or text me whenever you want, okay?'

'Cool!'

O'Brien appeared at the kitchen door. 'We'd better be off, Spider.'

'Coming,' said Shepherd.

'Am I in trouble, Dad?' asked Liam.

'No, of course not. Why do you ask?'

'Jack and Billy are bodyguards, aren't they?'

'They're here to take care of you, that's all.'

'But that's what Katra does.'

Shepherd didn't want to lie to his son, but he didn't want to worry him either. 'I just want to make sure you're safe,' he said.

'Why wouldn't I be safe?'

'You *are* safe, Liam. It's just I feel better knowing that Billy and Jack are here.'

Liam looked at the ground. 'You're coming back, right?'

'Of course I am.' He bent down and hugged his son. 'Everything's okay, Liam, I promise.' He kissed the boy's cheek. He wanted to say more, but couldn't think of the right words. He didn't really expect whoever was after Charlotte Button or Richard Yokely to target his family, but if the killer had accessed Button's phone records there was a possibility, no matter how remote, that he would identify Shepherd and where he lived. Billy and Jack were an insurance policy, nothing more. But that wasn't something he could explain to a ten-year-old. 'I'll call you when I get to Belfast.'

O'Brien drove Shepherd back to Birmingham airport. He kept slightly above the speed limit and moved out of the way whenever a sales rep with a deadline to meet hared by in a company car.

'Thanks for fixing up the boys,' said Shepherd.

'Where would you be if I wasn't around to pull your nuts out of the fire?' said O'Brien.

'I'm not arguing,' said Shepherd. 'But I could do with another favour.'

'Why am I not surprised?'

'Charlotte Button's going to need protecting.'

O'Brien frowned. 'I thought she was a big girl – former spook, right? She must know all about personal protection.'

'She doesn't know she's in the firing line.'

O'Brien's frown deepened. 'That makes no sense,' he said.

'Remember Yokely? The American we met in Baghdad?'

'The secret spook? Guy with tassels on his shoes?'

'Yeah. He tipped me off. Yokely doesn't want to tell her. He reckons if she knows she'll have to tell her bosses and they'll have no choice other than to make her do a Salman Rushdie. That'll be the end of her career and her family life.'

'As opposed to what? The end of her life?'

'It's early days,' said Shepherd. 'This bastard Salih doesn't know much about her yet. He's still at the gathering-intel stage. And, like the twins said, he's a Palestinian so he won't be too difficult to spot.'

'So why not tell her but make sure she doesn't pass it on to her bosses?'

'She's not like you and me. She won't bend the rules,' said Shepherd. 'And she'll want to protect her family.'

'That should be her choice, shouldn't it?'

Shepherd shook his head. 'Even if SOCA put her and her family under full police protection, they'll get her eventually. The guy who's paying this assassin has enough money to keep sending people until the job's done.'

'You want me to shadow her without her knowing?' O'Brien grimaced. 'Spider, shadowing someone like Charlie Button round the clock would take three seven-man teams, plus a minimum of three vehicles and two bikes.'

'It wouldn't be surveillance,' said Shepherd. 'We're not looking to see what she does, only to make sure Salih doesn't get close to her. The way I see it he's a pro, which means he'll be watching her before he strikes. So you'll be looking for him looking for her. I'll have a good idea of where she is.'

'But if she's shuttling between London and Belfast, she'll spot a tail on the plane.'

'So you'll need a couple of good guys in Belfast, and another in London,' said Shepherd. 'Plus a fourth watching her house. Guys who know what they're doing.'

'You don't want much, do you?'

Shepherd punched O'Brien's shoulder. 'I know what I'm asking, Martin,' he said, 'and I know who I'm asking.'

Salih flashed his headlights and Tariq waved, then headed for the car. He was wearing a shiny leather jacket, tight Versace jeans and wraparound sunglasses. 'You look like a pimp,' muttered Salih.

Tariq's mouth opened in surprise. 'This jacket cost six hundred pounds,' he said.

'Lesson number one,' said Salih. 'You dress to blend in, not to stand out. Lose the hair gel, lose the glasses, lose the gold chain round your neck. Lose everything that people can use to identify you. Wear mid-range high-street clothes. Not too cheap, not too expensive. Wear shoes or workboots, not expensive trainers.'

'I'll remember,' said Tariq.

'Drive a mid-range car, blue or grey. Don't speed, don't drive aggressively, do nothing to attract attention to yourself. Don't smile too much, don't frown, don't talk too much, don't talk too little. Fly economy, not first class, stay in three-star hotels, not five. Blend.'

'I understand,' said Tariq.

'I am putting a lot of faith in you, Tariq.'

'I will do whatever you ask,' said Tariq.

'Open the glove box. You'll find an envelope. Take it out.'

Tariq did as he was told.

'Inside that envelope is the name of a man and an address in Hereford. There is also the telephone number of the house. And five thousand pounds. I want you to kill the man, if he is there.'

Tariq frowned. 'Is there a photograph of him?'

'No.'

'You watch the house, see who comes and goes. You find out if the man is there. If he is, you kill him. If he is not, you find out who else is in the house. If there is a wife or child, you kill them.' Salih pointed at the glove box. 'There is a gun in there. With a silencer. There are eleven rounds in the magazine. That will be more than you need. Get in close, to within six feet. Put at least two bullets in the chest and one in the head. Wear gloves. When you have finished, drop the gun.'

'Drop the gun?'

'It's untraceable. There's no need to hide it. Use a hire car. Keep a change of clothes in the boot. Drive to an area where you will not be disturbed, remove your outer clothing and burn it. Change into fresh clothes and return the car.'

Tariq reached into the glove box and took out a leather case. He reached for the zip.

'Not here,' said Salih. 'Do not open the case unless you're wearing gloves. Do not touch the gun unless you're wearing gloves. Do not touch the magazine or the bullets unless you're wearing gloves. The tiniest flake of skin or drop of sweat could identify you.'

'I understand,' said Tariq.

'Buy another pay-as-you-go Sim card,' said Salih. 'Phone me just before you do it. Then call me once you're clear of the area. Once you've made the second phone call, destroy the Sim card.'

Tariq nodded. 'I won't let you down,' he said.

'I know you won't,' said Salih.

Charlotte Button had taken a suite at the Europa Hotel, which, during the Troubles, had acquired the unenviable reputation of being the most-bombed hotel in the world. These days, it was just one of Belfast's thriving luxury hotels and was full of tourists and businessmen. She had booked in under another name and hadn't told anyone where she was staying, so when her phone rang at nine that evening she assumed someone on the hotel staff was calling her. She was wrong. 'Long time no hear,' said a voice. 'How's Belfast?'

It was Patsy Ellis, her former boss at MI5's International

Counter-terrorism Branch. She had long been Button's mentor and had suggested that she take the job with SOCA. 'Raining, as usual,' said Button.

'When are you back in the Big Smoke?'

'Tomorrow morning,' said Button. 'Is everything okay?'

'We need a face-to-face, darling. Shall we say the wine bar, eight or thereabouts?'

'See you there,' said Button.

She put down the phone, worried. It had been three months since she'd seen Ellis, and that had been a social lunch. A glass of Chardonnay each, salad, and an hour of gossip. But this phone call had been as far from social as it was possible to get. Ellis hadn't identified herself or the place where they were to meet. And by saying 'eight or thereabouts' she had told Button to subtract two hours from the meeting time. Standard tradecraft. Which meant Ellis was concerned that someone might be listening in.

The display of Shepherd's pay-as-you-go mobile phone flashed. He had set it to silent and when he checked the display he saw it was Yokely. He went into the back garden to take the call. 'I took on board what you said about not using your cover phone,' said Yokely.

'Cheers,' said Shepherd.

'Have you been reading the English papers?'

'I've been rushed off my feet the last couple of days.'

'Hereford and back, I gather.'

'Have you been spying on me, Richard?'

'Just think of me as your guardian angel,' said Yokely. 'I don't know why you're so suspicious of me, Dan. I really do have your best interests at heart.'

'What do you want?' asked Shepherd. 'Why are you so interested in my reading habits?'

'Viktor Merkulov was pulled out of the Regent's Canal this morning. He'd been knifed but his wallet and phone were still on him so it wasn't a mugging.'

'What's that got to do with me?'

'Merkulov was working for Salih. He's a former KGB spook.'

'You don't think I did it, do you?'

Yokely chuckled. 'You didn't go near London.'

'Are your friends at the NSA tracking me?' asked Shepherd.

Yokely ignored the question. 'You weren't in Little Venice, but Salih was. And shortly afterwards he ditched his Sim card.'

'Why would he kill the Russian?'

'Because I'd turned Merkulov. He must have found out.'

'So now we've lost all track of him? Is that what you're telling me?'

'For the moment. But we've a good idea of where he's been.'

'Belfast?'

'No, he's not crossed the water yet. But he's been to Berkshire and Surrey.'

Shepherd's fingers tightened on the phone until his knuckles were white. Surrey was where Charlie lived.

'Spider, are you there?'

Shepherd realised he'd been holding his breath. 'I heard you.'

'I had my NSA people talk to their contacts in the UK and they pinned down where Salih went before he threw his Sim card away.'

'And you're saying he was at Charlie's house?'

'He went to Windsor, where her husband works. And Virginia Water. He was only in the area for a couple of hours, then went back to London.'

'Why would he be checking out her husband?'

'I'd only be guessing, Dan.'

'What about Hereford? Did he go anywhere near my home?'

'There's a definite negative on that.'

Shepherd relaxed a little. 'Can you put out an alert for Salih?'

'I can do that, sure. I can get the FBI liaison at the embassy to do it through SOCA, but even if I do, you know that Ireland leaks like a sieve, North and South. The ferries are a nightmare at the best of times and there's no need to show passports when travelling from the mainland to Northern Ireland.'

'Do you have a photograph yet?'

'I'm afraid not,' said Yokely. 'He stays under the radar, this guy. If he's travelled to the States he's done it under a different name, and none of the countries he's visited under the aliases we have take pictures at point of entry. But we're working on it.'

'Let me know as soon as you get anything, will you?'

'No problem,' said Yokely. 'No one's keener than I am to get this guy, Spider. It's me he's trying to kill, remember. Me and Charlotte.'

'You're a big boy, you can take care of yourself,' said Shepherd. 'It's collateral damage I'm worried about.'

The wine bar where Patsy Ellis wanted to meet was on the fringes of Covent Garden. Button spent half an hour wandering through crowds of tourists, checking she wasn't being followed, and assumed that Ellis would do the same. A man in a top hat and tails was balancing on stilts and juggling flaming torches. Button watched him for a while, then tossed a pound coin into a yellow plastic bucket.

When she walked into the wine bar, Ellis was at a corner table, two glasses in front of her. She stood up as Button came over and they hugged. 'I thought we'd try the Pinot Grigio,' said Ellis.

'So long as there's alcohol in it, I'm a happy bunny,' said Button. She sipped appreciatively. 'It's good.'

'You've got time to eat, I hope?'

'On my tab or yours?'

Ellis laughed. 'I've got the bigger budget,' she said. 'But after you've heard what I have to say, maybe you'll want to treat me.' Her face was serious now. 'You've got an admirer, Charlie, and not in a good way.'

'I'm all ears.'

Ellis reached into her handbag and passed across a surveillance photograph of a heavy-set man with a square face and a pig-like nose. 'Viktor Merkulov. Former KGB, hard man of the Seventh Directorate,' said Ellis. 'Switched over to the Sluzhba Vneshney Razvedki, then went freelance. Now he works for the highest bidder. Surveillance and intelligence, mainly. Or, rather, he used to work for the highest bidder.'

'Used to?'

'Mr Merkulov is no longer with us. He was fished out of the Regent's Canal yesterday with a very sore throat.'

'Can I keep this?' asked Button.

'Of course,' said Ellis. 'But I doubt he's the one interested in you. He was almost certainly acting for someone else. He was looking at your phone, Charlie. Location tracking and call listing. He has contacts with most of the mobile-phone companies and we've been looking at him for the past six months. Alarm bells rang when he made enquiries about your number.'

Button sipped her wine. 'I'm confused, Patsy. Are you telling me this because he was looking at my phone or because he's dead?'

'Good question, darling,' said Ellis. 'We got wind that someone was on your trail a few days ago, and we had a pretty good idea it was Merkulov. But knowing and proving are two different things. It was only when his body was fished out of the canal that we could forget about things like search warrants and took a look round his very well-appointed apartment in St John's Wood. Frankly, we're a bit annoyed at his untimely demise because it was of more use to us having him going about his business. Down the line we might have closed him down, but we were happy enough keeping an eye on what he was doing.'

'Any idea who he was working for?'

'Specifically, no. His clients included the great and the good, the bad and the ugly. He didn't care who he worked for so long as they could afford his fees. Our American cousins used him from time to time, and a couple of less than responsible Sunday newspapers had him on retainer. But we didn't have him under direct surveillance. Merkulov was a pro so it would have taken up too much in the way of resources to do it without him knowing. If he'd realised we were on to him, he'd have upped and left.'

'So we're none the wiser,' said Button.

'I have a list of clients we know about,' said Ellis. 'Cast your eyes over them, see if anyone rings a bell.' She passed Button an envelope.

Button pulled out a folded sheet of paper and scanned the list. She recognised several names – a big-time cannabis-dealer based in Amsterdam, a South London gang boss high on SOCA's wish list, half a dozen members of the Russian Mafia, which wasn't surprising, and several Bosnian and Serbian gangsters. Three others were top City financiers and one was a well-known documentary-maker. But she didn't see anyone who might want to cause her any grief.

'That's not an inclusive list by any means,' said Ellis. 'Much of his work is for cash and he's often approached by middle men.'

Button folded the sheet of paper and put it back into the envelope. 'No one there has it in for me,' she said.

'What about the cases you're working on now?'

'I have a man under cover in Belfast, but it's a murder case and I've got a very low profile.'

'IRA? Unionists? Could they be after you?'

Button smiled. 'I'm SOCA now, Patsy, totally non-political.'

'But you were in Belfast for three years on counter-terrorism, back in the day,' said Ellis. 'They've got long memories, the Provos.'

'As I said, I'm very low profile there, and why would they

bother tracking my phone? If they already know I'm in the city a couple of guys in ski masks could pay me a visit and that'd be that. The fact that whoever it is had to use Merkulov suggests they don't know much about me.'

'Agreed,' said Ellis.

'Do you know what they wanted to know?'

'Merkulov's contact in the phone company has provided him with a list of incoming and outgoing calls and texts, and the location of your phone.'

Button frowned. 'How could he have got my number?'

'It's your work phone, right?'

'That means he has to have got it from someone I work with, doesn't it?'

'Not necessarily,' said Ellis. 'You could have been scanned. Or he could have taken the number off someone else's mobile.'

'Do you think I should be worried?' asked Button.

Ellis smiled sympathetically. 'I'm not sure how to answer that, Charlie. Merkulov wasn't cheap, so whoever was paying him must have a good reason. But the fact that they have to ask for your location means they can't know much about you.'

'Which begs the question, why would a stranger want to know where I am? And why would they want a list of my calls?'

'I suppose it could be personal,' said Ellis.

'I'm too busy to be having an affair.'

'I'm glad to hear it,' said Ellis. 'How's Graham, these days?'

'As busy as always. You don't think he's checking up on me, do you?'

Ellis laid her hand on Button's. 'Don't get paranoid,' she said. 'I was only asking after him. One, he loves you to bits, and two, an estate agent in Surrey wouldn't know how to contact a man like Merkulov. There's no need to worry too much. We know someone's looking at you so we've got the edge.'

'He'll already have passed on the information, presumably?'

'I would assume so.'

'So whoever paid Merkulov knows I was in Belfast, and has a list of all the calls to and from my mobile.'

'Which, frankly, is no biggie. You can change your Sim card, and keep away from Belfast if necessary.'

'I'm running an operative,' said Charlie.

'Someone else can run him,' said Ellis. 'Or her.'

'It's a he,' she said, 'and it's a sensitive case so I'm not playing hide and seek just because someone's stalking me. But you're right, of course, it's not too serious. Yet.'

'And let's be positive. As I said, whoever it is, if he had to pay Merkulov for information he couldn't have known that much about you in the first place.'

'You always look on the bright side, don't you?' said Button. 'Or are you just trying to make me feel better?'

'How long have I known you, darling?' said Ellis. She raised her glass.

'Too long,' laughed Button. They clinked.

'Are you happy at SOCA?'

'Funnily enough, I am. They're not as cerebral as Five, that's for sure, but they get the job done.'

'You won't be there for ever, you know. You're far too valuable to be playing cops and robbers.'

Button sipped her wine. 'Nice to know I'm wanted.'

'You are, very much so. At some point I'm moving up, and when that happens there'll be a slot at the Joint Terrorism Analysis Centre.'

'I've only just got my feet under the table at SOCA.'

'It's a stepping-stone, Charlie. Don't think of it as anything other than that.'

Button picked up the menu. 'So, are we eating?'

Shepherd sipped his coffee as he looked out of the sitting-room window. His mobile rang. It was Button. 'Good morning, Charlie,' he said. 'Are you in Belfast?'

'I'm at home, actually,' she said. 'I've a couple of meetings and will probably be back in Belfast tonight.'

A black Vauxhall Vectra crawled up the hill towards Shepherd's house.

'But don't worry, Amar's listening in,' said Button.

'I feel like I'm in the *Big Brother* house,' said Shepherd, 'but without the chance of eviction.' Two big men were in the car, peering at the house numbers. There were no markings on the vehicle but it was obviously police. Less than a year old, with a radio aerial on the back, no dealer stickers. Official transport. Shepherd realised it was the car he'd seen when he'd been in Elaine's house, searching the attic.

'The reason I'm calling is that someone's just run a check on Jamie Pierce. Have you come across a Superintendent John Maplethorpe?'

'He's a friend of Elaine's,' said Shepherd, 'Robbie's best man at their wedding.'

'Well, he ran a check on you through the Police National Computer.'

'Probably just looking out for Elaine,' said Shepherd. The car stopped outside her house and the two men climbed out. 'She's got visitors,' said Shepherd. 'I'll call you back.'

He cut the connection and moved to the side of the window so that the two men couldn't see him from the road. They walked towards the front door, their eyes watchful. They were well over six feet, one a little taller than the other, in their mid-forties and slightly overweight. They pressed the bell. Shepherd picked up the financial brochures Elaine had given him and hurried outside. As he went across the garden, she opened her front door and began to talk to the men.

'Hi, Elaine, is everything okay?' Shepherd asked.

'Hi, Jamie. They're police. At least, they say they are.'

'Who are you?' said the taller man. He had a strong Scottish accent.

'I'm a neighbour,' said Shepherd, and indicated his house.

'We'd like to talk to Mrs Carter, if that's okay with you,' said the second. He was broad-shouldered with a hairline that had receded more than half-way across his skull. He also spoke with a Scottish accent, probably Glaswegian.

Shepherd looked at Elaine. 'I can stay if you want,' he said. Elaine nodded. 'Please.'

'We don't need an audience,' said the second man, more aggressively this time.

'Can I see your warrant cards, please?' said Shepherd.

'What?'

'Your warrant cards. I want to see them.'

'Are you a lawyer?'

'No, I'm not a lawyer. But you two are claiming to be police officers and you sound Scottish to me. This is Belfast so it's a fair enough request to ask you to identify yourselves.'

The two men looked at each other and the taller one nodded. They pulled out small black wallets and flipped them open. Shepherd peered at the two warrant cards. The taller man was Colin Staniford, a detective inspector. His companion was Sergeant Stevie Ferguson. Both warrant cards had been issued by the Strathclyde Police.

'You see, we've got a problem right there,' said Shepherd, pointing at the cards. 'You don't have jurisdiction here.'

'You sure you're not a lawyer?' said Staniford.

'I'm a website designer,' said Shepherd. 'But that's not the point. The point is that you two are from Strathclyde. And this is Northern Ireland.'

'We're on secondment to the Police Service of Northern Ireland,' said Staniford.

'Do you have something to back that up?' said Shepherd.

'What?'

Shepherd gestured at the warrant card in Staniford's hand. 'That just says you're a police officer. It doesn't say you have the right to be in here asking questions.'

'And you are?' asked Staniford.

'Pierce,' said Shepherd. 'Jamie Pierce.'

'And you live next door?'

'That's right.'

'What's your date of birth, Mr Pierce?'

'Are you planning to send me a birthday card?'

'I'd just like to know your date of birth.'

'That's none of your business,' he said.

'You won't tell me your date of birth?'

'I won't help you run a check on me, that's for sure.'

Staniford nodded slowly. 'Okay,' he said. He pulled a wallet from his trouser pocket and handed Shepherd a business card. It bore his name and rank, the crest of the Police Service of Northern Ireland and the address of the Historical Enquiries Team in Lisburn, County Antrim.

'I haven't heard of the Historical Enquiries Team,' said Shepherd.

'We're tasked with investigating deaths that occurred during the Troubles,' said Staniford.

Shepherd held up the card. 'Can I keep this?'

'Go ahead,' said Staniford. He looked at Elaine. 'Do you mind if we ask you a few questions now, Mrs Carter?'

'Please, come in,' she said. They followed her down the hall to the sitting room. Shepherd closed the door and went after them. Ferguson took off his overcoat, draped it over the arm of the sofa and sat down, Staniford next to him. The sergeant fished a notebook out of his overcoat pocket and rested it on his knee. Shepherd positioned himself in an armchair at an angle to the men. 'Can I get you tea or coffee?' asked Elaine. She stood by the fireplace, her arms crossed defensively. The picture of her with Robbie and Timmy was at her left shoulder. Shepherd wondered if she'd consciously chosen to stand next to it or if it was coincidence.

'We're fine,' said Staniford. 'Please, Mrs Carter, sit down. We're just here for a chat.'

Elaine went to the chair where Shepherd was sitting and perched on the arm. 'How can I help you?' she said.

'Did your husband have any diaries, Mrs Carter?' asked Staniford.

Elaine's brow furrowed. 'Any what?'

'Diaries. Work diaries. Or notebooks. We're trying to pin down his movements during the five years before he died.'

'Are you here about Robbie's murder?'

Shepherd realised she hadn't answered the detective's question. She must know about the diaries in the trunk in the attic, which meant that she was deliberately evading it.

'It's the years prior to his death that we're interested in, actually,' said Staniford.

'Why?' asked Elaine.

'Just part of our enquiries,' said Staniford.

'But Robbie's death has been resolved,' said Elaine. 'The men were found guilty and sentenced. We know who did it. Why would you reopen the investigation?'

'It's part of an ongoing investigation, Mrs Carter,' said Ferguson.

'Investigation into what?' asked Elaine.

'I'm not at liberty to reveal that,' said Ferguson.

'You're here to rubbish Robbie, aren't you? You're trying to prove that he did something wrong.'

'Please calm down, Mrs Carter,' said Staniford.

'Don't you tell me what to do,' snapped Elaine. 'I don't know you but I knew Robbie and what sort of cop he was. What do you think he did?'

'We're not saying he did anything,' said Staniford. He glanced at Ferguson.

'It's an ongoing investigation, Mrs Carter, that's all we can tell you,' said Ferguson.

'It sounds to me as if you're investigating her husband, not his murder,' said Shepherd.

Staniford put up a hand to silence him. 'Mr Pierce, I'm okay with you being here, but I'm not prepared to have you impede our investigation.'

'I'm not impeding anything,' said Shepherd. 'If you're here in connection with Robbie Carter's murder, that's all well and good. But if you've another agenda, it might be that Mrs Carter needs her solicitor present during questioning.'

'The more you talk, the more you sound like a lawyer, Mr Pierce,' said Ferguson, clearly annoyed.

'I'm just someone who knows his rights,' said Shepherd. 'Presumably you have Mr Carter's work diaries.'

'They're missing,' said Ferguson. 'In fact, there's a lot of paperwork gone missing from Special Branch. And several of the men who worked with Robbie Carter seem to have developed either amnesia or early Alzheimer's.'

'Have you spoken to John Maplethorpe?' asked Elaine. 'He was Robbie's boss. He's a superintendent now.'

'I can't reveal details of our investigation, I'm afraid,' said Ferguson.

'John can speak for Robbie,' said Elaine. 'They were tight. John was a rock after Robbie was killed.'

'Again, who I am or am not talking to is not something I can discuss with you,' said Ferguson.

'Get them out of my house, Jamie,' said Elaine. She lit a cigarette with trembling hands.

'What specifically is it you want from Mrs Carter?' asked Shepherd.

'I already said. Any diaries or notebooks Inspector Carter brought home, especially during the late eighties. Or any office paperwork.'

'Do you have anything like that?' Shepherd asked her. She shook her head. Shepherd looked back at the two detectives. 'That's that, then. Unless you've anything else you want to ask.'

'That about covers it for the moment,' said Ferguson, his eyes boring into Shepherd's.

Staniford pulled out his wallet and offered a business card to Elaine. 'Just on the off-chance, Mrs Carter, if you do find anything, please give us a call.'

'Stuff your card where the sun doesn't shine,' she spat.

Ferguson picked up his overcoat. 'Thank you for your time, Mrs Carter.' He nodded at Shepherd. 'I'm sure we'll meet again some time, Mr Pierce.'

'I'll look forward to it,' said Shepherd.

Shepherd led the two detectives into the hallway and let them out. When he came back into the room Elaine offered him a cigarette. 'Bastards,' she said.

'They're just doing their job,' said Shepherd, 'but you've got to stand up to them or they'll walk right over you.'

'You sound like you know cops.' She blew smoke at the ceiling.

'I watch a lot of cop shows,' he said, 'but you were married to one, so you must understand where they're coming from, right?'

She grimaced. 'Those two aren't concerned with policing,' she said bitterly. 'They're political. They're here to rubbish the work the RUC did during the years when they were all that stood between us and anarchy. Do you know how many members of the RUC were killed during the Troubles? Well, I do, Jamie. Three hundred and three. An average of one murder a month throughout the Troubles.' She jerked a thumb at the door. 'You think they know that? You think they care?'

'I'm sorry,' said Shepherd.

'It's not your fault,' she said. 'You've nothing to apologise for.' She gestured with her cigarette. 'But them, they're outsiders brought in by the British Government to shit on the work Robbie and the rest gave their lives for. They even changed the name of the force, Jamie. What the hell was wrong with "Royal Ulster Constabulary"? It was a name to be proud of, a name with a history that meant something. What is it now? The Police Service of Northern Ireland,' she sneered, and took another drag on her cigarette. 'Those bastards are here to prove that the RUC were the villains. Forget about the thousands the IRA murdered, forget about the bombings, the shootings and kneecappings. The IRA are the heroes because they put down their guns. And if they're the heroes there have to be villains, and who do you think's being lined up to play that role?'

She sagged on to the sofa, tears trickling down her cheeks.

'I guess it's part of the Peace Process,' said Shepherd.

She shook her head vehemently. 'It's got fuck all to do with peace,' she said. 'I want peace, of course I do. We all do. No one wanted the killing except the psychopaths in the paramilitaries. But the way to do it was to draw a line and say, "We move on from there." But that's not what happened, Jamie. John Major and then Tony Blair just caved in and gave the IRA everything they wanted. The British want rid of Northern Ireland, and everything they're doing is a step in that direction. Small steps, maybe, but the end result is that we're slowly but surely being sold down the line. They open the prisons and release the murders and bombmakers. They castrate the RUC. McGuinness and Adams are invited around for tea at Number Ten.' She stabbed out the cigarette in the ashtray. 'And what do I get? They want to dig up Robbie and piss on his corpse.'

She brushed away the tears with the back of her hand. Shepherd sat next to her and put his arm round her. She rested her head on his shoulder. Shepherd knew that her tears weren't for the political situation, but for her husband. It was Robbie she missed. He kissed the top of her head, and smelt her hair, hating himself for using her grief to get close to her but knowing that was exactly what he had to do. 'It's all right, love,' he said softly.

'It's not fair,' she sobbed.

'I know,' he said.

'They killed him, Jamie. They shot him dead in front of me and there was nothing I could do.'

She shuddered, and Shepherd held her close, smoothing her hair with his right hand. 'I'm sorry, love.'

She turned her face up to him, glistening with tears. 'Jamie . . .'

Shepherd didn't know what to say. There was nothing he could tell her that would ease her pain.

'Kiss me, Jamie. Please.'

Her hand slipped round his neck and she pulled him close, her mouth opening as she pressed her lips to his.

★   ★   ★

Shepherd felt something warm pressing against his back and a hand on his thigh. He opened his eyes and found himself looking at his clothes, piled untidily on an unfamiliar chair in the corner of the room. He closed his eyes again and cursed silently. His assignment had been to get close to Elaine Carter, not to climb into her bed.

'I know you're awake,' she whispered.

'How?'

'Your breathing changed,' she said.

Shepherd rolled over and smiled.

She smiled back. 'Well, this is awkward,' she said.

'It's fine,' he said.

'I don't make a habit of sleeping with the neighbours,' she said. 'Mind you, old man Hutcheson was in his eighties and did smell a bit.'

'I'm sorry,' said Shepherd.

'For what?' she asked. 'What the hell do you have to apologise about?'

'I sort of feel like I took advantage of you.'

Elaine sat up and wrapped the duvet round herself. 'I'm a big girl, Jamie. I don't let people talk me into doing things I don't want to do. Are you thinking you made a mistake, is that it?'

'No, it's not that.'

'What is it, then?'

'Elaine, you were pretty emotional last night, with the cops and everything. I was a shoulder to cry on, I didn't expect . . .'

'That I'd fuck your brains out?'

Shepherd laughed. 'Yeah, you did that right enough.'

'No complaints, then?'

'No complaints.' He sat up and propped his pillow behind his neck. 'Still awkward?'

'A bit.'

'I guess it's been a while, has it?' he said.

'What's been a while?'

'You know . . .'

She smiled mischievously. 'I've no idea what you're talking about.'

'You know, since you . . .'

'Had sex?' She was amazed. 'Do you think I'm a nun?'

Shepherd felt his cheeks flush. 'I just thought . . .'

She arched one eyebrow. 'Yes, Jamie, tell me what you thought.'

'You're making this really hard for me, Elaine.'

Her hand crept along his thigh. 'Hmm, yes, I can see that.'

He shuffled away from her and pushed the duvet down as a barrier between them. 'I'm serious.'

'Are you now?'

'You were upset because they were asking questions about your husband. You still . . . you know . . .'

'Love him?' Elaine sighed. 'Robbie's been dead for a long time, Jamie. Do I still love him? Of course, but it's the memory I love now, not the man. Timmy, too. I love them both as much as I ever did, but they're gone and I'm still here. Robbie's picture is on the mantelpiece because I can't move it. His parents come round every weekend. How could I tell them I've put their boy's picture in a drawer somewhere, locked it away like a dirty secret? I'll never put it away, no matter what happens in my life. The same goes for Timmy. Timmy's my son and will be until the day I die. I saw Robbie die on my kitchen floor and I saw Timmy die in a hospital bed, with tubes in him and a machine beeping. But that doesn't mean my life has stopped.' She pushed away the duvet and reached for him. 'You're not the first man I've slept with since Robbie died, and you probably won't be the last. So don't worry. I'm not a mad widow desperate for a man, much as that might appeal to your adolescent fantasies.'

'Elaine . . .'

'Now, if you tell me I was a one-night stand, I will get upset.'

'You weren't,' said Shepherd.

'I'm so glad to hear that,' she said, rolling on top of him. 'Now prove it.' Her hair cascaded over his face as she kissed him.

It was just before noon when Shepherd got back to his house. He shaved and showered, then changed into a clean polo shirt and jeans. He stared at his reflection as he splashed aftershave on his face. He hadn't planned to sleep with Elaine, and a sexual relationship would just complicate matters. He liked her, there was no question of that, and the sex had been good – better than good. It had been great. Shepherd swore. 'You cannot get too close,' he said to himself. 'She is under investigation. You cannot get too close.' He leant close to the mirror and stared himself in the eye. 'Listen to me, you daft bastard,' he whispered. 'It's going to end in tears if you carry on like this.' His breath fogged on the glass.

He pushed himself away from the mirror, went downstairs and switched on the kettle. He wanted to go for a run, and grinned as he wondered what SOCA's psychologist would make of that – he'd met a woman he really liked and his first instinct after getting out of her bed was to put on his running shoes.

Shepherd went through to the sitting room, sat on the sofa and put his feet on the coffee-table as he dialled Charlotte Button's number. She answered immediately and Shepherd asked what she knew about the Historical Enquiries Team. 'It was set up after the Good Friday Agreement,' said Button. 'There's a squad of about seventy-five officers headed by a guy from the Met. They're split into two teams, one staffed locally by PSNI officers, the other by officers from outside.'

'To ensure impartiality?'

'Horses for courses,' said Button. 'The HET has been tasked with looking at all murders that occurred between 1968 and the signing of the Good Friday Agreement in 1998. Some cases can't be dealt with by former RUC personnel so they've brought in outsiders. Why the sudden interest?'

'Two cops came round to talk to Elaine. They were asking questions about her husband.'

'Curiouser and curiouser. Robbie Carter's murder was cut and dried. There were no loose ends that I'm aware of.'

'They weren't asking about his death. They wanted his work diaries for the late eighties. She wasn't happy.'

'Understandable,' said Button.

'Thing is, she lied to them. They were asking about any diaries he might have kept and she didn't mention the ones in the trunk.'

'Trunk?'

'The trunk where I found the ammunition. There were diaries in there along with photograph albums and stuff. Look, I don't want to sound paranoid, but their visit wasn't part of some grand plan, was it?'

'What are you insinuating, Spider?'

'I just thought it might have been a way of putting her under pressure, a visit from heavy cops.'

'Good cop, bad cop, you mean? Them bad and you good? Spider, do you really think I'd play a game like that?'

'It's a complicated world.'

'It is indeed, but I wouldn't do that to you. You should know better. If I thought outside pressure was a good idea, I'd run it by you first.'

'Okay, I'm sorry,' said Shepherd. 'Doing what I do, you get to suspect everybody's motives. Is there any chance of you finding out what's going on? It occurred to me they might be trying to pin something on Carter.'

'On a dead RUC hero? Is that likely?'

'The dead can't defend themselves,' said Shepherd. 'I just thought you should know what was going on, that's all.'

'It's noted, Spider, but I'm not sure how much I'll be able to find out. I don't want to start alarm bells ringing, but I'll see what I can do. How's it going with Elaine?'

Shepherd's heart skipped a beat. He didn't want to lie to Button but he didn't want to tell her he'd made love to Elaine either. 'She trusts me,' said Shepherd. 'All I've got to do now is abuse that trust.'

'Spider . . .'

'I know, I shouldn't get all bitter and twisted,' said Shepherd. 'But it's a funny old world, isn't it? She's the widow of a dead hero and we're trying to put her away because the men who killed her husband were set free for political reasons. If they'd stayed where they belonged, they'd still be alive.'

'Interesting theory,' said Button. 'Setting them free is what killed them – is that what you're saying?'

'I'm saying that for bastards who shoot coppers' life should mean life, no matter what their politics.'

'No argument there,' said Button, 'but it's not our call.'

Shepherd left the phone on the coffee-table and went back to the kitchen. He made himself a cup of coffee, took it out into the garden with his pay-as-you-go mobile. He phoned Jimmy Sharpe and asked if he knew either Staniford or Ferguson. Sharpe had worked for the Strathclyde force for almost two decades before joining SOCA's undercover unit.

'Colin Staniford, I know,' said Sharpe. 'Good guy, but not averse to giving a villain a slap, if you get my drift.'

'But a straight arrow?'

'Sure, straight as they come,' said Sharpe. 'What's the story?'

'He's been seconded to the Northern Ireland cops, working for a unit clearing up the murders that took place during the Troubles.'

'That sounds right,' said Sharpe. 'He wouldn't take shit from anyone, least of all a Paddy.'

'I can see the racial-awareness courses are paying off.'

'Paddy's an affectionate term, like Yank or sheepshagger,' said Sharpe. 'Not been giving Staniford a hard time, have you?'

'Trying to make an impression on the girl next door, that's all. Thought if I stood up for her she'd see me as a white knight.'

'Just give her one,' said Sharpe.

'You really are in touch with your feminine side, aren't you?'

'I do what I can.'

'What are you up to at the moment? I could do with some help.'

'Worming my way into a marijuana syndicate in East Kilbride,' said Sharpe. 'Spreading lots of cash around, drinking champagne until it runs out of my arse and staying out until it's way past my bedtime. Nothing I can't slip away from for a few days.'

'I need you to find out why he's looking at this woman's husband. He's dead now, murdered by the IRA. His name was Robbie Carter.'

'Cold case?'

'Nah. His killers were caught and sent down. I'm trying to prove that the wife's knocking off the guys who killed her hubby, but Staniford's looking at Carter for something else and I need to know what.'

'So, I just ring Staniford and pick his brains?'

'I was hoping you might fly over and do a face to face. Less obvious.'

'Yeah, right,' said Sharpe, his voice loaded with sarcasm. 'I fly over for a chat, he won't suspect a thing.'

'I was assuming you'd be more circumspect,' said Shepherd. 'Crack on you're working on a case with a Belfast end.'

'Carter, you said?'

'Robbie Carter. Murdered by the IRA on the twenty-eighth of August nineteen ninety-six.'

'I'm on it,' said Sharpe. 'I'll call you for a pint when I'm done.'

'I owe you one, Razor.'

'You owe me another one,' Sharpe corrected him. 'But who's keeping score? Are you okay there?'

'I'm fine. It's just messy, that's all.'

'Northern Ireland's always been messy. Back in the old

days I was a uniform at the Old Firm games and you could feel the hatred there. They're never going to get on, no matter what the politicians say. Catholics and Protestants are natural enemies. Like cats and dogs.'

'With respect, Razor, that's bollocks. People are people.'

'Are you getting all Rodney King on me? Why can't we just get along? Because there's hundreds of years of history and hatred, that's why. Too much bad blood.'

'It's changing, Razor. It's not like it was.'

'Tell you what, Spider, you put on a Rangers shirt and take a walk down the Falls Road. See how far you get.'

'The barriers are down in the city centre. The troops have gone. The IRA has decommissioned its weapons. The UVF has called it a day. It's a different Belfast now.'

'On the surface, maybe,' said Sharpe, 'but if they're sending in cops to investigate sectarian killings, you need a guy like Colin Staniford. The villains in Belfast aren't scared of the local cops, no matter which foot they kick with. You watch your back, you hear?'

'I'll be fine.'

'I mean it, Spider. There's a lot of very hard men in that city, and I'm not just talking about the paramilitaries.' Sharpe cut the connection.

Tariq pulled in at the side of the road and consulted the street map for the twentieth time since he'd left London. The gun and silencer were in the glove box, with a pair of binoculars. He still wasn't sure where and when he was going to kill Daniel Shepherd. He kept having to fight the urge to phone Salih and ask his advice, but he knew he was being tested and that Salih would see any contact as a sign of weakness. Salih hadn't given him a photograph of the man he was supposed to kill. All he had was a name and address. Tariq knew that first he had to check out the house, find out what Shepherd looked like and what car he drove. Then he could decide on the when and where.

He ran his finger along the route to Shepherd's street. It was trembling and he fought to keep his hand steady. If he was shaking now, how would he be when he was pointing his gun at Shepherd? Or at the man's family? He clenched and unclenched his hand, then willed the shaking to stop. He could do what Salih wanted, and once he had proved himself, Salih would teach him everything else he needed to know.

Tariq put the map on the passenger seat. He looked at himself in the rear-view mirror. He had washed out the styling gel and given himself a parting. He was wearing a checked shirt, cargo pants and brown Hush Puppies. He had left his gold chains at home. He bared his teeth and snarled, then grinned. Anyone who saw him would think he was a nonentity, a waiter in an Indian restaurant or a shelf-filler at a corner shop. Nobody would suspect he was a killer. A stone-cold killer. 'I'm going to kill you, Daniel Shepherd,' he said to his reflection. 'I'm going to put a bullet in your head. Then I'm going to kill your family.'

A horn sounded behind him and Tariq jumped. It was a delivery van. The horn sounded again as the van sped by. The driver waved at a woman pushing a pram along the pavement. Tariq's heart was pounding and his hands were shaking again. He put them on the steering-wheel, took a deep breath, held it for a few seconds, then exhaled slowly.

He put the car in gear, had a final look at the map, then pulled away from the kerb. He drove slowly and indicated at every turn, even though there was little traffic. When he reached Shepherd's road he drove slowly until he saw a house number. Shepherd's was five away. Tariq accelerated; he didn't want it to be obvious that he was looking for something. He glanced to his left as he passed the house, a two-storey cottage with a small garden at the front. There was a separate garage, with a dark green Honda CRV and a black BMW SUV parked outside it.

He drove to the end of the road and turned left. He needed

a vantage point, somewhere he could get an overall view of the house and see who came and went. He stopped the car again and reached for the map.

Shepherd's personal mobile rang just before midday. It was Jimmy Sharpe. They arranged to meet at Belfast airport, and an hour later Shepherd was sitting next to his colleague with a cup of cappuccino and an almond croissant in front of him. Sharpe had a wheeled black carry-on case at his feet.

'I don't suppose I can put this trip on expenses, can I?' said Sharpe.

'I'll see you right,' said Shepherd.

'What about all the booze I had to buy to lubricate his tongue last night?' said Sharpe. 'He could drink for Scotland.'

'I'll see you right,' said Shepherd. 'Curry's on me next time we're in London. Now, what did Staniford tell you?'

'It's messy,' said Sharpe, 'and from what he says, it's going to get messier. You know what the Historical Enquiries Team is doing, right?'

'Investigating all the murders that took place during the Troubles.'

'Right. All three thousand two hundred and sixty-eight deaths since nineteen sixty-eight. Every case is being looked at and, where necessary, re-examined. Half of the murders committed during the Troubles are still unsolved. You had Catholics killing Protestants, Protestants killing Catholics, Catholics and Protestants killing the police and security services, and vice versa. The HET team is looking for miscarriages of justice, and at cold cases that still have to be solved.'

'And they've brought in outsiders like Staniford because they won't be tainted by the old regime.'

'Pretty much. HET is made up of two teams, one team made up of outsiders, the other made up of locals, former RUC now PSNI.' He grinned. 'You know they were going to call it the Northern Ireland Police Service until they realised that the newspapers would talk about the bad guys being grabbed by the NIPS?'

'Stick to the point, Razor. You've got a plane to catch.' Shepherd sipped his cappuccino.

'So, HET starts at 'sixty-eight and is working its way to the end of hostilities. The locals are doing the non-controversial cases. Staniford and his colleagues look at the ones that might benefit from an outsider's eye. And they've given Staniford one of the hottest potatoes to deal with.' He paused to make sure he had Shepherd's undivided attention, then leant across the table. 'Back in the late eighties and early nineties, RUC Special Branch was passing information to Loyalist paramilitaries. Information that led directly to the assassination of IRA members. Staniford is trying to identify the officers involved.'

'With a view to prosecution?'

'The powers-that-be want to show they're being even-handed,' said Sharpe. 'If they're investigating murders by the IRA, they want to clear up any RUC-sponsored killings as well.'

Shepherd picked at his croissant. 'That is messy,' he said.

'It gets messier,' said Sharpe. 'Seems that the funding for the RUC's intelligence operations came from our very own MI5.'

'MI5 was funding an RUC operation to use Protestant killers to murder IRA members? If ever there was a case for letting sleeping dogs lie, that would be it, don't you think?'

Sharpe shook his head. 'Nah, the powers-that-be want every case wrapped up so there can't be any comeback down the line that would give either side an excuse to start shooting and bombing again. This is a once-in-a-lifetime chance to get all the dirty laundry washed and hung out to dry.'

'And now Staniford's looking at Robbie Carter's murder?'

'I couldn't press Colin too hard without tipping him off that my interest's personal. But from what he told me, Robbie Carter probably wasn't whiter than white.'

'Oh, shit.' Shepherd sighed.

'Yeah,' said Sharpe. 'Staniford's trying to put Carter in the frame for a number of killings in the late eighties and early nineties, maybe not as the triggerman but as part of an RUC conspiracy.'

'This just gets better and better,' said Shepherd.

'Come on, Spider, you know how murky Ireland's been over the years. Your old mob pretty much ran shoot-to-kill operations all over the North.'

'Allegedly.'

'Aye, allegedly. Well the RUC, allegedly, decided that the odds had swung so heavily against the Loyalists that they were justified in giving them a little support now and then.'

'And how did this come to light?'

Sharpe took a quick look at his watch. There was just over an hour before his flight was due to leave. 'Detective superintendent by the name of Scott Devlin killed himself two years ago. Nothing untoward, he had terminal cancer and the doctors had done all they could. They gave him the phone number of a Macmillan nurse and sent him home to die, basically. Devlin decided there was no point in hanging around so he took a mouthful of water, put his gun in his mouth and pulled the trigger. It wasn't exactly a cry for help.'

Putting a gun in your mouth and pulling the trigger wasn't a guaranteed way of ending your life, but doing it with a mouthful of water meant your head literally exploded. 'He leave a note?' asked Shepherd.

'No. His wife died ten years ago and they had no children. There was no one to leave a note to. It was the gun that triggered the investigation.' He grinned. 'No pun intended.' He pointed at the croissant in front of Shepherd. 'Are you going to finish that?' Shepherd pushed the plate towards him. 'The gun was an automatic, a Browning Hi-power. But it wasn't his official gun. He'd handed that in when he left the service. Turns out that the gun he used to kill himself had been used in the murders of four IRA men.'

Shepherd grimaced. 'Unsolved murders, right?'

'One was, but three were sorted,' said Sharpe, breaking off a piece of croissant and shoving it into his mouth. 'The UFF did the actual killings and eight of their men were sent down for them. All are now out under the Good Friday Agreement. The cops have a pretty good idea who did the fourth but the two guys responsible did a runner to the South and are thought to be OTRs in Limerick.'

'OTRs?'

'On the run. There's several dozen IRA men in the States and Ireland who haven't served any time for their crimes. In theory, they could still be sent down to serve the two-year minimum required under the Good Friday Agreement. Sinn Fein's trying to thrash out a deal with the British Government to allow the OTRs back.'

'Hang on, you're saying the gun was involved in all four killings, but it was different men each time?'

'Exactly,' said Sharpe. 'Which means that the gun went back and forth. It was used in a killing, then given back, used again and returned. Backwards and forwards like a bloody yo-yo.'

'And it ends up with this guy Devlin.'

'The question is, did it end with Devlin or did it start with him? That's what Staniford's looking at. The suspicion is that Devlin was supplying the weapon and the intel, and that the UFF were doing the dirty work.'

'And how does this involve Carter?'

'The second killing took place when Devlin was on holiday with his wife in Spain, ten days after he'd left the country. And Robbie Carter was his aide at the time.'

'So it's circumstantial?'

'Devlin and Carter were tight, from what Staniford's been told. If Devlin was up to something, it's unlikely Carter wouldn't have known about it.'

'Knowing and taking part are two different things, Razor.'

'Assuming it was Devlin who was looking after the gun, someone must have given it to the UFF while he was out of the country.'

'But now both men are dead, what's the point?'

'Yeah, that's what Staniford thinks. But the powers-that-be want to be seen to be even-handed. Every single case has to be closed.'

Shepherd finished his coffee. 'And how close is he to fingering Carter?'

'Not very,' said Sharpe. 'That's why he was talking to the wife. He's tried interviewing the UFF men involved, but they're not talking. Truth be told, Staniford reckons he's banging his head against a brick wall.'

'His sidekick was asking Elaine for her husband's diaries. I guess he's trying to pin down where Carter was during all the killings. You don't think he plans to get a search warrant for the house, do you?'

'He didn't mention it. At the moment it's softly-softly. How is the merry widow, then? Given her one yet?'

'You're a class act, Razor.'

'Best place to get her talking's in bed, you know that.'

'Thanks for the tip,' said Shepherd, standing up, 'and thanks for talking to Staniford for me.'

'What are friends for?' said Sharpe. 'I'd better be going. Don't know how long the security checks'll take. It's bloody nonsense, isn't it? Look at me. I'm a middle-aged white male with a Scottish accent. How the hell could anyone think I'd be a bloody suicide-bomber?'

'Middle-aged?' repeated Shepherd, in disbelief. 'What? You're going to live to ninety-six, are you?'

Sharpe opened his mouth to retort but Shepherd had already walked away.

Liam pretended to kick the ball to his left, but at the last second he shifted his centre of balance and sent it sailing past Billy Bradford. 'Nice kick!' called Bradford.

'I'm on the school team,' said Liam, as Bradford retrieved the ball from the hedge.

'I can see why,' said Bradford. He threw it back to Liam,

who caught it on his chest, dropped it to his foot, then kicked it up and headed it half a dozen times before letting it fall to his feet again. Bradford clapped enthusiastically.

'Billy, what do you want to eat tonight?' called Katra, from the kitchen door.

'Bacon sandwich'll do me fine.'

'You had that last night,' said Katra. 'And this morning for breakfast.'

'What can I say, sweetheart? I like bacon sandwiches.'

'You've got to eat vegetables,' said Katra.

'Put ketchup on it,' said Bradford.

Katra laughed and went back into the house.

'Come on, Liam, take your best shot,' shouted Bradford.

Tariq put down the binoculars. He had parked his hire car on the brow of a hill overlooking the road where Daniel Shepherd lived. Earlier that afternoon he had seen Shepherd get into the dark green Honda CRV with a young woman he had assumed was his wife. They had returned half an hour later with a boy of twelve or thirteen, obviously Shepherd's son. But Tariq thought the girl could only be in her mid-twenties, which meant she was too young to be the boy's mother and too old to be his sister. That meant the boy's mother had gone and the girl was probably Shepherd's girlfriend. Not that the exact relationship mattered. They were clearly a family, which meant Salih wanted them dead.

The digital clock in the dashboard showed just after five, which meant it wouldn't be dark for a few hours. He couldn't stay parked where he was until then. There were several houses nearby and the road was reasonably busy. An old man had walked by twice with a small terrier on a leash and the second time he'd looked at Tariq's car. Tariq had quickly lowered the binoculars and he was fairly sure that the old man had been curious rather than suspicious, but it was better to be safe than sorry. He knew where the house was, he knew who the targets were. There was nothing to be gained from sitting in the car and watching the house. He decided to drive to the nearest motorway and find a motel. There, he could bathe, pray and prepare himself. Once it was dark he'd come back and keep the house under surveillance until he was sure everyone was asleep. Then he'd do what he had to do.

A silver Volvo was parked outside Shepherd's house. A man sat in the driving seat, his coat collar turned up. Shepherd slowed as he drove by and recognised the driver. It was John Maplethorpe.

Maplethorpe climbed out of his car as Shepherd parked in front of his garage. 'How's it going, Jamie?' he asked. He put his hands into his coat pockets.

'Fine,' said Shepherd. 'Are you here to see Elaine?' Her car wasn't outside her house.

'Thought I'd drop by and say hello to you, as it happens,' said Maplethorpe.

'Sure, come on in,' said Shepherd. 'Everything's okay, yeah?'

'Everything's fine,' said Maplethorpe. His right hand reappeared from his coat pocket. Shepherd tensed, but relaxed when he saw Maplethorpe was holding a packet of Benson & Hedges. Maplethorpe lit a cigarette and offered one to Shepherd.

He shook his head. 'I'm a Marlboro man.'

Maplethorpe chuckled. Shepherd took him into the house. 'Beer or something stronger?' he asked, as they went into the sitting room.

'Have you got whiskey?'

'Jameson's,' said Shepherd.

'Perfect,' said Maplethorpe.

'Ice?'

'Just a splash of water,' said Maplethorpe. He stretched out on the sofa.

As Shepherd poured a whiskey and soda for himself, then a whiskey and water for his visitor, he wondered what

Maplethorpe wanted. No red flags would have flown when the detective ran a PNC check on Jamie Pierce. He gave Maplethorpe his whiskey, then sat in an armchair facing him. 'So . . .' said Shepherd.

'Yes,' said Maplethorpe. 'So . . .'

'Is there anything in particular you wanted? Or is this purely social?'

'Elaine's a good friend of mine,' said Maplethorpe.

'I know that.'

'I was best man at their wedding.'

'I know that, too.'

Maplethorpe's eyes narrowed. 'How?'

Shepherd had made the cardinal error of an undercover agent – he had revealed that he knew something his character shouldn't. He knew that Maplethorpe had been Robbie Carter's best man because he'd seen the wedding photographs in the trunk in Elaine's attic. 'Elaine mentioned it,' he said. He cursed himself because now he'd been forced to tell a direct lie – which Maplethorpe could check.

'Robbie was like a brother to me,' said Maplethorpe.

'And Elaine?'

'What do you mean?' said Maplethorpe, leaning forward.

'You obviously care a lot about her. That's why you're here, right?'

'There's something not right about you.'

Shepherd's mind was racing. What had he done to make the detective suspicious? 'Specifically?'

'That's the thing, Jamie,' said Maplethorpe. 'There's nothing I can put my finger on. Bit by bit everything makes sense. Education, work record, no criminal offences. You're a model citizen.'

'You checked me out? Isn't that against the Data Protection Act?'

'Elaine's a good friend of mine, and I want to make sure she doesn't get hurt.'

'I'm a good guy, John,' said Shepherd.

'That's what the stats say,' agreed Maplethorpe. 'But it's a sum-of-the-parts thing. It doesn't add up.' He winced and put a hand to his temple.

'Are you okay?'

'It's nothing,' said Maplethorpe. 'Headache.'

'Do you want an aspirin or a paracetamol?'

Maplethorpe fumbled in his pocket, brought out a small plastic bottle containing white tablets and shook out a couple. He swallowed them and washed them down with whiskey.

'Sure you're supposed to take painkillers that way?' said Shepherd.

'Yeah, well, you're a website designer, not a doctor.' Maplethorpe put the bottle away. 'Are you with MI5, Jamie?'

Shepherd laughed. 'Don't be ridiculous.'

'There's something about you that makes the hairs stand up on the back of my neck. I don't think you're a serial killer or a paedophile, but I don't think you're a computer geek either.' He swirled his whiskey in his glass as he studied Shepherd with hard eyes.

'I could show you my CV.'

'If you were a spook, your CV would be perfect. Which it is.'

'I swear to you I don't work for MI5,' said Shepherd. 'But if I did, why would that concern you? I'm hardly likely to be spying on Elaine, am I?'

'It's a question of honesty, Jamie. I don't think you're bad, but I don't think you're being honest with her. And I don't want Elaine hurt. She's taken to you. She's not exactly been celibate since Robbie was killed, but she's very selective, and the few relationships she's had haven't lasted long.'

'I'm not surprised, if you paid her boyfriends a visit like this,' said Shepherd.

'I'm looking out for her,' said Maplethorpe.

'Are you sure that's all it is?'

Maplethorpe thrust out his chin. 'What are you getting at?'

'Are you married, John?'

Maplethorpe scowled at him. 'You want to be careful, Jamie,' he said. 'You shouldn't believe all the PR crap about Belfast being a changed city. It's still a very dangerous place to have a cop mad at you.'

'And are you?' asked Shepherd. 'Mad at me?'

Maplethorpe gave Shepherd a long, hard look. 'Not yet,' he said.

'That's a relief,' said Shepherd.

'You see, that's what worries me, Jamie,' said Maplethorpe. 'You're not intimidated by me, are you? I mean, you pretend to be, but under that soft exterior you're as hard as fucking nails, aren't you?'

'Wanna arm-wrestle? Or slap dicks on the table and see which of us has the biggest?'

Maplethorpe put his glass on the coffee-table and stood up. 'I'll be off,' he said.

'You're not drinking and driving, are you?'

Maplethorpe ignored him. 'Let me leave you with one thought,' he said. 'If you *are* up to something, if you have some agenda I'm not aware of, then leave Elaine out of it. Because if you cause her any pain, any pain at all, it will be revisited on you a thousandfold.'

'Message received and understood,' said Shepherd.

'I'll let myself out,' said Maplethorpe, heading for the front door.

Shepherd watched him drive away. His mobile rang. 'What the hell was that about?' Button asked.

'Marking his territory, maybe,' said Shepherd.

'There's no suggestion there was anything between him and Elaine Carter, is there?'

'I haven't picked up on it from her.'

'And if there was, you would, right?'

Shepherd frowned. Did Button know how close he and Elaine had become? 'She talks about him but always as a friend.'

'So maybe he's just looking out for a friend.'

'Maybe.'

'Any idea what set him off?'

'He's a senior police officer. You don't get to be a detective superintendent without being a good reader of people.'

'Suspicions are all he can have because your legend's watertight,' said Button.

'It had better be,' said Shepherd. 'He's right about what he said. If I fall foul of the cops here I'll have to get out sharpish.'

'If he was sure of anything, he wouldn't have come round for a chat,' said Button.

'That's true,' agreed Shepherd. 'Look, can you check on why he's taking early retirement? He said it was because he was fed up with the job, but he has bad headaches.'

'You think he's got a medical problem?'

'It's possible.'

'I'll get on it.'

Liam frowned at the book in front of him and chewed the end of his biro. Billy Bradford was sitting on the other side of the kitchen table, munching a bacon sandwich. Liam smiled hopefully at him. 'Do you know about factor trees?'

'I was never any good at biology,' said Bradford.

'It's maths,' said Liam, scornfully.

'I knew that,' said Bradford.

Katra put a mug of black coffee in front of him, then went to the sink and began to load dirty plates into the dishwasher.

'Did you used to work with my dad?' Liam asked Bradford.

'Me and Jack joined just as he left.' Bradford sipped his coffee. 'He was a bit of a legend, your dad.'

'What do you mean?'

'Because of his nickname, Spider. He ate a tarantula when he was on a jungle training exercise.'

'A tarantula?' Katra queried.

'It's a big hairy spider,' said Bradford. He used his free

hand to mime a spider scurrying across the table. 'They still talk about what a mad bastard he was.' He grinned apologetically at Liam. 'Sorry.'

'My dad's a mad bastard?' said Liam in mock-horror.

Suddenly Bradford was serious. 'Don't ever tell him I said that.'

'Your secret's safe with me, Billy,' said Liam. He pushed his exercise book across the table towards Bradford. 'If you help me with my homework.'

'Let's wait for Jack,' said Bradford. 'He's the smart one.'

'I thought you were the smart one,' said Katra.

Bradford shook his head. 'Nah, I'm the good-looking one,' he said. Headlights flashed across the hall window. 'Speak of the devil.'

Tariq watched through his binoculars as the black Range Rover drove up in front of the house and parked. He hadn't seen it before and the dark green CRV and the BMW SUV were parked in front of the garage. A man in a padded jacket climbed out and headed for the front door. It was Shepherd, Tariq realised. The man looked round, then slotted a key into the lock and let himself in. Tariq grinned. He'd made the right decision in waiting for it to get dark. While he'd been showering and praying in the motel, Shepherd must have left the house and just returned. If Tariq had gone straight in he'd have missed him. But now he was there, with the boy and the girl. The dashboard clock told him it was just before nine. His heart began to pound and he took deep breaths, trying to calm himself. A light went on in the front bedroom, and a few minutes later, it went off. The boy was going to bed. Tomorrow was a school day so he'd be up early. Except that tomorrow he wouldn't wake up. He'd be dead like his father.

Tariq's mouth had gone dry and he cursed himself for not bringing a bottle of water. He had a packet of chewing-gum in his pocket, though, so he took it out and popped a piece into his mouth.

An hour or so later the lights went out downstairs, except for the one in the hall. A moment later the upstairs lights went on. The girl and Shepherd were getting ready for bed. The lights stayed on for about half an hour and winked off just after eleven, leaving the upstairs windows dark.

Tariq watched the house as the digital clock ticked off the minutes. Midnight passed. Then one o'clock. His palms were soaked with sweat and he wiped them on his trousers. Then he took the back off his phone, removed his Sim card and slid in the pay-as-you-go card he'd bought from a shop in London's East End. He switched on the phone and took deep breaths as he waited for it to boot up.

Headlights moved slowly up the hill and Tariq lay across the passenger seat until the car had gone by. Then he sat up and tapped out Salih's number. He answered on the third ring. 'Now,' said Tariq. 'I'm going to do it now. They're all in bed. I'll call you when it's done.'

The line went dead.

Billy Bradford tossed a can of lager to his brother and popped the tab on his own. 'Are you heading off?'

'Think I'll watch the fight,' said Jack. 'Heavyweight championship.'

'Two black guys trying to kill each other. Might as well drive over to Manchester,' said Billy.

'Ha-ha,' said Jack. He sipped his lager and sat in the armchair opposite the plasma television. He lit a cigarette. His Glock, a bulbous silencer screwed into the barrel, lay next to the ashtray.

'Look, I'll do the night shift if you want. I'm not tired,' said Billy, as he sat on the sofa and swung his feet on to the coffee-table.

'You know Katra doesn't like feet on the furniture,' said Jack.

'Yeah, well, she doesn't like us smoking in the house, either.'

Jack chuckled. 'You're just pissed because she likes me more than you.'

'In your dreams,' said Billy.

'You asked her out yet?'

'Have you?'

'I'm here to work,' said Jack. 'And so are you.'

'This isn't working,' said Billy. 'It's babysitting.'

'Spider's not paranoid,' said Jack. 'If he says someone's after him, he's not making it up.'

'Arab terrorist, international hitman, it's all a bit Andy McNab, isn't it?'

'You ever meet McNab? He's out in Hollywood, I heard, advising on action movies.'

'Where did we go wrong?' asked Billy. 'He gets lost in the desert, now he's out in Hollywood and we're babysitting a boy and an au pair in Hereford.'

'Billy, stop bitching. Spider's Sass and he needs help. Watching TV and having Katra cook for us is hardly shit work, is it?' He sipped his lager. 'Anyway, we'll be back in Baghdad soon enough.'

Tariq crept around the side of the house. He had stuck the gun into the belt of his trousers, the silencer in his jacket pocket. He was carrying a brown-paper bag containing a sheet of sticky-backed plastic and a small hammer.

The kitchen was in darkness and he peered through the window. He hadn't seen a dog when he'd had the house under surveillance and there was no sign of a food or water bowl. He knelt down, peeled the back off the plastic, then pressed it against the pane of glass closest to the door lock. He listened for a few seconds, then drove his elbow into the glass. It splintered and most of the glass remained stuck to the plastic. Tariq peeled it away and kept it glass side up as he placed it carefully on the ground.

He pulled the gun from his belt and screwed in the silencer, then reached through the hole in the glass and flicked open the Yale lock. He turned the handle and pushed open the door. As he stepped into the kitchen his shoe crunched on a small piece of glass that had escaped the plastic. He realised he was holding his breath and forced himself to relax.

He cocked his head to one side, frowning. He could hear sounds from down the hall. A fight. A crowd roaring and the thud-thud-thud of punches. A boxing match. His heart started to pound again. Shepherd should have been in bed with the girl. His finger tightened on the trigger. It didn't matter. With the silencer on the gun, the girl and the boy wouldn't hear a thing. He could shoot Shepherd downstairs, then go up and kill his family. Salih had said he should kill Shepherd if he was in the house and his family if he wasn't, but in killing them all he would show he was committed to what he was doing, that it made no difference if his target was a man, a woman or a child. They were infidels. A human being who did not believe in Allah was not a human being. He was lower than an animal, lower even than the insects that crawled along the ground. He went up on tiptoe and moved silently across the kitchen floor. He paused at the door. The television was in the front room, the sound turned low so that it wouldn't disturb the sleepers upstairs.

Tariq moved along the hallway. The sitting-room door was open. He raised his gun. There were eleven bullets in the magazine. He'd taken them out in his room, counted and recounted them, wearing gloves as Salih had instructed. They were so small, the bullets. Just an inch long, bright and shiny. It was hard to believe that something so small could kill a man, but Tariq had seen at first hand the damage that bullets could do. As part of his training, at a camp near Malakand on the border with Afghanistan and Pakistan, he'd been taught how to shoot and how to kill, how to make explosives by mixing ammonium nitrate fertiliser and aluminium powder. His instructors had shown him how to strip and fire a Kalashnikov, and many different types of handgun.

Most of his training had been on target ranges, but during their second month three prisoners had been brought in, bloody, battered, begging for their lives, and tied to posts.

Tariq and five other British Muslims had been lined up in front of them and told to fire. Tariq had needed no urging. He had been the first to pull the trigger. His shot had hit the prisoner on the left, blowing away a big chunk of his head. His second shot had missed but then he had remembered his training and held the gun with both hands. His next three shots had hit the chest of the man in the middle. Tariq had turned the gun on the third man, even though he was already riddled with bullets, and he had carried on firing until the hammer clicked on empty casings. He had screamed then, as had the others, screamed and yelled and danced, kicking up dust, as the instructors clapped and cheered. Killing was easy, Tariq had learnt that day. It was easy and it was pleasurable. As he'd danced and chanted praise to Allah, he'd realised he had an erection. He'd been turned on by the killings. For a moment he'd been ashamed, but then he'd realised that the erection was a gift from Allah, a reward for what he'd done.

Tariq felt himself harden as he moved towards the open door. His left hand crept involuntarily towards the front of his trousers and his penis twitched in anticipation. He'd kill the man, then the boy – and then he'd rape the girl before he killed her too. He'd rape her in the name of Allah.

He took another step and saw Shepherd in an armchair, watching television, a bottle of beer and an ashtray containing a burning cigarette on the table beside him. As Tariq watched, the man picked up the cigarette, took a long drag on it, then blew smoke at the ceiling. To be sure of a clear shot, Tariq had to take at least two steps into the room.

Shepherd flicked ash, then groaned as the bell sounded for the end of the round. Tariq took a deep breath and readied himself. He wanted to say something to Shepherd before he killed him, to tell him why he was taking his life. He wanted to tell Shepherd that his son was going to be killed and his woman raped, that the last thing his woman would feel was Tariq coming inside her. His penis was rock hard now and his testicles ached. It was going to be the best sex he'd ever had, Tariq knew, sex followed by death. He shivered.

Upstairs, a toilet flushed. Tariq froze. It must be either the woman or the boy. He pressed himself against the wall. It wasn't a problem. Whoever it was would go back to bed. Tariq heard footsteps coming down the stairs. His heart pounded and for a moment he felt so light-headed that he thought he would pass out. Was it the boy or the woman? Whoever it was, they were half-way down the stairs and were only seconds from reaching the bottom – at which point they would see him. He would have to shoot them first, then turn and shoot Shepherd.

Tariq raised his gun and moved away from the wall. He stepped sideways, both hands on the butt of the gun, swinging it up to aim at the figure on the stairs. He gasped when he saw it was Shepherd. The man was wearing a denim shirt and over it a nylon shoulder holster. As Tariq hesitated, Shepherd ducked, reached for his gun and yelled, 'Jack!'

Tariq backed away from the stairs. He couldn't get a clear shot. He heard the man in the sitting room shout, 'Billy!' and turned, his finger tightening on the trigger. His mind whirled when he saw that the man in the sitting room was also Shepherd. Two Shepherds? How could that be? He felt as if he was moving through treacle. Was he dreaming? Was it all a nightmare? The Shepherd in the sitting room was reaching for a gun on the coffee-table next to the ashtray, a big automatic with a silencer.

Tariq pulled the trigger and there was a loud popping sound, but his hands were shaking so much that the shot went wide and buried itself in the sofa.

The man in the sitting room rolled on to the floor and Tariq pulled the trigger again. The gun kicked in his hands and there was another loud pop.

Then Tariq felt a thump in his back and gasped. His first thought was that he'd been punched, but a burning pain was spreading between his shoulder-blades. He'd been shot. He turned, his mouth open in surprise. The man on the stairs was holding his gun in both hands, a confident smile on his face. 'Drop the gun,' he said.

Tariq tried to breathe but a gurgling sound came from his lungs. His body felt as if all the energy was draining from it, and the slightest movement was an effort.

'Drop the gun,' repeated the man on the stairs.

Tariq lifted it. If he was about to die, at least he would take one of the infidels with him. *'Allahu Akbar,'* he whispered, and pointed his weapon at the man's chest.

The man fired twice and Tariq felt two blows to his chest. There was no burning pain this time, just a spreading coldness. The strength went from his legs and he fell to the floor. The last thing he saw was the smile on his killer's face.

Shepherd's phone rang. He groped for it as he squinted at the clock on his bedside table. He grunted, 'Yeah?'

'Spider, it's Jack.'

Shepherd sat up, immediately wide awake. It was after two o'clock in the morning and Jack Bradford could only be calling with bad news. 'What's happened?' he said, fighting to keep his voice steady. Bradford had called on Shepherd's personal phone and all the power sockets in the room were switched off so Shepherd knew they weren't being overheard.

'Spider, it's okay. Everyone here's fine.'

Shepherd exhaled deeply.

'We had a visitor, an Asian guy. He had a gun and a silencer. Could have been that Salih you were expecting. Anyway, we've taken care of it.'

'What about Liam?'

'Slept through the whole thing. Katra, too. A couple of shots went off but we've cleared up the damage. Bit of blood on the hall floor but we can clean that up. A bullet went into the sofa and another buried itself in a wall.'

'And the guy?'

'Dead as disco,' said Bradford. 'So, now we've got a decision to make. Do you want us to call the cops or not?'

As a SOCA officer Shepherd was duty-bound to call it in. But if he did, his home would be crawling with scene-of-crime officers in their white suits, and detectives from the local force. There'd be journalists too, from the local paper at first but they'd soon be joined by others from the nationals, and television crews. Within hours it would be a circus.

'Spider?'

'Give me a minute, Jack. I'm considering my options.'

'Whatever you decide is fine by us,' said Bradford. 'The guy took a couple of shots at me so he had it coming. We can take the body out of here and drop it in some very deep water long before it gets light. Won't ever be your problem.'

What Bradford was suggesting was legally wrong, no question. The brothers had killed a man, and while it was obviously in self-defence, disposing of the body would be a criminal offence. If they were ever caught, it would spell the end of Shepherd's career, and they would all be sent to prison. But if the killing was made public, there was a good chance it would end Shepherd's career anyway. There would be an inquest, and the journalists would keep digging until they found out who Shepherd was and what he did for a living. He'd have to move house, and that would mean uprooting Liam yet again when he was finally getting some stability in his life. There was another option. He could call Charlotte Button, tell her everything and hope she would protect him. If she had been his former boss, Sam Hargrove, he wouldn't have hesitated. But after what Major Gannon had told him, Shepherd wasn't sure how far he could trust Button. If Gannon was right and her loyalties lay solely with MI5, she might decide to hang Shepherd out to dry.

'Jack, if you and Billy did get rid of the evidence, how comfortable would you be with that?'

'I wouldn't give it a moment's thought, Spider.'

'No one heard the shots?'

'Silencers all round,' said Bradford.

'How did he get in?'

'Broke a glass pane in the kitchen door,' said Bradford. 'I'll tell Katra I did it accidentally and we'll get it fixed tomorrow.'

'He'd have had a car,' said Shepherd.

'I'll check for keys. He won't have parked it too far away. I'll take it somewhere and burn it.'

'Where did you shoot him?'

'The hall.'

Shepherd smiled, despite the seriousness of the situation. 'In his body, Jack. Where did the rounds go?'

'One in the back, two in the chest.' Bradford sounded crestfallen.

'Okay, I'm a bit dubious about dropping the guy in the drink with three rounds in him. If ever the body surfaces, the cops will be able to ID the gun.'

'We can dump the weapon.'

'Better to get the rounds out,' said Shepherd. 'Get the rounds out and put the body in the car. Use a can of petrol to get the blaze going, and leave the can on the lap of the body. Put a lighter in his hand before you start the fire. Do it somewhere where the car can burn out. The cops will probably put it down as suicide.'

'Sounds good to me,' said Bradford.

'Go through the body first, see if you can get an ID on the guy. But leave everything on him when you torch the car.'

'Got you.'

'Jack, if you have any reservations about this at all, I'd understand.'

'I know what cops are like,' said Bradford. 'No offence.'

'None taken.'

'If we come clean on this we'll be answering questions for weeks. Billy and I don't have time for that. We've got work to do. Plus the way the cops are now we might end up in court and then we're screwed work-wise for life, no matter how the case pans out. So, fire it is.'

'Call me if you need me. And if anything goes wrong, Jack, anything at all, it's on me, understand?'

'Nothing will go wrong, Spider.'

The line went dead. Shepherd got out of bed and went downstairs to make himself a cup of coffee. He doubted he'd get any more sleep that night.

Salih removed the back of his phone, lifted out the battery and the Sim card. It had been two hours since Tariq had phoned to say he was going inside the house. He hadn't called back. There was no point in Salih checking the number. If Tariq had succeeded, he would have heard. That Tariq hadn't called meant he was either dead or had been captured. Either way he was of no further use to Salih. He broke the Sim card in half and dropped it into the lavatory. It had probably been a set-up from the start. Whoever had turned Merkulov had wanted Salih to attack Daniel Shepherd so they could catch him in the act. Well, they'd failed. And forewarned was forearmed.

Dawn was breaking and the sky was streaked with orange behind the Belfast hills when Shepherd's phone rang. It was Jack Bradford. Shepherd went into the garden to take the call. 'Everything's done,' said Bradford. 'He was in a hire car, nothing of any interest in it. His name's Tariq Chadhar, twenty-three years old, had a driving licence with an address in Luton.'

'Twenty-three?'

'That's what the licence said.'

'And the guy looked twenty-three?'

'Sure. You think the licence is fake?'

'He's young to be a professional hitman,' said Shepherd.

'They start young, these days,' said Bradford. 'Especially if he cut his teeth in Iraq or Afghanistan.'

'Maybe,' said Shepherd. 'Liam and Katra still asleep?'

'Like logs,' said Bradford.

'I owe you big-time,' said Shepherd. 'Are you and Billy okay to stay there until I'm back?'

'As long as you need us,' said Bradford.

'And the house is like it never happened?'

'So far as we're concerned, Spider, it never did.'

Shepherd ended the call. He rubbed the back of his neck. He hadn't run since he'd moved to Belfast and being confined to the house for hours on end was driving him crazy. He went upstairs, changed into a pair of tracksuit bottoms and a French Connection T-shirt. He pulled on a pair of training shoes and laced them. He preferred army boots but they would attract too much attention.

He let himself out of the front door, then jogged in his driveway as he worked out a decent route. He ran down the hill, his feet pounding on the pavement. The roads were deserted and there were no pedestrians about. A couple of dogs watched him run by, and he scattered a flock of pigeons. He was angry, but he wasn't sure who with. The man who'd turned up at his house was dead, so there was no point in being angry with him. Shepherd doubted that the man the Bradfords had killed was the assassin who had been on Button's trail; he was too young. And a professional wouldn't have gone into a house where there were two bodyguards. So who was he, and what had he been doing at Shepherd's house? Maybe Yokely's mystery assassin was a red herring. Maybe the Asian had been working to a different agenda. Shepherd had come up against several Asians over the past few years. Maybe it was one of them or a relative out for revenge.

He upped the pace, his hands in tight fists. The big question was, how had the man known where Shepherd lived? He had only recently moved to Hereford and wasn't on the electoral roll. And if the man had staked out the house before he went in, he must have known Shepherd wasn't at home.

What if it had been the assassin Yokely had warned him about? Perhaps he had traced calls made from Shepherd's mobile and been able to trace the landline that would have given him Shepherd's home address – but, then, he'd also have known that Shepherd was in Belfast. So if the assassin had found Shepherd's address, why had he sent an amateur?

The more he tried to solve the puzzle, the more his mind whirled. For some reason he was under threat, and that had to be his prime concern. Jack and Billy would stay with Liam and Katra, but Shepherd himself needed protection. He'd not bothered with a weapon while he was in Belfast because the nature of the investigation didn't warrant it. But that had changed.

He ran for an hour through the streets of Belfast and was bathed in sweat by the time he arrived back at his house. He showered, changed into jeans and a denim shirt, then went into the garden and used his pay-as-you-go mobile to call Richard Yokely. He asked the American where he was. 'The embassy in London.'

'We need to talk,' said Shepherd. 'Face to face.'

'Where are you?' said Yokely.

'Belfast. But I'm planning to be in England later today.'

The American made a clicking sound, then sighed. 'I've got to fly later this morning so I could stop off where you are, but God help us if the press spots the plane. Last thing we want is another row over rendition flights.'

'It's important,' said Shepherd.

'I understand that. Let me see what I can arrange flight-plan-wise and I'll get back to you.' Yokely cut the connection.

Shepherd used his Jamie Pierce phone to call Button and asked her if he could take a couple of days off. 'Problems at home?' she asked.

'I want to spend a bit of time with Liam,' said Shepherd.

'What about Elaine Carter?'

'If Kinsella's in London, she can't do anything,' said Shepherd. 'She doesn't fly so all you've got to do is keep a watch on the ports. If she goes she'll take her car, so just red-flag her registration number.'

'She doesn't fly?'

'She's got a phobia.'

'Interesting,' said Button. 'Okay, a couple of days away shouldn't hurt. While you're over, fix up an appointment with Caroline Stockmann, will you?'

'It'll be a pleasure,' said Shepherd.

The general aviation terminal and apron were to the east of the main terminal at Belfast international airport and had their own entrance. Shepherd pulled up in his Audi and showed his ID card to a security guard, who checked his name against a list on a clipboard and waved him through.

A white Gulfstream with an American registration number was parked by a hangar belonging to a helicopter charter company. The steps were down but no one was around. Shepherd got out of his car and went up them.

Richard Yokely was sitting in one of the plane's eight luxurious chairs, drinking coffee. He grinned when Shepherd appeared at the doorway. 'Dan, come on in,' he said. 'We've got about twenty minutes. You want coffee?'

Shepherd shook his head. 'Someone tried to attack my family. A Pakistani, British-born.' He gave Yokely a piece of paper. 'All the details I have are there. I don't think it's your man.'

Yokely ran his eyes down Shepherd's notes. 'Twenty-three?' he said.

'I think he was working with your man.'

Yokely looked at him over the top of his mug. 'I'm not happy at you referring to him as my man.'

'You know what I mean, Richard. You said there was a Muslim hitman after you and Charlie Button and the next thing I know a Muslim is breaking into my house with a gun.'

'Your family okay?' asked Yokely.

Shepherd could see that the American's concern was genuine. 'They're fine, thanks. I had two guys looking after them and they took care of things.'

'Permanently?'

'There wasn't time for kid gloves,' said Shepherd. 'And no one will be filing a police report.'

Yokely took another look at the piece of paper. 'This isn't a name I know,' he said.

'I'm assuming he was recruited locally. Which means that your man could try again. There's enough fundamentalist nutters in this country for him to choose from. Do you have any idea where he is?'

'I had his phone tracked for a while but he destroyed the Sim card so he's off the radar again.'

'Photograph? Anything I can work with?'

Yokely shook his head. 'I'm sorry,' he said. 'But if I can get the information you want, what then?'

'I'd take care of it.'

Yokely slipped the piece of paper into his jacket pocket and sipped his coffee. 'Before, you said you weren't happy about being proactive,' he said.

Shepherd's jaw tightened. 'He attacked my family. He has to take the consequences. I haven't changed my view on assassinating potential terrorists.'

'I don't remember that being an option,' he said.

'You chose your words carefully,' said Shepherd, 'but I got the implication.'

'Remember when we first met, in the Special Forces Club in Knightsbridge? I ran a moral dilemma past you.'

'Sure. Would I kill a terrorist who was on his way to kill civilians but who wasn't a threat at the time?'

'Yeah, well, let me give you another. Some scientist in the States has been using it as part of an experiment to see how the brain reacts while it's making moral decisions.'

Shepherd sighed. 'If you must.'

Yokely ignored the sarcasm. 'Say you're standing by a railway line and a runaway wagon's racing towards you. You're beside a set of points. If the wagon carries on the way it's going, it'll hit six people on the line. They'll die unless you do something. If you pull the lever that controls the points you can divert the wagon along another line. But there's a man on the second line. He'll die if you change the direction of the runaway wagon. What do you do?'

'That's a no-brainer,' said Shepherd. 'You pull the lever. Six lives are more important than one.'

'And ninety-nine per cent of the population would agree with you,' said Yokely. 'Now, say you're standing on a bridge over the line and there's a runaway wagon heading towards six people. No points this time, but you could throw yourself off the bridge in front of the wagon. Problem is, you're not big enough to stop the wagon. But standing next to you is a fat guy. More than enough body mass to stop the wagon. Do you throw him off the bridge in front of the wagon to save the lives of the six people on the line?'

Shepherd smiled. 'I get it,' he said.

'It's a tougher call, isn't it? Yet the premise is the same. You perform an action that puts six lives ahead of one. But while most people would pull the lever without hesitation, most would not push the guy off the bridge. Why do think that is?'

'Because most people can't kill up close and personal. Pulling a lever detaches you from the killing, I guess.'

'The physical contact, you mean?' Yokely's brow furrowed. 'Maybe that's it. But you've never had a problem with that, have you?'

'I don't lose sleep over the people I've killed,' said Shepherd. 'But every time I've taken a life, I've had right on my side. A moral and legal right. And, more often than not, the people I've killed have been trying to kill me.'

'Sure, that makes the dilemma simpler, doesn't it? If you're the one standing in the way of the runaway wagon, you'll do whatever it takes. It's when you're on the bridge that your moral code kicks in. But Hassan Salih is a stone-cold killer. If we don't stop him he'll kill Charlotte Button, maybe taking out her family as well. And he'll carry on killing because that's what he does for a living.'

'I'm losing your metaphor. Is Salih the guy on the bridge or the runaway wagon?'

'He's the piece of shit that tried to kill your boy and who's going to kill your boss unless we do something to stop him.'

'You say "we" but you mean me, don't you?'

'She's your boss, and it's your country,' said Yokely. 'I can't go around killing people on your turf. It's only the Russians who do that.'

'So what are we talking about here, Richard? Are we talking about protecting Charlie, or about protecting you?'

Yokely smiled. 'Tomato, potato,' he said.

Shepherd drove from Belfast airport to Dublin and caught the Stena Line high-speed catamaran to Holyhead. The sea was mirror flat and the crossing took less than two hours. As he drove off the ferry he used his hands-free to call Martin O'Brien. O'Brien sounded out of breath. 'You're not having sex, are you, Martin?' he asked.

'Chance'd be a fine thing,' said O'Brien. 'Just done a twelve-mile run.'

'How fast?'

'Just over the hour,' said O'Brien.

'Well done you.'

'And I've lost three kilos in the last week.'

'Kudos.'

'Mind you, I'd kill for a burger. What's up?'

A Porsche drove past Shepherd at breakneck speed. The driver was barely out of his twenties with a mobile phone pressed to his ear. Shepherd's natural competitiveness kicked in and he had to fight the urge to stamp on his accelerator and give chase. 'How's it going with Charlotte?'

'Bloody hard work,' said O'Brien. 'I've got four guys in rotation but she's as slippery as an eel.'

'Yeah, I told you she was shit hot at surveillance.'

'You weren't wrong. But we haven't shown out and we haven't seen anyone else on her tail.'

'Have you spoken to the Bradford boys?'

'Yeah, they said you had a spot of bother in Hereford.'

'They handled it just fine.'

'So, all's well that ends well, as my old gran used to say.'

'I'm not sure about that, Martin,' said Shepherd. 'The guy who went to my house didn't fit the profile of a professional hitman. A bit young.'

'So there's more than one?'

'I don't know for sure, but I'm assuming so. I'm going to pick up a weapon from the major, just in case. And I'd like you to keep an eye on Charlie for a bit longer.'

'Pleasure,' said O'Brien.

Shepherd ended the call, then rang Caroline Stockmann and explained that he was back in England for two days. 'We can meet tomorrow evening, say six o'clock,' said the psychologist. 'How about the Stag?'

'In Hereford?' said Shepherd, surprised. He had assumed she'd want to see him in London.

'Mountains, Muhammad, and all that jazz,' she said. 'You're a busy man and I get a very generous allowance from SOCA.'

'Six it is,' said Shepherd. '*Inshallah.*'

'Indeed,' said Stockmann. 'God willing.'

It was late at night when Shepherd arrived at his house in Hereford. He parked the Audi in the street and let himself in. As he flicked on the light one of the Bradfords put away his gun and grinned. 'Sorry,' he said. 'Didn't hear you drive up.'

'Hey, my fault for not calling first,' said Shepherd. 'And I'm sorry – normally I'm good with faces but I can't tell you guys apart.'

'I'm Billy, the good-looking one.'

Shepherd grinned. 'Everyone asleep?'

'They went up at nine,' said Billy. 'Jack's coming at midnight. I was making a coffee. Do you want one?'

'Thanks,' said Shepherd. He went upstairs to his son's room. Liam was asleep, hugging a pillow. Shepherd knelt beside the bed and brushed the boy's hair away from his eyes. Liam muttered something but didn't wake. Shepherd kissed his forehead. 'Sweet dreams,' he whispered.

He went downstairs. Billy had made the coffee and handed him a mug. 'Everything okay?' Shepherd asked.

'No problems,' said Billy.

'Katra and Liam have no idea what went down?'

'Slept through it all. I'll show you the damage.' He took Shepherd to the sitting room and showed him the small hole in the sofa. 'Bullet's still in there,' he said. 'Probably lodged in the frame. I think you can leave it where it is.' He went to the wall by the fireplace. 'This one's a bit more complicated,' he said. There was a picture on the wall, a pen-and-ink drawing of the clock tower at the old Stirling Lines barracks. Engraved on it were the names of SAS members who had died in action. He moved the picture to reveal a hole that had been gouged in the wall. 'We dug out the bullet and moved the hook a few inches to the left so that the picture covers the hole but you'll have to get it patched up,' said Billy.

'I'll decorate the room as soon as I have a chance,' said Shepherd.

Billy put the picture back and sat in an armchair.

'The guy who came here, Tariq?'

'Tariq Chadhar,' said Billy.

'What sort of gun did he have?'

'Glock 17 with a silencer.'

'A professional rig,' said Shepherd. 'Did he seem like a pro to you?'

'Definitely not,' said Billy. 'Nervous as shit, slow reactions, damn near pissed himself. Is there a problem?'

'I don't know,' said Shepherd. 'I was warned there was a pro around, a pro who knew where I lived. But the guy you dealt with doesn't fit the profile.'

'Jack and I are here as long as you need us, you know that?'

'Thanks, Billy. For everything.'

Shepherd woke at dawn, pulled on a running vest, a pair of old tracksuit bottoms and two pairs of thick woollen socks. He retrieved his boots and a battered old rucksack from the cupboard under the stairs and carried them into the kitchen. The rucksack was packed with bricks wrapped in newspaper. One of the Bradfords was sitting at the kitchen table, nursing a mug of black coffee.

Shepherd squinted at him. 'Don't tell me,' he said. 'Jack?'

'Jack it is,' said Bradford.

'I'm starting to get it,' said Shepherd.

'I'm the good-looking one, right?'

Shepherd sat down to put on his boots. 'Actually, Billy's nose is slightly curved.'

'Yeah, he broke it when he was a kid.' Bradford grinned. 'On my tennis racquet, as it happens.' He nodded at the rucksack. 'Bricks?'

'Yeah.'

'I use old telephone directories. They don't move around as much.'

Shepherd pulled on the rucksack. He took a bottle of Evian water from the fridge and left by the front door. He ran for the best part of an hour, keeping at a fast pace. The rucksack banged uncomfortably against his back but he ignored it. He didn't run for pleasure. He ran to stay fit so that he could do his job properly.

He had worked up a sweat by the time he let himself in through the front door and went upstairs to shave, shower and change into clean black jeans and a denim shirt. He opened the door to the walk-in wardrobe. There were six drawers, all lockable, on one side. In the top ones, which he never secured, he kept his socks, underwear and ties. He took out his key-ring and unlocked the bottom drawer. Inside, a black case contained his official issue SIG-Sauer semi-auto-matic, two filled magazines and several boxes of nine-millimetre ammunition. One box was a different brand from the rest. He took it out and relocked the drawer. He slid the box into his pocket and went downstairs.

Liam was sitting at the kitchen table, studying a maths book and bolting down a bowl of cereal opposite Jack Bradford. 'How long are you here for, Dad?' he asked, through his breakfast.

'Just today. I'm off to Belfast again tomorrow,' said Shepherd. 'And don't talk with your mouth full.'

'Why are you working in Ireland?'

'It's Northern Ireland,' said Shepherd, 'part of the United Kingdom.'

'But I don't see why you have to work there,' said Liam. 'Don't they have their own policemen?'

'It's complicated,' said Shepherd.

Liam scowled. 'You always say that when you can't be bothered to answer my questions,' he said.

Shepherd sat down beside his son. 'Have you studied the Irish situation at school?' he asked. Liam shook his head. 'Okay, here's a crash course. Ireland used to be Ireland and everyone was Irish. Then the English took over the country and from the twelfth century we ruled it. Then in nineteen twenty-one the country was divided into the North, run by Westminster, and the South, which was Ireland. That's the way it is now. Under the law, anyone born in the North, the bit controlled by the British, is both Irish and British. But there's always been a lot of conflict between the two groups. The Irish Irish, if you like, are mainly Catholics, and the descendants of the British that moved there are mainly Protestant.'

'And the IRA are Catholics, right?'

'They are, but it's not really about religion. It's about who runs the country. Over the last few years they've hammered out a deal whereby both groups share power so they'll run the country together.'

'Why do they need you there?'

Shepherd sat back in his chair. 'Because Belfast is a relatively small city so everyone knows who the cops are. They needed a fresh face.'

'You're hardly fresh,' Liam giggled.

'Less of the cheek,' said Shepherd. He glanced at his watch. 'I've got to be going.'

Liam had noticed the plastic Casio wristwatch with its tiny calculator keyboard. 'That is such a lame watch,' he said.

'It's got lots of functions,' said Shepherd.

'It's a watch,' said Liam. 'All it has to do is tell the time.'

'You could say that about your expensive mobile phone,' Shepherd said. 'All it needs to do is make calls but you want it to take photographs and videos and play all sorts of stupid games, don't you?'

'It's not the same.'

'Tomato, potato,' said Shepherd.

'What?' said Liam, frowning.

'It's an expression,' said Shepherd. 'It's from an old song.'

'Oh, back in the days when dinosaurs roamed the earth?'

Shepherd patted his son's head. 'Get ready for school. I'll take you today.'

The pub Caroline Stockmann had chosen for their meeting was half a mile from Shepherd's house, and as it was a warm evening he decided to walk.

When he arrived she was sitting at the bar with a half-drunk pint of beer. Shepherd grinned as they shook hands. 'What's so funny?' she asked, as he sat down next to her.

'I was thinking your glass looked half empty, then wondered if I should pretend I'd thought it was half full, thereby showing a more optimistic frame of mind.'

Stockmann smiled. She picked up her glass, and drank the rest of the beer. 'No argument now,' she said. 'Empty, plain and simple. So, is everything okay?'

'Peachy keen,' said Shepherd.

'See, I've never understood that expression,' she said. 'Why are peaches keen? Lemons are zesty, bananas are bent, but what's keen about a peach?'

Shepherd caught a barmaid's eye. 'Jameson's, ice and soda,' he said, 'and whatever my friend's having.'

'You're in Northern Ireland, I gather,' said Stockmann.

'Belfast,' said Shepherd.

'Interesting part of the world,' she said. 'The enemies of the past now working together to bring about peace.'

'So much for not negotiating with terrorists,' said Shepherd.

'You don't think that peace is worth any compromise?' The barmaid brought their drinks, and Shepherd paid her.

'The IRA, a.k.a. Sinn Fein, wants a united Ireland,' said Shepherd. 'Nothing has changed on that front. They laid down their weapons because they sensed that the British Government's position on Ireland was weakening. But they're still the same heartless killers they always were. And if things don't continue to go their way, they'll buy new weapons.' He sipped his whiskey and put his glass on the bar. 'This isn't supposed to be a political discussion, is it?' he said. 'I thought I was here for a psychological assessment?'

'So, what would you like to talk about?'

Shepherd shrugged carelessly. 'Have you heard the one about the runaway wagon and the guy standing at the points? If he does nothing, six people die, if he changes the points just one dies.'

'Sure,' said Stockmann. 'It's first-year philosophy material. Then you make it more difficult by bringing in the fat guy on the bridge, right?'

'What's the right answer?'

'It's philosophy. There's no right or wrong answer. What's interesting is the way in which people consider the options. In the case of changing the points, most decide to sacrifice the one person and reach that decision very quickly. When it comes to pushing the fat guy off the bridge, the decision is more equally split but takes longer to reach.' She drank some beers. 'Let me give you another railway one. You're standing on an electrified railway line, with your leg trapped. You can't move. The power's off, so for the moment you're okay. But down the line a man is about to reconnect the supply. He doesn't know you're there, and he doesn't know that if he reconnects the power you'll die. Now, you happen to have a sniper's rifle with one bullet in the chamber.'

'We call them rounds,' said Shepherd, 'not bullets.'

Stockmann grinned. 'It's about philosophy, not ammunition,' she said. 'Anyway, you have a loaded rifle and you can kill the guy before he reconnects the power and kills you. Are you morally justified in killing him?'

'You do what you have to do to stay alive,' said Shepherd.

'Indeed,' said Stockmann. 'But think about this. If you shoot him, you've killed him deliberately. But if he kills you, he's done it by accident. There's a world of difference. Do you have the moral right to kill a man who might kill you by accident?'

'Why does morality have to come into it?' asked Shepherd. 'As I said, you do what you have to do to stay alive.'

Stockmann didn't say anything, but a smile spread across her face.

'What?' said Shepherd, defensively.

'You say it with such conviction, but have you thought about the ramifications?'

Shepherd toyed with his glass. 'If I do nothing, I die.'

'Agreed. But kill him and you'll have killed an innocent man. A man who was doing nothing wrong. Who was breaking no law.'

Shepherd stopped playing with his glass. 'It'd be murder, wouldn't it?'

'Well, that would probably be for a jury to decide. Or at least for the Crown Prosecution Service to take a view on.'

'So, what's the answer? I maintain the moral high ground by allowing the guy to kill me?'

Stockmann laughed. 'As I said, there's no right or wrong.

It's philosophy. But it's puzzles like that which help us analyse our thought processes.'

Deep furrows creased Shepherd's brow.

Stockmann patted his shoulder. 'It's hypothetical, Dan,' she said.

'I get that, but hypothetical or not, I'd pull the trigger, guaranteed.'

'Because your survival instinct would kick in. There's nothing to be ashamed of. It's your instinct for survival that makes you so good at what you do.'

'It worries me that I'd kill an innocent man to survive. But what if the positions were reversed? What if I was the one doing something that would kill someone else? Even inadvertently. Doesn't that mean he'd be justified in killing me?'

'Justice isn't what the conundrum is about. But it's good that it makes you think. Is it something you think about much?'

'Killing?'

Stockmann nodded.

'Every time it's happened, there's been no doubt in my mind that what I was doing was legally and morally right. When I was in the SAS I had to follow rules of engagement, and when I was a cop I had to follow PACE, the Police and Criminal Evidence Act. It's a bit greyer now that I'm with SOCA because I'm effectively a civil servant rather than a police officer, but there are still rules that have to be followed. If at any point I were to break the law I'd be out of a job and probably facing criminal charges.'

'And providing you're within the law, there's no guilt?'

'Pretty much, yeah. But there's more to it than just following the law. More often than not, when I took a life it was because my own was threatened. Either at the point of a gun or because the person I shot was about to detonate a bomb. It was self-defence, pretty much.'

Stockmann held up her glass. 'Half full again,' she said. 'The Belfast job's a bit different from what you normally do, isn't it?'

'I'm not trying to penetrate a gang, but basically it's the same old routine, getting a person to trust me so that I can betray them,' he said. 'It's what I do, and I do it well.'

'It can't be easy,' she said.

'Winning their trust is easy,' said Shepherd. 'It's the betrayal that takes its toll.'

'This latest job is a woman, right? That must make it harder. And it's not as if she's a drug-dealer or gangster.'

'We're not supposed to get specific about operational matters,' said Shepherd.

'That was when you were a policeman. SOCA has different rules.' She smiled. 'Actually, we can pretty much make up our own,' she said, 'and I do have a very high security clearance. Higher than yours, actually.'

'Because you worked for MI5?'

'I still do, from time to time,' she said. 'So, this woman you're trying to get close to, she might not be guilty of anything?'

'True.'

'Which makes it a very different job, because normally you'd be targeting hardened criminals, wouldn't you?'

'Yeah, we'd know in advance that the target was guilty. I'd be put in to gather the evidence. This case is different because at the end of the day she might not be a killer.'

'But she might be, so it's a valid investigation.'

Shepherd smiled ruefully. 'If she's guilty, what I'm doing is justifiable. But if she's just the widow of a hero cop, I'm a piece of shit for lying to her as I am.' He raised his glass in salute to her, then drained it and waved at the barmaid for a refill. Stockmann was looking at him anxiously. 'I'm fine, Caroline,' he said. 'It's what I do, but it doesn't get any easier. They're targets, but that doesn't make them less than human. Civilians probably assume that villains are villains, end of story, but they're sons, they're often fathers, they have friends, they go to weddings, they buy presents, they tell jokes. Some of the villains I've helped put inside have been great guys, guys I've got drunk with, guys who would have helped me without hesitation if I was in trouble. I'm not always proud of what I've done, but at the end of the day they're villains, and villains belong in jail.'

'I can't imagine how it must feel to live a lie.'

Shepherd shrugged. 'It's probably what acting's like, but there's no director to shout, "Cut." And no script. Everything's off-the-cuff, spur-of-the-moment stuff, reacting to what's going on around you.' The barmaid put a fresh drink in front of him and looked questioningly at Stockmann. She shook her head. 'You know what the hardest thing about it is?' he said. 'It's remembering what you don't know.' He smiled. 'I know that sounds crazy but it's true. It's easy enough to remember what you've been told, or what you've said, but as an undercover cop you know things about the target that your character wouldn't. So when you're in character a mental wall has to divide what you know from what you're supposed to know.'

'It sounds positively schizophrenic,' said Stockmann.

'It is,' said Shepherd. 'There's a constant battle between your two selves, a constant checking and rechecking. And while that's going on, you have to appear calm and collected.'

'The proverbial swan,' said Stockmann. 'Serene on the surface, paddling like crazy under the water.' She sipped some beer. 'Have you thought that the same would apply to the woman you're targeting? She has to be playing a part, too.'

'If she's guilty.'

'Agreed,' said the psychologist. 'But if she is, she'll also be playing a role. Like you, she'll be running anything she says through an internal filter, constantly checking her reality against how the world perceives her.'

'I hadn't thought of it that way,' said Shepherd. 'The thing is, she doesn't seem to be playing a part.'

'Can you tell?' asked Stockmann.

'I'm not sure.'

'Because if you can, isn't it possible that someone you're

targeting can tell that you're playing a role? Surely the only way you can function as an undercover agent is by being totally convincing.'

'But I'm a professional. It's my job. If she's guilty, she's an amateur who's killing the men who killed her husband. There should be signs, shouldn't there?'

Stockmann grinned. 'Like looking up to the left when she's lying? Or scratching her nose? It's not as easy as that, Dan. If it was, I'd be making a fortune playing Texas Hold 'Em. And she could be a sociopath, of course.'

Shepherd laughed. 'Now, that I would spot.'

'Actually, I doubt it. Sociopaths are natural mimics. They lack feelings of empathy with others and are totally uncaring about their effect on people, but can behave completely to the contrary. That's why serial killers are so effective. They can appear charming. And paedophiles can appear genuine and caring. If they looked like monsters, kids would never go near them.'

'What are you saying? That you can't judge a book by its cover?'

'It's a cliché, but it's true,' said Stockmann. 'You can't tell a murderer by looking them in the eye.'

Shepherd smiled. 'I'm not sure that's so,' he said.

'You can tell if someone's killed by looking at them?'

'There's a look that people who've been in combat have. They call it the thousand-yard stare. There's a coldness in their eyes as if they're looking through you.'

'And does everyone who's been in combat have it?'

'No,' said Shepherd. 'I know men who have killed several times and they're the most laid-back guys you'll ever meet. But I've never met someone with the thousand-yard stare who hasn't killed. I've seen it in the eyes of non-soldiers, too. Gangsters. Drug-dealers. Blaggers.'

'Blaggers?'

'Armed robbers,' said Shepherd. 'What I'm saying is, if they've got the look, they've killed.'

'Unless they're faking it,' said Stockmann.

'Faking it?'

'Say there's a hard man who wants you to think he's a killer. He fakes the thousand-yard stare. How would you know?'

'I'd know.'

Stockmann grinned. 'But if they were sociopaths, they'd be good at faking it.'

'So a sociopath would fake a thousand-yard stare to make me think he was a killer?' Shepherd exhaled through pursed lips. 'You're giving me a headache here, Caroline.'

'I just want you to understand that it's virtually impossible to tell if someone is guilty or not by looking at them,' said Stockmann. She beckoned the barmaid. 'If it was possible, the police's job would be a lot easier, wouldn't it?'

'Here's the thing,' said Shepherd. 'I look into Elaine's eyes and I see an honest person who wouldn't harm anyone. There's no guile, no deviousness. She shows no signs of lying.'

'Elaine is the woman in Belfast?'

Shepherd nodded. 'She's been hurt, and she's carrying a lot of baggage, but that's to be expected, considering the way her husband was killed and her son died.'

'You sound like you're empathising.'

'I am. A lot. And that's not good.'

'You're human,' she said. 'It's natural.'

'That means you're giving me a clean bill of health?'

'Buy me another pint and we'll talk about it,' laughed Stockmann.

Noel Kinsella looked around the hotel suite and sneered. 'This is the best you can do?' he asked.

'It's four hundred pounds a night,' said Patsy Ellis, folding her arms, 'and that's before you pick up the phone to order room service.'

'It's tiny.'

'It's a suite. And it's not for long.'

'Have you got the tickets yet?'

'They'll be here tomorrow.'

'First class, right?'

Ellis sighed. 'Yes.'

'Elizabeth insists on first class.'

'Well, maybe Elizabeth should be buying her own bloody ticket. It's not as if she's strapped for cash.'

'It's not her fault that everything turned to shit in Belfast,' said Kinsella, sitting down on the sofa. He took a bunch of grapes from the crystal bowl on the ornate coffee-table and popped one into his mouth.

'That's an exaggeration,' said Ellis. 'Frankly, I don't see why you need to go back to the States.'

'Because four of the guys who killed Robbie Carter are dead and I'm the only one left.'

'They weren't as protected as you are,' said Ellis. 'Lynn was riding around with two psychopathic gunmen, and McEvoy was sitting in his drug den on his own. And we still don't know that it's the same killer. McEvoy was a low-life with enemies all over the city, and plenty of people would happily have put a bullet in Gerry Lynn's head.'

'Please don't insult my intelligence. We both know what's going on.'

'And we both know how well protected you are. There'll be a man in the corridor outside and another in the next room.' She gestured at the connecting door. 'That will be unlocked at all times. Any problems and he can be here in a second.' She sat in an armchair by the window. The view was spectacular, across Hyde Park and beyond to North London. 'I do wish you'd reconsider. Now's a pivotal time for Northern Ireland and you could make a real difference to what happens in the province.'

'If I'm dead, I'm not going to be able to do anything.'

'And if you run away again, the people of Northern Ireland won't forget. Or forgive.'

'Don't screw around with me, Patsy,' said Kinsella. 'You owe me, remember?'

Ellis smiled tightly. 'We owe each other,' she said quietly. 'Don't forget that.'

'You said it would be safe to come back.'

'It *is* safe.'

'Are you stupid?' hissed Kinsella.

Ellis stood up. 'I don't want to fight with you, Noel. Sleep on it. Talk to Elizabeth.'

'She wants to go home.'

'Belfast is your home. In the States, you're just another Irishman on the make. In Belfast, you could be a leader. You could be in the inner circle, making real decisions.'

'Which is where you want me, right? This isn't about me, it's about you. You just want to use me again.' He threw a grape at her. It bounced off her chest.

'Very mature,' she said.

Kinsella tossed a handful of grapes at her. Ellis stalked out of the room, fuming.

Shepherd drove off the motorway into the service-station car park and saw the grey Jaguar beside a strip of grass. As he pulled up beside it, the Major climbed out, grinning. 'Nice car, SOCA must pay well,' he said.

'It goes with the legend,' said Shepherd. He flashed his Casio watch with its calculator keyboard. 'Same as this.'

The Major opened the boot of the Jaguar. 'I've got what you wanted, Spider, but are you sure about this?'

'I don't have any choice,' said Shepherd. 'He sent a man to kill my son. If it hadn't been for Billy and Jack, he'd have succeeded. I can't take the chance that he'll try again.'

'You don't have to do it yourself.'

'Yes, I do.'

'There are guys who'd do it for you at the drop of a hat.'

'I know, but this is personal.'

'If it goes wrong, you'll lose everything, you know that?

He's a stone-cold killer, no question, but if you handle this yourself you'll be a vigilante in the eyes of the law.'

'I know you've got my best interests at heart, and I know you're talking sense,' said Shepherd, 'but we both know that if our positions were reversed there's nothing I could say to you that would change your mind.'

'I can't argue with that.'

'So I appreciate what you're saying, but this is my fight. That bastard attacked my family, and it's up to me to take care of business.'

The Major stepped forward, put his arms around Shepherd and hugged him. 'You be careful,' he whispered, then released him. He pulled the metal case out of the boot and gave it to him. 'Okay, I've configured it for the nine-millimetre, like you asked. You've got rounds, right?'

'I'm sorted,' said Shepherd. 'I had some over from an undercover operation I was on a year ago. Untraceable.'

The Major nodded. 'Once you've used it, remove the bolt, the barrel and the magazine, wreck them and lose them. Make sure you screw up the inside of the barrel with a file, then cut it into pieces so it can't be used again. If it can't be test-fired it can never be identified.' He pointed at the case. 'In there is a replacement bolt, barrel and magazine for the .45 ACP. Reassemble the UMP in the .45 configuration and get it back to me. No one will ever know.'

Shepherd put it into the boot of his Audi.

'You're going to take that on the ferry to Belfast?' asked the Major.

'I'll take it apart and hide it under the back seat,' said Shepherd. 'But they never check, anyway. And if they do, my SOCA credentials should get me through.'

'You need anything, you call me,' said the Major.

'It'll be fine,' said Shepherd.

Shepherd climbed into his car, waved at the Major and drove off.

Gannon watched him go. 'I wish I had your confidence, Spider,' he murmured.

Shepherd arrived in Belfast at just after seven that evening. Customs had waved him through. He drove the Audi into the garage, switched on the light and pulled down the door.

He took the UMP from its hiding place under the back seat of the car, stripped and reassembled it, then checked the firing mechanism. He ejected the magazine and loaded it with the nine-millimetre rounds he'd taken from his house in Hereford. He unlocked the door that led from the garage to the kitchen, went upstairs and slid the weapon under his bed.

As he sat down in front of the television, the doorbell rang. Elaine, in camouflage cargo pants and a yellow T-shirt, was on the step, holding a bottle of white wine. 'Drink?' she said.

Shepherd got a corkscrew and two glasses from the kitchen, then poured the wine. 'To neighbours,' he said, as he sat beside her.

'Neighbours,' she said. 'So, where have you been the last couple of days?'

'Manchester,' he said. 'Couple of clients wanted meetings so I took the ferry over.'

'See? You're getting into the ferry thing, aren't you?'

'It's easier to have the car with me,' said Shepherd, 'and it cuts out the hassle of security checks. The airports are such a pain. The last time I flew I had to take my shoes, belt and jacket off, and I still got patted down. Do I look dangerous to you?'

Elaine smiled suggestively. 'Define dangerous.' She put down her glass and kissed him. Shepherd kissed her back, then stood up and switched off the lights. He lit two candles in the fireplace, then switched off the power at the sockets for the television and DVD player. He didn't want Singh or Button listening in.

'You are a smoothie, aren't you, Jamie?'

'I look better in candlelight,' said Shepherd.

'Because of your scar?'

'What scar?'

'Jamie, I've seen you naked, remember? The scar on your shoulder. It looks like a gunshot wound.'

'It was a long time ago.'

She kissed him on the lips, slipping her hand around his neck. When she released him she smiled at him with amused eyes. 'Who would want to shoot a nice guy like you?' she asked.

There had been no military service in the Jamie Pierce legend, but Elaine seeing him naked hadn't been part of the plan. He had to think on his feet, which was always dangerous. 'It was another life,' he said. 'I was in the army.'

'No way.'

'I'm afraid so,' said Shepherd. 'Infantry, but I was trained as an electrician. Thought I was learning a trade. Then Saddam Hussein invaded Kuwait and I was packed off with a gun and a prayer. I got hit by a sniper and that was the end of my soldiering.'

'It looks bad.'

'It wasn't, but the doctors who treated me weren't that hot.'

'You never said you were in the army.'

'I don't talk about it much,' said Shepherd.

Elaine stroked the back of his head. 'What was it like, getting shot?'

'I don't remember much about it,' he said. That was a lie. He still had nightmares about the dull thump of the bullet slamming into his shoulder, the crunch as he'd hit the ground, the wetness of the blood that seeped from the gaping wound into his shirt as he lay on the sand.

'My hero,' she said.

'There's nothing heroic about getting shot,' he said. Instantly he regretted what he'd said. 'Elaine, I'm sorry . . .'

'It's okay.'

'What happened to me doesn't compare with what happened to your husband.'

'Jamie, it's okay,' she said, and kissed him again, harder this time.

Shepherd woke to find Elaine propped up on her pillow, looking down at him and smiling. 'You snore,' she said.

'I've been told that before.'

She leant over to kiss him. 'I have to go,' she said. 'I've got clients to see in Bangor.'

'Dinner tonight? I'll cook.'

'I'll be back late,' she said. 'Raincheck?'

'I'll hold you to that.'

She slid out of bed and pulled on her clothes. 'I'm going to London the day after tomorrow for a financial-services exhibition. Earls Court.'

'Driving?'

'Of course. I'll probably go down to Dublin and across to Holyhead.'

'For long?'

'A few days. Why? Will you miss me?' She tickled him.

Shepherd pushed her away and grinned. 'Of course I will.'

He waited until he heard her leave, then reached for his mobile and phoned Button. 'We have a problem,' he said. 'Elaine's heading for London the day after tomorrow. She says she's got a conference or something at Earls Court. Financial services.'

'Now, that is interesting,' said Button. 'It's either a hell of a coincidence or she's going after Kinsella. How would she know where he is, though?'

'Maplethorpe told her the Kinsellas are in London. And she's got a lot of friends in the Intelligence Branch. I don't think she'd find it too difficult to get his location. Look, I had a thought. I should go with her.'

'Sure – but what reason would you have for going to London at short notice?'

'I'm sure we could think of something. What's the story with Kinsella?'

'Under wraps,' said Button. 'Hotel near Hyde Park.'

'How do we play this?'

'Let's see what she does when she gets to London.'

'You still think it's her?' asked Shepherd.

'I'm keeping an open mind,' said Button. 'You?'

'I really don't think she's a killer,' said Shepherd.

'You're not too close, are you, Spider?'

Shepherd cut the connection.

Shepherd's doorbell rang. He groaned and went to the bedroom window. He couldn't see who it was and there was no car parked outside. He pulled on a towelling robe and went downstairs.

Elaine looked as if she'd just got out of bed. 'My car's been stolen,' she said.

'You're kidding!'

She ran a hand through her unkempt hair. 'Jamie, if I wanted to wake you with a joke, I'd have thought of something better than that. Did you hear anything last night?'

'Nah, and I was up until one. Have you called the cops?'

'They'll send someone round, they said. But what can they do?'

'Keep an eye out for it, I guess.'

'If it's joyriders they'll have set fire to it by now, and if it was stolen for parts it'll have been stripped. Either way I doubt I'll get it back in one piece. Bastards.'

'I'm sorry.'

Elaine smiled. 'You're always apologising for things that aren't your fault.'

He held the door open for her. 'Come on, I'll make you a coffee.'

Elaine went through to the kitchen. 'Can I have one of your cigarettes?'

'Sure,' said Shepherd, switching on the kettle.

Elaine sat down and lit a Marlboro. 'I am so screwed,' she said.

'And not in a good way, I suppose,' said Shepherd.

'I'm supposed to be driving to London tomorrow. Now I'll have to hire a car. If they'll let me take it to the mainland.'

'Why don't I drive you?' asked Shepherd.

She blew smoke up at the ceiling. 'That doesn't make sense, Jamie.'

'It makes perfect sense. There's a couple of guys I need to see in London. I was going to fly next week but I could bring the meetings forward. I'll drive you tomorrow.'

'Where would you stay?'

'I'll go to a hotel. You?'

'My sister. Are you sure about this?'

Shepherd made coffee. 'It'll be fun, a road trip. You've already booked your ticket, right? Just change the car registration number on it and we're sorted.'

'You're such a sweetie.'

Shepherd grinned. 'That's what my mum says.'

'Okay, but we share the driving.'

They drank coffee and smoked for half an hour, then Elaine went home. Shepherd phoned Button. 'Were you listening?' he asked.

'Every word,' she said.

'She loves her car, you know.'

'We'll get it back for her – assuming she isn't a serial killer, of course.'

'I'll go through her bags first chance I get. If she has her husband's gun, we'll know for sure. What about you? Will you go to London?'

'Sure. I'll set up surveillance on her sister's house. I'll take a morning flight and be there before you.'

Shepherd ended the call, then took his personal mobile into the garden, called Martin O'Brien and told him Button was flying to London. O'Brien confirmed that he'd be at Heathrow to keep tabs on her.

As Shepherd turned back to the house, his eyes strayed up to Elaine's attic. He wondered if she was up there, taking the rounds from the trunk, preparing to kill Kinsella. Was she capable of cold-blooded murder? Could she shoot a man in the knees and the back of the head, then act as if it had never happened?

Elaine rang Shepherd's doorbell at just before six in the morning. It was a two-hour drive to Dublin, which would give them plenty of time to catch the high-speed ferry to Holyhead. She was wearing a black blazer over a dark blue dress and carrying a large Louis Vuitton bag and her brief-case. 'Ready?' she said brightly.

'I'm all packed and ready to go,' he said. 'I left my car in the garage in case the joyriders were on the rampage again.' He took her bag. 'I'll put it in the boot for you. The kettle's just boiled so why don't you make us both a coffee?'

'Yes, sir,' she said.

'I'll take your briefcase, too, yeah?'

'I'll keep it with me,' she said. 'It's got my mobile and cigarettes in it.'

They went into the kitchen together and Shepherd opened the door to the garage. He closed it behind him, then opened the car boot and put Elaine's bag next to his hard-shelled suitcase. He took a deep breath and slowly unzipped the bag. On the top were two magazines, then a toiletries bag. Shepherd opened it and peered inside – toothbrush, tooth-paste, dental floss, moisturiser, hairbrush. There was a Prada leather case containing cosmetics, neatly folded underwear, silk pyjamas, two shirts, a pair of jeans and a pullover. Shepherd groped around in the bottom.

The door opened. He pulled his hand from the bag and closed the boot, heart racing. 'Toast?' asked Elaine.

'Just coffee, please,' said Shepherd.

'It's ready,' she said. 'Is everything okay?'

'Just a last-minute check,' he said. 'Don't want to forget

anything.' She pulled the door to but didn't close it. Shepherd couldn't risk searching the bag any further. He opened the boot again, zipped up the bag, then slammed the boot.

Elaine gave him his coffee as he went back into the kitchen. She had put her briefcase on the floor by the table. She offered him a cigarette, and as they smoked and drank their coffee, she seemed totally at ease, laughing, smiling and flirting with him. Shepherd found it impossible to believe she could be so relaxed if she was going to London to shoot Noel Kinsella. He remembered Stockmann's words, that a true sociopath could fake all emotions. Was Elaine Carter a sociopath?

'Penny for them?' said Elaine.

Shepherd realised he hadn't been listening to her. 'Sorry, what?'

'You were miles away, Jamie.'

'Sorry. Just getting my head straight.' He smiled. 'I'm not really a morning person.' He hated it when she called him Jamie. It was a reminder that everything she thought she knew about him was a lie. She had made love to him, she had shared her innermost thoughts with him, but in return he had done nothing but lie to her.

There was little traffic on the motorway to Dublin, and theirs was one of the first cars on to the Stena Line ferry, which was packed. Elaine and Shepherd found two seats at the rear of the boat. Shepherd wanted to go back down and search Elaine's bag and briefcase but passengers weren't allowed on the vehicle deck while the ferry was at sea. He had his SOCA identification in a hidden compartment in his wallet but he wasn't sure that the ferry staff would know what it was. His police warrant card had always been accepted without question, but SOCA was a relatively new agency and, more often than not, his credentials were met with frowns and head-scratching. The last thing he wanted was to attract attention to himself so he made small-talk as the ferry powered across the Irish Sea.

★　★　★

Martin O'Brien looked over the top of the *Evening Standard*. He had already seen two British Midland flights arrive and there had been no sign of Charlotte Button on either. She was not on the third, either. It had been twenty minutes since the flight had landed and Button never flew with checked-in luggage. He took out his mobile to phone Shepherd when someone tapped his shoulder. He whirled round. The woman herself, with a Samsonite carry-on case, was at his side, smiling. O'Brien's heart sank.

'Hello, Martin,' she said cheerfully. 'You look like you've lost weight.'

'I'm training for the Marathon des Sables,' he said.

'People die running that race, you know.'

'I know.'

'You be careful.'

'I will.'

'And following me is part of your training, is it?'

O'Brien smiled ruefully. He knew there was no point in lying. 'You're good,' he said.

'Yes, Martin, I am. So are you. How long have you been on my case?'

'Not long.'

'But you've had someone else in Belfast, right?'

'A few pals of mine from the Ranger Wing have been helping me out.'

'Tall man with curly hair and a Tag diving watch? And a heavyset fellow with a limp?'

'Diving accident a few years back,' said O'Brien. 'They were that obvious, were they?'

'Actually, they were damned good. And I only spotted the two. Most of the time I had no idea where they were. Are you here alone?'

O'Brien jerked a thumb at the exit. 'I've a driver outside. Black cab.'

'Am I right in thinking that Spider's behind this?'

O'Brien looked pained.

'Special forces' code of silence? I hardly think you've developed a crush so I assume someone's asked you to keep an eye on me. The common link between us is Spider.'

'You ought to be a detective,' said O'Brien.

Button ignored his attempt at sarcasm. 'So the question I need answering, Martin, is why did he want you tailing me? Why is he suddenly interested in my comings and goings?'

'It was more a case of protecting you than tailing you,' he said.

'Protecting me from what?'

'He thought someone might want to hurt you.'

'Spit it out, Martin. We're both big boys and I don't have all day.'

O'Brien sighed. 'He said there was a contract out on you. Some raghead. Hassan Salih, a Palestinian. He didn't know what the guy looked like, he just had the name.'

'This Palestinian, is he the one offering the contract or the killer?'

'He was the hitman. He didn't say who put up the contract.'

Button nodded thoughtfully. 'Okay,' she said. 'Well, as of now you're off the case. I don't need minding and Spider should know that by now. There's nothing I can say that'll stop you phoning him thirty seconds after I've walked out of here, so all I'll ask is that you tell him you're rumbled and that if I find anyone else on my tail he can look for employment elsewhere. Are we clear?'

'Crystal,' said O'Brien.

'Excellent,' said Button. 'So, I'll wish you good day and good luck with your run in the desert. I did the Marathon des Sables in my gap year. Drink plenty of water, and pop any blisters with a sterilised needle.' She gave him a final tight smile and walked away, her high heels clicking on the hard floor.

As soon as she had left the terminal building, O'Brien rang Shepherd's number. His call went to voicemail but he decided not to leave a detailed message – it would be better to give

him the bad news in person. 'Spider, call me.' As he put the
phone away he saw Button through the terminal window.
She gave him a thumbs-up and climbed into a taxi.

About two hours outside London, Shepherd told Elaine
that he needed the washroom and pulled into a service
station. Elaine said she wanted to buy cigarettes so she
headed for the shop. Shepherd had listened to O'Brien's
brief message as he had driven off the ferry in Holyhead
but hadn't wanted to call him while Elaine was in the car.
As soon as he went into the men's room he punched in
O'Brien's number.

A sales representative had taken off his jacket and tie and
was shaving with a disposable razor, a leather attaché case
at his feet. He nodded at Shepherd and carried on. O'Brien
answered. 'Martin, hey. What's up?' asked Shepherd.

'Good news, bad news,' said O'Brien.

'You lost her?'

'No, she found me.'

'Shit.'

'Sorry,' said O'Brien. 'She blindsided me.'

'And what's the good news?'

'She wasn't as mad as I thought she'd be. Quite laid back,
actually. She said we had to lay off her and that she'd sack
you if you ever did anything like that again, but other than
that she was pretty relaxed.'

'How much did you tell her?' asked Shepherd.

'I couldn't lie to her, Spider.'

'It's okay,' said Shepherd. 'Just tell me what you told her.'

'That you had her best interests at heart, that you knew
there was a contract out on her.'

'Terrific,' muttered Shepherd.

'Spider, you know her background. If she gets pissed off
at me, she could do me a lot of damage.'

'It's not your fault. I should have been up front with her.'

'That was the strange thing,' said O'Brien. 'She wasn't in

the least bit fazed when I said there was a hitman after her.
It's like she already knew.'

'Maybe she did,' said Shepherd.

'What do you want to do?' asked O'Brien.

The salesman was splashing water over his face.

'There's nothing we can do,' said Shepherd. 'If Charlie
says back off, we don't have a choice. Like you said, she's a
heavy hitter.'

'Did you know she was a runner? She said she did the
Marathon des Sables when she left university.'

'No, I didn't,' said Shepherd. 'But then the woman is
constantly surprising me.'

'Wouldn't want to get on the wrong side of her,' said
O'Brien.

'I think I've left it a bit late to worry about that,' said
Shepherd.

'I'll call the guys in Belfast and stand them down.'

Shepherd thanked him and cut the connection. He used
the urinal and washed his hands. As he left, the salesman
was brushing his teeth with slow, even strokes.

Elaine was standing outside the service station, smoking.
She offered him a cigarette. He took one and lit it. 'Do you
want me to share the driving?' she asked.

'Sure,' said Shepherd.

She looked at him quizzically. 'You're a funny one, Jamie.'

'Now what?'

'Most men wouldn't give up the steering-wheel no matter
how tired they were. Same way they'll never ask for direc-
tions if they get lost.'

'Ah, that's because I'm in touch with my feminine side.'

'Yeah, that's glaringly obvious.'

'I am,' said Shepherd, seriously. 'I cry at movies.'

She looked at him in disbelief. 'What was the last movie
you cried at?'

Shepherd pretended to consider the question. '*Snow White
and the Seven Dwarfs*,' he said eventually.

'Rubbish,' she said.

'Yeah,' he said. 'That first night when she stayed with the dwarfs and they all got into bed feeling sleepy. Sleepy had to get out again. I felt so sorry for him.'

Elaine laughed as she was taking a drag on her cigarette and began to cough. She bent over and Shepherd patted her on the back. 'Do you need the Hindenburg manoeuvre?' he asked.

She stopped coughing and put a hand on his shoulder. 'You mean the Heimlich manoeuvre. That's for choking.'

'No, it's the Hindenburg,' said Shepherd. 'I fill you full of hydrogen and set fire to you. Guaranteed to stop coughing fits.'

She started to laugh again. Shepherd put an arm round her and kissed her cheek. He couldn't believe she was a serial killer. The Elaine Carter he knew simply wasn't capable of murder.

As they drove off the M1 and into central London, Shepherd asked Elaine if she wanted him to drop her at her sister's. 'What hotel are you staying at?' she asked.

'The Ibis in Earls Court. Opposite the exhibition centre.'

Elaine's surprise was written on her face. 'Why did you book in there?'

'Thought it would be easy for you, and they've got car parking.'

'You didn't have an ulterior motive, did you?'

Shepherd chuckled. 'Such as?'

'Such as hoping to persuade me to stay over. I did say I was going to stay with my sister.'

'Elaine, you have so little faith in me.'

'Double bed?'

'King size,' said Shepherd. 'I move around a lot when I sleep.'

She slid her hand along his thigh. 'I know,' she said, and grinned. 'Okay, let's go to the hotel first.'

It had started to rain by the time they reached Earls Court.

They parked the Audi and checked in, then went up to the room. She kissed him as soon as he'd closed the door, a long, slow kiss as she pressed herself against him. Eventually she broke away. 'I need a shower,' she said. 'Don't start without me.'

Her bag was by the door and her briefcase was on the bed but she'd left the bathroom door open and the walls were mirrored so he couldn't risk going through her things. 'Hey, I'm out of cigarettes,' he called. 'I'll just pop down and get some.'

'Don't be long,' she said. 'I'm hungry.'

As soon as he got down to Reception, Shepherd called Button on his mobile. 'I've checked in,' he said. 'We'll have dinner together and she's going to the conference tomorrow. I'll probably go with her.'

'My spies tell me you're sharing a room,' said Button.

'Are you checking up on me, Charlie?' said Shepherd, coldly.

'The surveillance team outside her sister's house said she hasn't been there, that's all,' said Button. 'Is there anything you need to tell me?'

'She's left some of her things in my room. We're at the Ibis, right opposite the exhibition centre. I thought it was the best way to keep an eye on her.'

'Well, I look forward to seeing your expense claim,' said Button.

'What about Kinsella? How long will he be in London?'

'Two more nights, then he's off to the States. Once he's left the UK, he's no longer our responsibility.'

'What do I do then?' asked Shepherd. 'Does the investigation continue?'

'We're tasked with identifying the killer,' said Button. 'We stay on the job until that's resolved.'

Maplethorpe took the lift to the fifteenth floor. Kinsella's suite was to the left, half-way down the corridor. The man in the door was in his early forties, stocky in a blue pinstripe suit that was too baggy in the trousers. He was Russ Williamson, a detective sergeant in the PSNI. Maplethorpe had known him for eighteen years, and for more than half that time they'd served in the RUC's Special Branch.

'Looks like you're putting on weight, Russ,' said Maplethorpe, as he strode down the corridor. 'Too much hotel food, I suppose.'

'John, what the hell are you doing in London?'

'Just checking everything's okay,' he said. 'The top brass are scared shitless that something might happen to Kinsella. He's heading back to the States, I gather.'

'I'll be glad when he's gone,' said Williamson. 'He's a right pain in the arse.'

'Who are you with?' asked Maplethorpe.

'Owen Crompton. He's one of the new intake, a Catholic, but he's a solid guy.' He indicated the room next door. 'He's in there.'

'How's he feel about Kinsella?'

'No love lost there,' said Williamson. 'Reckons Kinsella's just a scrote who got lucky.'

Maplethorpe grinned. 'His head's obviously screwed on right. Is the wife with him?'

'They're in for the afternoon,' said Williamson. 'Out this evening for dinner and a show with friends.'

'You both go out with them?' asked Maplethorpe.

'The two of us and a driver, Paul Cadman.'

Maplethorpe knew Cadman. He was a detective sergeant, a twenty-five-year veteran. 'You must be pulling in some overtime,' he said.

'Paying for my place in Bulgaria,' said Williamson. 'Three bedrooms, pool, it's going to be my retirement place. What about you? I heard you were quitting.'

'I'll never leave Belfast,' said Maplethorpe. 'What time are you off? I'll take you for a drink.'

'I'm on the clock until midnight,' said Williamson. 'We can hit the hotel bar.'

Maplethorpe grinned. 'It's a date,' he said.

Shepherd and Elaine had breakfast in the hotel restaurant, then walked over to the exhibition centre. 'Are you sure you want to come in?' she asked.

'My first meeting isn't until this afternoon,' he said, 'and I might find something interesting to do with my money.'

'Well, no impulse buying,' she said. 'Run anything past me first. There'll be a lot of sharks about.'

The giant hall was filled with booths offering the wares of banks, building societies, insurance companies and investment firms. They were staffed by earnest young men and women in suits, half of whom seemed to have Bluetooth headsets glued to their ears. Shepherd walked with Elaine from booth to booth. Hundreds of visitors were milling around, inspecting the displays and collecting glossy brochures.

At eleven they had coffee, then watched a presentation by two blonde girls with pneumatic breasts promoting a property fund that was investing in shopping malls in the former Communist bloc, and another by two slick men in black Armani suits with Russian accents who were pitching shares in an oil-exploration company.

Afterwards they went out for a cigarette, then wandered round the booths again. Elaine said she needed to wash her hands and redo her makeup. Shepherd went off for another coffee, then sat and read the *Daily Mail*. By the time he'd finished his coffee she hadn't returned. He realised it had been almost thirty minutes since he'd seen her. He went down to the cloakroom area but she wasn't there, then walked the length of the exhibition hall. There was no sign of her. He called her but her mobile went straight to answering-machine. He put his phone back into his pocket, went up to the mezzanine floor and scanned the exhibition below.

He left the hall and went to the hotel on the off-chance that Elaine had gone back to the room. She hadn't. He phoned Button. 'I've lost her,' he said.

'How long?'

'I last saw her an hour ago. I spent half an hour looking for her in the exhibition centre, and she's not in the hotel room. Her mobile phone's off.'

'You checked for a weapon, right?'

'As best I could.'

Button clicked her tongue. 'What do you think, Spider?'

'I don't know,' he said. 'Maybe she met a client and went off for a meeting.'

'Without telling you?'

'We're not joined at the hip.'

'Is it possible she's going after Kinsella?'

'Charlie, I don't know. My gut feeling is that it's not her.'

'I'm not sure we can risk everything on a gut feeling,' she said. 'Okay, meet me at Kinsella's hotel. In Reception. Soon as you can.'

Shepherd ended the call and hurried to the car park for his Audi.

The lift door opened and Russ Williamson moved his hand closer to the gun in a nylon holster under his left armpit. He relaxed when he saw John Maplethorpe. 'You can't stay away, can you?' he said.

'How's your head?' asked Maplethorpe. The two men had spent three hours drinking the previous night, ending up in an after-hours club in Soho.

'Throbbing,' said Williamson. 'I could do with a hair of the dog but the wife has a thing about alcohol.'

'Thought I'd see if you wanted a cigarette break,' said Maplethorpe. 'I'm supposed to have a chat with Kinsella before he departs these shores so we can kill two birds with one stone.'

'You sure? I could do with a coffee as well.'

'Take half an hour. I'll have my debrief and wait until you get back. You said the wife was going out shopping, right?'

'Yeah, she's at Harrods with Paul.' He pointed to the door down the corridor. 'Owen's in there. I'll let him know I'm taking a break.'

Maplethorpe patted his shoulder. 'I'll tell him,' he said.

'You're a star, John, thanks.'

'You'd do the same for me,' said Maplethorpe.

Williamson went to the lift. When it arrived he waved at Maplethorpe, who waved back as the doors closed. Then Maplethorpe undid his jacket. A Smith & Wesson .357 Magnum stuck out of his belt.

Shepherd parked his Audi at a meter down the road from the hotel and phoned Button as he hurried along the pavement. 'On my way,' he said.

'I'm here already,' she said. A uniformed doorman saluted Shepherd as he went in. Button was in the lobby. 'They're on the fifteenth floor,' she said. They got into the lift and she pressed the button.

'We might be worrying about nothing,' said Shepherd.

'I agree,' said Button, 'but I'll feel happier if we check for ourselves.' She jabbed at the button to close the doors. 'Come on, come on,' she muttered.

Maplethorpe knocked at the door to Kinsella's suite. After a few seconds it opened on the safety chain. Maplethorpe flashed his PSNI identification. 'John Maplethorpe, Intelligence Branch.'

Kinsella squinted at the ID card. 'Where's Russ?'

'Family problems in Belfast. His wife.'

'How long will he be gone?'

'I'm to fill in until you leave for the States,' said Maplethorpe. 'Can I come in and do a visual check, please?'

'What?'

'It's procedure when there's a personnel change,' said Maplethorpe, putting away his ID.

'Now?'

'It's supposed to be done as soon as I come on duty,' said Maplethorpe.

Kinsella grunted, took off the chain and opened the door. He was wearing a dark blue denim shirt with the sleeves rolled up to his elbows and faded blue jeans. He hadn't shaved and his hair was tousled as if he'd only just got out of bed.

Maplethorpe walked into the suite. 'Nice room,' he said. There were two beige sofas, a desk and a large plasma television on one wall. A half-eaten plate of sandwiches and a pot of tea stood on a coffee-table in front of the television.

'You should try living here,' said Kinsella.

Maplethorpe pointed at the door that led to the room on the left. 'Is that where Owen is?'

'Yeah. I think he listens in when I'm having sex with my wife,' said Kinsella.

'I'll have a word with him about that,' said Maplethorpe.

'Don't bother, it's quite a turn-on knowing that I'm having sex and he isn't,' said Kinsella. He sat on the sofa and put his feet on the coffee-table. 'Do you want tea? I'll get them to send up an extra cup.'

'I'm fine, thanks,' said Maplethorpe. He went to the connecting door and opened it. A man in a grey suit was sitting on the bed, pointing a remote control at the television. He stood up awkwardly and reached for the gun in his underarm holster.

'Whoa, lad, I'm on the job,' said Maplethorpe, holding up a hand. 'Detective Superintendent Maplethorpe. John to my friends. Didn't Russ mention I'd be dropping by?'

'No, he didn't,' said Owen Crompton, visibly relaxing. 'He was out on the town with you last night, wasn't he?'

'Just a few drinks,' said Maplethorpe. 'I said I'd swing by and review the security arrangements.' He closed the door behind him.

'It's a babysitting job,' said Crompton. 'He's off soon, anyway.'

'Got to be done right, though, Owen,' said Maplethorpe. He nodded at the window. 'I saw a car down there this morning. Didn't look right.'

Crompton went to look outside. 'Is it still there?'

'I'm not sure,' said Maplethorpe, as he took his gun from his belt and held it by the barrel. 'Grey Toyota.' Crompton craned his neck to look down at the road below. Maplethorpe slammed the butt of the revolver against Crompton's temple, then caught him under the arms as he slumped to the ground. 'Sorry, lad,' he whispered.

He lowered Crompton to the carpeted floor, then laid down his gun, took a roll of insulation tape from his jacket pocket and used it to bind the man's hands and feet. He picked up his weapon then strode across the room to the adjoining door. He pulled it open and stepped into Kinsella's suite.

The doors to the lift rattled open and a robotic female voice informed Shepherd and Button that they had arrived at the fifteenth floor. Button looked at the signs indicating where the rooms were and pointed left. 'This way.' She rushed down the corridor and Shepherd hurried after her. His phone rang and he pulled it from his pocket. It was Elaine Carter. He rejected the call and put the phone away.

There was a chambermaid's trolley at the far end of the corridor but other than that it was deserted. 'There should be a man on guard here,' said Button. 'Something's wrong.'

'Turn around,' said Maplethorpe, pointing his gun at Kinsella's face. 'Turn around or I'll shoot you in the face.'

Kinsella was trembling and breathing heavily. 'You're a cop – what are you doing?' he said.

'I'm a cop and you killed a cop,' said Maplethorpe. 'Now turn around.'

'You can't do this,' said Kinsella.

Maplethorpe stepped forward and whipped the barrel across Kinsella's face. He yelped and blood spurted from his nose. 'Turn around,' said Maplethorpe.

At a knock on the door both men jumped.

Maplethorpe raised the gun. 'Turn around or I'll shoot you in the face,' he said.

Button knocked on the door again. 'Could they have gone out?' asked Shepherd. The chambermaid came out of a room down the corridor, loaded with dirty towels.

Button shook her head. 'I checked with Reception. The wife went out but Kinsella ordered room service half an hour ago.'

Shepherd banged on the door.

The chambermaid was West Indian with a gold tooth that glinted as she spoke. She waddled over to them. 'He's in there,' she said. 'Maybe he's in the shower.'

Button showed the woman her SOCA identification. 'Can you open the door for us?' she said.

The chambermaid had a master keycard on a chain attached to her belt. 'Sure I can,' she said.

'Charlie, maybe we should wait for back-up,' said Shepherd.

'We don't have time,' said Button.

'If someone's in there with a gun, we're going to be in a lot of trouble,' said Shepherd.

'A gun?' said the chambermaid, covering her mouth with a ring-covered hand.

'It's okay,' said Shepherd. He held out his hand. 'Give me the keycard, please.'

She landed it over. 'Now, please leave the floor,' said Button. The chambermaid didn't need to be asked twice. She set off as fast as she could to the lift.

'There should be security in the next room,' said Button.

Shepherd went to the door of the adjoining room, knocked, then slid the keycard into the slot on the door. The green light winked on. He twisted the handle and stepped inside. A man in a grey suit was lying on the floor, his hands and feet bound with blue tape. 'Charlie, come on,' he said.

'Please don't shoot me,' cried Kinsella. 'I've got a wife. She's pregnant. I'm going to be a father.' Tears were running down his cheeks.

'You killed Robbie Carter and he was a father,' said Maplethorpe. 'You shot him in the legs and you shot him in the head. Now it's your turn.'

'You can't do this,' said Kinsella.

'Turn around, Noel. Be a man.'

'You killed Gerry Lynn?'

'And McFee, and Dunne, and McEvoy.'

The door to the adjoining room crashed open.

Shepherd aimed Crompton's gun at Maplethorpe. It was a Glock so there was no safety to worry about. 'Drop the gun, John,' he said.

Maplethorpe sneered at Shepherd, and kept his revolver aimed at Kinsella's face. 'I knew something wasn't right about you, Jamie,' he said. 'What are you? Special Branch? MI5?'

'I'm the guy who's pointing a gun at you, John. That's the only thing you should be worried about.'

'Do I look worried?' said Maplethorpe. 'Who's the woman?'

'Armed police are on their way,' said Button.

'So?' said Maplethorpe. He took aim at Kinsella's left leg. 'You can watch as I take care of this little scrote.'

'Shoot him!' shouted Kinsella. 'He's crazy – shoot him, for God's sake!'

'John, put down the gun.'

'Don't talk to him, just shoot him!' shouted Kinsella.

'Maybe he wants you dead as much as I do,' said Maplethorpe. 'He's a good friend of Robbie Carter's widow. Maybe he wants me to kill you.'

'John, enough,' said Shepherd.

'Am I right, Jamie? Don't you think that this little scrote deserves to die?'

Shepherd said nothing.

'You're a detective superintendent with almost thirty years' service. You know that what you're doing is wrong,' said Button.

'Legally, but not morally,' said Maplethorpe. 'He killed Robbie Carter and didn't serve a day for it. How can that be right? He murdered a good man but the Government pats him on the head and lets him go. Now he's going to get what's coming to him, what he gave to Robbie.'

'Robbie Carter was a killer,' muttered Kinsella. 'A goddamned killer.'

'Bollocks!' said Maplethorpe.

'He was passing info to the UFF, info that got Republicans killed. Info that came from his MI5 handler.'

'You're telling us that Carter was working with MI5 and the UFF?' said Button.

'He was a conduit. If MI5 wanted to put someone in the firing line they gave the info to Carter and he fed it to his UFF contact. He might not have pulled the trigger himself but he was responsible for the murders of at least eight good Republicans.'

'And that's why you killed him?' asked Button.

'I didn't kill him. No one ever said I put a bullet in Carter. I was there but I didn't shoot him. I fired into the floor. It was Adrian Dunne who put the bullet in Carter's head. And there was nothing I could do to stop him.'

'And why the hell would you have wanted to stop him?' asked Shepherd.

Kinsella stared at him, sweat beading on his forehead. 'Because I was an MI5 agent,' he said.

'Like fuck,' said Maplethorpe.

'I was a paid agent of MI5. Had been since 1992.'

'You're lying,' said Maplethorpe.

'Why would I lie about something like that?'

'Because you know I'm going to put a bullet in your head, same as you did with Robbie.'

'I didn't shoot anyone,' said Kinsella.

'If Carter worked for MI5 and you worked for MI5, why didn't you stop it?' asked Shepherd.

'Carter didn't work for MI5. They used him. I was a paid agent.'

'But you let the IRA team kill him,' said Shepherd, his gun still aimed at Maplethorpe's head.

'There was nothing I could do. It was all kick, bollock, scramble,' said Kinsella. 'The guy running the operation was Gerry Lynn. The rest of us didn't even know who the target was. It was only when we pulled up outside the house that I realised we were there for Carter.'

'And you let them kill him?' said Maplethorpe.

'I was outgunned,' said Kinsella. 'If I'd done anything they'd have killed me as well.'

'Bollocks,' said Maplethorpe, his finger tightening on the trigger.

'Don't do it, John,' said Shepherd. 'If you shoot him, I'll kill you.'

'Easy to say, Jamie,' said Maplethorpe, 'but it's not that easy to pull the trigger.'

'Just put the gun down and we can talk this through.'

'He's a liar. He helped kill Robbie.'

'I had no choice!' shouted Kinsella. '*I had no bloody choice.*'

'If you were working for MI5, why didn't you say something when the Brits were trying to extradite you?' asked Maplethorpe. 'Why didn't you come clean then?'

'Because once a tout, always a tout, and you know what the IRA does to touts,' said Kinsella. 'Peace Process or not, they'd have killed me. Look what happened to Denis Donaldson, shot dead in two thousand and six. The IRA didn't care about the Peace Process then, and they sure as hell wouldn't care about it now if they found out I'd been working for MI5.'

Shepherd knew of Donaldson, a dyed-in-the-wool Republican who had been an active IRA member right through the Troubles. After the ceasefire he became Sinn Fein's office administrator in Stormont but he was blasted four times with a shotgun in his cottage in County Donegal after being exposed as a long-time informer and British agent. Shepherd knew that Kinsella was right. If it became known that he'd worked for MI5 he'd be a marked man.

'You hear what he's saying, John?' said Button. 'You can't shoot an MI5 agent.'

'He's an IRA killer who didn't serve a day for the death of Robbie Carter, and now he's going to get what he deserves,' said Maplethorpe. 'Just because he says he worked for MI5 doesn't make it so. He'd say anything to save his skin.' Maplethorpe's finger tightened on the trigger.

'John, don't!' shouted Shepherd.

'Wait!' said Button. 'Noel, if what you're saying is true, who was your handler?'

'Why does that matter?' asked Kinsella.

'If you really were working for MI5, you'd have had a handler,' said Button.

'Who the hell are you?' asked Maplethorpe.

'It doesn't matter who I am,' said Button.

'She's your boss?' Maplethorpe asked Shepherd. 'Or does she work for you?'

'Like the lady said, it doesn't matter who we are,' said Shepherd. 'What matters is what happens over the next few seconds. Lower your weapon, John.'

'That's not going to happen,' said Maplethorpe. He took half a step closer to Kinsella. Kinsella flinched and put his hands in front of his face.

'Ellis!' shouted Kinsella. 'My handler was Patsy Ellis!'

Button's eyes widened. 'Do you know Ellis?' asked Shepherd.

'Yes, I know her,' said Button. She looked at Maplethorpe.

'John, listen to me. Patsy Ellis works at the Joint Terrorism Analysis Centre and used to head up MI5's Belfast office.'

'Makes no difference,' said Maplethorpe, through gritted teeth.

'It makes a world of difference,' said Button. 'Ellis wouldn't be handling small-fry. If she was his handler, he was an important intelligence source.'

'He's a murderer,' said Maplethorpe, 'and now he's going to get what he deserves.'

'Tell me one thing before you pull that trigger and this all turns to shit,' said Shepherd.

'What?'

'Why would you throw everything away for this scumbag? You killed McFee, Dunne, McEvoy and Lynn, right?'

'Bloody right,' said Maplethorpe.

'And you did a good job. Got clean away. No forensics, no witnesses.'

Maplethorpe grinned. 'I knew what I was doing.'

'Agreed,' said Shepherd. 'So why this? Why in front of witnesses? Why throw it all away? You want to spend the rest of your life behind bars, is that it? Do penance for what you've done?'

'He doesn't care any more,' said Button. 'He wanted all five dead, and Kinsella's the fifth. Once Kinsella dies, it's over. He doesn't care what happens to him.'

'That doesn't make any sense,' said Shepherd.

'It does when you know he's dying,' said Button.

'How did you—' Maplethorpe stopped mid-sentence. He glared at her. 'Who the hell are you?'

'He's got a brain tumour,' said Button. 'Inoperable. He's getting headaches now, and blurred vision, but in a few months he'll be having more serious symptoms. Fits. Hallucinations. Memory loss. How long did the doctors give you, John?'

'Long enough to put my affairs in order,' said Maplethorpe. 'Long enough to do what I have to do.'

'He's taking early retirement on medical grounds,' said Button. 'But the doctors have told him there's nothing they can do and that at best he's got six months.'

'Do you understand now, Jamie?' said Maplethorpe. 'Do you understand I've got absolutely nothing to lose?'

'I will shoot you, John.'

'You keep saying that, Jamie. But here's two things to think about. One, are you capable of pulling that trigger?'

'Yes,' said Shepherd, emphatically.

'And, two, will you be able to shoot me before I pull mine?'

'Yes,' said Shepherd.

'Because that will make you a murderer, and that's something you'll have to live with for a lot longer than six months. Killing changes you, Jamie. It changes you for the worse. I've no regrets about what I've done, but I'm able to do it because I know I don't have much time left. If you kill me, you'll spend the rest of your life knowing you killed a man who was doing the right thing. They killed Robbie Carter, they took away a good husband and a loving father. They killed my friend. So killing them is the least I can do.'

'Don't do it, John,' said Shepherd.

'He will,' said Button. 'He will shoot you.'

Maplethorpe's finger tightened on the trigger. He smiled at Kinsella. 'See you in hell, you murdering—'

The bang was deafening in the confines of the hotel room. The side of Maplethorpe's head exploded and a red spray splattered across the wall. The acrid cordite made Shepherd's eyes water and he blinked hard, took aim again and put a second shot in Maplethorpe's chest. Maplethorpe slumped to the floor.

Kinsella backed away from the body, his mouth hanging open.

Maplethorpe stared at Shepherd with unseeing eyes. The gun fell from his nerveless fingers and clattered to the floor.

'You stupid bastard!' Kinsella shouted at Shepherd.

Shepherd turned to Kinsella as if noticing him for the first time. His gun was pointing at the Irishman and his finger was still on the trigger.

'Why did you wait so long?' Kinsella hissed. 'He could have killed me.'

'Maybe I should have let him,' said Shepherd, quietly. 'He was worth ten of you.'

Kinsella sneered at Shepherd. 'I don't give a toss what you think.' He went to the door.

'If I were you, I'd go back to the States,' said Shepherd.

Kinsella paused. 'I'm going to Ireland,' he said. 'That's where my future lies.'

Shepherd shook his head slowly. 'Not any more it doesn't,' he said. 'You're an MI5 informer and pretty soon the whole world will know it. The IRA might have decommissioned its weapon stocks but that doesn't mean there aren't a hell of a lot of psychopaths out there who'll be gunning for you as soon as the news gets out.' He smiled cruelly. 'And, trust me, the news will get out.'

'You can't do that,' said Kinsella.

'I can do what the hell I want,' said Shepherd. 'Now sod off or I'll shoot you myself.' He raised the gun and aimed it at Kinsella's face.

Kinsella's hand shook as he pulled open the door and hurried out of the room.

Shepherd ejected the magazine from the Glock, cleared the chamber, and handed the weapon to Button. 'I wasn't really going to shoot him,' he said.

'I wouldn't have cared overmuch if you had, frankly,' she said.

'What now?' said Shepherd, glancing at Maplethorpe's body. 'Do we call the police?'

'I'll handle it. No one'll want to have to explain a renegade RUC officer.'

'MI5?'

'I'll call Kinsella's handler. She can get her people to clean up her mess.'

'Who's going to tell Elaine Carter?'

'It'll be taken care of, but not by you. You're off the case as of now.'

Shepherd nodded. 'Where are you going?'

'I'll make sure this is squared away, then I'm going to see Patsy Ellis. She's got some explaining to do.'

Shepherd took a final look round his hotel room. The only things left there belonged to Elaine. Her clothes, her toiletries, her magazines. When he walked out, it would look as though he had never been there. He wouldn't be going back to the house in Belfast. Jenny Lock, the dresser, was on her way with a removal crew, and Amar Singh would already be in the house, removing his surveillance equipment. All that was left of Jamie Pierce was the Audi and he'd be returning that to the SOCA pool by the end of the week.

He walked out of the room with his holdall and took the lift to the ground floor. As he walked across the lobby he saw her coming through the revolving door and moved behind a pillar. She was talking animatedly into her mobile phone as she headed for the lifts. Shepherd watched her go. There was so much he wanted to say to her. He wanted to tell her that he'd killed Maplethorpe because she deserved to hear it from him. He wanted to tell her he had feelings for her, that he was close to falling in love with her. He wanted to tell her he was sorry he'd lied to her but that he was only doing his job.

He watched her take away the phone from her ear and press the button to call the lift. She dialled another number and Shepherd's mobile rang. He took the call.

'Jamie, where are you?' It was her.

'Still at the exhibition,' he said. 'What happened to you?'

'I'm sorry,' she said. 'I bumped into someone I knew in the ladies'. She's CEO of a company in Londonderry and wanted me to put together a pensions proposal for her. We ended up in a wine bar round the corner.'

'Why didn't you call?'

'I did. I went through to your voicemail. Didn't you get my message?'

Shepherd closed his eyes. She had rung when he was in Kinsella's hotel. He hadn't taken the call and he hadn't checked his voicemail.

'Jamie, I'm sorry I didn't call you right away but we were straight down to business. Are you okay?'

Shepherd was far from okay. He wanted to tell her John Maplethorpe had killed the men who had taken her husband from her, but he was fairly sure she already knew that. When he had opened the trunk in her attic, her husband's watch had been ticking. Someone must have been handling it, and that someone must have been Elaine. The ammunition had been in the trunk, and rounds had been missing from the box. Shepherd had no way of knowing whether she had kept the gun in the trunk, but he was reasonably sure that she had given the rounds to Maplethorpe. It wasn't something he could prove, even if he wanted to. Maplethorpe had killed the men and now he was dead. Case closed.

'Jamie? Are you there?'

There were so many things Shepherd wanted to say to her, but he knew that nothing he said would make any difference. He was working under cover and he wasn't Jamie Pierce, the man she liked and trusted. He was Dan Shepherd, a SOCA undercover agent and a professional liar. Almost everything she thought she knew about him was untrue and for that reason, and that reason alone, he could never talk to her again.

'I'm here.'

'Look, I'm just going to the room to freshen up. I'll be over at the centre in about half an hour. We'll have coffee.'

'Okay.'

'I'm going into the lift now. I'll phone you later.'

'Okay.'

'Jamie?'

'Yes?'

'I love you.'

Shepherd watched her get into the lift. He waited until the doors closed before he walked out of the hotel. As he went to his car he checked his voicemail. There was a message from Elaine, telling him what wine bar she was in and asking him to join her. He switched off his phone, took out the Sim card and broke it in half.

Charlie Button was sitting at a table with a bottle of red wine in front of her when Patsy Ellis walked in. She raised her glass as Ellis sat down. 'Red?' said Ellis. 'I thought you liked Chardonnay.'

'You like Chardonnay,' said Button. 'I've always preferred claret.' She picked up the bottle, filled the glass in front of Ellis, then topped up her own. She put down the bottle. It was almost empty.

'Thank you,' said Ellis.

Button lit a cigarette and inhaled deeply.

'I thought you'd quit,' said Ellis.

Button blew a tight plume of smoke at the ceiling. 'So did I,' she said. She waved at a waitress and mimed for her to bring over a second bottle. 'Why did you lie to me, Patsy?'

Ellis sipped her wine and put the glass on the table, her fingers lightly touching the stem. 'I didn't lie,' she said frostily.

'You should have told me that Noel Kinsella was an MI5 agent.'

'That was a long time ago,' she said. 'And I didn't lie.'

'You must have known what I was doing in Belfast.'

Ellis shrugged. 'You're with a different agency now,' she said. 'You're not family.'

'I'm not used to having guns pointed at me, Patsy, and it's not an experience I want to repeat.'

'If I'd known what was going to happen, obviously I'd have stepped in,' said Ellis.

'You had an IRA killer on the payroll,' said Button.

'Kinsella was a valuable source of intelligence,' said Ellis. 'You take your intel where you can, you know that – *and* that the people you get information from aren't usually the sort you'd invite around for tea and crumpets.'

'And Carter? What was he?'

Ellis sighed. 'Carter was a grey area. Nothing to do with me, I swear.'

'Black ops?'

Ellis smiled without warmth. 'We don't have a black-ops department, darling, as you also know. We leave that sort of thing to our American cousins.'

'But he fed information to the Loyalists, didn't he? Information that resulted in the murder of Republicans?'

'That wasn't official policy.'

'You're playing with words, Patsy.' Button drained her glass. 'Where is that damn waitress?'

'There was never a policy of murdering Republicans, if that's what you're suggesting.'

'The guys on Gibraltar in 1988 might argue with that,' said Button. 'If they weren't dead, of course.'

'That was an SAS operation, and you know it,' said Ellis. 'The Gibraltar team were planning to detonate a car bomb.'

'The SAS acted on MI5 intel on Gibraltar,' said Button, 'and the UFF were using MI5 intel in Belfast to kill IRA Volunteers. Robbie Carter was the conduit for that information.'

The waitress returned with a bottle. She smiled apologetically. 'I'm sorry, madam, you can't smoke here.'

Button stabbed out her cigarette as the waitress showed her the label on the bottle. Then the two women sat in silence until the waitress had pulled the cork, set the bottle on the table and gone away. 'Charlie, you're making a mountain out of a molehill, you really are,' said Ellis.

'Well, having a gun pointed at you can distort your perception, I suppose.'

'That was nothing to do with me,' said Ellis.

Button refilled her glass. 'The IRA hit team went after Robbie Carter because he was feeding information to a UFF hit team. Information supplied by MI5. So, whichever way you look at it, MI5 was involved in Carter's death. Maybe not responsible, but certainly involved.'

Ellis said nothing.

Button lit another cigarette, then leant across the table. 'If MI5 hadn't fed information to Carter, there'd have been no reason for the IRA to go after him.' She jabbed the cigarette at Ellis, punctuating her words.

'I get what you're saying, Charlie. I'm not stupid. And please stop waving that cigarette in my face.'

Button flicked ash on the floor. 'So I'm called in to protect the men who killed Robbie Carter, and what do I find? That one of his killers was an MI5 agent. How perverse is that, Patsy? One of your men helped kill another of your men.'

'Strictly speaking, neither of them was my man. Or Five's man for that matter. As you said, Carter was a conduit. He was an RUC officer and never on Five's payroll. And Noel Kinsella was an informer.'

'Informer, agent, it's the same thing.'

Ellis sipped some wine, granite-faced.

'Why didn't he stop them, Patsy? Why did he let them kill Robbie Carter?'

'He couldn't, without revealing who he was. What he was. If the IRA had found out he was an informer, he'd have been a dead man.'

'You could have pulled him out, given him a new identity, protection.'

'It wasn't like that, Charlie. He wasn't staff. He wasn't someone we'd put into the IRA. He was an IRA man through and through. He just had an axe to grind with some of his bosses and we were a means to an end. We paid him for information but he was using us to get rid of people who were giving him trouble.'

'He was betraying IRA men he didn't get on with. Is that what you're saying?'

'Pretty much. It was a symbiosis. We were using him and he was using us.'

'So, rather than spoil his cosy little arrangement, he helped murder Robbie Carter?'

Ellis nodded but didn't say anything.

'I'm not wired for sound, Patsy. I'm not recording this.'

'It wouldn't matter if you were, darling. You've signed the Official Secrets Act and a recording of this conversation wouldn't be of any use to anyone.' She smiled. 'Besides, I know you. You're upset, but you're not stupid.'

'Kinsella put his own life ahead of Carter's. By not doing anything, he was responsible.'

'Charlie, he stood up in court and pleaded guilty.'

'Because he knew he'd be released immediately. Why are you defending him?' She shook her head in frustration. 'When he decided to come back and go into Irish politics, I bet you thought your ship had come in.'

Ellis toyed with the stem of her glass.

'Was that the plan, Patsy? To have your own man embedded in Sinn Fein? Your own agent at Stormont, a conduit to the inner sanctum?'

'You're not crying, are you, darling?' asked Ellis.

Button blinked away the tears that were threatening to fill her eyes. She was absolutely not going to cry in front of Ellis. 'I don't think you realise how angry I am, Patsy,' she said.

'I do, and I'm sorry you're angry but I'm not sorry for what I did. Noel Kinsella was gold. He gave us grade-A intel on the IRA leadership at a time when RUC informers were being found in country lanes with bags over their heads. And he could give us intel now on what's going on in Sinn Fein. Can you imagine how valuable that would be?'

'You don't get it, do you?' Button gulped some wine, then took a long drag on her cigarette. 'We're supposed to be the guardians of this society. We're supposed to be defending our way of life against people who want us to live under a different regime. The Communists, the IRA, the Islamic fundamentalists. We're supposed to have right on our side. If we were backing both sides in Northern Ireland, then what's the point?'

'That's not what happened, Charlie. We took intel from some sources and fed intel to others. But the interests of our country always came first.'

'Noel Kinsella was an IRA killer. Robbie Carter was helping to kill Republicans.'

'And we were fighting on two fronts. The Loyalists on one hand, the IRA on the other.'

'And now the killers on both sides are back on the streets. Like it never happened. Like those three thousand or so people weren't murdered.'

'That was the politicians. It was their call. It had nothing to do with our work.'

The manager came over. He was a young man in a shiny suit with slicked-back hair and a tuft of hair below his lower lip. 'I'm sorry, madam, but you really can't smoke in here,' he said, in a nasal whine. 'If you continue to smoke I shall have to ask you to leave.'

Button regarded him coldly. 'Listen, you officious little prick, have you ever heard of SOCA, the Serious Organised Crime Agency? Well, I work for them.' Button gestured at Ellis. 'And she works for MI5. So if you want to send a plod over, feel free. I'll explain to him why I need a cigarette, and then I'll go out of my way to make your miserable little life a great deal more miserable than it already is.' She smiled brightly. 'Trust me, I can do it. Okay?'

The manager's face reddened. He turned and walked away.

'That was out of order, Charlie,' said Ellis.

Button blew smoke at the ceiling. 'I'll tell you why I'm so angry, Patsy. I'll tell you why I'm starting to question everything I've ever worked for. What's the biggest threat we're facing today? Islamic fundamentalists, right? Al-Qaeda infiltrators from overseas or home-grown terrorists. Everything from shoe bombs on planes to bio-hazards on our transport systems. We're running around like those guys who keep spinning plates balanced. Except if one of our plates falls, people die. A lot of people.'

'Charlie, I think you've had enough to drink, don't you?'

Button pointed her cigarette at Ellis. 'Don't patronise me, Patsy. Don't you dare patronise me.'

Ellis sat back in her chair, her hands flat on the table. 'I think I'd better go.'

'Here's what's getting me all riled up. Then, we were backing both sides against the middle. What if the powers-that-be are playing the same game now? What if one or more of those guys who went down the Tube with haversacks full of explosives was working for MI5? Or the ones that were planning to kidnap a Muslim soldier and behead him on the Internet. Or the London car bombs – were MI5 agents behind them? What if we've got agents in place among the Islamic fundamentalists and we're letting them run, like we let Noel Kinsella and Robbie Carter run?'

'That's not how it works,' said Ellis.

'It's how it used to work in Belfast, so why can't it be happening now? And if you tell me it's not, why should I believe you?'

'I'm not saying we don't have agents in the Muslim community. Of course we do.'

Button waved her cigarette in the air. 'And what if there are other parallels? What if these fundamentalists we're putting away, these bastards who want to kill and maim the citizens of this country, what if one day in the not-too-distant future our politicians decide to set them free? What if al-Qaeda sets up a political wing and our government agrees to release its people in return for them laying down their arms? What if we start setting murderers free again?'

Ellis shrugged.

'Don't you see, Patsy? Don't you get it? Everything we're

doing now in this so-called War on Terror could be a lie. Smoke and mirrors.'

'Now you really are sounding paranoid.'

'Would you have said I was paranoid if I'd said twenty years ago that we had agents in the IRA and agents in the RUC and that they were killing each other?'

'You're trying to sum up a very difficult situation in a handy soundbite,' said Ellis. 'Life is more complex than that.'

'Too complex for a tiny brain like mine, is that what you mean?'

'You got a double first at Cambridge. This isn't about your intellect,' said Ellis.

'So who was making those decisions back then?' hissed Button. 'And who's making the decisions now? The Prime Minister? Of course not. The Home Secretary – with the *Sunday Times* Insight Team watching his every move? Doubtful. Who decided back then that Robbie Carter should be allowed to pass information to the paramilitaries? And was it the same person who said it was okay for Noel Kinsella to be part of an IRA assassination squad?'

'Those decisions were taken at a salary grade much higher than mine,' said Ellis.

'Now who's using handy soundbites?' snapped Button. 'Was it men in wood-panelled rooms, smoking cigars and spinning their webs? Thinking up their grubby little schemes, then nipping off to their Mayfair mistresses for a bit of S and M? Was it our bosses, Patsy? And if it was, are they playing the same games now?'

'Enough, Charlie,' said Ellis, coldly.

'No,' Button spat. 'It's not enough. You make it sound as if my work with SOCA is somehow inferior to the great game you're playing, that I'm dabbling in the shallows while you're taking on the big fish. Well, let me tell you, Patsy, at least I'm fighting real criminals. At least I'm upholding real laws. When I put a drug-dealer or a murderer behind bars I know I'm making the streets a bit safer, and that a few years down the line they're not going to be released because of a change of heart on the part of our political masters.'

Ellis tried to take Button's hand, but she jerked it back as if she'd been stung. 'Don't touch me. I don't want you to touch me.'

'I'm going,' said Ellis, standing up.

'Good.'

'I'll put this down to the drink,' said Ellis, 'and the stress.'

'Screw you,' said Button. 'Screw you and screw MI5. Screw the lot of you.'

Ellis opened her mouth to say something, but when she saw how intensely Button was glaring at her she shut it and left.

Graham Pickering opened the kitchen door and whistled for his dog. The Labrador barked from the bottom of the garden but made no move to come back to the house. 'Poppy, get in here or you can sleep outside tonight!' shouted Pickering. The dog's nose was buried in the hedgerow, her tail swishing from side to side. 'Damn you,' muttered Pickering. 'Come on, Poppy, let's call it a night!' he shouted.

It made no sense to him that his daughter was at boarding-school hundreds of miles away, yet every day he was at the beck and call of a four-year-old animal whose only thoughts seemed to be of food and hedges. His wife had agreed to the dog only after their daughter had gone to boarding-school, and Pickering had always felt he was being offered a consolation prize.

Charlie was right, of course, and he hadn't argued when she had suggested sending Zoë away. They both had demanding careers and it wouldn't have been fair to turn Zoë into a latch-key kid, with or without an au pair. She was blossoming now, and so were their careers, so it had worked out for the best, though there were times when Pickering missed watching her grow. He'd read her bedtime stories when she was four, taught her to swim when she was five and how to ride a bike when she was six, but now it seemed that all she needed from him were the school fees and pocket money.

It was the way of the world, Pickering knew. You give birth to children and you spend a few years teaching them the skills to survive on their own, then they leave to start families of their own. Pickering wished he'd had a few more years with Zoë before she'd been packed off to school. Throwing sticks in the park for Poppy came a poor second to watching movies and eating popcorn with a giggling thirteen-year-old.

The doorbell rang and Pickering frowned. He wasn't expecting anyone other than Charlie, and she had her key. 'Poppy, get the hell in here now!' he shouted. The dog ignored him.

Pickering closed the kitchen door and hurried to the hallway. The bell rang again. He opened the door to find an Arab man in his thirties on the step smiling amiably.

'Mr Pickering, it's Mr Hassan, from your office. I hope I'm not imposing.'

'Of course I remember you, Mr Hassan,' he said. 'I just didn't expect to see you here, that's all.'

Salih smiled. 'You made Virginia Water sound so attractive that I thought I'd take a drive round the area and see for myself,' he said. 'You weren't exaggerating. It's quite lovely. And your house is spectacular.'

'Thank you,' said Pickering, 'but as I said, it's not for sale.'

Salih flashed a broad smile and held up the fistful of brochures Pickering had given him. 'I understand that. I just thought you might have time to go over a few of these with me. I'm a cash buyer and I do want to move quickly.'

Pickering looked at his watch.

'I'm sorry. You're busy with your family. How thoughtless of me,' said Salih.

'No, my wife's not back yet,' said Pickering. A two-million-pound sale generated a lot of commission. 'Come on in, we can chat until my wife returns. Who knows? Maybe you can make her an offer she can't refuse.'

'You are a kind man, Mr Pickering,' said Salih, walking into the hall. 'This is quite beautiful, your wife has wonderful taste.'

'Thank you,' said Pickering, closing the door. 'Mr Hassan, I don't remember giving you my home address.'

Salih smiled. 'You didn't.' He dropped the brochures. The knife slid down his sleeve and the handle into the palm of his hand. He stepped forward and drove the blade between the third and fourth rib on Pickering's left side, forcing it into his heart. He clamped his left hand over Pickering's open mouth and pushed him back against the wall. He kept the knife pressed hard into Pickering's heart. A trickle of blood ran down the handle. Pickering grunted. Most of the blood from his pierced heart was pooling inside his body, and as long as Salih kept the knife in place there would be none on the floor.

Pickering's legs gave out and Salih moved down with him, keeping the knife in the man's heart and his hand over his mouth. He eased Pickering on to his back so that there would be no spillage. Pickering's eyelids fluttered, his body went into spasm and his heels drummed against the floor. The reflex lasted three or four seconds, then Pickering was still.

Salih took his hand off the man's mouth and slid out the knife. He wiped the blade on Pickering's shirt and stood up. '*Allahu Akbar,*' he whispered. 'God is great.'

Charlotte Button poured more wine into her glass. As she lifted it to her lips, she saw Shepherd smiling down at her. 'What are you doing here?' she asked.

'Fancied a drink,' said Shepherd. 'Can I?'

'You may,' she said. She lifted the bottle and showed him the label. 'I'm on red, but I suppose we could order some of the Irish whiskey you love.'

Shepherd took it from her and poured some into an empty water glass. 'Wine is fine,' he said.

'So now you're a poet,' she said. 'How did you know where I was?'

'I followed you from the hotel,' said Shepherd. 'You didn't do much in the way of counter-surveillance. I guess you had other things on your mind.'

She pushed her packet of cigarettes across the table towards him. Shepherd shook his head. 'Strong will?' she said.

'Just never liked them,' said Shepherd. 'Never saw the point. Now that the Carter case is over, I'm not touching them.'

Button blew smoke at him and laughed when he coughed. 'The point is that smokers smoke,' she said, 'and I'm a smoker.'

'I'm a drinker,' said Shepherd, raising his glass to her.

'At least you've got one vice.' Button took another lungful, held it, then exhaled slowly, this time keeping the smoke away from him.

'You know you can't smoke here?'

'I had a word with the manager,' she said.

'Are you okay?' Shepherd asked.

'Define your terms,' she said.

'Who was she, that woman?'

'That woman was Patsy Ellis, Kinsella's handler in Belfast and my old boss at MI5. And I thought she was my friend.'

'But now you're not sure?'

'Oh, no, I'm sure.' She rubbed the bridge of her nose. 'I've got a headache,' she said.

'From the look of you, it's not all sweetness and light with Miss Ellis.'

'You think you know someone, and then you find out you never knew them at all.'

'Story of my life,' said Shepherd.

'You're an undercover agent, lying goes with the job,' she said. 'I've been lied to by people I thought were on my side.' She gulped more wine.

'Elaine Carter called me,' said Shepherd.

'And?'

'What's going to happen to her?'

Button pulled a face, as if she had a bad taste in her mouth. 'John Maplethorpe was the killer and he's dead.'

Shepherd nodded slowly. 'So that's the end of it?'

'Sleeping dogs,' said Button. 'Even if she was involved, even if she was helping Maplethorpe, what's to be gained by proving it?'

'Nothing,' said Shepherd.

'Exactly . . . Tell me something, Spider. I know she didn't actually pull the trigger, but do you think she was helping Maplethorpe?'

Shepherd thought about the ticking watch in the trunk. Did it mean she'd helped Maplethorpe, that she'd given him the rounds for her husband's gun? Or did it just mean she'd been through the trunk, handling her husband's things? And even if she'd helped Maplethorpe, what would be gained by punishing her? He looked into Button's eyes and prepared to lie to her. 'No,' he said.

'There you go, then,' she said. 'Sleeping dogs.' She refilled her glass, but her hand was unsteady and wine sloshed over the table.

'Come on. My car's outside,' said Shepherd.

Button giggled. 'You're not trying to pick me up, are you, Spider?'

'I'm driving you home,' he said. 'Your husband will be waiting for you.' He opened his wallet, dropped a handful of banknotes on the table, then helped Button to her feet. She stumbled and bumped against him, and he put an arm round her waist to steady her.

'You're my knight in shining armour, aren't you, Spider?' she said, slurring her words. 'My guardian angel.'

'Charlie,' he said, guiding her towards the door, 'you'll never know the half of it.'

Salih stood at the window. The sky was streaked with red as the sun prepared to dip below the horizon. It was time to pray. He took a small compass from his pocket and noted the direction in which Mecca lay. Salih would have preferred to cleanse himself before praying but there was a chance that he'd not hear Button return if he was in the bathroom. The bedroom he was in belonged to the daughter. There were cuddly toys on the bed and posters of pop stars on the walls. Also on the bed, beside a toy cocker spaniel, lay a carving knife he'd taken from the kitchen.

From the bedroom he could see the driveway and, through the trees, most of the road, left and right. He moved into the centre of the room, turned towards Mecca, lowered his head and closed his eyes. 'Thanks be to Allah,' he said. 'We thank him, turn to him, ask his forgiveness, and seek refuge in him from our wicked souls and evil deeds. Whomever Allah enlightens will not be misguided, and the deceiver will never be guided. I declare that there is no God but Allah alone. He has no partners. I also declare that Muhammad is his servant and prophet.'

Salih knelt down and placed his hands on the carpet in front of him. He leant forward and continued to pray. Outside, the sky darkened.

They drove past the entrance to Wentworth golf club and Charlotte Button pointed at a turning ahead. 'Left there,' she said. Shepherd flicked on his indicator.

'Nice area,' he said, as he made the turn, the Audi's head-lights cutting across the trees that blanketed either side of the road. To the right were the forests of the Crown Estate but much of the land to the left was taken up with the multi-million-pound residences of the Wentworth Estate, gated communities with their own security force.

'We like it,' said Button. 'To be honest, with the way the job is, I'm hardly ever here to enjoy it.' She pointed at a large detached house set back from the road, with decorative white shutters on all the windows. 'That's it.' The lights were off inside the house but twin coach lamps illuminated the front door.

'Nice,' said Shepherd.

'Now you're being sarcastic,' she said.

'It *is* a nice house.'

'You're using "nice" in a not very nice way,' slurred Button.

'Charlie, it's a nice house in a nice area.' Shepherd turned the Audi into the driveway and stopped next to a large Mercedes parked in front of the double garage. 'Is that your husband's?' he asked.

Button nodded. 'Come in and say hello.'

'Some other time,' said Shepherd. 'I want to get back to Hereford.'

'At least have a coffee.'

'Really, Charlie, I'd rather get off.'

'Raincheck?'

'Absolutely.'

'I do need to talk to you about what happened.'

'A debriefing?'

'More to get my thoughts straight than anything else,' she said. 'I'm pretty confused about a lot of things just now.'

'It's a confusing trade we're in,' said Shepherd. 'Now's probably not the best time to talk about it. Certainly not over coffee with your husband.'

'You're right, of course. You're always right. You're my rock, Spider, you know that?'

Shepherd smiled. 'I know you've had a lot to drink,' he said.

'Thank you,' she said.

'You're welcome. Go on with you.'

Button sighed. 'Don't suppose you've got a cigarette, have you?' she asked. 'Graham won't have them in the house.'

Shepherd opened the glove box and gave her a packet of Marlboro. 'On me,' he said.

She took out a cigarette and Shepherd lit it for her. She inhaled deeply, held the smoke in her lungs, then exhaled with a sigh of pleasure. She climbed out of the car and went to the lawn. Shepherd laughed as she bent down, stubbed out the cigarette and covered the butt with soil, like a cat covering its traces. Then she went unsteadily to the front door, gave him a final wave and put the key into the lock. As she entered the house, Shepherd put the Audi in gear and reversed down the driveway.

Button pushed open the door. 'It's me!' she called, then smiled as she realised how stupid that was. Who else would be letting themselves in with a key at that time of night? 'Sorry I'm late. No rest for the wicked.' She took off her coat and opened the hall cupboard. 'Graham, where are you?' There was no reply. She hung up her coat and closed the door.

She heard a scratching noise from the kitchen. Poppy was outside, scrabbling to get in. Button opened the door and the Labrador bowled in, tail wagging frantically. Button knelt down and made a fuss of her. 'What are you doing outside?' she asked. The dog tried to lick her face and she pushed it away. Poppy scampered across the tiled floor to her dish and pushed it with her nose, then made a soft grunting sound. She looked up expectantly, her tail swishing from side to side. 'Has he not fed you?' asked Button. 'What's he playing at? Did he forget you, Poppy?' Poppy woofed and pushed her bowl again. 'I guess he did,' said Button. 'Shame on him.'

She went to the cupboard where they kept the dog's tinned food, opened a can of Pal and spooned the contents into Poppy's bowl. The dog started to bolt the food, and by the time Button had taken a box of dog biscuits from the cupboard, half the meat had gone. She pushed Poppy away, scattered some biscuits into the bowl, then stood up and smiled as Poppy started to wolf her food again. 'Where are your manners, girl?' She switched on the kettle. 'And where's your lord and master?'

She went to the kitchen door. 'Graham, where are you?' she called. There was no answer. She looked round the kitchen. It was spotless. There was a Tesco carrier-bag on the counter by the fridge and she peered inside. Two steaks, a bunch of asparagus, a microwaveable pouch of new potatoes and two individual chocolate mousses. At least he hadn't eaten without her. The kitchen clock told her it was just before nine. Occasionally Graham went to the pub at weekends but rarely during the week. He made a point of being first in the office, which meant getting up at seven each morning. He was probably showering. Button smiled to herself. It had been a while since she'd surprised Graham in the bathroom. Last time it had led to an eventful evening. The steaks could wait.

She headed for the stairs, closing the kitchen door behind her. The last thing she wanted was the dog jumping up on to the bed.

Shepherd flicked on his indicator to make a right turn on the A30 back to London. Opposite him he saw an entrance to the Crown Estate land and, beyond, a rutted track that led through the forest. A blue car was parked beside the gate. Shepherd turned on to the main road, noticing idly that the vehicle was empty. Suddenly he braked. He peered at the car in his rear-view mirror. It was a dark blue saloon, a Ford Mondeo. There was nothing unusual about it, which was why it seemed out of place in Virginia Water. He couldn't imagine anyone wealthy enough to live in the area driving a common-or-garden Ford. It was a place where BMWs, Jaguars and petrol-guzzling SUVs were the norm. The nanny might drive a Ford, or the gardener, but neither was likely to park it at the side of the road. It might have belonged to a Crown Estate worker – but why would they have parked outside the gate and not driven through it?

Shepherd wondered if he was worrying about nothing. Charlie was at home, and so was her husband. He put the car in gear and accelerated away. He had travelled only a few yards when he stamped on the brake. He couldn't shake off the feeling that something was wrong, that the car shouldn't have been parked where it was. He sighed and reached for his mobile phone. It would take only a few minutes to check it out. He tapped in the number of SOCA's intelligence unit in a nondescript office building in Pimlico, central London, not far from MI6's more dramatic riverside headquarters.

A man answered. 'Hello.' It was standard procedure for SOCA operatives at all levels not to identify their location or function. If Shepherd had asked if he was talking to SOCA or to Intel, the call would have been terminated immediately.

'PNC vehicle check, please,' said Shepherd.

'Name, ID number and radio call sign?' said the voice.

Shepherd gave his full name and the two numbers.

'Registration number?'

Shepherd read the digits off the front numberplate of the car.

There was a short pause before the man spoke again. 'It's a blue Ford Mondeo 2.0 LX. The registered keeper is shown as the Hertz Rental Company and they have been the keeper since the tenth of January two thousand and seven. There are no reports.'

Shepherd's jaw tightened. A hire car was a bad sign. 'It doesn't by any chance say to which Hertz office the car was assigned?'

'Just the company name, sorry.'

'Can you do me a favour?' asked Shepherd. 'I'm in the field and pressed for time. Can you contact Hertz and find out which office the car was hired from, and get me the name of the customer?'

'Not a problem,' said the voice. 'Is it okay to call you on this number?'

'That would be great,' said Shepherd.

The line went dead. Shepherd rarely used the intelligence unit but when he did he was always impressed with the can-do attitude. If he'd called the Metropolitan Police for help they would have given him half a dozen reasons why they couldn't make the call to the car-hire company. He settled back in his seat. Maybe he was worrying about nothing. Maybe one of the locals had put his BMW or Jaguar in for servicing and hired a car to tide him over. Maybe.

Button stared round the empty bathroom. 'Graham, where are you?' she called. Poppy barked from the kitchen. She went back into the bedroom. He couldn't have gone far because his car was parked outside and he wasn't one of life's great walkers. The bedroom window overlooked the garden and she peered out. She didn't expect to see him there because he wasn't one of life's gardeners, either.

Her jacket was on the bed where she'd thrown it and she retrieved her mobile phone from the pocket. She'd called Graham just before she'd met Patsy Ellis in the wine bar so she scrolled through her calls list and pressed her husband's number. She put the phone to her ear as she looked round the bedroom. For a crazy moment she imagined her husband had walked out on her, but that made no sense because he would have taken the car. She opened the sliding mirrored door to the wardrobe. All his clothes were there, of course. She shut it and smiled at her reflection. Graham didn't have time for an affair, and she doubted that any other woman would put up with the hours he worked.

The phone rang, and kept on ringing. Button frowned. That didn't make sense because Graham never went anywhere without it. He took calls from clients at any time of day or night, no matter where he was or what he was doing, and usually he answered on the second or third ring.

She began to pace round the room. She had often joked with him that only a stroke or a heart-attack would stop him answering his phone, and now a coldness was spreading through her, tightening round her chest like a steel band. The phone stopped ringing and went to voicemail. She cut the connection, then pressed redial as she went on to the landing. As soon as she did, she heard his ringtone downstairs. The James Bond theme. He'd chosen it initially as an ironic comment on her job, but after a while he'd grown to like the tune and had steadfastly refused to change it. Every time it rang he'd look at her, smile slyly, and she would say, 'Boys will be boys.'

Button moved along the landing, holding out her phone in front of her. If the phone was in the house, so was Graham. The band round her chest was so tight now that she could barely breathe. Something was wrong. Something was terribly wrong.

She walked slowly down the stairs. 'Graham!' she called, hearing the uncertainty in her voice. 'Graham, where are you?'

Poppy barked from the kitchen.

Button reached the bottom of the stairs. The phone went to voicemail and the James Bond music stopped. She cut the connection and pressed redial again. She put her head on one side, her brow furrowed as she concentrated. The ring-tone kicked into life again. It was coming from the study. She reached for the door handle and took a deep breath as she tried to convince herself that everything was all right, that when she pushed open the door she'd see Graham at his desk, listening to Phil Collins on his Bose headphones, oblivious to his ringing phone.

Her jaw dropped when she saw him on the floor, lying on his back. His eyes were wide and staring and there was a damp patch at his groin.

'Graham?' she whispered. 'Oh, Graham.' She hurried across the carpet and knelt beside him. She put her hand to his neck and felt for a pulse, but even as she did so she knew she was wasting her time. He was dead. She sat back and looked at his chest. She opened his jacket and saw a red stain on his shirt. She began to tremble, but fought to stop her hands shaking, and undid the buttons round the glistening stain. 'Oh, Graham, my poor darling,' she whispered. The wound was narrow, less than an inch, a clean cut. He had been killed with a knife. A very sharp knife. A single blow to the heart. There was no sign of the murder weapon.

She stood up, her mind in a whirl. She put a hand to her forehead, trying to focus. Graham's mobile was still ringing in his pocket and she pressed the red button on hers to end the call. She stared down at the body, suddenly aware that the only sound in the room was her breathing. She looked at her phone, wondering who to call.

The door to the study slammed and she spun round, the phone slipping from her fingers to the floor. An Arab was standing there, a smile on his face. There was no need for Button to ask who he was or what he wanted. He was holding a carving knife and he swished it from side to side as he walked across the carpet towards her.

Shepherd jumped when the phone buzzed, then pressed the green button. 'Shepherd,' he said.

'It was hired from their Marble Arch location, thirty-five Edgware Road, by a Hassan Salih, using a United Arab Emirates driving licence.'

Shepherd thanked the man and ended the call. His heart pounded as his adrenal glands kicked into overdrive. An Arab renting a car and driving out to Virginia Water could mean only one thing. He climbed out of the Audi, opened the rear door on the driver's side and groped under the seat for the UMP. He ripped off the plastic wrapping and slotted in the magazine, then slammed the door. He looked around. There was no one nearby. He hid the machine-gun under his jacket as best he could and started to run back to Charlie's house.

The Arab bared his teeth at Button but said nothing. Button crouched, her hands up defensively. She had done some hand-to-hand combat during basic training, but her instructors had always told her that if you were unarmed and facing a combatant with a blade, the best option by far was to turn and run. But the only door was behind the Arab and she had no other escape route. 'What do you want?' she said, knowing the question was meaningless but wanting to say something because talking was the only thing that might slow him.

He took a step towards her and she took a step back. Her husband's body was to her right. Between it and the window there was a desk with a computer on it. The window was double-glazed and she wasn't sure how hard she'd have to hit it to be sure of it breaking but she was sure that the Arab wouldn't give her a chance to find out. 'You know the name Abdal Jabbaar bin Othman al-Ahmed? And that of his brother, Abdal Rahmaan?'

Button curled her fingertips. If he stabbed with the knife she had a chance of catching his wrist but if he slashed with it he'd cut her. Of course she knew who Abdal Jabbaar bin Othman al-Ahmed was. And his brother. And now she realised why the killer was in her house, why he'd stabbed her husband and why he was going to kill her. She'd watched in horror as Abdal Rahmaan had been burnt to death by men working for Richard Yokely. And she'd interrogated Abdal Jabbaar while he was being tortured in the basement at the American embassy in London. It hadn't been her idea, but she had played a part and she had always thought that one day her actions might come back to haunt her. That day had come, but the man with the knife was no ghost. 'No,' she said. 'The name means nothing to me.'

'Abdal Jabbaar bin Othman al-Ahmed? Abdal Rahmaan bin Othman al-Ahmed?'

'Never heard of them.'

He stopped swishing the knife. 'You're lying,' he said.

'Why would I lie? Abdul what?'

'Abdal Jabbaar bin Othman al-Ahmed. Abdal Rahmaan. Do not lie to me.'

Button shook her head again, more emphatically this time. 'I don't know why you think those names should mean something to me, but I can assure you they don't.'

The man's eyes narrowed.

'You're making a mistake,' said Button. 'I don't know who

you're talking about, I don't know why you're here, but I'm not the person you're looking for.'

'I know who you are. I have your photograph. There is no mistake.'

Button pointed at him. 'I know who you are, and I know why you're here. Your name is Hassan Salih and you're a marked man.'

A look of confusion flashed across Salih's face. 'How did you . . .'

Button bent down, picked up her mobile phone and threw it hard at him. It hit his shoulder and shattered against the wall. Button moved forward, ready to grab the knife, but he was too quick for her and jabbed at her hand, just missing her. She jumped back, then rushed to the desk. There was a glass paperweight, a birthday present from Zoë to her father. She grabbed it. Salih lashed out with the knife again, catching her in the shoulder, cutting through her shirt and slicing into her flesh. She screamed and hurled the paper-weight at him. It smashed into his jaw, breaking two front teeth. He glared at her as blood ran down his chin and he slowly raised the knife.

Shepherd's feet pounded on the pavement, his breathing regular although he had run several hundred yards at full pelt. He hurtled through the gate and down the driveway towards the house. As he neared it, he heard a scream, followed by shouting. A man. He kicked at the front door, but it was solid mahogany and barely moved. He had the carbine in his hands but he knew it was only in movies that you could blow open a door with nine-millimetre rounds. The SAS used shotguns to shoot out the hinges of locked doors but the weapon he was holding was useless against the inch-thick wood. He stood back and kicked again. It barely moved.

Shepherd swore and ran to his left, round the house. A dog was barking and there were more shouts from inside the house. The shouts were a good sign. They meant that Charlie was still alive.

Salih stabbed at Button with the knife. She turned to the side and grabbed at his wrist with her right hand, but he was too quick for her and jerked the knife back. The blade cut into her palm and she felt blood spurt between her fingers. She screamed, more in anger than pain. Salih had killed her husband, the father of her child, but she was powerless to do anything. She wished with all her heart that she had a gun but she hadn't been issued one by SOCA and she'd never carried a weapon when she'd worked for MI5. As blood dripped from her hand on to the carpet she looked for something, anything, to use as a weapon.

Salih said nothing as he slashed at her with the knife. Blood was pouring from his mouth where she'd hit him with the paperweight, but the only sound he made was a gentle whistling as he breathed.

Button glanced at the desk. There was a letter-opener that went with the paperweight, a steel blade embedded in a piece of carved crystal. It was next to the computer keyboard. She lurched towards it, but Salih anticipated her and slashed at her, screaming. The knife caught her side, slicing easily through her shirt and ripping into her flesh. The blade bit deep and she tried to twist away from the searing pain, tripped over Graham's legs and went sprawling on her hands and knees.

She heard Salih grunt, then fell forward as something thumped into her right shoulder, followed by a sharp pain. She realised that the blade was embedded in her shoulder. She screamed as he pulled it out and the serrated edge ripped through skin and muscle. Tears filled her eyes. She didn't want to die like this, cut to pieces in her own home. She didn't want to leave her daughter. She didn't want to die on the floor. She didn't want the man who'd killed her to defile her as she bled to death. She rolled over. He was standing over her, blood dripping down his chin. Still he said nothing, though she could feel the hatred pouring out of him.

Button pulled her legs up and scrabbled away from him. She could feel blood running down her hip. It wasn't life-threatening, she knew. There were no major blood vessels there, and the knife hadn't gone deep enough to cut any organs. The wound in the shoulder was just muscle damage. She could still feel her fingers so there was no nerve damage. She was hurt but not dead yet.

Salih grinned. 'Abdal Jabbaar bin Othman al-Ahmed,' he said. 'And Abdal Rahmaan. You are to die hearing those names.'

'Screw you!'

Salih grunted and slashed the knife at her legs. The tip nicked her ankle, drawing blood. Button yelped and pulled her legs close to her body.

She shuffled to the left and he moved with her, waving the knife menacingly. He lunged at her but as he did so she lashed out with her right foot and caught him in the groin with her heel. Salih grimaced and stabbed at her thigh. The blade went in deep and Button screamed. She screamed again as he pulled it out and blood spurted down her leg. She shuffled back to the wall and pushed herself up against it, then almost fell over as her injured leg gave way beneath her. She staggered along a bookcase, scattering books on the floor. She grabbed at a book and threw it at her attacker as hard as she could. It hit his forehead and spun across the room. He laughed. 'Is that the best you can do?' he snarled. He stabbed at her with the knife and she jumped away.

The door was to her left, a few yards away, but Salih realised that too and took a step to the side, blocking her escape. As he moved she saw Shepherd at the window, a machine-gun in his hands. For a brief moment they had eye contact. 'Down,' he mouthed.

As Shepherd raised the carbine, Button grinned at Salih.

'No,' she said. 'This is the best I can do,' and she dropped to the floor.

Shepherd brought the UMP to his shoulder as Button fell. He was firing through glass so he knew there was no guarantee that the first or second shot would hit the target. He pulled the trigger, the gun kicked in his hands and the window shattered into a thousand shards. The Arab turned, the knife raised above his head. Shepherd fired again, and saw him lurch as a bullet hit his shoulder. Glass was falling to the paved path outside the window, tinkling like wind chimes.

The Arab's face was contorted in a mask of rage. He yelled something in Arabic and Shepherd fired a short burst into his chest. The man fell backwards, a red rose blossoming on the front of his shirt.

Shepherd rushed forward and leant through the window. The Arab was sitting on the floor, his back to the door, his left hand clutched to his chest, the knife still in his right hand, his mouth working. Shepherd fired twice at his head and his face imploded. He sagged forward and the knife fell to the floor.

Shepherd used the butt of the UMP to clear the glass that was still in the window frame, then tossed the weapon on to the desk and climbed inside after it. 'Charlie, are you okay?' he shouted. There was no answer. He scrambled across the desk, knocking over several framed photographs. Button was on the floor, curled into a ball, not far from the dead Arab. Another man lay on his back, a bloodstain on his shirt.

Shepherd rolled off the desk and rushed to Button. Her shirt was sodden with blood and there were cuts on her legs, but she was breathing and her eyes were open. Shepherd checked her out, running his fingers along the length of her body, then checked for a pulse at her wrist. She'd lost a lot of blood but none appeared to be arterial and her pulse was strong and steady. 'You're going to be fine,' he said.

She didn't appear to hear him and stared into the middle distance, eyes glassy with shock.

'Charlie, you're going to be all right,' he said.

Button blinked. She turned to look at her husband's body. 'Graham?' she whispered.

Shepherd knelt in front of her. 'Charlie, come on, snap out of this.'

Button frowned. 'I didn't even get to wear the underwear,' she said.

'What?'

'I bought underwear and he didn't even see it.'

Shepherd put his hands on either side of her face and stared into her eyes. 'Charlie, stop this,' he said. 'I need you with me.'

Her eyes were filling with tears. 'Graham's dead,' she faltered.

'I know,' he said. 'But we've got to get you to hospital. Do you understand?' Button nodded slowly but there was no recognition in her eyes. Shepherd shook her. 'Come on, Charlie, stay with me. Focus.'

She nodded. 'Okay,' she whispered. 'I'm okay.'

Shepherd helped her into a sitting position, and pulled her back against the wall. 'You've got to get to hospital,' he said.

'I know,' she said. She took a deep breath and winced.

Shepherd stood up and went to the desk. He picked up the phone and dialled nine-nine-nine. A woman who sounded as if she had better things to do asked him which emergency service he wanted. 'Ambulance,' he said.

'What's the nature of the emergency?' asked the woman.

'A heart-attack, I think,' said Shepherd. Button frowned and he made a patting motion, telling her to relax. 'She's on the floor and in a lot of pain, her breathing's ragged and she's as white as a sheet.'

'I'll transfer you to the ambulance service,' said the woman. She put the call through and this time it was a man. He asked Shepherd for his name and address, then the nature of the problem. Shepherd repeated what he'd told the first operator and hung up. He went to Button and knelt in front of her again.

'What was that about?' she asked.

'If they know shots have been fired or knives used the paramedics will stand back until they're sure the area's safe. That means waiting for an armed-response vehicle, and who knows how long that'll take? This way the paramedics will be right here and by the time they see what the damage is they'll already be treating you.'

'You know all the tricks,' she said.

'I know what the rules are, and I know how to get around them,' he said. 'I need towels.'

'Down the hallway. First on the right, there's a loo,' she said.

Shepherd hurried out and returned with three small cotton towels. He knelt down beside her. Her shirt was sodden with blood at her right hip and he pulled it gently away from her skirt and pressed a towel to the wound. 'How do you feel?' he asked.

'Like I'm bleeding to death,' she said. 'I'll be okay, Spider.'

'Where does it hurt?'

'My side. My shoulder. My hand. My legs. Pretty much all over, really.'

Shepherd eased her forward and looked at her back. The shirt was soaked with blood there too. He placed a towel over the wet patch and leant her against the wall. He took her right hand and examined it. A deep cut ran right across her palm and blood was dripping from it on to the carpet. Shepherd got her to hold her hand up while he wrapped a towel round it. 'Keep it high, if you can,' he said. The wounds on her legs were superficial. 'No arteries cut but you'll have a few nice scars.' He took the towel from her side and examined the wound there. Blood was trickling out but there was no pulsing. He replaced the towel and kept up a light pressure on it.

'I'm going to have to put my hand down,' she said. 'Sorry.' She put her towel-wrapped hand into her lap and looked past Shepherd at the body by the desk. 'My husband,' she said. 'Graham.'

'I'm sorry,' said Shepherd.

'It's so bloody unfair,' she said. 'He never hurt anyone in his whole life.' Her eyes closed.

Shepherd shook her. 'Stay with me, Charlie, don't sleep now. Wait until the paramedics get here.'

'I'm so tired,' she said, her voice barely a whisper.

'Open your eyes, Charlie. Come on.'

She did as he asked. 'He's dead. The bastard's dead, isn't he?' she whispered.

'Absolutely,' said Shepherd.

'I suppose I was lucky he wanted to use a knife and not a gun,' she said. Tears ran down her face. 'I was so scared, Spider.'

'That's okay,' he said. 'It's over now.'

She wiped away her tears with her left hand. 'I felt so bloody helpless,' she said.

'He had a knife, Charlie,' said Shepherd.

'If it had been you, you'd have done some flashy *kung-fu* stuff and taken it off him,' she said.

'Not if he'd cut my throat from behind,' said Shepherd. 'And we never did *kung-fu* in the SAS.'

'You know what I mean,' she said. 'I was throwing books at him, for God's sake. How pathetic is that?'

The towel around her right hand was soaked with blood. Shepherd lifted her hand from her lap and held it at shoulder height. 'You did medical training in the SAS?' she asked.

'The basics, but I was never a medic,' he said. 'My speciality was hostage rescue as part of CRW,' he said. 'Counter-revolutionary Warfare. I was trained for putting rounds into people rather than patching them up afterwards.' In the distance Shepherd heard an ambulance siren. 'Here they come,' he said.

'I need to make a call,' she said.

'It can wait,' said Shepherd.

'No, it can't,' she said. 'As soon as they see two dead bodies and the state of me they'll call the police and we can't have that.' She held out her right hand. 'Let me have my mobile.'

Shepherd went over to it. 'It's broken,' he said. 'Use mine.'

'They'll keep a record of the call and I don't want your name in the frame.' She pointed to her husband's body. 'Give me Graham's.'

Her husband's mobile was in a leather holster clipped to his belt. Shepherd pulled it out and gave it to her. She nodded at the desk. 'Hide the gun,' she said. She tapped out a number with her thumb, brow furrowed. Shepherd stood up and went over to get the UMP. 'Thinking about it, Spider, it might be best if you get as far away from here as you can,' she said.

Shepherd took the Tube to Knightsbridge and wandered around the Harrods food hall for ten minutes to check that he wasn't being followed, then took a circuitous route through the surrounding streets to the red-brick mansion that housed the Special Forces Club. He pushed open the door, signed in at the reception desk in the hallway and headed upstairs. Yokely was already at the bar with a vodka and tonic.

'Your usual?' asked Yokely.

Shepherd nodded and the American ordered a Jameson's with soda and ice, then went over to a quiet table in the window. It had been at the Special Forces Club that Shepherd had first met Yokely. Shepherd dropped into a winged leather armchair. 'What's so urgent that I have to be dragged out of the bowels of the American embassy?' asked Yokely.

'It's done,' said Shepherd.

'What's done?' asked the American.

'Your man. Hassan Salih.'

'Dead?'

'Very.'

Yokely raised his glass in salute. 'Well done you. Details?'
Shepherd told the American everything, only pausing when
a white-jacketed waiter brought his whiskey. When he'd
finished, Yokely was grinning like a Cheshire cat. 'And
Charlie?'

'She'll be okay. She's in hospital. I'm going to see her after
this.'

'Tell her I was asking about her, will you?'

'You should pop around yourself,' said Shepherd.

'I was never one for flowers,' said Yokely. 'And, frankly,
we're not that close.'

'What about her husband's funeral? Will you go to that?'

Yokely's eyes narrowed. 'Dan, I'm picking up a vibe here.'

Shepherd shrugged. 'There's no vibe,' he said. 'I just can't
help but think that if you'd warned Charlie of the danger
she was in, her husband might still be alive and she wouldn't
be in hospital.'

'Trust me, if we'd warned her the killer would have just
bided his time and eventually killed them both.'

'And maybe gone after you, too?'

'I told you before, I'm very hard to get.' He sipped his
vodka and tonic. 'What about you? Where do you go from
here?'

'I'm not sure.'

'Do you ever wonder what the world's coming to, Dan?
Down the john, that's where we're headed. Unless we do
something about it.'

'By "we", who do you mean exactly?' asked Shepherd.

'You and me,' said Yokely. 'And those like us. We're the
only ones who stand between what we have and anarchy.'

'That's the job of governments. I'm a civil servant, working
within government guidelines.'

'Do you think your government is up to the job?'

Shepherd threw up his hands. 'Who knows?'

'I know,' said Yokely. 'The answer is, no, sir, they are not.
You only have to read the papers to know that. You saw what

happened to those sailors and marines who were taken hostage by the Iranians. Paraded in front of television cameras, saying they were sorry to have offended their Iranian hosts. Whatever happened to "Name, rank and serial number"? The Iranians are responsible for half the deaths in Iraq and they made the Brits look as if they were in the wrong. Your government's weak and they've reduced your armed forces to a shadow of what they used to be. They've hamstrung your cops with rules and regulations and brought in so-called human-rights legislation that means terrorists and murderers can't be deported, no matter what atrocities they're planning to commit. I'm offering you the chance to make a difference, Dan. A real difference. To fight on the front line against the real villains in the world, and to fight on their terms.'

'To kill them, you mean?'

'If that's what it takes, then that's what it takes,' said Yokely. He leant forward and stared at Shepherd with his pale blue eyes. For the first time Shepherd realised the American was wearing contact lenses. 'Anyone close to you ever die of cancer?'

Shepherd shook his head.

'You're a lucky man. With all the bullshit about terrorist attacks and Aids and airplane crashes, you know what people die of?'

'Cancer,' said Shepherd. 'Cancer, strokes and heart disease.'

'Damn right,' said Yokely. 'And cancer's the big one. My father died of colon cancer. He was a big man, big and strong, but before he died I could carry him to the bathroom like he was a kid.'

'I'm sorry,' said Shepherd.

Yokely waved away Shepherd's comment, as if it were an irritating insect. 'My sister died of breast cancer a few years ago. Fought it right to the end. She let the doctors cut her, pour poison into her veins, zap her with radiation and she still died. Cancer's a bitch. It puts everything else into perspective.'

Shepherd wasn't sure where the conversation was going.

'The thing about cancer is that it starts small, a single rogue cell. But once that cell has grown and spread and the tumours have taken hold, it's too late to do anything about it. The trick is to take out the single rogue cell. Take it out before it becomes fatal.'

Realisation dawned. 'I get the analogy.'

'So you understand the logic?'

'I understand that there's a difference between a human being and cancerous cells. And I understand there are laws, and above laws there's morality.'

'Where's the morality in flying airliners into office blocks, Dan? In chopping the heads off aid workers? Blowing up commuters?'

'If we go down to their level, they've won,' said Shepherd.

'That's what they want you to think,' said Yokely. 'That's one of the great lies. The idea that because we meet fire with fire we're somehow the poorer for it. That's crap. All that matters is that our way of life continues, and we have the right, the God-given right, to do whatever's necessary to preserve it.' He shook his head. 'Your talents are being wasted, Dan. What has the lovely Charlie got you doing now? Protecting IRA assassins? You do see how incongruous that is, don't you? Back in the eighties, if they'd caught you in Northern Ireland they'd have pulled out your fingernails, broken your legs and put a bullet in the back of your head.'

'Things change,' agreed Shepherd.

'Yeah, well, I don't believe that one-man's-terrorist-is-another-man's-freedom-fighter bullshit. The IRA were terrorists. Now they're terrorists who no longer kill people. But I don't understand why the organisation you work for thinks it's a justifiable use of your time to keep former terrorists alive.'

'You and me both, as it happens. But ours not to reason why.'

'The Charge of the Light Brigade mentality. The problem

is that if you're following orders issued by morons, it's going to end in tears.'

'What exactly do you want me to do? What are you offering me?'

'As we're sitting here drinking and chewing the fat, men and women all over the world are planning to kill and maim innocent civilians. Now, I don't care what their motives are, I don't care if they're freedom-fighters or terrorists. All I care about is stopping them before they commit whatever carnage they're planning.'

'Pre-emptive strikes?'

'Killing cancer cells before they form tumours,' said Yokely. 'Taking them out with surgical precision.'

'You're doing this already?'

Yokely nodded. 'We started in Afghanistan and Iraq, but we've expanded our operations. Don't get me wrong, we're not some sort of vigilante group. Our operations are sanctioned at the highest level. But we're not signed off by judges or district attorneys, there's no paper trail, no recordings. Everything we do is deniable by those who sanction it.'

'I thought assassination was specifically outlawed in the US? Didn't Ronald Reagan sign Executive Order 12333 back in 1981?'

'You and your trick memory,' sighed Yokely.

'It's a gift,' said Shepherd. 'According to Executive Order 12333, "No person employed by or acting on behalf of the United States Government shall engage in, or conspire to engage in, assassination." And then it goes on to say that "No agency of the Intelligence Community shall participate in or request any person to undertake activities forbidden by this Order." Am I right?'

'You are right,' said Yokely. 'But let's not forget that Bill Clinton himself gave the CIA *carte blanche* to kill bin Laden.'

'Which, really, he shouldn't have done,' said Shepherd.

'It's a grey area, Dan. An executive order isn't a law, it's more a statement of political policy.'

'Actually, it's not,' said Shepherd. 'It's black and white. Assassination is illegal. It's murder.'

'So is crashing a plane into an office block,' said Yokely. 'But it happens.' He grinned. 'I'm not here to argue politics or law with you. The world has changed since Nine Eleven. It's like George W said back then – you're either with us or you're against us. If a country or an individual chooses to stand against us, they have to deal with the consequences.'

'Let's say I did work for you. Who would I . . .' He hesitated. 'What word do you use?'

'"Kill" sounds good to me, Dan. Providing no one's listening.'

'So, who would I kill?'

'You'd kill individuals who are working to kill others. Look, your own head of MI5 said a while back that there were some three hundred terror cells in the UK, all beavering away at getting guns, explosives or poisons, all preparing to kill for a place in Heaven. Your security services keep them under observation, but when it's time to move in they have to hand over to the cops. And then what happens? The cops go charging in, local communities are up in arms about the heavy-handed response, and more often than not there isn't even enough evidence to get a conviction. It's a lose-lose situation. You might have averted one catastrophe, but the bad guys are still free to plot again. And, believe me, they will.'

'And why me?

'Because you're good at what you do – you're one of the most professional operatives I've ever met. You're capable of looking down the barrel of a gun and pulling the trigger.'

'You must have hundreds of men with those qualifications in the States,' said Shepherd.

'Agreed,' said Yokely. 'But there are times when it would be useful to have a Brit. And you've got undercover skills that most of the American special-forces guys don't. They'll allow you to get up close and personal in situations where a gung-ho former Navy Seal would be spotted a mile away.'

Shepherd snorted softly. 'And how would I be expected to get up close and personal with Islamic fundamentalists?'

'Not all our enemies are Arabs and Asians,' said Yokely. 'But that's not the point. There's a hundred different roles you could play that would get you in, roles that would be more believable because of your accent. Trust me, Dan, I want you on my team.'

'You know I spoke to Charlie about this, the first time you raised it?'

Yokely's eyes tightened a fraction. 'I didn't, but of course that's your prerogative.'

'She said you weren't in a position to issue me with a get-out-of-jail-free card. That if I did work for you and something went wrong, I'd be left swinging in the wind.'

Yokely nodded thoughtfully. 'Okay,' he said. 'Let me see if I can find some way to reassure you that you'd be fully protected.' He smiled thinly. 'Trust me, Dan, I've got friends in high places.'

'I bet you have,' said Shepherd. 'And some pretty low places, too.'

Yokely laughed and stamped his foot on the floor. 'Ain't that the truth,' he said.

Shepherd sipped his whiskey. 'I've got a question for you,' he said quietly.

'Sure.'

'You knew that Salih had my home address, right?'

'Merkulov had your home phone number so it would have been easy enough for him to get the address.'

'But my question is, why did Salih think I was a target?'

'I don't follow you,' said the American.

'If all Salih had was my name, address and phone number, why did he attack me? Why did he send the guy with a gun?'

'I still don't follow you.'

'He didn't know I worked for Button. All he knew was that Charlie had been in contact with me. But she must have been in contact with dozens of people. Why did he single me out?'

'He must have known you were with SOCA.'

Shepherd nodded. 'And that worries me,' he said. 'I don't see how Merkulov could have found out that I worked for SOCA. Unless someone told him.'

'Someone?'

'SOCA is pretty much leakproof,' said Shepherd.

'I guess the fact that you were in Belfast suggested you were working with her.'

'That's a hell of a leap.' Shepherd shrugged. 'I guess it'll remain a mystery.'

'I guess so.' Yokely frowned. 'Something on your mind, Dan?'

Shepherd shook his head. 'No, nothing.'

Shepherd walked out of the lift. A sign that read 'Intensive Care Unit' pointed to the left. His shoes squeaked on the gleaming linoleum as he headed for the glass cubicles that housed the seriously ill patients. In the centre cubicle Button was lying on a bed, her eyes closed. A nurse appeared in front of Shepherd and raised her clipboard as if she was going to hit him with it. 'Can I help you?' she said, in a tone that suggested helping him was the last thing on her mind.

'I'm here to see Charlotte Button,' said Shepherd. 'That's her there.'

'It's nearly midnight. Are you a relative?'

'No, I work with her.' Shepherd took out his ID card and held it out to her, but she glared at him over the top of it.

'I don't care who you work for. You can't go in there.' She pointed down the corridor. 'Please talk to Reception. They can tell you when she's allowed visitors.'

'I don't want to talk to Reception. I want to talk to her.'

'That's not going to happen,' she said.

Shepherd pointed a finger at her. 'Look, sweetheart, I've already shot one arsehole today. I don't want to have to do it again.' He pushed past her and went into the ICU. He closed the glass door in the nurse's face and held it shut.

Button smiled at him. She was ashen and there were dark patches under her eyes. Her right hand was bandaged, there was a drip into her left arm, and a heartbeat monitor beeped in the background. 'I can see you're winning friends and influencing people,' she said. She gestured with her bandaged right hand at the glass window. On the other side the nurse was talking angrily to the doctor and pointing at Shepherd.

'She didn't want you disturbed,' said Shepherd.

'Didn't you tell her that you were my knight in shining armour?' She grimaced.

'Are you okay?'

'I said I didn't want them to go over the top on the painkillers and they took me at my word. I'll be interviewed soon so I need a clear head.'

'IPCC?' The Independent Police Complaints Commission investigated all police-related shootings.

'Home Office,' she said. 'Plod's been squared away. They're not even sending in a SOCO crew. So far as the police are concerned, it never happened. The nine-nine-nine call you made has been wiped and the paramedics have been briefed.'

A young doctor with receding hair and red-framed spectacles appeared at the glass door, the nurse at his shoulder. Shepherd held up his SOCA card. The doctor read it through the glass, then held up a hand, fingers splayed. 'Five minutes,' he mouthed.

Shepherd nodded, and the doctor ushered the nurse away. Shepherd went back to the bed and took Button's left hand. 'Charlie, I'm so sorry,' he said.

'For what?'

'I should have taken you inside the house. I should have gone in with you.'

'If you had he'd have killed you straight away. You saw what he did to Graham. He'd have killed you and then he'd have tortured me. We'd both have died, Spider. There's no question about that.'

'Maybe,' said Shepherd.

'Spider, you saved my life and that's the end of it. I'm just grateful you turned up when you did.'

'What about your daughter?'

'She doesn't know yet. I'll wait until I can tell her myself. I don't want her finding out over the phone.'

'I can drive you when you're ready.'

'Thanks.' She lay back and stared at the ceiling. 'I need a cigarette.'

Shepherd chuckled. 'I think it's an arrestable offence, these days, smoking in a hospital.'

'You're probably right.'

Shepherd sat down on a chair next to the bed. 'What will you tell the Home Office people?' he said.

'Not much,' said Button. 'My old firm's on the case. I'm a SOCA employee but MI5 takes precedence. They'll cite national security and take over the investigation. There'll be a full D Notice on everything that happened at the house. As far as the world's concerned, it never happened.'

'Two men died, Charlie.'

'No one's going to care about what happened to the assassin or how he died. His body'll be disposed of by some very clever people at MI5. The damage to my house is being repaired as we speak.'

'And your husband?'

'A stroke or a heart-attack. It's better that way – better all round. I wouldn't want Zoë knowing her father was stabbed to death. No one will ever know what happened. Except the two of us. And a few select people at MI5. The gun you used, where is it?'

'Taken care of.'

'It wasn't your SIG-Sauer, was it?'

Shepherd shook his head. 'It was something special.'

'I sense the hand of Major Gannon in there somewhere.'

'It'll never be traced,' said Shepherd. 'Is that going to be a problem because I'm not prepared to go into details with any investigators.'

'Playing hardball, Spider?'

'I asked the Major to do me a favour and I'm not going to let him down.'

'And I respect that,' said Button. 'They won't be here to investigate. They just want to know what happened and what, if anything, is needed in the way of damage limitation.' She winced. 'Damn it.'

'What?'

'Nothing,' she said. 'Just my shoulder. It was a deep wound but I can't be in any other position because of the other cuts. You knew, didn't you?'

'Knew what?'

'That someone was after me.'

After what O'Brien had told her, Shepherd knew there was no point in lying. 'I had a hunch,' he said, which wasn't quite a lie but wasn't exactly the truth.

'Must have been a pretty strong hunch to have Martin O'Brien tailing me.'

Shepherd sat back and folded his arms, then realised he was adopting a defensive pose. He unfolded his arms and rested his hands on his knees. 'Was he easy to spot?'

'Give me a break, Spider.'

'Not long, obviously.'

'The thing is, O'Brien and his pals were tailing me before I got the nod from my former colleagues at MI5,' said Button, 'so that must have been one hell of a hunch. I know you've got a photographic memory, but I didn't realise you also had supernatural powers.'

At least he hadn't actually lied to her, Shepherd thought.

'Was Richard Yokely involved in your hunch by any chance?'

Shepherd nodded. 'Yes.'

'Spider, Yokely is one dangerous son-of-a-bitch.'

'I know.'

'He knew I was under threat? O'Brien said you told him there was a contract out on me.'

'He thought it possible.'

'Possible enough for you to assign me protection? But not possible enough for you to mention it to me?'

Button winced again, and Shepherd knew that this time it wasn't because her shoulder was hurting. 'Yokely thought it best you weren't told,' he said.

'Because?'

'It's complicated,' he said. 'I'm sorry, Charlie.'

'You dance with Yokely, you dance with the devil,' said Button.

'I know that,' said Shepherd.

A man and a woman appeared at the door, and Shepherd turned to look at them through the glass. They were both wearing dark coats. The man was grey-haired with steel-rimmed spectacles, tall and thin with the sombre face of an undertaker consoling the recently bereaved. The woman was a decade younger, with short blonde hair framing a sharp face and inquisitive eyes. The man knocked on the door with a gloved hand.

'Time for my debrief,' she said.

'What will you tell them about me?'

'Nothing,' she said.

'They'll want to know, surely.'

'Screw them,' she said. 'The gun can't be traced, right?'

'Everything identifiable has been destroyed and the weapon is back where it belongs.'

'So I'll tell them my husband was murdered, the bastard was about to kill me and someone got to him first. I was out of it, didn't see who it was, et cetera et cetera.'

'They won't believe that.'

'Screw them. I'm going to quit anyway.'

Shepherd's jaw dropped. It was the last thing he'd expected to hear. 'You can't,' he said.

'I can do what the hell I want,' she said flatly. 'My husband's dead and my daughter's going to need all the support she can get.'

'You're good at what you do,' he said.

'That's not true,' she said. 'I don't have what it takes. I'm not hard enough.'

'It's not about being hard,' said Shepherd. 'It's about caring. It's about giving a damn.' The man knocked on the door again but Shepherd ignored him. 'I might not know much, Charlie, but I know one thing for sure. The world would be a much kinder and safer place if it was run by women.'

Button smiled tightly. 'Not the sort of women I know,' she said.

'You know what I mean. There's too much testosterone around at the moment, too much chest-beating and men trying to prove how hard they are. Don't let the bastards beat you. You're better than they are.'

She smiled, this time with warmth. 'You should go, Spider.' Shepherd stood up. Button reached for his hand and squeezed it gently. 'Thank you,' she said.

Shepherd winked at her, then opened the door. 'She's all yours,' he said, and walked past the two visitors. The nurse glared at him with undisguised loathing as he passed her on the way to the lifts. He gave her a friendly wave and blew her a kiss.

Othman bin Mahmuud al-Ahmed smiled as the hawk slammed into the dove and ripped off the bird's head. What was left of it tumbled to the ground, its white feathers spattered with blood. The smile was for his host's benefit. The Kuwaiti prince who had arranged the trip into the desert was proud of his hawks. Othman did not want to offend him, but they were of poor quality and the prince thought it acceptable to have them hunt caged birds. The prince's falconer was also incompetent. The hawks were not hungry enough and two had refused to fly. Othman's manservant stood behind him, shading the old man with an umbrella. The two American bodyguards stood by the cars that had been provided by the prince, their eyes, as always, hidden behind wraparound sunglasses. The prince's bodyguards were Gurkhas, wiry men with leathered faces. Othman didn't like the way they whispered to each other in their own language. He hadn't enjoyed his three-day trip to Kuwait and was looking forward to returning to Saudi Arabia.

The trip had been forced on him by one of his longest-standing Saudi patrons, who had set his heart on acquiring a top New York hotel owned by the Kuwaiti prince. Money was no object but the Kuwaiti had been reluctant to sell, mainly because one of his favourite mistresses was ensconced in a penthouse suite there. Othman knew the prince well so he had been sent to broker a deal. It had been hard work. The Kuwaiti was a renowned womaniser and, on the second night, had invited Othman to a party at his palace where there had been more than fifty girls, all young and pretty. There had been blondes, brunettes, Africans, Asians, Orientals, though noticeably no Arabs. The Kuwaiti had kept asking Othman to choose, but he had politely declined, citing his inflamed prostate. The truth was that the old man had long since lost interest in sex as anything other than a means of procreation and had no intention of allowing a prostitute to bear his child. At one point during the party one of the prince's servants had walked round with a huge silver tray piled high with Rolex and Cartier watches. The squealing girls had been told to help themselves. Othman had smiled serenely, privately disgusted by the ostentatious display. As far as he was concerned, money should be treated with respect. Like power and love, it was not to be squandered.

Othman's host walked over, clearly elated by the kill. He was accompanied by two of his fifteen sons, both toddlers. Othman smiled his appreciation and made small-talk as they walked together to the waiting cars. The prince was driving in the second car with his fourth wife, who was barely twenty and the mother of the toddlers. There were four of the prince's bodyguards in the first car, Othman was in the third Mercedes with his bodyguards and a driver provided by the prince.

Bringing up the rear a white Toyota Landcruiser contained four more Gurkha bodyguards. The vehicles sat low on reinforced suspension, weighed down by armour plating and bulletproof glass.

One of Othman's bodyguards opened the rear door to the third Mercedes and the old man climbed in. One bodyguard sat next to him as the second got into the front passenger seat.

Othman settled back and closed his eyes as the convoy drove off. He had much on his mind. Muhammad Aslam had come to see him in Riyadh two days before Othman had flown to Kuwait. The assassin had failed. He had been killed by the infidels before he had been able to exact revenge on either the American man or the English woman. The one small piece of good news was that the woman's husband had been killed, so at least she would know some of the pain Othman had felt when he had learnt of his sons' deaths.

Muhammad Aslam had been profuse in his apologies but Othman had put him at ease. It wasn't Aslam's fault that the assassin had failed. And Othman had more than enough money to try again. And again. He would keep sending assassins until they were both dead. He would not rest until he had avenged his sons. It was the Bedouin way.

He sighed and opened his eyes. It was half an hour's drive to the palace. The prince had arranged a dinner with his three brothers, all of whom Othman knew and had done business with in the past. He wasn't looking forward to it. The prince had already agreed to sell the hotel for double what he had paid for it three years earlier, so his business was concluded, but the Kuwaiti had insisted that Othman accept his hospitality. The brothers, like the prince, enjoyed the pleasures of the flesh, and Othman had no doubt that the palace would again be filled with prostitutes. He shuddered.

Off in the distance he saw something streak through the sky. His eyesight was perfect but whatever it was moved so quickly that it was hard to focus on it. It was metallic, glinting in the sun, and left behind it a trail of white vapour. As Othman watched, it curved through the air as if guided by an unseen hand.

The bodyguard in the front passenger seat of the Mercedes had seen it, too. 'Incoming!' he screamed and punched the driver's shoulder. The driver swung the wheel hard to the right and Othman banged into the man sitting next to him, who put his hand on the back of the seat in front to steady himself. The tyres screeched across the Tarmac and Othman tasted bile at the back of his throat. The driver swung the wheel in the opposite direction and Othman was flung across the car so roughly that his head struck the window hard enough to daze him. Then the missile hit and the car exploded in a ball of flame.

'Perfect,' said Simon Nichols, twisting around in his seat. 'They don't come much better than that.'

Richard Yokely raised his Coke can in salute. 'You're the man, Simon.' Nichols turned back to study the screens in front of him. One showed an aerial view of the carnage on the road below, transmitted from the unmanned Predator drone some two hundred feet above the ground. The lead Mercedes had pulled round and three Gurkhas in dark suits were racing towards the car that had been hit by the four-hundred-pound Hellfire missile. 'Bring her back, Phillip,' said Yokely.

'Your wish is my command,' said Phillip Howell, who was piloting the Predator. He toyed with a joystick and the aerial view on the LCD screen panned to the left. The Predator's cameras were so powerful that they could have picked out the numberplates of the cars on the ground from as high as thirty thousand feet. A variable-aperture television camera gave them the live feed and an infra-red camera provided real-time images at night or in low-light conditions.

Yokely, Howell and Nichols were seven thousand miles

away from Kuwait at Nellis air-force base in Las Vegas. The Predator had taken off from Balad air base, forty miles north-west of Baghdad, under the control of the US military, but once it had reached four thousand feet, control had been handed to Yokely and his team in Las Vegas. No flight plan had been filed and the US military kept no record of where the Predator went or what it was doing. The Predator's hundred gallons of fuel allowed it to stay in the air for a full twenty hours if it was cruising or to fly 450 miles at its top speed of eighty miles an hour and was more than enough for it to fly into Kuwait, carry out its mission, and fly back to land at Balad air base. Howell had piloted the drone at just under twenty thousand feet across the Iraqi desert until it had reached Kuwaiti airspace, then taken it down to just a hundred feet above the sand, flying higher only when it got to within five miles of the target. Nichols had fired the Hellfire missile, one of two carried by the twenty-seven-foot-long Predator. There had been no need to fire the second.

As the Predator continued to bank to the left, still flying low, Nichols centred the nose-cone camera on the burning Mercedes. The car was lying on its side and clouds of black smoke were being blown across the road by the desert wind. The Landcruiser had run off the road to avoid the explosion. The Gurkha bodyguards were standing in the sand, their hands on their heads as they stared helplessly at the wreckage.

Yokely's face tightened as he watched the car burn. He had known the bodyguard sitting in the front passenger seat of Othman's car. He had been a former Navy Seal who had served with Delta Force and worked with Yokely on an anti-drugs operation in Colombia during the mid-nineties. Unlike Yokely, Rick Dawson had quit working for the Government and moved into the more lucrative private sector. It was simply bad luck that he had been in the wrong place at the wrong time, but it had been his choice. No one had forced him to work for Othman. There was no way that Yokely could have warned him of what was to happen. The bodyguard would have had to come up with some excuse to get himself off the convoy, which might have tipped off the target.

'Who was he?' asked Howell, interrupting Yokely's train of thought.

'Just an angry old man,' said Yokely. 'He won't be missed.'

The phone rang, dragging Shepherd out of a dreamless sleep. He groped for the receiver, fumbled, and pressed it to his ear. 'Yes?'

'Mr Daniel Shepherd?' It was a woman, upper class. Her voice alone could have frozen water.

'Who is this?' growled Shepherd. The only person who ever called him Daniel was his mother-in-law, but this definitely wasn't Moira.

'Hold the line, please, Mr Shepherd. I have the Prime Minister for you.'

'What?' said Shepherd. He shook his head, trying to clear his thoughts. Music started to play. Classical, something with lots of violins. 'Hello?' said Shepherd.

He wondered if this was a practical joke, but then a man was on the line and he knew immediately that it wasn't a prank. He recognised the Prime Minister's measured tones and the soft Scottish burr he'd heard so many times on news broadcasts.

'Sorry to call you so late, Mr Shepherd, but I've been trying to get our Education Bill through and I'm having to grease an awful lot of wheels.'

Shepherd tried to focus on the digital clock on his bedside table. It was just after one o'clock. 'That's all right, sir. Not a problem.'

'I've been asked to give you a call to reassure you that we are aware of the approach that has recently been made to you by your American counterparts.'

'Right, sir. Thank you.'

'The fight against terrorism is one we absolutely have to

win. There's no question about that. And sometimes measures have to be taken that fall outside the remit of our law-
enforcement agencies.' The Prime Minister spoke slowly,
almost as if he was reading from a script.

'I understand, sir.'

'We're very grateful for the work you've done for us in
the past, your exemplary army career and the excellent job
you've done as a police officer and with SOCA. There's no
pressure on you to accept the offer that has been made. All
I'm doing is calling to let you know that if you do accept,
you do so with our blessing and that you will be accorded
whatever protection we're able to offer. Subject to total deni-
ability, of course.'

'Of course,' said Shepherd.

'So, that's it, then. Good night, and God bless.'

'Good night, sir.'

The line went dead and Shepherd hung up. Richard Yokely
had been right. He did have friends in high places.